Praise for bestselling author Debbie Macomber

"Bestselling Macomber . . . sure has a way of pleasing readers."
—*Booklist*

"Debbie Macomber writes characters who are as warm and funny as your best friends."
—*New York Times* bestselling author Susan Wiggs

"Macomber . . . is no stranger to the *New York Times* best-seller list. She knows how to please her audience."
—*Oregon Statesman Journal*

"Macomber's assured storytelling and affirming narrative is as welcoming as your favorite easy chair."
—*Publishers Weekly* on *Twenty Wishes*

"Prolific Macomber is known for her portrayals of ordinary women in small-town America. [She is] an icon of the genre."
—*Publishers Weekly*

"Readers won't be able to get enough of Macomber's gentle storytelling."
—*RT Book Reviews*

"Poignant story of real women with real problems becoming real friends."
—*Booklist* on *A Good Yarn*

Midnight Sons
Alaska Skies
  (*Brides for Brothers* and
  The Marriage Risk)
Alaska Nights
  (*Daddy's Little Helper* and
  Because of the Baby)
Alaska Home
  (*Falling for Him, Ending in
  Marriage* and *Midnight
  Sons and Daughters*)

This Matter of Marriage
Montana
Thursdays at Eight
Between Friends
Changing Habits
The Sooner the Better
Three Brides, No Groom
Summer Breezes
  (*Fallen Angel* and
  The Way to a Man's Heart)
Seaside Springtime
  (*For All My Tomorrows*
  and *Yours and Mine*)
Fairy-Tale Forever
  (*Cindy and the Prince* and
  Some Kind of Wonderful)
Perfect Partners
  (*Rainy Day Kisses* and
  Love 'n' Marriage)
Finally You
  (*All Things Considered*
  and *No Competition*)
Winning Hearts
  (*Laughter in the Rain*
  and *Love by Degree*)
Finding You Again
  (*White Lace and Promises*
  and *Jury of His Peers*)

A Second Glance
  (*Shadow Chasing* and
  Yesterday Once More)
Longing for Yesterday
  (*Reflections of Yesterday*
  and *Yesterday's Hero*)
The Night We Met (*Starlight*)
Time for Love
  (*A Friend or Two* and
  The Trouble with Caasi)
Their Perfect Match
  (*Promise Me Forever* and
  Adam's Image)
Married in Seattle
  (*First Comes Marriage* and
  Wanted: Perfect Partner)
Right Next Door
  (*Father's Day* and *The
  Courtship of Carol Sommars*)
Wyoming Brides
  (*Denim and Diamonds* and
  The Wyoming Kid)
A Wish Upon a Dress
  (*The First Man You Meet*
  and *The Man You'll Marry*)
Weddings in Orchard Valley
  (*Valerie* and *Stephanie*)
Married in Texas
  (*Norah* and *Lone Star Lovin'*)
An Engagement in Seattle
  (*Groom Wanted* and
  Bride Wanted)
North to Alaska
  (*That Wintry Feeling* and
  Borrowed Dreams)

*Debbie Macomber's
  Cedar Cove Cookbook*
*Debbie Macomber's
  Christmas Cookbook*

DEBBIE MACOMBER

Romance and Peppermint Lattes

HERE COMES TROUBLE and *THE FORGETFUL BRIDE*

/IIMIRA

/II MIRA™

ISBN-13: 978-0-7783-6022-3

Romance and Peppermint Lattes

Copyright © 2025 by Harlequin Enterprises ULC

All illustrations by Lucy Davey

Here Comes Trouble
First published in 1991. This edition published in 2025.
Copyright © 1991 by Debbie Macomber

The Forgetful Bride
First published in 1991. This edition published in 2025.
Copyright © 1991 by Debbie Macomber

Recycling programs
for this product may
not exist in your area.

For questions and comments about the quality of this book, please contact us at
CustomerService@Harlequin.com.

TM is a trademark of Harlequin Enterprises ULC.

MIRA
22 Adelaide St. West, 41st Floor
Toronto, Ontario M5H 4E3, Canada
MIRABooks.com

HarperCollins Publishers
Macken House, 39/40 Mayor Street Upper,
Dublin 1, D01 C9W8, Ireland
www.HarperCollins.com

Printed in U.S.A.

Contents

Romance and Peppermint Lattes

Here Comes Trouble

Prologue

"Tomorrow's Christmas Eve, Mom!" nine-year-old Courtney Adams said.

"Mom, you have my list for Santa, don't you?" seven-year-old Bailey asked anxiously. She knelt on her bed, her large brown eyes beseeching.

This, Maryanne Adams recognized, was a blatant attempt to postpone bedtime. Both girls were supposed to turn out their lights ten minutes ago but, as usual, they were looking for any excuse to delay the inevitable. The one thing Maryanne hoped to avoid was yet another discussion about the top item on both their Christmas lists—a puppy.

"What about *my* list?" Courtney asked from her bed. She, at least, had crawled between the covers, but remained in a sitting position.

"Don't worry, I'm sure Santa has both your lists by now," Maryanne reassured her daughters. She stood in the doorway, her hand poised over the light switch. Both her daughters slept in canopy beds their Simpson grandparents had insisted on purchasing for them. It was their prerogative to spoil the grandkids, her father had told her, so she didn't argue too much. The grandchildren were the delight of their grandparents' lives and could do no wrong.

"Did you read the list before you gave it to Santa?" Courtney asked.

At nine, Courtney was well aware that Santa was actually her mom and dad, but she was generous enough not to spoil the fantasy for her younger sister.

"You said your prayers?" Maryanne asked, wanting to turn the subject away from a dog.

Bailey nodded. "I prayed for a puppy."

"I did, too," Courtney echoed.

They were certainly persistent. "We'll see what happens," Maryanne said.

Bailey glanced at her older sister. "Is 'we'll see' good news?"

Courtney looked uncertain. "I don't know." She turned pleading eyes to her mother. "Mom, we *have* to know."

"Mom, please, I beg of you," Bailey cried dramatically. "We've just got to have a dog. We've *got* to."

Maryanne sighed. "I hate to disappoint you, but I don't think it's a good idea for our family to get a puppy now."

"Why not?" Courtney demanded, her sweet face filling with disappointment.

Instinctively, Maryanne pressed her hand to her stomach. It was time to tell the girls that there'd be a new family member in six months—past time, really, for them to know. She'd wanted to share the news earlier, but this baby was a complete surprise; she and Nolan had needed time to adjust to the idea first.

Stepping all the way into the room, Maryanne sat on the edge of Courtney's bed. She'd prefer to tell the girls with Nolan at her side, but her husband was on deadline and had barricaded himself in his home office, coming out once or twice a day.

The last fifty pages of a book were always the most difficult for him to write, winding down the plot and tying up all the loose ends. It was never easy, according to Nolan, to part with the characters he'd lived with for the past number of months. They were as real to him as his own flesh and blood, and because she was a writer, too, she understood that.

"We'll discuss this later." Checking her watch, she frowned. "It's past your bedtime as it is."

"Aw, Mom," Bailey moaned.

"Mom, please," Courtney chimed in. "I won't be able to sleep if you don't tell me now."

"Tell them what?" Nolan asked from the doorway.

At the sight of their father both girls squealed with delight. Bailey was out of bed first, flying across the room at breakneck speed. Anyone would think it'd been weeks since she'd last seen their father, when in fact he'd had breakfast with the girls that morning.

"Daddy!" Courtney leaped off the bed, as well.

Bailey was in Nolan's arms, fiercely hugging his neck, and Courtney clasped her skinny arms around his waist.

"Are you finished the book?" Maryanne asked, her gaze connecting with his. She remained seated on the bed, tired out from a long day of Christmas preparations.

"I typed *The End* about five minutes ago," her husband said, smiling down at her.

"What do you think?" she asked. As a wildly popular suspense author, Nolan generally had an excellent feel for his own work.

"I think it's good, but I'll wait for your feedback."

Maryanne loved the way they worked together as husband and wife and as two professional writers. Nolan wrote his novels, and it was the income he generated from the sales of his books that supported their family. Maryanne tackled nonfiction projects. She wrote a weekly column for the *Seattle Review* and contributed articles to various parenting magazines. One day, she might try her hand at fiction, but for the present she was content.

"Mom says now isn't a good time for us to get a puppy," Courtney whined, and it wasn't long before her younger sister added her own disconsolate cries.

"Why can't we, Daddy?" Bailey cried. "Every kid should have a puppy."

"A puppy," Nolan repeated, locking eyes with Maryanne. He sat down on the bed beside her and exhaled slowly. "Well, the truth is, there are other considerations."

"Like what?" Courtney asked. It was inconceivable to her that anything should stand in the way of her heart's desire.

Nolan placed his arm around Maryanne's shoulders, indicating that perhaps now was the time to explain. "Well," he began in thoughtful tones. "When a man and a woman fall in love and marry, they sometimes . . ." He paused and waited for Maryanne to finish.

"They love each other so much that they . . ." She hesitated, thinking this might not be the right approach.

"They make babies," Nolan supplied.

"You were a baby once," Maryanne continued, reaching out to tickle Bailey's tummy.

"And you, too," Nolan told Courtney.

The girls sat cross-legged on Bailey's bed, their attention on Nolan and Maryanne. Their long brown hair spilled over their shoulders.

"What has this got to do with a puppy?" Courtney asked, cocking her head to one side, a puzzled frown on her face. How like Nolan she looked just then, Maryanne thought. The Nolan she remembered from the days of their courtship, the newspaper reporter who always seemed to be frowning at her for one reason or another.

"What your mother and I are attempting to explain is that . . ." He paused and a smile crept across his face.

"You're both going to be big sisters," Maryanne said.

Courtney understood the implications before her little sister did. "Mom's going to have a *baby*?"

Maryanne nodded.

The girls screamed with happiness. As if they'd been practicing the move for a week, they leaped off the bed and immediately started jumping up and down. Soon Nolan was laughing at their antics.

"I want another sister," Bailey insisted.

"No, no, a brother," Courtney said.

"Personally I'll be overjoyed with either," Nolan assured them all. His arm tightened around Maryanne's shoulders, and he buried his face in her neck as she hid a smile. While this baby was certainly unexpected, he was most welcome. Yes, he! Earlier in the day Maryanne had been at the doctor's, had her first ultrasound and received the news. How appropriate for Christmastime . . . She'd tell Nolan as soon as the kids were asleep.

"Are you excited, Mom?" Courtney asked.

Maryanne nodded and held out her arms to her daughter. "Very much so."

Courtney came into the circle of Maryanne's arms. "A baby is even better than a puppy." She grinned. "But a puppy's good, too!"

"Yeah," Bailey said. She climbed into Nolan's lap, leaning her head against his chest.

"But you girls understand that a baby *and* a puppy at the same time would be too much, don't you?"

"Yes." Both girls nodded.

"Later," Courtney said in a solemn voice. "When the baby's older."

"Yeah," Bailey said again.

"Isn't it bedtime yet?" Nolan asked.

"Not yet," Bailey said. "I can't sleep, I'm too excited."

"I can't either." Courtney gazed up at her mother.

"Tell us a story," Bailey suggested. "A *long* story."

"You should get into bed first," Nolan said, and both girls reluctantly climbed back into their beds, and pulled the covers all the way up to their chins.

"Do you want me to read to you?" Nolan asked.

"Not a book," Courtney said. "Tell us a *real* story."

"About Grandpa and the newspaper business?" Maryanne knew how much her daughters loved to hear about their grandfather Simpson when he'd first started his business.

"No." Courtney shook her head. "Tell us about how you and Daddy met."

"You already know that story," Nolan said.

"We want the unabridged version this time," Bailey piped up.

Unabridged? Only the seven-year-old daughter of a writer would know the meaning of that word.

"What do you think, Annie?" Nolan asked.

Grinning, Maryanne lowered her head. When they'd first met, Nolan had been convinced she was nothing more than a spoiled debutante. From that point on, he'd taken to referring to her as *Deb, Trouble* and, with obvious affection, Annie.

"It was love at first sight," Nolan told his children.

Maryanne smiled again. Despite his sometimes cynical manner, her husband could be a real romantic.

"Your mother was head over heels in love with me the minute we met," he went on.

"I don't remember it quite that way," Maryanne protested.

"You don't?" Nolan feigned surprise.

"No, because you infuriated me no end." She remembered the notorious column he'd written about her—"My Evening with the Debutante."

"Me?" His expression turned to one of exaggerated indignation.

"You thought I was a spoiled rich kid."

"You *were* spoiled."

"I most certainly was not." Although Maryanne could see the gleam in his eye, she wasn't going to let him get away with this. It was true her father owned the newspaper and had arranged for her position, but that didn't mean she didn't deserve the opportunity. She might not have worked her way up through the normal channels, but in time she'd proved herself to the staff at the *Seattle Review*. She'd also proved herself to Nolan—in a rather different way.

Courtney and Bailey exchanged glances.

"Are you fighting?" Bailey asked.

Nolan chuckled. "No, I was just setting your mother straight."

Maryanne raised her eyebrows. "Apparently your father remembers things differently from the way I do."

"Start at the beginning," Bailey urged.

Excitedly clapping her hands, Courtney added, "Don't forget to tell us about the time Daddy embarrassed you in front of the whole city."

Nolan had worked for the *Sun*, the rival paper in town. It wasn't as if Maryanne would ever forget the column he'd written about his evening with her. Even now, after all these years, she bristled at the memory. He'd informed the entire city of Seattle that she was a naive idealist, and worst of all, he'd announced that she was away from home for the first time and lonely.

"I still don't get why that column upset your mother so much," Nolan said, gesturing helplessly toward his daughters. "All I did was thank her for making me dinner."

"Did Daddy kiss you that night?" Bailey asked.

"No, he—"

"Don't tell us," Courtney cried, interrupting Maryanne. "Start at the *very* beginning and don't leave anything out."

Nolan looked at Maryanne. "Why don't you tell them, sweetheart?"

"I'll tell them everything, then."

"Everything?" Nolan repeated.

Courtney rubbed her hands together. "Oh, boy, this is going to be good."

"It all started fifteen years ago . . ."

One

"Maryanne Simpson of the New York Simpsons, I presume?"

Maryanne glared at the man standing across from her in the reception area of the radio station. She pointedly ignored his sarcasm, keeping her blue eyes as emotionless as possible.

Nolan Adams—Seattle's most popular journalist—looked nothing like the polished professional man in the black-and-white photo that headed his daily column. Instead he resembled a well-known disheveled television detective. He even wore a wrinkled raincoat, one that looked as if he'd slept in it for an entire week.

"Or should I call you Deb?" he taunted.

"Ms. Simpson will suffice," she said in her best finishing-school voice. The rival newspaperman was cocky and arrogant—and the best damn journalist Maryanne had ever read. Maryanne was a good columnist herself, or at least she was desperately striving to become one. Her father, who owned the *Seattle Review* and twelve other daily newspapers nation-wide, had seen to it that she was given this once-in-a-lifetime opportunity with the Seattle paper. She was working hard to prove herself. Perhaps too hard. That was when the trouble had begun.

"So how's the heart?" Nolan asked, reaching for a magazine and flipping idly through the dog-eared pages. "Is it still bleeding from all those liberal views of yours?"

Maryanne ignored the question, removed her navy-blue wool coat and neatly folded it over the back of a chair. "My heart's just fine, thank you."

With a sound she could only describe as a snicker, he threw himself down on a nearby chair and indolently brought an ankle up to rest on his knee.

Maryanne sat across from him, stiff and straight in the high-backed chair, and boldly met his eyes. Everything she needed to know about Nolan Adams could be seen in his face. The strong well-defined lines of his jaw told her how stubborn he could be. His eyes were dark, intelligent and intense. And his mouth . . . well, that was another story altogether. It seemed to wrestle with itself before ever breaking into a smile, as if a gesture of amusement went against his very nature. Nolan wasn't smiling now. And Maryanne wasn't about to let him see how much he intimidated her. But some emotion must have shone in her eyes, because he said abruptly, "You're the one who started this, you know?"

Maryanne was well aware of that. But this rivalry between them had begun unintentionally, at least on her part. The very morning that the competition's paper, the *Seattle Sun*, published Nolan's column on solutions to the city's housing problem, the *Review* had run Maryanne's piece on the same subject. Nolan's article was meant to be satirical, while Maryanne's was deadly serious. Her mistake was in stating that there were those in the city who apparently found the situation amusing, and she blasted anyone who behaved so irresponsibly. This was not a joking matter, she'd pointed out.

It looked as if she'd read Nolan's column and set out to reprimand him personally for his cavalier attitude.

Two days later, Nolan's column poked fun at her, asking what Ms. High Society could possibly know about affordable housing. Clearly a debutante had never had to worry about the roof over her head, he'd snarled. But more than that, he'd made her suggestions to alleviate the growing problem sound both frivolous and impractical.

Her next column came out the same evening and referred to tough pessimistic reporters who took themselves much too seriously. She went so far as to make fun of a fictional Seattle newsman who resembled Nolan Adams to a T.

Nolan retaliated once more, and Maryanne seethed. Obviously she'd have to be the one to put an end to this silliness. She hoped that not responding to Nolan's latest attack would terminate their rivalry, but she should've known better. An hour after her column on community spirit had hit the newsstands, KJBR, a local radio station, called, asking Maryanne to give a guest editorial. She'd immediately agreed, excited and honored at the invitation. It wasn't until later that she learned Nolan Adams would also be speaking. The format was actually a celebrity debate, a fact of which she'd been blithely unaware.

The door opened and a tall dark-haired woman walked into the station's reception area. "I'm Liz Walters," she said, two steps into the room. "I produce the news show. I take it you two know each other?"

"Like family," Nolan muttered with that cocky grin of his.

"We introduced ourselves five minutes ago," Maryanne rebutted stiffly.

"Good," Liz said without glancing up from her clipboard. "If you'll both come this way, we'll get you set up in the control booth."

From her brief conversation with the show's host, Brian Campbell, Maryanne knew that the show taped on Thursday night wouldn't air until Sunday evening.

When they were both seated inside the control booth, Maryanne withdrew two typed pages from her bag. Not to be outdone, Nolan made a show of pulling a small notepad from the huge pocket of his crumpled raincoat.

Brian Campbell began the show with a brief introduction, presenting the evening's subject: the growing popularity of the Seattle area. He then turned the microphone over to Maryanne, who was to speak first.

Forcing herself to relax, she took a deep calming breath, tucked her long auburn hair behind her ears and started speaking. She managed to keep her voice low and as well modulated as her nerves would allow.

"The word's out," she said, quickly checking her notes. "Seattle has been rated one of the top cities in the country for several years running. Is it any wonder Californians are moving up in droves, attracted by the area's economic growth, the lure of pure fresh air and beautiful clean waters? Seattle has appeal, personality and class."

As she warmed to her subject, her voice gained confidence and conviction. She'd fallen in love with Seattle when she'd visited for a two-day stopover before flying to Hawaii. The trip had been a college graduation gift from her parents. She'd returned to New York one week later full of enthusiasm, not for the tourist-cluttered islands, but for the brief glimpse she'd had of the Emerald City.

From the first, she'd intended to return to the Pacific Northwest. Instead she'd taken a job as a nonfiction editor in one of her father's New York publishing houses; she'd been so busy that travelling time was limited. That editorial job lasted almost eighteen months, and although Maryanne had thoroughly enjoyed it, she longed to write herself and put her journalism skills to work.

Samuel Simpson must have sensed her restlessness because he mentioned an opening at the *Seattle Review*, a long-established paper, when they met in Nantucket over Labor Day weekend. Maryanne had plied him with questions, mentioning more than once that she'd fallen in love with Seattle. Her father had grinned, chewing vigorously on the end of his cigar, and looked toward his wife of twenty-seven years before he'd casually reached for the telephone. After a single call lasting less than three minutes, Samuel announced that the job was hers. Within two weeks, Maryanne was packed and on her way west.

"In conclusion I'd like to remind our audience that there's no turning back now," Maryanne said. "Seattle sits as a polished jewel in the beautiful Pacific Northwest. Seattle, the Emerald City, awaits even greater prosperity, even more progress."

She set her papers aside and smiled in the direction of the host, relieved to be finished. She watched in dismay as Nolan scowled at her, then slipped his notepad back inside his pocket. He apparently planned to wing it.

Nolan—who needed, Brian declared, no introduction—leaned toward the microphone. He glanced at Maryanne, frowned once more, and slowly shook his head.

"Give me a break, Ms. Simpson!" he cried. "Doesn't anyone realize it *rains* here? Did you know that until recently, if Seattle went an entire week without rain, we sacrificed a virgin? Unfortunately we were running low on those until you moved to town."

Maryanne barely managed to restrain a gasp.

"Why do you think Seattle has remained so beautiful?" Nolan continued. "Why do you think we aren't suffering from the pollution problems so prevalent in Southern California and elsewhere? You seem to believe Seattle should throw open her arms and invite the world to park on our unspoiled doorstep. My advice to you, and others like you, is to go back where you came from. We don't want you turning Seattle into another L.A.—or New York."

The hair on the back of Maryanne's neck bristled. Although he spoke in general terms, his words seemed to be directed solely at her. He was telling her, in effect, to pack up her suitcase and head home to Mommy and Daddy where she belonged.

When Nolan finished, they were each given two minutes for a rebuttal.

"Some of what you have to say is true," Maryanne admitted through clenched teeth. "But you can't turn back progress. Only a fool," she said pointedly, "would try to keep families from settling in Washington state. You can argue until you've lost your voice, but it won't help. The population in this area is going to explode in the next few years whether you approve or not."

"That's probably true, but it doesn't mean I have to sit still and let it happen. In fact, I intend to do everything I can to put a stop to it," he said. "We in Seattle have a way of life to protect and a duty to future generations. If growth continues in this vein, our schools will soon be overcrowded, our homes so overpriced that no one except those from out of state will be able to afford housing—and that's only if they can find it. If that's what you want, then fine, bask in your ignorance."

"What do you suggest?" Maryanne burst out. "Setting up road blocks?"

"That's a start," Nolan returned sarcastically. "Something's got to be done before this area becomes another urban disaster."

Maryanne rolled her eyes. "Do you honestly think you're going to single-handedly turn back the tide of progress?"

"I'm sure as hell going to try."

"That's ridiculous."

"And that's our Celebrity Debate for this evening," Brian Campbell said quickly, cutting off any further argument. "Join us next week when our guests will be City Council candidates Nick Fraser and Robert Hall."

The microphone was abruptly switched off. "That was excellent," the host said, flashing them a wide enthusiastic smile. "Thank you both."

"You've got your head buried in the sand," Maryanne felt obliged to inform Nolan, although she knew it wouldn't do any good. She dropped her notes back in her bag and snapped it firmly shut, as if to say the subject was now closed.

"You may be right," Nolan said with a grin. "But at least the sand is on a pollution-free beach. If you have your way, it'll soon be cluttered with—"

"If I have my way?" she cried. "You make it sound as though I'm solely responsible for the Puget Sound growth rate."

"You *are* responsible, and those like you."

"Well, excuse me," she muttered sarcastically. She nodded politely to Brian Campbell, then hurried back to the reception room where she'd left her coat. To her annoyance Nolan followed her.

"I don't excuse you, Deb."

"I asked you to use my name," she said furiously, "and it isn't Deb."

Crossing his arms over his chest, Nolan leaned lazily against the doorjamb while she retrieved her wool coat.

Maryanne crammed her arms into the sleeves and nearly tore off the buttons in her rush to leave. The way he stood there studying her did little to cool her temper.

"And another thing . . ." she muttered.

"You mean there's more?"

"You're darn right there is. That crack about virgins was intolerably rude! I . . . I expected better of you."

"Hell, it's true."

"How would you know?"

He grinned that insufferable grin of his, infuriating her even more.

"Don't you have anything better to do than follow me around?" she demanded, stalking out of the room.

"Not particularly. Fact is, I've been looking forward to meeting you."

Once she'd recovered from the shock of learning that he'd be her opponent in this radio debate, Maryanne had eagerly anticipated this evening, too. Long before she'd arrived at the radio station, she'd planned to tell Nolan how much she admired his work. This silly rivalry between them was exactly that: silly. She hadn't meant to step on his toes and would've called and cleared the air if he hadn't attacked her in print at the earliest opportunity.

"Sure you wanted to meet me. Hurling insults to my face must be far more fun."

He laughed at that and Maryanne was astonished at how rich and friendly his amusement sounded.

"Come on, Simpson, don't take everything so personally. Admit it. We've been having a good time poking fun at each other."

Maryanne didn't say anything for a moment. Actually he was partially right. She *had* enjoyed their exchanges, although she wouldn't have admitted that earlier. She wasn't entirely sure she wanted to now.

"Admit it," he coaxed, again with a grin.

That uneven smile of his was her undoing. "It hasn't exactly been *fun*," she answered reluctantly, "but it's been . . . interesting."

"That's what I thought." He thrust his hands into his pockets, looking pleased with himself.

She glanced at him appraisingly. The man's appeal was definitely of the rugged variety: his outrageous charm—Maryanne wasn't sure charm was really the right word—his craggy face and solid compact build. She'd been surprised to discover he wasn't as tall as she'd imagined. In fact, he was probably under six feet.

"Word has it Daddy was the one responsible for landing you this cushy job," he commented, interrupting her assessment.

"Cushy?" she repeated angrily. "You've got to be kidding!" She often put in twelve-hour days, trying to come up with a column that was both relevant and entertaining. In the four weeks since she'd joined the *Seattle Review*, she'd worked damn hard. She had something to prove, not only to herself but to her peers.

"So being a journalist isn't everything it's cracked up to be?"

"I didn't say that," she returned. To be perfectly honest, Maryanne had never tried harder at anything. Her pride and a whole lot more was riding on the outcome of the next few months. Samuel Simpson's daughter or not, she was on probation, after which her performance would be reviewed by the managing editor.

"I wonder if you've ever done anything without Daddy's approval."

"I wonder if you've always been this rude."

He chuckled at that. "Almost always. As I said, don't take it personally."

With her leather purse tucked securely under her arm, she marched to the exit, which Nolan was effectively blocking. "Excuse me, please."

"Always so polite," he murmured before he straightened, allowing her to pass.

Nolan followed her to the elevator, annoying her even more. Maryanne felt his scrutiny, and it flustered her. She knew she was reasonably attractive, but she also knew that no one was going to rush forward with a banner and a tiara. Her mouth was just a little too full, her eyes a little too round. Her hair had been fire-engine red the entire time she was growing up, but it had darkened to a deep auburn in her early twenties, a fact for which she remained truly grateful. Maryanne had always hated her red hair and the wealth of freckles that accompanied it. No one else in her family had been cursed with red hair, let alone freckles. Her mother's hair was a beautiful blonde and her father's a rich chestnut. Even her younger brothers had escaped her fate. If it weren't for the distinctive high Simpson forehead and deep blue eyes, Maryanne might have suspected she'd been adopted. But that wasn't the case. Instead she'd been forced to discover early in life how unfair heredity could be.

The elevator arrived, and both Maryanne and Nolan stepped inside. Nolan leaned against the side—he always seemed to be leaning, Maryanne noticed. Leaning and staring. He was studying her again; she could feel his eyes as profoundly as a caress.

"Would you kindly stop?" she snapped.

"Stop what?"

"Staring at me!"

"I'm curious."

"About what?" She was curious about him, too, but far too civilized to make an issue of it.

"I just wanted to see if all that blue blood showed."

"Oh, honestly!"

"I am being honest," he answered. "You know, you intrigue me, Simpson. Have you eaten?"

Maryanne's heart raced with excitement at the offhand question. He seemed to be leading up to suggesting they dine together. Unfortunately she'd been around Nolan long enough to realize she couldn't trust the man. Anything she said or did would more than likely show up in that column of his.

"I've got an Irish stew simmering in a pot at home," she murmured, dismissing the invitation before he could offer it.

"Great! I love stew."

Maryanne opened her mouth to tell him she had no intention of asking him into her home. Not after the things he'd said about her in his column. But when she turned to tell him so, their eyes met. His were a deep, dark brown and almost . . . she couldn't be sure, but she thought she saw a faint glimmer of admiration. The edge of his mouth quirked upward with an unmistakable hint of challenge. He looked as if he expected her to reject him.

Against her better judgment, and knowing she'd live to regret this, Maryanne found herself smiling.

"My apartment's on Spring Street," she murmured.

"Good. I'll follow you."

She lowered her gaze, feeling chagrined and already regretful about the whole thing. "I didn't drive."

"Is your chauffeur waiting?" he asked, his voice and eyes mocking her in a manner that was practically friendly.

"I took a cab," she said, glancing away from him. "It's a way of life in Manhattan and I'm not accustomed to dealing with a car. So I don't have one." She half expected him to make some derogatory comment and was thankful when he didn't.

"I'll give you a lift, then."

He'd parked his car, a surprisingly stylish sedan, in a lot close to the waterfront. The late-September air was brisk, and Maryanne braced herself against it as Nolan cleared the litter off the passenger seat.

She slipped inside, grateful to be out of the chill. It didn't take her more than a couple of seconds to realize that Nolan treated his car the same way he treated his raincoat. The front and back seat were cluttered with empty paper cups, old newspapers and several paperback novels. Mysteries, she noted. The great Nolan Adams read mysteries. A container filled with loose change was propped inside his ashtray.

While Maryanne searched for the seatbelt, Nolan raced around the front of the car, slid inside and quickly started the engine. "I hope there's a place to park off Spring."

"Oh, don't worry," Maryanne quickly assured him. "I've got valet service."

Nolan murmured something under his breath. Had she made an effort, she might've been able to hear, but she figured she was probably better off not knowing.

He turned up the heater and Maryanne was warmed by a blast of air. "Let me know if that gets too hot for you."

"Thanks, I'm fine."

"Hot" seemed to describe their relationship. From the first, Maryanne had inadvertently got herself into scalding water with Nolan, water that came closer to the boiling point each time a new column appeared. "Hot" also described the way they seemed to ignite sparks off each other. The radio show had proved that much. There was another popular meaning of "hot"—one she refused to think about.

Nevertheless, Maryanne was grateful for the opportunity to bridge their differences, because, despite everything, she genuinely admired Nolan's writing.

They chatted amicably enough until Nolan pulled into the crescent-shaped driveway of The Seattle, the luxury apartment complex where she lived.

Max, the doorman, opened her car door, his stoic face breaking into a smile as he recognized her. When Nolan climbed out of the driver's side, Maryanne watched as Max's smile slowly turned into a frown, as though he wasn't certain Nolan was appropriate company for a respectable young lady.

"Max, this is Mr. Adams from the *Seattle Sun*."

"Nolan Adams?" Max's expression altered immediately. "You don't look like your picture. I read your work faithfully, Mr. Adams. You gave ol' Larson hell last month. From what I heard, your column was what forced him to resign from City Council."

Nolan had given Maryanne hell, too, but she refrained from mentioning it. She doubted Max had ever read her work or was even aware that Nolan had been referring to her in some of his columns.

"Would you see to Mr. Adams's car?" Maryanne asked.

"Right away, Ms. Simpson."

Burying his hands in his pockets, Nolan and Maryanne walked into the extravagantly decorated foyer with its huge crystal chandelier and bubbling fountain. "My apartment's on the eleventh floor," she said, pushing the elevator button.

"Not the penthouse suite?" he teased.

Maryanne smiled weakly in response. While they rode upward, she concentrated on taking her keys from her bag to hide her sudden nervousness. Her heart was banging against her ribs. Now that Nolan was practically at her door, she wondered how she'd let this happen. After the things he'd called her, the least of which were Ms. High Society, Miss Debutante and Daddy's Darling, she felt more than a little vulnerable in his company.

"Are you ready to change your mind?" he asked. Apparently, he'd read her thoughts.

"No, of course not," she lied.

She noticed—but sincerely hoped Nolan didn't—that her hand was shaking when she inserted the key.

She turned on the light as she walked into the spacious apartment. Nolan followed her, his brows raised at the sight of the modern white leather-and-chrome furniture. There was even a fireplace.

"Nice place you've got here," he said, glancing around.

She thought she detected sarcasm in his voice, then decided it was what she could expect from him all evening; she might as well get used to it.

"I'll take your raincoat," she said. Considering the fondness with which he wore the thing, he might well choose to eat in it, too.

To Maryanne's surprise, he handed it to her, then walked over to the fireplace and lifted a family photo from the mantel. The picture had been taken several summers earlier, when they'd all been sailing off Martha's Vineyard. Maryanne was facing into the wind and laughing at the antics of her younger brothers. It certainly wasn't her most flattering photo. In fact, she looked as if she was gasping for air after being underwater too long. The wind had caught her red hair, its color even more pronounced against the backdrop of white sails.

"The two young men are my brothers. My mom and dad are at the helm."

Nolan stared at the picture for several seconds and then back at her. "So you're the only redhead."

"How kind of you to mention it."

"Hey, you're in luck. I happen to like redheads." He said this with such a lazy smile that Maryanne couldn't possibly be offended.

"I'll check the stew," she said, after hanging up their coats. She hurried into the kitchen and lifted the lid of the pot. The pungent aroma of stewing lamb, vegetables and basil filled the apartment.

"You weren't kidding, were you?" Nolan asked, sounding mildly surprised.

"Kidding? About what?"

"The Irish stew."

"No. I put it on this morning, before I left for work. I've got one of those all-day cookers." After living on her own for the past couple of years, Maryanne had become a competent cook. When she'd rented her first apartment in New York, she used to stop off at a deli on her way home, but that had soon become monotonous. Over the course of several months, she'd discovered some excellent recipes for simple nutritious meals. Her father wasn't going to publish a cookbook written by her, but she did manage to eat well.

"I thought the stew was an excuse not to have dinner with me," Nolan remarked conversationally. "I didn't know what to expect. You're my first deb."

"Some white wine?" she asked, ignoring his comment.

"Please."

Maryanne got a bottle from the refrigerator and expertly removed the cork. She filled them each a glass, then gave Nolan his and carried the bottle into the living room, where she set it on the glass-topped coffee table. Sitting down on one end of the white leather sofa, she slipped off her shoes and tucked her feet beneath her.

Nolan sat at the other end, resting his ankle on his knee, making himself at home. "Dare I propose a toast?" he asked.

"Please."

"To Seattle," he said, his mischievous gaze meeting hers. "May she forever remain unspoiled." He reached over and touched the rim of her glass with his.

"To Seattle," Maryanne returned. "The most enchanting city on the West Coast."

"But, please, don't let anyone know," he coaxed in a stage whisper.

"I'm not making any promises," she whispered back.

They tasted the wine, which had come highly recommended by a colleague at the paper. Maryanne had only recently learned that wines from Washington state were quickly gaining a world reputation for excellence. Apparently the soil, a rich sandy loam over a volcanic base, was the reason for that.

They talked about the wine for a few minutes, and the conversation flowed naturally after that, as they compared experiences and shared impressions. Maryanne was surprised by how much she was enjoying the company of this man she'd considered a foe. Actually, they did have several things in common. Perhaps she was enjoying his company simply because she was lonely, but she didn't think that was completely true. Still, she'd been too busy with work to do any socializing; she occasionally saw a few people from the paper, but other than that she hadn't had time to establish any friendships.

After a second glass of wine, feeling warm and relaxed, Maryanne was willing to admit exactly how isolated she'd felt since moving to Seattle.

"It's been so long since I went out on a real date," she said.

"There does seem to be a shortage of Ivy League guys in Seattle."

She giggled and nodded. "At least Dad's not sending along a troupe of eligible men for me to meet. I enjoyed living in New York, don't get me wrong, but every time I turned around, a man was introducing himself and telling me my father had given him my phone number. You're the first man I've had dinner with that Dad didn't handpick for me since I moved out on my own."

"I hate to tell you this, sugar, but I have the distinct impression your daddy would take one look at me and have me arrested."

"That's not the least bit true," Maryanne argued. "My dad isn't a snob, only . . . only if you do meet him take off the raincoat, okay?"

"The raincoat?"

"It looks like you sleep in it. All you need is a hat and a scrap

of paper with 'Press' scrawled on it sticking out of the band—
you'd look like you worked for the *Planet* in Metropolis."

"I hate to disillusion you, sugar, but I'm not Ivy League and
I'm not Superman."

"Oh, darn," she said, snapping her fingers. "And we had such
a good thing going." She was feeling too mellow to remind him
not to call her sugar.

"So how old are you?" Nolan wanted to know. "Twenty-
one?"

"Three," she amended. "And you?"

"A hundred and three in comparison."

Maryanne wasn't sure what he meant, but she let that pass,
too. It felt good to have someone to talk to, someone who was
her contemporary, or at least close to being her contemporary.

"If you don't want to tell me how old you are, then at least
fill in some of the details of your life."

"Trust me, my life isn't nearly as interesting as yours."

"Bore me, then."

"All right," he said, drawing a deep breath. "My family was
dirt-poor. Dad disappeared about the time I was ten and Mom
took on two jobs to make ends meet. Get the picture?"

"Yes." She hesitated. "What about women?"

"I've had a long and glorious history."

"I'm not kidding, Nolan."

"You think I was?"

"You're not married."

"Not to my knowledge."

"Why not?"

He shrugged as if it was of little consequence. "No time for
it. I came close once, but her family didn't consider my writing
career noble enough. Her father tried to fix me up with a job
in his insurance office."

"What happened?"

"Nothing much. I told her I was going to work for the paper, and she claimed if I really loved her I'd accept her father's generous offer. It didn't take me long to decide. I guess she was right—I didn't love her."

He sounded nonchalant, implying that the episode hadn't cost him a moment's regret, but just looking at him told Maryanne otherwise. Nolan had been deeply hurt. Every sarcastic irreverent word he wrote suggested it.

In retrospect, Maryanne mused one afternoon several days later, she'd thoroughly enjoyed her evening with Nolan. They'd eaten, and he'd raved about her Irish stew until she flushed at his praise. She'd made them cups of café au lait while he built a fire. They'd sat in front of the fireplace and talked for hours. He'd told her more about his own large family, his seven brothers and sisters. How he'd worked his way through two years of college, but was forced to give up his education when he couldn't afford to continue. As it turned out, he'd been grateful because that decision had led to his first newspaper job. And, as they said, the rest was history.

"You certainly seem to be in a good mood," her coworker, Carol Riverside, said as she strolled past Maryanne's desk later that same afternoon. Carol was short, with a pixielike face and friendly manner. Maryanne had liked her from the moment they'd met.

"I'm in a fabulous mood," Maryanne said, smiling. Nolan had promised to pay her back by taking her out to dinner. He hadn't set a definite date, but she half expected to hear from him that evening.

"In that case, I hate to be the bearer of bad tidings, but someone has to tell you, and I was appointed."

"Tell me? What?" Maryanne glanced around the huge open office and noted that several faces were staring in her direction, all wearing sympathetic looks. "What's going on?" she demanded.

Carol moved her arm out from behind her and Maryanne noticed that she was holding a copy of the rival paper's morning edition. "It's Nolan Adams's column," Carol said softly, her eyes wide and compassionate.

"Wh-what did he say this time?"

"Well, let's put it this way. He titled it, 'My Evening with the Debutante.'"

Two

Maryanne was much too furious to stand still. She paced her living room from one end to the other, her mind spitting and churning. A slow painful death was too good for Nolan Adams.

Her phone rang and she went into the kitchen to answer it. She reached for it so fast she nearly ripped it off the wall. Rarely did she allow herself to become this angry, but complicating her fury was a deep and aching sense of betrayal. "Yes," she said forcefully.

"This is Max," her doorman announced. "Mr. Adams is here. Shall I send him up?"

For an instant Maryanne was too stunned to speak. The man had nerve, she'd say that much for him. Raw courage, too, if he knew the state of mind she was in.

"Ms. Simpson?"

It took Maryanne only about a second to decide. "Send him up," she said with deceptive calm.

Arms hugging her waist, Maryanne continued pacing. She was going to tell this man in no uncertain terms what she thought of his duplicity, his treachery. He might have assumed from their evening together that she was a gentle, forgiving soul who'd quietly overlook this. Well, if that was his belief, Maryanne was looking forward to enlightening him.

Her doorbell chimed and she turned to glare at it. Wishing her heart would stop pounding, she gulped in a deep breath, then walked calmly across the living room and opened the door.

"Hello, Maryanne," Nolan said, his eyes immediately meeting hers.

She stood exactly where she was, imitating his tactic of leaning against the door frame and blocking the threshold.

"May I come in?" he asked mildly.

"I haven't decided yet." He was wearing the raincoat again, which looked even more disreputable than before.

"I take it you read my column?" he murmured, one eyebrow raised.

"Read it?" she nearly shouted. "Of course I read it, and so, it seems, did everyone else in Seattle. Did you really think I'd be able to hold my head up after that? Or was that your intention—humiliating me and . . . and making me a laughingstock?" She stabbed her index finger repeatedly against his solid chest. "And if you think no one'll figure out it was me just because you didn't use my name, think again."

"I take it you're angry?" He raised his eyebrows again, as if to suggest she was overreacting.

"Angry! Angry? That isn't the half of it, buster!" The problem with being raised in a God-fearing, flag-loving family was that the worst thing she could think of to call him out loud was *buster*. Plenty of other names flashed through her mind, but none she dared verbalize. No doubt Nolan would delight in revealing this in his column, too.

Furious, she grabbed his tie and jerked him into the apartment. "You can come inside," she said.

"Thanks. I think I will," Nolan said wryly. He smoothed his tie, which drew her attention to the hard defined muscles of his chest. The last thing Maryanne wanted to do was notice how virile he looked, and she forced her gaze away from him.

Because it was impossible to stand still, she resumed her pacing. With the first rush of anger spent, she had no idea what to say to him, how to make him realize the enormity of what he'd done. Abruptly, she paused at the edge of her living room and pointed an accusing finger at him. "You have your nerve."

"What I said was true," Nolan stated, boldly meeting her glare. "If you'd bothered to read the column all the way through, objectively, you'd have noticed there were several complimentary statements."

"'A naive idealist, an optimist . . .'" she said, quoting what she remembered, the parts that had offended her the most. "You made me sound like Mary Poppins!"

"Surprisingly unspoiled and gentle," Nolan returned, "and very much a lady."

"You told the entire city I was *lonely*," she cried, mortified to even repeat the words.

"I didn't say you were lonely," Nolan insisted, his voice all too reasonable and controlled. That infuriated her even more. "I said you were away from your family for the first time."

She poked his chest again, punctuating her speech. "But you made it sound like I should be in a day-care center!"

"I didn't imply anything of the kind," he contended. "And I did mention what a good cook you are."

"I'm supposed to be grateful for that? As I recall you said, I was 'surprisingly adept in the kitchen'—as if you were amazed I knew the difference between a goldfish bowl and an oven."

"You're blowing the whole thing out of proportion."

Maryanne barely heard him. "The comment about my being

insecure was the worst. You want security, buster, you're looking at security. My feet could be molded in cement, I'm that secure." Defiant angry eyes flashed to him as she pointed at her shoes.

Nolan didn't so much as blink. "You work twice as hard as anyone else at the *Review*, and twice as many hours. You push yourself because you've got something to prove."

A strained silence followed his words. She *did* work hard, she *was* trying to prove herself, and Nolan knew it. Except for high school and college, she'd had no experience working at a newspaper.

"Did you wake up one morning and decide to play Sigmund Freud with my life?" she demanded. "Who, may I ask, gave you that right?"

"What I said is true, Maryanne," he told her again. "I don't expect you to admit it to me, but if you're honest you'll at least admit it to yourself. Your family is your greatest asset and your weakest link. From everything I've read about the Simpsons, they're good people, but they've cheated you out of something important."

"Exactly what do you mean by that?" she snapped, ready to defend her father to the death, if need be. How dared this pompous, arrogant, argumentative man insult her family?

"You'll never know if you're a good enough journalist to get a job like this without your father's help. He handed you this plum position, and at the same time cheated you out of a just reward."

Maryanne opened her mouth, an argument on the tip of her tongue. Instead, she lowered her gaze, since she couldn't deny what he'd just said. From the moment she arrived at the *Seattle Review*, she'd known that Carol Riverside was the one who'd earned the right to be the local-affairs columnist, not her. And yet Carol had been wonderfully supportive and kind.

"It wasn't my intention to insult you or your family," Nolan continued.

"Then why did you write that column?" she asked, her voice quavering. "Did you think I was going to be flattered by it?"

He'd been so quick with the answers that his silence caught her attention more effectively than anything he could've said. She watched as he started pacing. He drew his fingers through his hair and his shoulders rose in a distinct sigh.

"I'm not sure. In retrospect, I believe I wanted to set the record straight. At least that was my original intent. I wrote more than I should have, but the piece was never meant to ridicule you. Whether you know it or not, you impressed the hell out of me the other night."

"Am I supposed to be grateful you chose to thank me publicly?"

"No," he answered sharply. Once more he jerked his fingers roughly through his hair. He didn't wince, but Maryanne did— which was interesting, since only a few minutes earlier she'd been daydreaming about the joy she'd experience watching this man suffer.

"Inviting myself to dinner the other night was an impulse," he admitted grudgingly. "The words slipped out before I realized what I was saying. I don't know who was more surprised, you or me. I tried to act like I knew what I was doing, play it cool, that sort of thing. The fact is, I discovered I like you. Trust me, I wasn't in any frame of mind to talk civilly to you when you got to the radio station. All along I'd assumed you were a spoiled rich kid, but I was wrong. Since I'd published several pieces that suggested as much, I felt it was only fair to set the record straight. Besides, for a deb you aren't half-bad."

"Why is it every time you compliment me I feel a knife between my shoulder blades?"

"We certainly don't have a whole lot in common," Nolan said thoughtfully. "I learned most everything I know on the streets, not in an expensive private school. I doubt there's a single political issue we can agree on. You're standing on one side of the fence and I'm way over on the other. We're about as far apart as any two people could ever be. Socially. Economically. And every other way I could mention. We have no business even speaking to each other, and yet we sat down and shared a meal and talked for hours."

"I felt betrayed by that column today."

"I know. I apologize, although the damage is already done. I guess I wasn't aware it would offend you. Like I said, that wasn't what I intended at all." He released a giant sigh and paused, as though collecting his thoughts. "After I left your place, I felt good. I can't remember a time I've enjoyed myself more. You're a charming, interesting—"

"You might have said *that* in your column!"

"I did, only you were obviously too upset to notice it. When I got home that night, I couldn't sleep. Every time I'd drift off, I'd think of something you'd said, and before I knew it I'd be grinning. Finally I got up and sat at my desk and started writing. The words poured out of me as fast as I could type them. The quality that impressed me the most about you was your honesty. There's no pretense in you, and the more I thought about that, the more I felt you've been cheated."

"And you decided it was your duty to point all this out—for everyone in town to read?"

"No, it wasn't. That's why I'm here. I admit I went further than I should have and came over to apologize."

"If you're telling me this to make me feel better, it isn't working." Her ego was rebounding somewhat, but he still had a lot of apologizing to do.

"To be honest, I didn't give the column a second thought

until this afternoon, when someone in the office said I'd really done it now. If I was hoping to make peace with you, I'd failed. This friend said I was likely to get hit by the wrath of a woman scorned and suggested I run for cover."

"Rightly so!"

"Forgive me, Maryanne. It was arrogant in the extreme of me to publish that piece. If it'll make you feel any better, you can blast me to kingdom come in your next column. I solemnly promise I'll never write another word about you."

"Don't be so humble—it doesn't suit you," she muttered, gnawing on her lower lip. "Besides, I won't be able to print a rebuttal."

"Why not?"

"I don't plan on working for the *Review* anymore, or at least not after tomorrow." The idea seemed to emerge fully formed; until that moment she hadn't known what she was going to say.

The silence following her words was fraught with tension. "What do you mean?"

"Don't act so surprised. I'm quitting the paper."

"What? Why?" Nolan had been standing during their whole conversation, but he suddenly found it necessary to sit. He lowered himself slowly to the sofa, his face pale. "You're overreacting! There's no need to do anything so drastic."

"There's every need. You said so yourself. You told me I've been cheated, that if I'm even half as good a reporter as I think I am I would've got this 'plum position' on my own. I'm just agreeing with you."

He nodded stiffly.

"As painful as this is to admit, especially to you," she went on, "you're right. My family is wonderful, but they've never allowed me to fall on my face. Carol Riverside is the one who deserved the chance to write that column. She's been with the paper for five years—I'd only been there five minutes. But because my name is Simpson, and because my father made a simple phone call, I was given the job. Carol was cheated. She should've been furious. Instead, she was kind and helpful." Maryanne sat down next to Nolan and propped her feet on the coffee table. "And maybe worse than what happened to Carol is what happened to me as a result of being handed this job. What you wrote about me wondering if I had what it takes to make it as a journalist hit too close to home. All my life my father's been there to tell me I can be anything I want to be and then he promptly arranges it."

"Quitting the *Review* isn't going to change that," Nolan argued. "Come on, Maryanne, you're taking this too seriously."

"Nothing you say is going to change my mind," Maryanne informed him primly. "The time has come for me to cut myself loose and sink or swim on my own."

Her mind was galloping ahead, adjusting to the coming changes. For the first time since she'd read Nolan's column that afternoon, she experienced the beginnings of excitement. She glanced around the apartment as another thought struck her. "Naturally I'll have to move out of this place."

"Are you going back to New York?"

"Heavens, no!" she declared, unaccountably thrilled at the reluctance she heard in his voice. "I love Seattle."

"Listen to me, would you? You're leaping into the deep end, you don't know how to swim and the lifeguard's off duty."

Maryanne hardly heard Nolan, mainly because she didn't like what he was saying. How like a man to start a bonfire and then rush to put out the flames. "The first thing I need to worry about is finding another job," she announced. "A temporary one, of course. I'm going to continue writing, but I don't think I'll be able to support myself on that, not at first, anyway."

"If you insist on this folly, you could always freelance for the *Sun*."

Maryanne discounted that suggestion with a shake of her head. "I'd come off looking like a traitor."

"I suppose you're right." His eyebrows drew together as he frowned.

"You know what else I'm going to do?" She shifted her position, tucking her legs beneath her. "I've got this trust fund that provides a big interest payment every month. That's what I've been using to pay my bills. You and I both know I couldn't afford this place on what I make at the paper. Well, I'm not going to touch those interest payments and I'll live solely on what I earn."

"I . . . wouldn't do that right away, if I were you."

"Why not?"

"You just said you were quitting your job." Nolan sounded uneasy. "I can see that I've set off an avalanche here, and I'm beginning to feel mildly concerned."

"Where do you live?"

"Capitol Hill. Listen, if you're serious about moving, you need to give some thought as to what kind of neighborhood you're getting into. Seattle's a great town, don't get me wrong, but like any place we have our problem areas." He hesitated. "Annie, I don't feel comfortable with this."

"No one's ever called me Annie before." Her eyes smiled into his. "What do you pay in rent?"

With his hands buried deep in his pants pockets, he mumbled something under his breath, then mentioned a figure that was one-third of what she was currently dishing out every month.

"That's more than reasonable."

Maryanne saw surprise in his eyes, and smiled again. "If you're so concerned about my finding the right neighborhood, then you pick one for me. Anyplace, I don't care. Just remember, you're the one who got me into this."

"Don't remind me." Nolan's frown darkened.

"I may not have appreciated what you said about me in your column," Maryanne said slowly, "but I'm beginning to think good things might come of it."

"I'm beginning to think I should be dragged to the nearest tree and hanged," Nolan grumbled.

"Hi." Maryanne slipped into the booth opposite Nolan at the greasy spoon called Mom's Place. She smiled, feeling like a child on a grand adventure. Perhaps she *was* going off the deep end, as Nolan had so adamantly claimed the day before. Perhaps, but she doubted it. Everything felt so *right*.

Once the idea of living on her own—on income she earned herself, from a job she'd been hired for on her own merits— had taken hold in her mind, it had fast gained momentum. She could work days and write nights. That would be perfect.

"Did you do it?"

"I handed in my notice this morning," she said, reaching for the menu. Nolan had insisted on meeting her for a late lunch and suggested this greasy spoon with its faded neon sign that flashed Home Cooking. She had the impression he ate there regularly.

"I talked to the managing editor this morning and told him I was leaving."

"I don't imagine he took kindly to that," Nolan muttered, lifting a white ceramic mug half-full of coffee. He'd been wearing a frown from the moment she'd entered the diner. She had the feeling it was the same frown he'd left her apartment with the night before, but it had deepened since she'd last seen him.

"Larry wasn't too upset, but I don't think he appreciated my suggestion that Carol Riverside take over the column, because he said something I'd rather not repeat about how he was the one who'd do the hiring and promoting, not me, no matter what my name was."

Nolan took a sip of coffee and grinned. "I'd bet he'd like my head if it could be arranged, and frankly I don't blame him."

"Don't worry, I didn't mention your name or the fact that your column was what led to my decision."

Maryanne doubted Nolan even heard her. "I'm regretting that column more with each passing minute. Are you sure I can't talk you out of this?"

"I'm sure."

He sighed and shook his head. "How'd the job hunting go?"

The waitress came by, automatically placing a full mug of coffee in front of Maryanne. She fished a pad from the pocket of her pink apron. "Are you ready to order?"

"I'll have a turkey sandwich on rye, no sprouts, a diet soda and a side of potato salad," Maryanne said with a smile, handing her the menu.

"You don't need to worry, we don't serve sprouts here," she said, scribbling down the order.

"I'll have the chili, Barbara," Nolan said. The waitress nodded and strolled away from the booth. "I was asking how your job hunting went," Nolan reminded Maryanne.

"I found one!"

"Where? What will you be doing? And for how much?"

"You're beginning to sound like my father."

"I'm beginning to *feel* like your father. Annie, you're a babe in the woods. You don't have a clue what you're getting involved in. Heaven knows I've tried to talk some sense into you, but you refuse to listen. And, as you so delight in reminding me, I'm the one responsible for all this."

"Stop blaming yourself." Maryanne leaned across the table for her water glass. "I'm grateful, I honestly am—though, trust me, I never thought I'd be saying that. But what you wrote was true. By insulting me, you've given me the initiative to make a name for myself without Dad's help and—"

He closed his eyes. "Just answer the question."

"Oh, about the job. It's for a . . . service company. It looks like it'll work out great. I didn't think I'd have any chance of getting hired, since I don't have much experience, but they took that into consideration. You see, it's a new company and they can't afford to pay much. Everyone seems friendly and helpful. The only drawback is my salary and the fact that I won't be working a lot of hours at first. In fact, the money is a lot less than I was earning at the paper. But I expect to be able to sell a couple of articles soon. I'll get along all right once I learn to budget."

"How much less than the paper?"

"If I tell you, you'll only get angry." His scowl said he'd be even angrier if she didn't tell him. From the way he was glaring at her, Maryanne knew she'd reached the limits of his patience. She muttered the amount and promptly lowered her gaze.

"You aren't taking the job," Nolan said flatly.

"Yes, I am. It's the best I can do for now. Besides, it's only temporary. It isn't all that easy to find work, you know. I must've talked to fifteen companies today. No one seemed too impressed with my double degree in Early American History and English. I wanted to find employment where I can use my writing skills, but that didn't happen, so I took this job."

"Annie, you won't be able to live on so little."

"I realize that. I've got a list of community newspapers and I'm going to contact them about freelance work. I figure between the writing and my job, I'll do okay."

"Exactly *what* will you be doing?" he demanded.

"Cleaning," she mumbled under her breath.

"What did you say?"

"I'm working for Rent-A-Maid."

"Dear Lord," Nolan groaned. "I hope you're kidding."

"Get your mind out of the gutter, Adams. I'm going to work six hours a day cleaning homes and offices and I'll spend the rest of the time doing research for my articles. Oh, and before I forget, I gave your name as a reference."

"You're going to go back and tell whoever hired you that you're terribly sorry, but you won't be able to work there, after all," Nolan said, and the hard set of his mouth told her he brooked no argument.

Maryanne was saved from having to say she had no intention of quitting, because the waitress, bless her heart, appeared with their orders at precisely that moment.

"Now what about an apartment?" Maryanne asked. After his comment about living in a safe neighborhood, she was more than willing to let him locate one for her. "Have you had a chance to check into that for me?"

"I hope you didn't give your notice at The Seattle."

Swallowing a bite of her sandwich, Maryanne nodded eagerly. "First thing this morning. I told them I'd be out by the fifteenth, which, in case you were unaware of it, happens to be early next week."

"You shouldn't have done that."

"I can't afford the place! And I won't be able to eat in restaurants every day or take cabs or buy things whenever I want them." She smiled proudly as she said it. Money had never been a problem in her life—it had sometimes been an issue, but never a problem. She felt invigorated just thinking about her new status.

"Will you stop grinning at me like that?" Nolan burst out.

"Sorry, it's sort of a novelty to say I can't afford something, that's all," she explained. "It actually feels kind of good."

"In a couple of weeks it's going to feel like hell." Nolan's face spelled out apprehension and gloom.

"Then I'll learn that for myself." She noticed he hadn't touched his meal. "Go ahead and eat your chili before it gets cold."

"I've lost my appetite." He immediately contradicted himself by grabbing a small bottle of hot sauce and dousing the chili with several hard shakes.

"Now did you or did you not find me a furnished studio apartment to look at this afternoon?" Maryanne pressed.

"I found one. It's nothing like you're used to, so be prepared. I'll take you there once we're finished lunch."

"Tell me about it," Maryanne said eagerly.

"There's one main room, small kitchen, smaller bathroom, tiny closet, no dishwasher." He paused as if he expected her to jump to her feet and tell him the whole thing was off.

"Go on," she said, reaching for her soda.

"The floors are pretty worn but they're hardwood."

"That'll be nice." She didn't know if she'd ever lived in a place that didn't have carpeting, but she'd adjust.

"The furniture's solid enough. It's old and weighs a ton, but I don't know how comfortable it is."

"I'm sure it'll be fine. I'll be working just about every day, so I can't see that there'll be a problem," Maryanne returned absently. As soon as she'd spoken, she realized her mistake.

Nolan stabbed his spoon into the chili. "You seem to have forgotten you're resuming your job hunt. You won't be working for Rent-A-Maid, and that's final."

"You sound like a parent again. I'm old enough to know what I can and can't do, and I'm going to take that job whether you like it or not, and *that's final.*"

His eyes narrowed. "We'll see."

"Yes, we will," she retorted. Nolan might be an astute journalist, but there were several things he had yet to learn about her, and one of them was her stubborn streak. The thought produced a small smile as she realized she was thinking of him in a way that suggested a long-term friendship. He was right when he said they stood on opposite sides of the fence on most issues. He was also right when he claimed they had no business being friends. Nevertheless, Nolan Adams was the most intriguing man she'd ever met.

Once they'd finished their meal, Nolan reached for the bill, but Maryanne insisted on splitting it. He clearly wasn't pleased about that but let it pass. Apparently he wasn't going to argue with her, which suited Maryanne just fine. He escorted her to his car, parked outside the diner, and Maryanne slid inside, absurdly pleased that he'd cleaned up the front seat for her.

Nolan hesitated when he joined her, his hands on the steering wheel. "Are you sure you want to go through with this?"

"Positive."

"I was afraid you were going to say that." His mouth twisted. "I can't believe I'm aiding and abetting this nonsense."

"You're my friend, and I'm grateful."

Without another word, he started the engine.

"Where's the apartment?" Maryanne asked as the car progressed up the steep Seattle hills. "I mean, what neighborhood?"

"Capitol Hill."

"Oh, how nice. Isn't that the same part of town you live in?" It wasn't all that far from The Seattle, either, which meant she'd still have the same telephone exchange. Maybe she could even keep her current number.

"Yes," he muttered. He didn't seem to be in the mood for conversation and kept his attention on his driving, instead. He pulled into a parking lot behind an eight-storey post–World War II brick building. "The apartment's on the fourth floor."

"That'll be fine." She climbed out of the car and stared at the old structure. The Dumpster was backed against the wall and full to overflowing. Maryanne had to step around it before entering by a side door. Apparently there was no elevator, and by the time they reached the fourth floor she was so winded she couldn't have found the breath to complain, anyway.

"The manager gave me the key," Nolan explained as he paused in the hallway and unlocked the second door on the right. Nolan wasn't even breathing hard, while Maryanne was leaning against the wall, dragging deep breaths into her oxygen-starved lungs.

Nolan opened the door and waved her in. "As I said, it's not much."

Maryanne walked inside and was struck by the sparseness of the furnishings. One overstuffed sofa and one end table with a lamp on a dull stained-wood floor. She blinked, squared her shoulders and forced a smile to her lips. "It's perfect."

"You honestly think you can live here after The Seattle?" He sounded incredulous.

"Yes, I do," she said with a determination that would've made generations of Simpsons proud. "How far away is your place?"

Nolan walked over to the window, his back to her. He exhaled sharply before he announced, "I live in the apartment next door."

Three

"I don't need a babysitter," Maryanne protested. She had some trouble maintaining the conviction in her voice. In truth, she was pleased to learn that Nolan's apartment was next door, and her heart did a little jig all its own.

Nolan turned away from the window. His mouth was set in a thin straight line, as if he was going against his better judgment in arranging this. "That night at the radio station," he mumbled softly. "I knew it then."

"Knew what?"

Slowly, he shook his head, apparently lost in his musings. "I took one look at you and deep down inside I heard a small voice cry out, 'Here comes trouble.'"

Despite his fierce expression, Maryanne laughed.

"Like a fool I ignored it, although Lord only knows how I could have."

"You're not blaming me for all this, are you?" Maryanne asked, placing her hands on her hips, prepared to do battle. "In case you've forgotten, you're the one who invited yourself to dinner that night. Then you got me all mellow with wine—"

"You were the one who brought out the bottle. You can't blame me for *that*." He was muttering again and buried his hands deep in the pockets of his raincoat.

"I was only being a good hostess."

"All right, all right, I get the picture," he said through clenched teeth, shaking his head again. "I was the one stupid enough to write that column afterward. I'd give a week's pay to take it all back. No, make that a month's pay. This is the last time," he vowed, "that I'm ever going to set the record straight. Any record." He jerked his hand from his pocket and stared at it.

Maryanne crossed to the large overstuffed sofa covered with faded chintz fabric and ran her hand along the armrest. It was nearly threadbare in places and nothing like the supple white leather of her sofa at The Seattle. "I wish you'd stop worrying about me. I'm not as fragile as I look."

Nolan snickered softly. "A dust ball could bowl you over."

A ready argument sprang to her lips, but she quickly swallowed it. "I'll take the apartment, but I want it understood, right now, that you have no responsibilities toward me. I'm a big girl and I'll manage perfectly well on my own. I have in the past and I'll continue to do so in the future."

Nolan didn't respond. Instead he grumbled something she couldn't hear. He seemed to be doing a lot of that since he'd met her. Maybe it was a long-established habit, but somehow she doubted it.

Nolan drove her back to The Seattle, and the whole way there Maryanne could hardly contain a feeling of delight. For the first time, she was taking control of her own life. Nolan, however, was obviously experiencing no such enthusiasm.

"Do I need to sign anything for the apartment? What about a deposit?"

"You can do that later. You realize this studio apartment is the smallest one in the entire building? My own apartment is three times that size."

"Would you stop worrying?" Maryanne told him. A growing sense of purpose filled her, and a keen exhilaration unlike anything she'd ever felt.

Nolan pulled into the circular driveway at her building. "Do you want to come up for a few minutes?" she asked.

His dark eyes widened as if she'd casually suggested they play a round of Russian roulette. "You've got to be kidding."

She wasn't.

He held up both hands. "No way. Before long, you'll be serving wine and we'll be talking like old friends. Then I'll go home thinking about you, and before I know how it happened—" He stopped abruptly. "No, thanks."

"Goodbye, then," she said, disappointed. "I'll see you later."

"Right. Later." But the way he said it suggested that if he didn't stumble upon her for a decade or two it would be fine with him.

Maryanne climbed out of his car and was about to close the door when she hesitated. "Nolan?"

"Now what?" he barked.

"Thank you," she said softly.

Predictably, he started mumbling and drove off the instant she closed the door. In spite of his sour mood, Maryanne found herself smiling.

Once inside her apartment, she was immediately struck by the contrast between this apartment at The Seattle and the place Nolan had shown her. One was grey, cramped and dingy, the other polished and spacious and elegant. Her mind's eye went over the dreary apartment on Capitol Hill, and she felt a growing sense of excitement as she thought of different inexpensive ways to bring it color and character. She'd certainly faced challenges before, but never one quite like this. Instinctively she knew there'd be real satisfaction in decorating that place with her newly limited resources.

Turning her new apartment into a home was the least of her worries, however. She had yet to tell her parents that she'd quit her job. Their reaction would be as predictable as Nolan's.

The phone seemed to draw her. Slowly she walked across the room toward it, sighing deeply. Her fingers closed tightly around the receiver. Before she could change her mind, she closed her eyes, punched out the number and waited.

Her mother answered almost immediately.

"I was sitting at my desk," Muriel Simpson explained. She seemed delighted to hear from Maryanne. "How's Seattle? Are you still as fascinated with the Northwest?"

"More than ever," Maryanne answered without a pause; what she didn't say was that part of her fascination was now because of Nolan.

"I'm pleased you like it so well, but I don't mind telling you, sweetie, I miss you terribly."

"I haven't lived at home for years," Maryanne reminded her mother.

"I know, but you were so much closer to home in Manhattan than you are now. I can't join you for lunch the way I did last year."

"Seattle's lovely. I hope you'll visit me soon." But not too soon, she prayed.

"Sometime this spring, I promise," Muriel said. "I was afraid once you settled there all that rain would get you down."

"Mother, honestly, New York City has more annual rainfall than Seattle."

"I know, dear, but in New York the rain all comes in a few days. In Seattle it drizzles for weeks on end, or so I've heard."

"It's not so bad." Maryanne had been far too busy to pay much attention to the weather. Gathering her courage, she forged ahead. "The reason I called is that I've got a bit of exciting news for you."

"You're madly in love and want to get married."

Muriel Simpson was looking forward to grandchildren and had been ever since Maryanne's graduation from college. Both her brothers, Mark and Sean, were several years younger, so Maryanne knew the expectations were all focused on her. For the past couple of years they'd been introducing her to suitable young men.

"It's nothing that dramatic," Maryanne said, then, losing her courage, she crossed her fingers behind her back and blurted out, "I've got a special assignment . . . for the—uh—paper." The lie nearly stuck in her throat.

"A special assignment?"

All right, she was stretching the truth about as far as it would go, and she hated doing it. But she had no choice. Nolan's reaction would look tame compared to her parents' if they ever found out she was working as a janitor. Rent-A-Maid gave it a fancy name, but basically she'd been hired to clean. It wasn't a glamorous job, nor was it profitable, but it was honest work and she needed something to tide her over until she made a name for herself in her chosen field.

"What kind of special assignment?"

"It's a research project. I can't really talk about it yet." Maryanne decided it was best to let her family assume the "assignment" was with the newspaper. She wasn't happy about this; in fact, she felt downright depressed to be misleading her mother this way, but she dared not hint at what she'd actually be doing. The only comfort she derived was from the prospect of showing them her published work in a few months.

"It's not anything dangerous, is it?"

"Oh, heavens, no," Maryanne said, forcing a light laugh. "But I'm going to be involved in it for several weeks, so I won't be mailing you any of my columns, at least not for a while. I didn't want you to wonder when you didn't hear from me."

"Will you be travelling?"

"A little." Only a few city blocks, as a matter of fact, but she couldn't very well say so. "Once everything's completed, I'll get in touch with you."

"You won't even be able to phone?" Her mother's voice carried a hint of concern.

Not often, at least not on her budget, Maryanne realized regretfully.

"Of course I'll phone," she hurried to assure her mother. She didn't often partake in subterfuge, and being new to the game, she was making everything up as she went along. She hoped her mother would be trusting enough to take her at her word.

"Speaking of your columns, dear, tell me what happened with that dreadful reporter who was harassing you earlier in the month."

"Dreadful reporter?" Maryanne repeated uncertainly. "Oh," she said with a flash of insight. "You mean Nolan Adams."

"That's his name?" Her mother's voice rose indignantly. "I hope he's stopped using that column of his to irritate you."

"It was all in good fun, Mother." All right, he *had* irritated her, but Maryanne was willing to forget their earlier pettiness. "We're friends now. As it happens, I like him quite a lot."

"Friends," her mother echoed softly. Slowly. "Your new-found friend isn't married, is he? You know your father and I started our own relationship at odds with each other, don't you?"

"Mother, honestly. Stop matchmaking."

"Just answer me one thing. Is he married or not?"

"Not. He's in his early thirties and he's handsome." A no-ticeable pause followed the description. "Mother?"

"You're attracted to him, aren't you?"

Maryanne wasn't sure she should admit it, but on the other hand she'd already given herself away. "Yes," she said stiffly, "I am . . . a little. There's a lot to like about him, even though we don't always agree. He's very talented. I've never read a column of his that didn't make me smile—and think. He's got this—er—interesting sense of humor."

"So it seems. Has he asked you out?"

"Not yet." *But he will*, her heart told her.

"Give him time." Muriel Simpson's voice had lowered a notch or two. "Now, sweetie, before we hang up, I want you to tell me some more about this special assignment of yours."

They talked for a few minutes longer, and Maryanne was astonished at her own ability to lie by omission—and avoid answering her mother's questions. She hated this subterfuge, and she hated the guilt she felt afterward. She tried to reason it away by reminding herself that her motives were good. If her parents knew what she was planning, they'd be sick with worry. But she couldn't remain their little girl forever. She had something to prove, and for the first time she was going to compete like a real contender—without her father standing on the sidelines, bribing the judges.

Maryanne didn't hear from Nolan for the next three days, and she was getting anxious. At the end of the week, she'd be finished at the *Review*; the following Monday she'd be starting at Rent-A-Maid. To her delight, Carol Riverside was appointed as her replacement. The look the managing editor tossed Maryanne's way suggested he'd given Carol the job not because of her recommendation, but despite it.

"I'm still not convinced you're doing the right thing," Carol told her over lunch on Maryanne's last day at the paper.

"But *I'm* convinced, and that's what's important," Maryanne returned. "Why is everyone so afraid I'm going to fall flat on my face?"

"It's not that, exactly."

"Then what is it?" she pressed. "I don't think Nolan stopped grumbling from the moment I announced I was quitting the paper, finding a job and moving out on my own."

"And well he should grumble!" Carol declared righteously. "He's the one who started this whole thing. You're such a nice girl. I can't see you getting mixed up with the likes of him."

Maryanne had a sneaking suspicion her friend wasn't saying this out of loyalty to the newspaper. "Mixed up with the likes of him? Is there something I don't know about Seattle's favorite journalist?"

"Nolan Adams may be the most popular newspaper writer in town, but he's got a biting edge to him. Oh, he's witty and talented, I'll give him that, but he has this scornful attitude that makes me want to shake him till he rattles."

"I know he's a bit cynical."

"He's a good deal more than cynical. The problem is, he's so darn entertaining that his attitude is easy to overlook. I'd like two minutes alone with that man just so I could set him straight. He had no business saying what he did about you in that 'My Evening with the Debutante' piece. Look where it's led!"

For that matter, Maryanne wouldn't mind spending two minutes alone with Nolan, either, but for an entirely different reason. The speed with which the thought entered her mind surprised her enough to produce a soft smile.

"Only this time his words came back to bite him," Carol continued.

"Everything he wrote was true," Maryanne felt obliged to remind her friend. She hadn't been all that thrilled when he'd decided to share those truths with the entire western half of Washington state, but she couldn't fault his perceptions.

"Needless to say, I'm not as concerned about Nolan as I am about you," Carol said, gazing down at her sandwich. "I've seen that little spark in your eye when you talk about him, and frankly it worries me."

Maryanne immediately lowered her betraying eyes. "I'm sure you're mistaken. Nolan and I are friends, but that's the extent of it." She wasn't sure Nolan would even want to claim her as a friend; she rather suspected he thought of her as a nuisance.

"Perhaps it's friendship on his part, but it's a lot more on yours. I'm afraid you're going to fall in love with that scoundrel."

"That's crazy," Maryanne countered swiftly. "I've only just met him." Carol's gaze narrowed on her like a diamond drill bit and Maryanne sighed. "He intrigues me," she admitted, "but that's a long way from becoming emotionally involved with him."

"I can't help worrying about you. And, Maryanne, if you're falling in love with Nolan, that worries me more than the idea of you being a Rent-a-Maid or finding yourself an apartment on Capitol Hill."

Maryanne swallowed tightly. "Nolan's a talented, respected journalist. If I was going to fall in love with him, which I don't plan to do in the near future, but if I *did* fall for him, why would it be so tragic?"

"Because you're sweet and caring and he's so . . ." Carol paused and stared into space. "Because he's so scornful."

"True, but underneath that gruff exterior is a heart of gold. At least I think there is," Maryanne joked.

"Maybe, but I doubt it," Carol went on. "Don't get me wrong—I respect Nolan's talent. It's his devil-may-care attitude that troubles me."

But it didn't trouble Maryanne. Not in the least. Perhaps that was what she found most appealing about him. Yet everything Carol said about Nolan was true. He did tend to be cynical and a bit sardonic, but he was also intuitive, reflective and, despite Carol's impression to the contrary, considerate.

Since it was her last day at the paper, Maryanne spent a few extra minutes saying goodbye to her co-workers. Most were sorry to see her go. There'd been a fair amount of resentment directed at her when she arrived, but her hard work seemed to have won over all but the most skeptical doubters.

On impulse, Maryanne stopped at the diner where Nolan had met her earlier in the week, hoping he'd be there. Her heart flew into her throat when she saw him sitting in a booth by the window, a book propped open in front of him. He didn't look up when she walked in.

Nor did he notice her when she approached his booth. Without waiting for an invitation, she slid in across from him.

"Hi," she murmured, keeping her voice low and secretive. "Here comes trouble to plague you once more."

Slowly, with obvious reluctance, Nolan dragged his gaze from the novel. Another mystery, Maryanne noted. "What are you doing here, Trouble?"

"Looking for you."

"Why? Have you thought up any other ways to test my patience? How about walking a tightrope between two skyscrapers? That sounds right up your alley."

"I hadn't heard from you in the past few days." She paused, hoping he'd pick up the conversation. "I thought there was something I should do about the apartment. Sign a lease, give the manager a deposit, that sort of thing."

"Annie—"

"I hope you realize I don't even know the address. I only saw it that one time."

"I told you not to worry about it."

"But I don't want anyone else to rent it."

"They won't." He laid the book aside just as the waitress appeared carrying a glass of water and a menu. Maryanne recognized her from the other day. "Hello, Barbara," she said, reading the woman's name tag. "What's the special for the day? Mr. Adams owes me a meal and I think I'll collect it while I've got the chance." She waited for him to ask her what she was talking about, but apparently he remembered his promise of dinner to pay her back for the Irish stew he'd eaten at her house the first evening they'd met.

"Cabbage rolls, with soup or salad," Barbara said, pulling out her pad and pencil while Maryanne quickly scanned the menu.

"I'll have a cheeseburger and a chocolate shake," Maryanne decided.

Barbara grinned. "I'll make sure it comes up with Mr. Adams's order."

"Thanks," she said, handing her back the menu. Barbara sauntered off toward the kitchen, scribbling on her order pad as she walked.

"It was my last day at the paper," Maryanne said.

"I'll ask you one more time—are you *sure* you want to go through with this?" Nolan demanded. "Hell, I never thought for a moment you'd want that apartment. Damn it all, you're a stubborn woman."

"Of course I'm taking the apartment."

"That's what I thought." He closed his eyes briefly. "What did the Rent-A-Maid agency say when you told them you wouldn't be taking the job?"

Maryanne stared purposely out the window. "Nothing."

He cocked an eyebrow. "Nothing?"

"What could they say?" she asked, trying to ignore the doubt reflected in his eyes. Maybe she was getting good at this lie-telling business, which wasn't a comforting thought. The way she'd misled her mother still bothered her.

Nolan drew one hand across his face. "You didn't tell them, did you? Apparently you intend to play the Cinderella role to the hilt."

"And you intend to play the role of my wicked stepmother to perfection."

He didn't say anything for a long moment. "Is there a part in that fairy tale where Cinderella gets locked in a closet for her own good?"

"Why?" she couldn't resist asking. "Is that what you're going to do?"

"Don't tempt me."

"I wish you had more faith in me."

"I do have faith in you. I have faith that you're going to make my life hell for the next few months while you go about proving yourself. Heaven knows what possessed me to write that stupid column, but, trust me, there hasn't been a minute since it hit the streets that I haven't regretted it. Not a single minute."

"But—"

"Now you insist on moving into the apartment next to mine. That's just great. Wonderful. Whatever peace I have in my life will be completely and utterly destroyed."

"That's not true!" Maryanne cried. "Besides, I'd like to re-mind you, you're the one who found that apartment, not me. I have no intention of pestering you."

"Like I said, I figured just seeing the apartment would be enough to put you off. Now I won't have a minute to myself. I know it, and you know it." His eyes were darker and more brooding than she'd ever seen them. "I wasn't kidding when I said you were trouble."

"All right," Maryanne said, doing her best to disguise her crushing sense of defeat. "It's obvious you never expected me to take the place. I suppose you arranged it to look as bleak as you could. Don't worry, I'll find somewhere else to live. Another apartment as far away from you as I can possibly get." She was out of the booth so fast, so intent on escaping, that she nearly collided with Barbara.

"What about your cheeseburger?" the waitress asked.

Maryanne glanced at Nolan. "Wrap it up and give it to Mr. Adams. I've lost my appetite."

The tears that blurred her eyes only angered her more. Furious with herself for allowing his words to wound her, she hurried down the street, headed in the direction of the Seattle waterfront. It was growing dark, but she didn't care; she needed to vent some of her anger, and a brisk hike would serve that purpose nicely.

She wasn't concerned when she heard hard quick footsteps behind her. As the wind whipped at her, she shivered and drew her coat closer, tucking her hands in her pockets and hunching her shoulders forward.

Carol and Nolan both seemed to believe she needed a keeper! They apparently considered her incompetent, and their doubts cut deeply into her pride.

Her head bowed against the force of the wind, she noticed a pair of male legs matching steps with her own. She looked up and discovered Nolan had joined her.

For the longest time, he said nothing. They were halfway down a deserted pier before he spoke. "I don't want you to find another apartment."

"I think it would be for the best if I did." He'd already told her she was nothing but trouble, and if that wasn't bad enough, he'd implied she was going to be a constant nuisance in his life. She had no intention of bothering him. As far as she was concerned, they could live on opposite sides of town. That was what he wanted and that was what he was going to get.

"It isn't for the best," he argued.

"It is. We obviously rub each other the wrong way."

Nolan turned and gripped her by the shoulders. "The apartment's been cleaned. It's ready for you to move into anytime you want. The rent is reasonable and the neighborhood's a good one. As I recall, this whole ridiculous business between us started over an article about the lack of affordable housing. You're not going to find anyplace else, not with what you intend to live on."

"But you live next door!"

"I'm well aware of that."

Maryanne bristled. "I won't live beside a man who considers me a pest. And furthermore, you still owe me dinner."

"I said you were trouble," he pointed out, ignoring her claim. "I didn't say you were a pest."

"You did so."

"I said you were going to destroy my peace—"

"Exactly."

"—of mind," he went on. He closed his eyes briefly and expelled a sharp frustrated sigh, then repeated, "You're going to destroy my peace of mind."

Maryanne wasn't sure she understood. She stared up at him, intrigued by the emotion she saw in his intense brown eyes.

"Why the hell should it matter if you live next door to me or in The Seattle?" he exclaimed. "My serenity was shot the minute I laid eyes on you."

"I don't understand," she said, surprised when her voice came out a raspy whisper. She continued to look up at him, trying to read his expression.

"You don't have a clue, do you?" he whispered. His fingers found their way into her hair as he lowered his mouth with heart-stopping slowness toward hers. "Heaven keep me from redheaded innocents."

But heaven apparently didn't receive the message, because even as he whispered the words Nolan's arms were pulling her toward him. With a sigh of regret—or was it pleasure?—his mouth settled over hers. His kiss was light and undemanding, and despite her anger, despite his words, Maryanne felt herself melting.

With a soft sigh, she flattened her hands on his chest and slid them up to link behind his neck. She leaned against him, letting his strength support her, letting his warmth comfort her.

He pulled her even closer, wrapped his arms around her waist and half lifted her from the pier. Maryanne heard a low hungry moan; she wasn't sure if it came from Nolan or from her.

It didn't matter. Nothing mattered except this wonderful feeling of being cherished and loved and protected.

Over the years, Maryanne had been kissed by her share of men. She'd found the experience pleasant, but no one had ever set her on fire the way Nolan did now.

"See what I mean," he whispered unsteadily. "We're in trouble here. Big trouble."

Four

Maryanne stood in the doorway of her new apartment, the key held tightly in her hand. She was embarking on her grand adventure, but now that she'd actually moved out of The Seattle her confidence was a bit shaky.

Carol joined her, huffing and puffing as she staggered the last few steps down the narrow hallway. She sagged against the wall, panting to catch her breath.

"This place doesn't have an elevator?" she demanded, when she could speak.

"It's being repaired."

"That's what they always say."

Maryanne nodded, barely hearing her friend. Her heart in her throat, she inserted the key and turned the lock. The door stuck, so she used the force of one hip to dislodge it. The apartment was just as she remembered: worn hardwood floors, the bulky faded furniture, the kitchen appliances that would soon be valuable antiques. But Maryanne saw none of that.

This was her new life.

She walked directly to the window and gazed out. "I've got a great view of Volunteer Park," she announced to her friend.

She hadn't noticed it the day Nolan had shown her the apartment. "I had no idea the park was so close." She turned toward Carol, who was still standing in the threshold, her expression one of shock and dismay. "What's wrong?"

"Good heavens," Carol whispered. "You don't really intend to live here, do you?"

"It isn't so bad," Maryanne said with a smile, glancing around to be sure she hadn't missed anything. "I've got lots of ideas on how to decorate the place." She leaned back against the windowsill, where much of the dingy beige paint was chipped away to reveal an even dingier grey-green. "What it needs is a fresh coat of paint, something light and cheerful."

"It's not even half the size of your other place."

"There was a lot of wasted space at my apartment." That might be true, Maryanne thought privately, but she wouldn't have minded bringing some of it with her.

"What about your neighbor?" Carol asked in a grudging voice. "He's the one who started this. The least he could do is offer a little help."

Straightening, Maryanne brushed the dust from her palms and looked away. "I didn't ask him to. I don't think he even knows when I was planning to move in."

Nolan was a subject Maryanne wanted to avoid. She hadn't talked to him since the night he'd followed her to the waterfront . . . the night he'd kissed her. He'd stopped off at The Seattle to leave the apartment key and a rental agreement with the doorman. Max had promptly delivered both. The implication was obvious; Nolan didn't want to see her and was, in fact, doing his best to avoid her.

Clearly he disapproved of the way things had developed on the pier that night. She supposed he didn't like kissing her. Then again, perhaps he did. Perhaps he liked it too much for his oft-lamented "peace of mind."

Maryanne knew how *she* felt about it. She couldn't sleep for two nights afterward. Every time she closed her eyes, the image of Nolan holding her in his arms danced through her mind like a waltzing couple from a 1940s movie. She remembered the way he'd scowled down at her when he'd broken off the kiss and how he'd struggled to make light of the incident. And she remembered his eyes, so warm and gentle, telling her another story.

"Hey, lady, is this the place where I'm supposed to bring the boxes?" A lanky boy of about fourteen stood in the doorway, carrying a large cardboard box.

"Y-yes," Maryanne said, recognizing the container as one of her own. "How'd you know to bring it up here?"

"Mr. Adams. He promised a bunch of us guys he'd play basketball with us if we'd help unload the truck."

"Oh. How nice. I'm Maryanne Simpson," she said, her heart warming at Nolan's unexpected thoughtfulness.

"Nice to meet you, lady. Now where do you want me to put this?"

Maryanne pointed to the kitchen. "Just put it in the corner over there." Before she finished, a second and third boy appeared, each hauling boxes.

Maryanne slipped past them and ran down the stairs to the parking area behind the building. Nolan was standing in the back of Carol's husband's pickup, noisily distributing cardboard boxes and dire warnings. He didn't see her until she moved closer. When he did, he fell silent, a frown on his face.

"Hi," she said, feeling a little shy. "I came to thank you."

"You shouldn't have gone up and left the truck unattended," he barked, still frowning. "Anyone could've walked off with this stuff."

"We just arrived."

"We?"

"Carol Riverside and me. She's upstairs trying to regain her breath. How long will it be before the elevator's fixed?"

"Not soon."

She nodded. Well, if he'd hoped to discourage her, she wasn't going to let him. So what if she had to walk up four flights of stairs every day! It was wonderful aerobic exercise. In the past she'd paid good money to attend a health club for the same purpose.

Nolan returned to his task, lifting boxes and handing them to a long line of teenage boys. "I'm surprised you didn't have a moving company manage this for you."

"Are you kidding?" she joked. "Only rich people use moving companies."

"Is this all of it, or do you need to make a second trip?"

"This is it. Carol and I put everything else in storage earlier this morning. It's only costing me a few dollars a month. I have to be careful about money now, you know."

He scowled again. "When do you start with the cleaning company?"

"Monday morning."

Nolan placed his hands on his hips and glared down at her. "If you're really intending to take that job—"

"Of course I am!"

"Then the first thing you'll need to do is ask for a raise."

"Oh, honestly, Nolan," she protested, walking backward. "I can't do that!"

"What you can't do is live on that amount of money, no matter how well you budget," he muttered. He leapt off the back of the truck as agilely as a cat. "Will you listen to me for once?"

"I am listening," she said. "It just so happens I don't agree. Quit worrying about me, would you? I'm going to be perfectly all right, especially once I start selling articles."

"I'm not a knight in shining armor, understand?" he shouted after her. "If you think I'll be racing to your rescue every time you're in trouble, then you need to think again."

"You're insulting me by even suggesting I'd accept your help." She tried to be angry with him but found it impossible. He might insist she was entirely on her own, but all the while he was lecturing her he was doling out her boxes so she wouldn't have to haul them up the stairs herself. Nolan might claim not to be a knight riding to her rescue, but he was behaving suspiciously like one.

Two hours later, Maryanne was alone in her new apartment for the first time. Standing in the middle of her living room, she surveyed her kingdom. As she'd told Carol, it wasn't so bad. Boxes filled every bit of available space, but it wouldn't take her long to unpack and set everything in order.

She was grateful for the help Carol, Nolan and the neighborhood teenagers had given her, but now it was up to her. And she had lots of plans—she'd paint the walls and put up her pictures and buy some plants—to make this place cheerful and attractive. To turn it into a home.

It was dark before she'd finished unpacking, and by that time she was both exhausted and hungry. Actually *famished* more adequately described her condition. Her hunger and exhaustion warred with each other: she was too tired to go out and buy herself something to eat, but too hungry to go to bed without eating. Making the decision about which she should do created a dilemma of startling proportions.

She'd just decided to make do with a bowl of cornflakes, without milk, when there was a loud knock at her door. She jerked it open to find Nolan there, wearing grey sweatpants and a sweat-soaked T-shirt. He held a basketball under one arm and clutched a large white paper sack in his free hand.

"Never open the door without knowing who's on the

other side," he warned, walking directly into the apartment. He dropped the basketball on the sofa and placed his sack—obviously from a fast-food restaurant—on the coffee table. "That security chain's there for a reason. Use it."

Maryanne was still standing at the door, inhaling the aroma of french fries and hamburgers. "Yes, your majesty."

"Don't get testy with me, either. I've just lost two years of my life on a basketball court. I'm too old for this, but luckily what I lack in youth I make up for in smarts."

"I see," she said, closing the door. For good measure she clipped the chain in place and turned the lock.

"A little show of appreciation would go a long way toward soothing my injuries," he told her, sinking on to the sofa. He rested his head against the cushion, eyes drifting shut.

"You can't be that smart, otherwise you'd have managed to get out of playing with boys twenty years younger than you," she said lightly. She had trouble keeping her eyes off the white sack on the scratched mahogany coffee table.

Nolan straightened, wincing as he did so. "I thought you might be hungry." He reached for the bag and removed a wrapped hamburger, which he tossed to her before taking a second for himself. Next he set out two cardboard cartons full of hot french fries and two cans of soda.

Maryanne sat down beside him, her hand pressed against her stomach to keep it from growling. "You'd better be careful," she said. "You're beginning to look suspiciously like that knight in shining armor."

"Don't kid yourself."

Maryanne was too hungry to waste time arguing. She devoured the hamburger and fries within minutes. Then she relaxed against the back of the sofa and sighed, content.

"I came to set some ground rules," Nolan explained. "I think you and I need to get a few things straight."

"Sure," she agreed, although she was fairly certain she knew what he wanted to talk about. "I've already promised not to pester you."

"Good. I intend to stay out of your way, too."

"Perfect." It didn't really sound all that wonderful, but it seemed to be what he wanted, so she didn't have much choice. "Anything else?"

Nolan hesitated. Then he leaned forward, resting his forearms on his knees. "Yes, one other thing." He turned to her with a frown. "I don't think we should . . . you know, kiss again."

A short silence followed his words. At first Maryanne wasn't sure she'd heard him correctly.

"I realize talking about this may be embarrassing," Nolan continued, sounding as detached as if he'd introduced the subject of football scores. "I want you to know I'm suggesting this for your own good."

"I'm pleased to hear that." It was an effort not to mock him by rolling her eyes.

He nodded and cleared his throat, and Maryanne could see he wasn't nearly as indifferent as he wanted her to believe.

"There appears to be a certain amount of physical chemistry between us," he said, avoiding even a glance in her direction. "I feel that the sooner we settle this, the less likelihood there'll be for misunderstandings later on. The last thing I need is for you to fall in love with me."

"That's it!" she cried, throwing up her arms. The ridiculousness of his comment revived her enough to indulge in some good-natured teasing. "If I can't have your heart and soul, then I'm leaving right now!"

"Damn it, Annie, this is nothing to joke about."

"Who's joking?" she asked. She made her voice absurdly melodramatic. "I knew the minute I walked into the radio station for the Celebrity Debate that if I couldn't taste your lips there was nothing left to live for."

"If you're going to make a joke out of this, then you can forget the whole discussion." He vaulted to his feet and stuffed the wrappers from their burgers and fries into the empty sack. "I was hoping we could have a mature talk, one adult to another, but that's obviously beyond you."

"Don't get so bent out of shape," she said, trying not to smile. "Sit down before you do something silly, like leave in a huff. We both know you'll regret it." She didn't know anything of the sort, but it sounded good.

He complied grudgingly, but he stared past her, training his eyes on the darkened window.

Maryanne got stiffly to her feet, every muscle and joint protesting. "It seems to me that you're presuming a great deal with this hands-off decree," she said with all the dignity she could muster. "What makes you think I'd even *want* you to kiss me again?"

A slow cocky grin raised the corners of his mouth. "A man can tell. My biggest fear is that you're going to start thinking things I never meant you to think. Eventually you'd end up getting hurt. I intend to make damn sure nothing romantic develops between us. Understand?"

"You're saying my head's in the clouds when it comes to you?"

"That's right. You're a sweet kid, stubborn and idealistic, but nonetheless naive. One kiss told me you've got a romantic soul, and frankly I don't want you fluttering those pretty blue eyes at me and dreaming of babies and a white picket fence. You and I are about as different as two people can get."

"Different?" To Maryanne's way of thinking, she had more in common with Nolan Adams than with any other man she'd ever dated.

"That's right. You come from this rich upstanding family—"

"Stop!" she cried. "Don't say another word about our economic differences. They're irrelevant. If you're looking for excuses, find something else."

"I don't need excuses. It'd never work between us and I want to make sure neither of us is ever tempted to try. If you want someone to teach you about being a woman, go elsewhere."

His words were like a slap in the face. "Naturally a man of your vast romantic experience gets plenty of requests." She turned away, so angry she couldn't keep still. "As for being afraid I might fall in love with you, let me assure you right now that there's absolutely no chance of it. In fact, I think you should be more concerned about falling for me!" Her voice was gaining strength and conviction with every word. The man had such colossal nerve. At one time she might have found herself attracted to him, but that possibility had disappeared the minute he walked in her door and opened his mouth.

"Don't kid yourself," he argued. "You're halfway in love with me already. I can see it in your eyes."

Carol had said something about her eyes revealing what she felt for Nolan, too.

Maryanne whirled around, intent on composing a suitably sarcastic retort, away from his searching gaze. But before any mocking words could pass her lips, a sharp pain shot through her neck, an ache so intense it brought immediate tears to her eyes. She must have moved too quickly, too carelessly.

Her hands flew to the back of her neck.

Nolan was instantly on his feet. "What's wrong?"

"Nothing," she mumbled, easing her way back to the sofa. She sat down, hand still pressed to her neck, waiting a moment before slowly rotating her head, wanting to test the extent of her injury. Quickly, she realized her mistake.

"Annie," Nolan demanded, kneeling in front of her, "what is it?"

"I . . . don't know. I moved wrong, I guess."

His hands replaced hers. "You've got a crick in your neck?"

"If I do, it's all your fault. You say the most ridiculous things."

"I know." His voice was as gentle as his hands. He began to knead softly, his fingers tenderly massaging the tight muscles.

"I'm all right."

"Of course you are," he whispered. "Just close your eyes and relax."

"I can't." How could he possibly expect her to do that when he was so close, so warm and sensual? He was fast making a lie of all her protestations.

"Yes, you can," he said, his voice low and seductive. He leaned over her, his face, his lips, scant inches from hers. His hands were working the tightness from her neck and shoulders and at the same time creating a dizzying heated sensation that extended to the tips of her fingers and the soles of her feet.

She sighed and clasped his wrist with both hands, wanting to stop him before she made a fool of herself by swaying toward him or doing something equally suggestive. "I think you should stop. Let me rephrase that. I *know* you should stop."

"I know I should, too," he admitted quietly. "Remember what I said earlier?"

"You mean the hands-off policy?"

"Yes." She could hardly hear him. "Let's delay it for a day— what do you think?"

At that moment, clear organized thought was something of a problem. "Wh-whatever you feel is best."

"Oh, I know what's best," he whispered. "Unfortunately that doesn't seem to make a damn bit of difference right now."

She wasn't sure exactly when it happened, but her hands seemed to have left his wrists and were splayed across the front of his T-shirt. His chest felt rigid and muscular; his heart beneath her palms pounded hard and fast. She wondered if her own pulse was keeping time with his.

With infinite slowness, Nolan lowered his mouth to hers. Maryanne's eyes drifted closed of their own accord and she moaned, holding back a small cry of welcome. His touch was even more compelling than she remembered. Nolan must have felt something similar, because his groan followed, an echo of hers.

He kissed her again and again. Maryanne wanted more, but he resisted giving in to her desires—or his own. It was as if he'd decided a few kisses were of little consequence and wouldn't seriously affect either one of them.

Wrong. Maryanne wanted to shout it at him, but couldn't.

His mouth left hers and blazed a fiery trail of kisses across her sensitized skin. His lips brushed her throat, under her chin to the vulnerable hollow. Only minutes earlier, moving her neck without pain had been impossible; now she did so freely, turning it, arching, asking—no, demanding—that he kiss her again the way he had that night at the waterfront.

Nolan complied, and he seemed to do it willingly, surrendering the battle. He groaned anew and the sound came from deep in his throat. His fingers tangled in the thick strands of her hair as his mouth rushed back to hers.

Maryanne was experiencing a renewal of her own. She felt as if she had lain dormant and was bursting to life, like a flower struggling out of winter snows into the light and warmth of spring.

All too soon, Nolan pulled away from her. His eyes met and held hers. She knew her eyes were filled with questions, but his gave her no answers.

He got abruptly to his feet.

"Nolan," she said, shocked that he would leave her like this.

He looked back at her and she saw it then. The regret. A regret tinged with compassion. "You're so exhausted you can barely sit up. Go to bed and we'll both forget this ever happened. Understand?"

Too stunned to reply, she nodded. Maybe Nolan could forget it, but she knew she wouldn't.

"Lock the door after me. And next time don't be so eager to find out who's knocking. There isn't any doorman here."

Once more she nodded. She got up and followed him to the door, holding it open.

"Damn it, Annie, don't look at me like that."

"Like what?"

"Like that," he accused, then slowly shook his head as if to clear his thoughts. He rubbed his face and sighed, then pressed his knuckle under her chin. "The two of us are starting over first thing tomorrow. There won't be any more of this." But even as he was speaking, he was leaning forward to gently brush her mouth with his.

It was the sound of Nolan pounding furiously away on his electric typewriter—a heavy, outdated office model—that woke Maryanne the next morning. She yawned loudly, stretching her arms high above her head, arching her back. Her first night in her new apartment, and she'd slept like a rock. The sofa, which opened into a queen-size sleeper, was lumpy and soft, nearly swallowing her up, but she'd been too exhausted to care.

Nolan's fierce typing continued most of the day. Maryanne hadn't expected to see him, so she wasn't disappointed when she didn't. He seemed determined to avoid her and managed it successfully for most of the week.

Since she'd promised not to make a nuisance of herself, Maryanne kept out of his way, too. She started work at the cleaning company and wrote three articles in five days, often staying up late into the night.

The work for Rent-A-Maid was backbreaking and arduous. She spent three afternoons a week picking up after professional men who were nothing less than slobs. Maryanne had to resist the urge to write them each a note demanding that they put their dirty dishes in the sink and their soiled clothes in the laundry basket.

Rent-A-Maid had made housekeeping sound glamorous. It wasn't. In fact, it was the hardest, most physically exhausting job she'd ever undertaken.

By the end of the week, her nails were broken and chipped and her hands were red and chapped.

It was by chance rather than design that Maryanne bumped into Nolan late Friday afternoon. She was carrying a bag of groceries up the stairs when he bounded past her, taking the steps two at a time.

"Annie." He paused on the landing, waiting for her to catch up. "How's it going?"

Maryanne didn't know what to say. She couldn't very well inform him that the highlight of her week was scraping a crusty patch off the bottom of an oven at one of the apartments she cleaned. She'd had such lofty expectations, such dreams. Nor could she casually announce that the stockbroker she cleaned for had spilled wine on his carpet and she'd spent an hour trying to get the stain out and broken two nails in the process.

"Fine," she lied. "Everything's just wonderful."

"Here, let me take that for you."

"Thanks." She handed him the single bag, her week's allotment of groceries. Unfortunately it was all she could afford. Everything had seemed so exciting when she started out; her plans had been so promising. The reality was proving to be something else again.

"Well, how do you like cleaning?"

"It's great, really great." It was shocking how easily the lie came. "I'm finding it . . . a challenge."

Nolan smiled absently. "I'm glad to hear it. Have you got your first paycheck yet?"

"I cashed it this afternoon." She used to spend more each week at the dry cleaners than she'd received in her first paycheck from Rent-A-Maid. The entire amount had gone for food and transportation, and there were only a few dollars left. Her budget was tight, but she'd make it. She'd have to.

Nolan paused in front of her door and waited while she scrabbled through her bag, searching for the key. "I hear you typing at night," she said. "Are you working on anything special?"

"No."

She eyed him curiously. "How fast do you type? Eighty words a minute? A hundred? And for heaven's sake, why don't you use a computer like everyone else?"

"Sixty words a minute on a good day. And for your information, I happen to like my electric. It may be old, but it does the job."

She finally retrieved her key, conscious of his gaze on her hands.

Suddenly he grasped her fingers. "All right," he demanded. "What happened to you?"

Five

"Nothing's happened to me," Maryanne insisted hotly, pulling her hand free of Nolan's.

"Look at your nails," he said. "There isn't one that's not broken."

"You make it sound like I should be dragged before a firing squad at dawn. So I chipped a few nails this week. I'll survive." Although she was making light of it, each broken fingernail was like a small loss. She took pride in her perfect nails, or at least she once had.

His eyes narrowed as he scrutinized her. "There's something you're not telling me."

"I didn't realize you'd appointed yourself my father confessor."

Anger flashed in his dark eyes as he took the key from her unresisting fingers. He opened the door and, with one hand at her shoulder, urged her inside. "We need to talk."

"No, we don't." Maryanne marched into the apartment, plunked her bag of groceries on the kitchen counter and spun around to confront her neighbor. "Listen here, buster, you've made it perfectly clear that you don't want anything to do with me. That's your choice, and I'm certainly not going to bore you with the sorry details of my life."

He ignored her words and started pacing the small living area, pausing in front of the window. His presence filled the apartment, making it seem smaller than usual. He pivoted sharply, pointing an accusatory finger in her direction. "These broken nails came from swinging a dust mop around, didn't they? What the hell are you doing?"

Maryanne didn't answer him right away. She was angry, and his sudden concern for her welfare made her even angrier. "I told you before, I don't need a guardian."

"Against my advice, you took that stupid job. Anyone with half a brain would know it wasn't going to—"

"Will you stop acting like you're responsible for me?" Maryanne snapped.

"I can't help it. I *am* responsible for you. You wouldn't be here if I hadn't written that damn column. I don't want to intrude on your life any more than you want me to, but let's face it, there's no one else to look out for you. Sooner or later someone's going to take advantage of you."

That did it. Maryanne stalked over to him and jabbed her index finger into his chest with enough force to bend what remained of her nail. "In case you need reminding, I'm my own woman. I make my own decisions. I'll work any place I damn well please. Furthermore, I can take care of myself." She whirled around and opened her front door. "Now kindly leave!"

"No."

"No?" she repeated.

"No," he said again, returning to the window. He crossed his arms over his chest and sighed impatiently. "You haven't eaten, have you? I can tell, because you get testy when you're hungry."

"If you'd leave my apartment the way I asked, that wouldn't be a problem."

"How about having dinner with me?"

The invitation took Maryanne by surprise. Her first impulse was to throw it back in his face. After an entire week of pretending she didn't exist, he had a lot of nerve even asking.

"Well?" he prompted.

"Where?" As if that made a difference. Maryanne was famished, and the thought of sharing her meal with Nolan was more tempting than she wanted to admit, even to herself.

"The diner."

"Are you going to order chili?"

"Are you going to ask them to remove the nonexistent bean sprouts from your sandwich?"

Maryanne hesitated. She felt confused by all her contradictory emotions. She was strongly attracted to Nolan and every time they were together she caught herself hoping they could become friends—more than friends. But, equally often, he infuriated her or left her feeling depressed. He made the most outlandish remarks to her. He seemed to have appointed himself her guardian. When he wasn't issuing decrees, he neglected her as if she were nothing more than a nuisance. And to provide a finishing touch, she was lying to her parents because of him! Well, maybe that wasn't quite fair, but . . .

"I'll throw in dessert," he coaxed with a smile.

That smile was her Waterloo, yet she still struggled. "A la mode?"

His grin widened. "You drive a hard bargain."

Maryanne's eyes met his and although Nolan could make her angrier than anyone she'd ever known, a smile trembled on her own lips.

They agreed to meet a half hour later. That gave Maryanne time to unpack her groceries, change clothes and freshen her makeup. She found herself humming as she applied lip gloss, wondering if she was reading too much into this impromptu dinner date.

When Nolan came to her door to pick her up, Maryanne noted that he'd changed into jeans and a fisherman's sweater. It was the first time she'd seen him without the raincoat, other than the day he'd played basketball with the neighborhood boys. He looked good. All right, she admitted grudgingly, he looked fantastic.

"You dressed up," she said before she could stop herself, grateful she'd understated her attraction to him.

"So did you. You look nice."

"Thanks."

"Before I forget to tell you, word has it the elevator's going to be fixed Monday morning."

"Really? That's the best news I've heard all week." Goodness, could she take all these glad tidings at once? First Nolan had actually invited her out on a date, and now she wouldn't have to hike up four flights of stairs every afternoon. Life was indeed treating her well.

They were several blocks from the apartment building before Maryanne realized Nolan was driving in the opposite direction of the diner. She said as much.

"Do you like Chinese food?" he asked.

"I love it."

"The diner's short-staffed—one of the waitresses quit. I thought Chinese food might be interesting, and I promise we won't have to wait for a table."

It sounded heavenly to Maryanne. She didn't know how significant Nolan's decision to take her to a different restaurant might be. Perhaps it was foolish, but Maryanne hoped it meant she was becoming special to him. As if he could read her mind, Nolan was unusually quiet on the drive into Seattle's International District.

So much for romance. Maryanne could almost hear his thoughts. If she were a betting woman, she'd place odds on the way their dinner conversation would go. First Nolan would try to find out exactly what tasks had been assigned to her by Rent-A-Maid. Then he'd try to convince her to quit.

Only she wasn't going to let him. She was her own woman, and she'd said it often enough to convince herself. If this newsman thought he could sway her with a fancy dinner and a few well-spoken words, then he was about to learn a valuable lesson.

The restaurant proved to be a Chinese version of the greasy spoon where Nolan ate regularly. The minute they walked into the small room, Maryanne was greeted by a wide variety of tantalizing scents. Pungent spices and oils wafted through the air, and the smells were so appealing it was all she could do not to follow them into the kitchen. She knew before sampling a single bite that the food would be some of the best Asian cuisine she'd ever tasted.

An elderly Chinese gentleman greeted Nolan as if he were a long-lost relative. The two shared a brief exchange in Chinese before the man escorted them to a table. He shouted into the kitchen, and a brightly painted ceramic pot of tea was quickly delivered to their table.

Nolan and Maryanne were never given menus. Almost from the moment they were seated, food began appearing on their table. An appetizer plate came first, with several items Maryanne couldn't readily identify. But she was too hungry to care. Everything was delicious and she happily devoured one after another.

"You seem well acquainted with the waiter," Maryanne commented, once the appetizer plate was empty. She barely had time to catch her breath before a bowl of thick spicy soup was brought to them by the same elderly gentleman. He paused and smiled proudly at Nolan, then glanced at Maryanne, before nodding in a profound way.

"Wong Su's the owner. I went to school with his son."

"Is that where you picked up Chinese?"

"Yes. I only know a few words, just enough to get the gist of what he's saying," he answered brusquely, reaching for his spoon.

"What was it he said when we first came in? I noticed you seemed quick to disagree with him."

Nolan dipped his spoon into the soup, ignoring her question. "Nolan?"

"He said you're too thin."

Maryanne shook her head, immediately aware that he was lying. "If he really thought that, you'd have agreed with him."

"All right, all right," Nolan muttered, looking severely displeased. "I should've known better than to bring a woman to Wong Su's place. He assumed there was something romantic between us. He said you'd give me many fine sons."

"How sweet."

Nolan reacted instantly to her words. He dropped his spoon beside the bowl with a clatter, planted his elbows on the table and glared at her heatedly. "Now don't go all sentimental on me. There's nothing between us and there never will be."

Maryanne promptly saluted. "Aye, aye, Captain," she mocked.

"Good. Well, now that's settled, tell me about your week."

"Tell me about yours," she countered, unwilling to change the subject to herself quite so easily. "You seemed a whole lot busier than I was."

"I went to work, came home . . ."

". . . worked some more," she finished for him. Another plate, heaped high with sizzling hot chicken and crisp vegetables, was brought by Wong Su, who offered Maryanne a grin.

Nolan frowned at his friend and said something in Chinese that caused the older man to laugh outright. When Nolan returned his attention to Maryanne, he was scowling again. "For heaven's sake, don't encourage him."

"What did I do?" To the best of her knowledge she was innocent of any wrongdoing.

Nolan thought it over for a moment. "Never mind, no point in telling you."

Other steaming dishes arrived—prawns with cashew nuts, then ginger beef and barbecued pork, each accompanied by small bowls of rice until virtually every inch of the small table was covered.

"You were telling me about your week," Maryanne reminded him, reaching for the dish in the center of the crowded table.

"No, I wasn't," Nolan retorted.

With a scornful sigh, Maryanne passed him the chicken. "All right, have it your way."

"You're going to needle me to death until you find out what I'm working on in my spare time, aren't you?"

"Of course not." If he didn't want her to know, then fine, she had no intention of asking again. Acting as nonchalant as possible, she helped herself to a thick slice of the pork. She dipped it into a small dish of hot mustard, which proved to be a bit more potent than she'd expected; her eyes started to water.

Mumbling under his breath, Nolan handed her his napkin. "Here."

"I'm all right." She wiped the moisture from her eyes and blinked a couple of times before picking up her water glass. Once she'd composed herself, she resumed their previous discussion. "On the contrary, Mr. Adams, whatever project so intensely occupies your time is your own concern."

"Spoken like a true aristocrat."

"Obviously you don't care to share it with me."

He gave an exaggerated sigh. "It's a novel," he said. "There now, are you satisfied?"

"A novel," she repeated coolly. "Really. And all along, I thought you were taking in typing jobs on the side."

He glared at her, but the edges of his mouth turned up in a reluctant grin. "I don't want to talk about the plot, all right? I'm afraid that would water it down."

"I understand perfectly."

"Damn it all, Annie, would you stop looking at me with those big blue eyes of yours? I already feel guilty as hell without you smiling serenely at me and trying to act so blasé."

"Guilty about what?"

He expelled his breath sharply. "Listen," he said in a low voice, leaning toward her. "As much as I hate to admit this, you're right. It's none of my business where you work or how many nails you break or how much you're paid. But damn it all, I'm worried about you."

She raised her chopsticks in an effort to stop him. "It seems to me I've heard this argument before. Actually, it's getting downright boring."

Nolan dropped his voice even lower. "You've been sheltered all your life. I know you don't want me to feel responsible for what you're doing—or for you. And I wish I didn't. Unfortunately I can't help it. Believe me, I've tried. It doesn't work. Every night I lie awake wondering what trouble you're going to get into next. I don't know what's going to happen first—you working yourself to death, or me getting an ulcer."

Maryanne's gaze fell to her hands, and the uneven length of her once perfectly uniform fingernails. "They are rather pitiful, aren't they?"

Nolan glanced at them and grimaced. "As a personal favor to me would you consider giving up the job at Rent-A-Maid?" He ran his fingers through his hair, sighing heavily. "It doesn't come easy to ask you this, Annie. If for no other reason, do it because you owe me a favor for finding you the apartment. But for heaven's sake, quit that job."

She didn't answer him right away. She wanted to do as he asked, because she was falling in love with him. Because she craved his approval. Yet she wanted to reject his entreaties, flout his demands. Because he made her feel confused and contrary and full of unpredictable emotions.

"If it'll do any good, I'll promise not to interfere again," he said, his voice so quiet it was almost a whisper. "If you'll quit Rent-a-Maid."

"As a personal favor to you," she repeated, nodding slowly. So much for refusing to be swayed by dinner and a few well-chosen words.

Their eyes met and held for a long moment. Deliberately, as though it went against his will, Nolan reached out and brushed an auburn curl from her cheek. His touch was light yet strangely intimate, as intimate as a kiss. His fingers lingered on her cheek and it was all Maryanne could do not to cover his hand with her own and close her eyes to savor the wealth of sensations that settled around her.

Nolan's dark eyes narrowed, and she could tell he was struggling. She could read it in every line, every feature of his handsome face. But struggling against what? She could only speculate. He didn't want to be attracted to her; that much was obvious.

As if he needed to break contact with her eyes, he lowered his gaze to her mouth. Whether it was intentional or not, Maryanne didn't know, but his thumb inched closer to her lips, easing toward the corner. Then, with an abrupt movement, he pulled his hand away and returned to his meal, eating quickly and methodically.

Maryanne tried to eat, but her own appetite was gone. Wong Su refused payment although Nolan tried to insist. Instead the elderly man said something in Chinese that sent every eye in the place straight to Maryanne. She smiled benignly, wondering what he could possibly have said that would make the great Nolan Adams blush.

The drive back to the apartment was even more silent than the one to the restaurant had been. Maryanne considered asking Nolan exactly what Wong Su had said just before they'd left, but she thought better of it.

They took their time walking up the four flights of stairs. "Will you come in for coffee?" Maryanne asked when they arrived at her door.

"I can't tonight," Nolan said after several all-too-quiet moments.

"I don't bite, you know." His eyes didn't waver from hers. The attraction was there—she could feel it as surely as she had his touch at dinner.

"I'd like to finish my chapter."

So he was going to close her out once again. "Don't work too hard," she said, opening the apartment door. Her disappointment was keen, but she managed to disguise it behind a shrug. "Thank you for dinner. It was delicious."

Nolan thrust his hands into his pockets. It might have been her imagination, but she thought he did it to keep from reaching for her. The idea comforted her ego and she smiled up at him warmly.

She was about to close the door when he stopped her. "Yes?" she asked.

His eyes were as piercing and dark as she'd ever seen them. "My typing. Does it keep you awake nights?"

"No," she told him and shook her head for emphasis. "The book must be going well."

He nodded, then sighed. "Listen, would it be possible . . ." He paused and started again. "Are you busy tomorrow night? I've got two tickets to the Seattle Repertory Theatre and I was wondering . . ."

"I'd love to go," she said eagerly, before he'd even finished the question.

Judging by the expression on his face, the invitation seemed to be as much a surprise to him as it was to her. "I'll see you tomorrow, then."

"Right," she answered brightly. "Tomorrow."

The afternoon was glorious, with just the right mixture of wind and sunshine. Hands clasped behind her back, Maryanne strolled across the grass of Volunteer Park, kicking up leaves as she went. She'd spent the morning researching an article she hoped to sell to a local magazine and she was taking a break.

The basketball court was occupied by several teenage boys, a couple of whom she recognized from the day she'd moved. With time on her hands and an afternoon to enjoy, Maryanne paused to watch the hotly contested game. Sitting on a picnic table, she swung her legs, content to laze away the sunny afternoon. Everything was going so well. With hardly any difficulty she'd found another job. Nolan probably wasn't going to approve of this one, either, but that was just too bad.

"Hi." A girl of about thirteen, wearing a jean jacket and tight black stretch leggings, strolled up to the picnic table. "You're with Mr. Adams, aren't you?"

Maryanne would've liked to think so, but she didn't feel she could describe it quite that way. "What makes you ask that?"

"You moved in with him, didn't you?"

"Not exactly. I live in the apartment next door."

"I didn't believe Eddie when he said Mr. Adams had a woman. He's never had anyone live with him before. He's just not the type, if you know what I mean."

Maryanne did know. She was learning not to take his attitude toward her personally. The better acquainted she became with Nolan, the more clearly she realized that he considered all women a nuisance. The first night they met, he'd mentioned that he'd been in love once, but his tone had been so casual it implied this romance was merely a long-ago mistake. He'd talked about the experience as if it meant little or nothing to him. Maryanne wasn't sure she believed that.

"Mr. Adams is a really neat guy. All the kids like him a lot." The girl smiled, suggesting she was one of his legion of admirers. "I'm Gloria Masterson."

Maryanne held out her hand. "Maryanne Simpson."

Gloria smiled shyly. "If you don't live with him, are you his girlfriend?"

"Not really. We're just friends."

"That's what he said when I asked him about you."

"Oh." It wasn't as though she could expect him to admit anything more.

"Mr. Adams comes around every now and then and talks to us kids in the park. I think he's checking up on us and making sure no one's into drugs or gangs."

Maryanne smiled. That sounded exactly like the kind of thing Nolan would do.

"Only a few kids around here are that stupid, but you know, I think a couple of the boys might've been tempted to try something if it wasn't for Mr. Adams."

"Hey, Gloria," a lanky boy from the basketball court called out. "Come here, woman."

Gloria sighed loudly, then shouted. "Just a minute." She turned back to Maryanne. "I'm really not Eddie's woman. He just likes to think so."

Maryanne smiled. She wished she could say the same thing about her and Nolan. "It was nice to meet you, Gloria. Maybe I'll see you around."

"That'd be great."

"Gloria," Eddie shouted, "are you coming or not?"

The teenage girl shook her head. "I don't know why I put up with him."

Maryanne left the park soon afterward. The first thing she noticed when she got home was an envelope taped to her door.

She waited until she was inside the apartment to open it, and as she did a single ticket and a note slipped out. "I'm going to be stuck at the office," the note read. "The curtain goes up at eight—don't be late. N."

Maryanne was mildly disappointed that Nolan wouldn't be driving her to the play, but she decided to splurge and take a taxi. By seven-thirty, when the cab arrived, she was dressed and ready. She wore her best evening attire, a long black velvet skirt and matching blazer with a cream-colored silk blouse. She'd even put on her pearl earrings and cameo necklace.

The theatre was one of the nicest in town, and Maryanne's heart sang with excitement as the usher escorted her to her seat. Nolan hadn't arrived yet and she looked around expectantly.

The curtain was about to go up when a man she mentally categorized as wealthy and a bit of a charmer settled in the vacant seat next to hers.

"Excuse me," he said, leaning toward her, smiling warmly. "I'm Griff Bradley. Nolan Adams sent me."

It didn't take Maryanne two seconds to figure out what Nolan had done. The low-down rat had matched her up with someone he considered more appropriate. Someone he assumed she had more in common with. Someone wealthy and slick. Someone her father would approve of.

"Where's Nolan?" Maryanne demanded. She bolted to her feet and grabbed her bag, jerking it so hard the gold chain strap threatened to break.

Griff looked taken aback by her sharp question. "You mean he didn't discuss this with you?"

"He invited me to this play. I assumed . . . I believed the two of us would be attending it together. He didn't say a word about you. I'm sorry, but I can't agree to this arrangement." She started to edge her way out of the row just as the curtain rose.

To her dismay, Griff followed her into the aisle. "I'm sure there's been some misunderstanding."

"You bet there has," Maryanne said, loudly enough to attract the angry glares of several patrons sitting in the aisle seats. She rushed toward the exit with Griff in hot pursuit.

"If you'll give me a moment to explain—"

"It won't be necessary."

"You are Maryanne Simpson of the New York Simpsons?"

"Yes," she said, walking directly outside. Moving to the curb, she raised her hand and shouted, "Taxi!"

Griff raced around to stand in front of her. "There isn't any need to rush off like this. Nolan was just doing me a good turn."

"And me a rotten one. Listen, Mr. Bradley, you look like a very nice gentleman, and under any other circumstances I would've been more than happy to make your acquaintance, but there's been a mistake."

"But—"

"I'm sorry, I really am." A cab raced toward her and squealed to a halt.

Griff opened the back door for her, looking more charming and debonair than ever. "I'm not sure my heart will recover. You're very lovely, you know."

Maryanne sighed. The man was overdoing it, but he certainly didn't deserve the treatment she was giving him. She smiled and apologized again, then swiftly turned to the driver and recited her address.

Maryanne fumed during the entire ride back to her apartment. Rarely had she been more furious. If Nolan Adams thought he could play matchmaker with her, he was about to learn that everything he'd ever heard about redheads was true.

"Hey, lady, you all right?" the cabbie asked.

"I'm fine," she said stiffly.

"That guy you were with back at the theatre didn't try anything, did he?"

"No, some other man did, only he's not going to get away with it." The driver pulled into her street. "That's the building there," Maryanne told him. She reached into her bag for her wallet and pulled out some of her precious cash, including a generous tip. Then she ran into the apartment building, heedless of her clothes or her high-heeled shoes.

For the first time since moving in, Maryanne didn't pause to rest on the third-floor landing. Her anger carried her all the way to Nolan's apartment door. She could hear him typing inside, and the sound only heightened her temper. Dragging breath through her lungs, she slammed her fist against the door.

"Hold on a minute," she heard him grumble.

His shocked look as he threw open the door would have been comical in different circumstances. "Maryanne, what are you doing here?"

"That was a rotten underhanded thing to do, you deceiving, conniving, low-down . . . rat!"

Nolan did an admirable job of composing himself. He buried his hands in his pockets and smiled nonchalantly. "I take it you and Griff Bradley didn't hit it off?"

Six

Maryanne was so furious she couldn't find the words to express her outrage. She opened and closed her mouth twice before she collected herself enough to proceed.

"I told you before that I don't want you interfering in my life, and I meant it."

"I was doing you a favor," Nolan countered, clearly unmoved by her angry display. In fact, he yawned loudly, covering his mouth with the back of his hand. "Griff's a stockbroker friend of mine and one hell of a nice guy. If you'd given him half a chance, you might have found that out yourself. I could see the two of you becoming good friends. Why don't you give it a try? You might hit it off, after all."

"The only thing I'd consider hitting is *you*." To her horror, tears of rage flooded her eyes. "Don't ever try that again. Do you understand?" Not waiting for his reply, she turned abruptly, stalked down the hall to her apartment and unlocked the door. She flung it shut with sufficient force to rattle the windows on three floors.

She paced back and forth several times, blew her nose once and decided she hadn't told him nearly enough. Throwing open her door, she rushed down the hall to Nolan's apartment again. She banged twice as hard as she had originally.

Nolan opened the door, wearing a martyr's expression. He cocked one eyebrow expressively. "What is it this time?"

"And furthermore you're the biggest coward I've ever met. If I still worked for the newspaper, I'd write a column so all of Seattle would know exactly what kind of man you are." Her voice wobbled just a little, but that didn't diminish the strength of her indignation.

She stomped back to her own apartment and she hadn't been there two seconds before there was a pounding on her door. It didn't surprise her to find Nolan Adams on the other side. He might have appeared calm, but his eyes sparked with an angry fire. They narrowed slightly as he glowered at her.

"What did you just say?" he asked.

"You heard me. You're nothing but a coward. Coward, coward, coward!" With that she slammed her door so hard that a framed family photo hanging on the wall crashed to the floor. Luckily the glass didn't break.

Her chest heaving, Maryanne picked up the photo, wiped it off and carefully replaced it. But for all her outward composure, her hands were trembling. No sooner had she completed the task than Nolan beat on her door a second time.

"Now what?" she demanded, whipping open the door. "I would have thought you got my message."

"I got it all right. I just don't happen to like it."

"Tough." She would have slammed the door again, but before she could act, a loud banging came from the direction of the floor. Not knowing what it was, Maryanne instinctively jumped back.

Nolan drew a deep breath, and Maryanne could tell he was making an effort to compose himself. "All right, Mrs. Mc-Bride," Nolan shouted at the floor, "we'll hold it down."

"Who's Mrs. McBride?"

"The lady who lives in the apartment below you."

"Oh." Maryanne had been too infuriated to realize she was shouting so loudly half the apartment building could hear. She felt ashamed at her loss of control and guilty for disturbing her neighbors—but she was still furious with Nolan.

The man in question glared at her. "Do you think it's possible to discuss this situation without involving any more doors?" he asked sharply. "Or would you rather wait until someone phones the police and we're both arrested for disturbing the peace?"

She glared back at him defiantly. "Very funny," she said, turning around and walking into her apartment. As she knew he would, Nolan followed her inside.

Maryanne moved into the kitchen. Preparing a pot of coffee gave her a few extra minutes to gather her dignity, which had been as abused as her apartment door. Mixed with the anger was a chilling pain that cut straight through her heart. Nolan's thinking so little of her that he could casually pass her on to another man was mortifying enough. But knowing he considered it a favor only heaped on the humiliation.

"Annie, please listen—"

"Did it ever occur to you that arranging this date with Griff might offend me?" she cried.

Nolan seemed reluctant to answer. "Yes," he finally said, "it did. I tried to catch you earlier this afternoon, but you weren't in. This wasn't the kind of situation I felt comfortable explaining in a note, so I took the easy way out and left Griff to introduce himself. I didn't realize you'd take it so personally."

"How else was I supposed to take it?"

Nolan glanced away uncomfortably. "Let's just say I was hoping you'd meet him and the two of you would spend the evening getting to know each other. Griff comes from a well-established family and—"

"That's supposed to impress me?"

"He's the type of man your father would arrange for you to meet," Nolan said, his voice sandpaper-gruff.

"How many times do I have to tell you I don't need a second father?" His mention of her family reminded her of the way she was deceiving them, which brought a powerful sense of remorse.

He muttered tersely under his breath, then shook his head. "Obviously I blew it. Would it help if I apologized?"

An apology, even a sincere one, wouldn't dissolve the hurt. She looked up, about to tell him exactly that, when her eyes locked with his.

He stood a safe distance from her, his expression so tender that her battered heart rolled defencelessly to her feet. She knew she ought to throw him out of her home and refuse to ever speak to him again. No one would blame her. She tried to rally her anger, but something she couldn't explain or understand stopped her.

All the emotion must have sharpened her perceptions. Never had she been more aware of Nolan as a man. The space separating them seemed to close, drawing them toward each other. She could smell the clean scent of the soap he used and hear the music of the rain as it danced against her window. She hadn't even realized, until this moment, that it was raining.

"I am sorry," he said quietly.

Maryanne nodded and wiped the moisture from her eyes. She wasn't a woman who cried easily, and the tears were a surprise.

"What you said about my being a coward is true," Nolan admitted. He sighed heavily. "You frighten me, Annie."

"You mean my temper?"

"No, I deserved that." He grinned that lazy insolent grin of his.

"What is it about me you find so unappealing?" She had to know what was driving him away, no matter how much the truth damaged her pride.

"Unappealing?" His abrupt laugh was filled with irony. "I wish I could find something, *anything*, unappealing about you, but I can't." Dropping his gaze, he stepped back and cleared his throat. When he spoke again, his words were brusque, impatient. "I was a lot more comfortable with you before we met."

"You thought of me as a debutante."

"I assumed you were a pampered immature . . . girl. Not a woman. I expected to find you ambitious and selfish, so eager to impress your father with what you could do that it didn't matter how many people you stepped on. Then we did the Celebrity Debate, and I discovered that none of the things I wanted to believe about you were true."

"Then why—"

"What you've got to understand," Nolan added forcefully, "is that I don't *want* to become involved with you."

"That message has come through loud and clear." She moistened her lips and cast her gaze toward the floor, afraid he'd see how vulnerable he made her feel.

Suddenly he was standing directly in front of her, so close his breath warmed her face. With one gentle finger, he lifted her chin, raising her eyes to his.

"All evening I was telling myself how noble I was," he said. "Griff Bradley is far better suited to you than I'll ever be."

"Stop saying that!"

He wrapped his arms around her waist and pulled her against him. "There can't ever be any kind of relationship between us," he said, his voice rough. "I learned my lesson years ago, and I'm not going to repeat that mistake." But contrary to everything he was saying, his mouth lowered to hers until their lips touched.

The kiss was slow and familiar. Their bottom lips clung as Nolan eased away from her.

"That wasn't supposed to happen," he murmured.

"I won't tell anyone if you won't," she whispered.

"Just remember what I said," he whispered back. "I don't do well with rich girls. I already found that out. The hard way."

"I'll remember," she said softly, looking up at him.

"Good." And then he kissed her again.

It was three days before Maryanne saw Nolan. She didn't need anyone to tell her he was avoiding her. Maybe he thought falling in love would wreak havoc with his comfortable well-ordered life. If he'd given her a chance, Maryanne would've told him she didn't expect him to fill her days. She had her new job, and she was fixing up her apartment. Most importantly, she had her writing, which kept her busy the rest of the time. She'd recently queried a magazine about doing a humorous article on her experiences working for Rent-A-Maid.

"Here's Nolan now," Barbara whispered as she hurried past Maryanne, balancing three plates.

Automatically Maryanne reached for a water glass and a menu and followed Nolan to the booth. He was halfway into his seat when he saw her. He froze and his narrowed gaze flew across the room to the middle-aged waitress.

Barbara didn't appear in the least intimidated. "Hey, what did you expect?" she called out. "We were one girl short, and when Maryanne applied for the job she gave you as a reference. Besides, she's a good worker."

Nolan didn't bother to look at the menu. Standing beside the table, Maryanne took her green order pad out of her apron pocket.

"I'll have the chili," he said gruffly.

"With or without cheese?"

"Without," he bellowed, then quickly lowered his voice. "How long have you been working here?"

"Since Monday morning. Don't look so angry. You were the one who told me about the job. Remember?"

"I don't want you working here!"

"Why not? It's a respectable establishment. Honestly, Nolan, what did you expect me to do? I had to find another job, and fast. I can't expect to sell any articles for at least a month, if then. I've got to have some way of paying the bills."

"You could've done a hell of a lot better than Mom's Place if you wanted to be a waitress."

"Are we going to argue? Again?" she asked with an impatient sigh.

"No," he answered, grabbing his napkin just in time to catch a violent sneeze.

Now that she had a chance to study him, she saw his nose was red and his eyes rheumy. In fact he looked downright miserable. "You've got a cold."

"Are you always this brilliant?"

"I try to be. And I'll try to ignore your rudeness. Would you like a glass of orange juice or a couple of aspirin?"

"No, Florence Nightingale, all I want is my usual bowl of chili, *without* the cheese. Have you got that?"

"Yes, of course," she said, writing it down. Nolan certainly seemed to be in a rotten mood, but that was nothing new. Maryanne seemed to bring out the worst in him.

Barbara met her at the counter. "From the looks your boyfriend's been sending me, he'd gladly cut off my head. What's with him, anyway?"

"I don't think he's feeling well," Maryanne answered in a low worried voice.

"Men, especially sick ones, are the biggest babies on earth," Barbara said wryly. "They get a little virus and think someone should rush in to make a documentary about their life-threatening condition. My advice to you is let him wallow in his misery all by himself."

"But he looks like he might have a fever," Maryanne whispered.

"And he isn't old enough to take an aspirin all on his own?" The older woman glanced behind her. "His order's up. You want me to take it to him?"

"No . . ."

"Don't worry, if he gets smart with me I'll just whack him upside the head. Someone needs to put that man in his place."

Maryanne picked up the large bowl of chili. "I'll do it."

"Yes," Barbara said, grinning broadly. "I have a feeling you will."

Maryanne got home several hours later. Her feet hurt and her back ached, but she felt a pleasant glow of satisfaction. After three days of waitressing, she was beginning to get the knack of keeping orders straight and remembering everything she needed to do. It wasn't the job of her dreams, but she was making a living wage, certainly better money than she'd been getting from Rent-A-Maid. Not only that, the tips were good. Maryanne didn't dare imagine what her family would say if they found out, though. She suffered a stab of remorse every time she thought about the way she was deceiving them. In fact, it was simpler not to think about it at all.

After his initial reaction, Nolan hadn't so much as mentioned her working at Mom's Place. He clearly wasn't thrilled, but that didn't surprise her. Little, if anything, she'd done from the moment she'd met him had gained his approval.

Maryanne had grown accustomed to falling asleep most nights to the sound of Nolan's typing. She found herself listening for it when she climbed into bed. But she didn't hear it that night or the two nights that followed.

"How's Nolan?" Barbara asked her on Friday afternoon.

"I don't know." Maryanne hadn't seen him in days, but then, she rarely did.

"He must have got a really bad bug."

Maryanne hated the way her heart lurched. She'd tried not to think about him. Not that she'd been successful . . .

"His column hasn't been in the paper all week. The *Sun's* been running some of his old ones—Nolan's Classics. Did you read the one last night?" Barbara asked, laughing. "It was about how old-fashioned friendly service has disappeared from restaurants today." She grinned. "He said there were a few exceptions, and you know who he was talking about."

As a matter of fact, Maryanne had read the piece and been highly amused—and flattered, even though the column had been written long before she'd even come to Seattle, let alone worked at Mom's Place. As always she'd been impressed with Nolan's dry wit. They often disagreed—Nolan was too much of a pessimist to suit her—but she couldn't help admiring his skill with words.

Since the afternoon he'd found her at Mom's, Nolan hadn't eaten there again. Maryanne didn't consider that so strange. He went to great lengths to ensure that they didn't run into each other. She did feel mildly guilty that he'd decided to stay away from his favorite diner, but it *was* his choice, after all.

During the rest of her shift, Maryanne had to struggle to keep Nolan out of her mind. His apartment had been unusually quiet for the past few days, but she hadn't been concerned about it. Now she was.

"Do you think he's all right?" she asked Barbara some time later.

"He's a big boy," the older woman was quick to remind her. "He can take care of himself."

Maryanne wasn't so sure. After work, she hurried home,

convinced she'd find Nolan hovering near death, too ill to call for help. She didn't even stop at her own apartment, but went directly to his.

She knocked politely, anticipating all kinds of disasters when there was no response.

"Nolan?" She pounded on his door and yelled his name, battling down a rising sense of panic. She envisioned him lying on his bed, suffering—or worse. "Nolan, please answer the door," she pleaded, wondering if there was someone in the building with a passkey.

She'd waited hours, it seemed, before he yanked open the door.

"Are you all right?" she demanded, so relieved to see him she could hardly keep from hurling herself into his arms. Relieved, that was, until she got a good look at him.

"I was feeling just great," he told her gruffly, "until I had to get out of bed to answer the stupid door. Which, incidentally, woke me up."

Maryanne pressed her fingers over her mouth to hide her hysterical laughter. If Nolan felt anywhere near as bad as he looked, then she should seriously consider phoning for an ambulance. He wore grey sweatpants and a faded plaid robe, one she would guess had been moth fodder for years. His choice of clothes was the least of her concerns, however. He resembled someone who'd just surfaced from a four-day drunk. His eyes were red and his face ashen. He scowled at her and it was clear the moment he spoke that his disposition was as cheery as his appearance.

"I take it there's a reason for this uninvited visit?" he growled, then sneezed fiercely.

"Yes . . ." Maryanne hedged, not knowing exactly what to do now. "I just wanted to make sure you're all right."

"Okay, you've seen me. I'm going to live, so you can leave in good conscience." He would have closed the door, but Maryanne stepped forward and boldly forced her way into his apartment.

In the weeks they'd lived next door to each other, she'd never seen his home. The muted earth colors, the rich leather furniture and polished wood floors appealed to her immediately. Despite her worry about his condition, she smiled; this room reminded her of Nolan, with papers and books littering every available space. His apartment seemed at least twice the size of hers. He'd once mentioned that it was larger, but after becoming accustomed to her own small rooms, she found the spaciousness of his a pleasant shock.

"In case you haven't noticed, I'm in no mood for company," he informed her in a surly voice.

"Have you been to a doctor?"

"No."

"Do you need anything?"

"Peace and quiet," he muttered.

"You could have bronchitis or pneumonia or something."

"I'm perfectly fine. At least, I was until you arrived." He walked across the carpet—a dark green-and-gold Persian, Maryanne noted automatically—and slumped onto an over-stuffed sofa piled with blankets and pillows. The television was on, its volume turned very low.

"Then why haven't you been at work?"

"I'm on vacation."

"Personally, I would've chosen a tropical island over a sofa in my own apartment." She advanced purposefully into his kitchen and stopped short when she caught sight of the dirty dishes stacked a foot high in the stainless-steel sink. She was amazed he could cram so much into such a tight space.

"This place is a mess!" she declared, hands on her hips.

"Go ahead and call the health department if you're so concerned."

"I probably should." Instead, she walked straight to the sink, rolled up her sleeves and started stacking the dishes on the counter.

"What are you doing now?" Nolan shouted from the living room.

"Cleaning up."

He muttered something she couldn't hear, which was probably for the best.

"Go lie down, Nolan," she instructed. "When I'm done here, I'll heat you some soup. You've got to get your strength back in order to suffer properly."

At first he let that comment pass. Then, as if she was taxing him to the limit of his endurance, he called out, "The way you care is truly touching."

"I was hoping you'd notice." For someone who'd been outraged at the sight of her dishpan hands a week earlier, he seemed oddly unconcerned that she was washing his dirty dishes. Not that Maryanne minded. It made her feel good to be doing something for him.

She soon found herself humming as she rinsed the dishes and set them in his dishwasher.

Fifteen minutes passed without their exchanging a word. When Maryanne had finished, she looked in the living room and wasn't surprised to find him sound asleep on the sofa. A curious feeling tugged at her heart as she gazed down at him. He lay on his back with his left hand flung across his forehead. His features were relaxed, but there was nothing remotely angelic about him. Not about the way his thick dark lashes brushed the arch of his cheek—or about the slow hoarse breaths that whispered through his half-open mouth.

Maryanne felt a strong urge to brush the hair from his forehead, to touch him, but she resisted. She was afraid he'd wake up. And she was even more afraid she wouldn't want to stop touching him.

Moving about the living room, she turned off the television, picked up things here and there and straightened a few piles of magazines. She should leave now; she knew that. Nolan wouldn't welcome her staying. She eyed the door regretfully, looking for an excuse to linger. She closed her eyes and listened to the sound of Nolan's raspy breathing.

More by chance than design, Maryanne found herself standing next to his typewriter. Feeling brave, and more than a little foolish, she looked down at the stack of paper resting beside it. Glancing over her shoulder to make sure he was still asleep, Maryanne carefully turned over the top page and quickly read the last couple of paragraphs on page 212. The story wasn't finished, but she could tell he'd stopped during a cliff-hanger scene.

Nolan had been so secretive about his project that she dared not invade his privacy any more than she already had. She turned the single sheet back over, taking care to place it exactly as she'd found it.

Once again, she reminded herself that she should go back to her own apartment, but she felt strangely reluctant to end these moments with Nolan. Even a sleeping Nolan who would certainly be cranky when he woke up.

Seeking some way to occupy herself, she moved down the hall and into the bathroom, picking up several soiled towels on the way. His bed was unmade. She would've been surprised to find it in any other condition. The sheets and blankets were sagging onto the floor, and two or three sets of clothing were scattered all about.

Without questioning the wisdom of her actions, she bundled up the dirty laundry to take to the coin-operated machine in the basement. She loaded it into a large garbage bag, then set about vigorously cleaning the apartment. Scrubbing, scouring and sweeping were skills she'd perfected in her Rent-A-Maid days. If nothing else, she'd had lots of practice cleaning up after messy bachelors.

Studying the contents of his refrigerator, more than an hour later, proved to be a humorous adventure. She found an unopened bottle of wine, a carton of broken eggshells and one limp strand of celery. Concocting anything edible from that would be impossible, so she searched the apartment until she found his keys. Then, with his garbage bag full of laundry in her arms, she let herself out the door, closing it softly.

She returned a half hour later, clutching two bags of groceries bought with her tip money. Then she went down to put his laundry in the dryer. To her relief, Nolan was still asleep. She smiled down at him indulgently before she began preparing his dinner. After another forty-five minutes she retrieved his clean clothes and put them neatly away.

She was in the kitchen peeling potatoes when she heard Nolan get up. She continued her task, knowing he'd discover she was there soon enough. He stopped cold when he did.

"What are you doing here?"

"Making your dinner."

"I'm not hungry," he snapped with no evidence of appreciation for her efforts.

His eyes widened as he glanced around. "What happened here? Oh, you've cleaned the place up."

"I didn't think you'd notice," she answered sweetly, popping a small piece of raw potato in her mouth. "I'll get soup to the boiling stage before I leave you to your . . . peace of mind. It should only take another ten or fifteen minutes. Can you endure me that much longer?"

He made another of his typical grumbling replies before disappearing. No more than two seconds had passed before he let out a bellow loud enough to shake the roof tiles.

"What did you do to my bed?" he demanded as he stormed into the kitchen.

"I made it."

"What else have you been up to? Damn it, a man isn't safe in his own home with you around."

"Don't look so put out, Nolan. All I did was straighten up the place a bit. It was a mess."

"I happen to like messes. I thrive in messes. The last thing I want or need is some neat-freak invading my home, organizing my life."

"Don't exaggerate," Maryanne said serenely, as she added a pile of diced carrots to the simmering broth. "All I did was pick up a few things here and there and run a load of laundry."

"You did my laundry, too?" he exploded, jerking both hands through his hair. Heaven only knew, she thought, what would happen if he learned she'd read a single word of his precious manuscript.

"Everything's been folded and put away, so you needn't worry."

Nolan abruptly left the kitchen, only to return a couple of moments later. He circled the table slowly and precisely, then took several deep breaths.

"Listen, Annie," he began carefully, "it isn't that I don't appreciate what you've done, but I don't need a nurse. Or a housekeeper."

She looked up, meeting his eyes, her own large and guileless. "I quite agree," she answered.

"You do?" Some of the stiffness left his shoulders. "Then you aren't going to take offence?"

"No, why should I?"

"No reason," he answered, eyeing her suspiciously.

"I was thinking that what you really need," she said, smiling at him gently, "is a wife."

Seven

"A wife," Nolan echoed. His dark eyes widened in undisguised horror. It was as if Maryanne had suggested he climb to the roof of the apartment building and leap off.

"Don't get so excited. I wasn't volunteering for the position."

With his index finger pointing at her like the barrel of a shotgun, Nolan walked around the kitchen table again, his journey made in shuffling impatient steps. He circled the table twice before he spoke.

"You cleaned my home, washed my clothes and now you're cooking my dinner." Each word came at her like an accusation.

"Yes?"

"You can't possibly look at me with those baby-blues of yours and expect me to believe—"

"Believe what?"

"That you're not applying for the job. From the moment we met, you've been doing all these . . . these sweet *girlie* things to entice me."

"Sweet girlie things?" Maryanne repeated, struggling to contain her amusement. "I don't think I understand."

"I don't expect you to admit it."

"I haven't the foggiest idea what you're talking about."

"You know," he accused her with an angry shrug.

"Obviously I don't. What could I possibly have done to make you think I'm trying to *entice* you?"

"Sweet girlie things," he said again, but without the same conviction. He chewed on his bottom lip for a moment while he mulled the matter over. "All right, I'll give you an example— that perfume you're always wearing."

"Windchime? It's a light fragrance."

"I don't know the name of it. But it hangs around for an hour or so after you've left the room. You know that, and yet you wear it every time we're together."

"I've worn Windchime for years."

"That's not all," he continued quickly. "It's the way I catch you looking at me sometimes."

"*Looking* at you?" She folded her arms at her waist and rolled her eyes toward the ceiling.

"Yes," he said, sounding even more peevish. He pressed his hand to his hip, cocked his chin at a regal angle and fluttered his eyelashes like fans.

Despite her effort to hold in her amusement, Maryanne laughed. "I can only assume that you're joking."

Nolan dropped his hand from his hip. "I'm not. You get this innocent look and your lips pout just so . . . Why, a man—any man—couldn't keep from wanting to kiss you."

"That's preposterous." But Maryanne instinctively pinched her lips together and closed her eyes.

Nolan's arm shot out. "That's another thing."

"What now?"

"The way you get this helpless flustered look and it's all a simpleminded male can do not to rush in and offer to take care of whatever's bothering you."

"By this time you should know I'm perfectly capable of taking care of myself," Maryanne felt obliged to remind him.

"You're a lamb among wolves," Nolan said. "I don't know how long you intend to play out this silly charade, but personally I think you've overdone it. This isn't your world, and the sooner you go back where you belong, the better."

"Better for whom?"

"Me!" he cried vehemently. "And for you," he added with less fervor, as though it was an afterthought. He coughed a couple of times and reached for a package of cough drops in the pocket of his plaid robe. Shaking one out, he popped it in his mouth with barely a pause.

"I don't think it's doing you any good to get so excited," Maryanne said with unruffled patience. "I was merely making an observation and it still stands. I believe you need a wife."

"Go observe someone else's life," he suggested, sucking madly on the cough drop.

"Aha!" she cried, waving her index finger at him. "How does it feel to have someone interfering in *your* life?"

Nolan frowned and Maryanne turned back to the stove. She lifted the lid from the soup to stir it briskly. Then she lowered the burner. When she was through, she saw with a glimmer of fun that Nolan was standing as far away from her as humanly possible, while still remaining in the same room.

"That's something else!" he cried. "You give the impression that you're in total agreement with whatever I'm saying and then you go about doing exactly as you damn well please. I've never met a more frustrating woman in my entire life."

"That's not true," Maryanne argued. "I quit my job at Rent-A-Maid because you insisted." It had worked out for the best, since she had more time for her writing now, but this wasn't the moment to mention that.

"Oh, right, bring *that* up. It's the only thing you've ever done that I wanted. I practically had to get down on my knees and beg you to leave that crazy job before you injured yourself."

"You didn't!"

"Trust me, it was a humbling experience and not one I intend to repeat. I've known you how long? A month?" He paused to gaze at the ceiling. "It seems like an eternity."

"You're trying to make me feel guilty. It isn't going to work."

"Why should you feel anything of the sort? Just because living next door to you is enough to drive a man to drink."

"You're the one who found me this place. If you don't like living next door to me, then I'm not the one to blame!"

"Don't remind me," he muttered.

The comment about Nolan finding himself a wife had been made in jest, but he'd certainly taken it seriously. In fact, he seemed to have strong feelings about the entire issue. Realizing her welcome had worn extremely thin, Maryanne headed for his apartment door. "Everything's under control here."

"Does that mean you're leaving?"

She hated the enthusiastic lift in his voice, as if he couldn't wait to be rid of her. Although he wasn't admitting it, she'd done him a good turn. Fair exchange, she supposed; Nolan had been generous enough to her over the past month.

"Yes, I'm leaving."

"Good." He didn't bother to disguise his delight.

"But I still think you'd do well to consider what I said." Maryanne had the irresistible urge to heap coals on the fires of his indignation. "A wife could be a great help to you."

Nolan frowned heavily, drawing his eyebrows into a deep V. "I think the modern woman would find your suggestion downright insulting."

"What? That you marry?"

"Exactly. Haven't you heard? A woman's place isn't in the home anymore. It's out there in the world, forging a career for herself. Living a fuller life, and all that. It's not doing the mundane tasks you're talking about."

"I wasn't suggesting you marry for the convenience of gaining a live-in housekeeper."

His brown eyes narrowed. "Then what *were* you saying?"

"That you're a capable talented man," she explained. She glanced surreptitiously at his manuscript, still tidily stacked by the typewriter. "But unfortunately, that doesn't mean a whole lot if you don't have someone close—a friend, a companion, a . . . wife—to share it with."

"Don't you worry about me, Little Miss Muffet. I've lived my own life from the time I was thirteen. You may think I need someone, but let me assure you, I don't."

"You're probably right," she said reluctantly. She opened his door, then hesitated. "You'll call if you want anything?"

"No."

She released a short sigh of frustration. "That's what I thought. The soup should be done in about thirty minutes."

He nodded, then, looking a bit chagrined, added, "I suppose I should thank you."

"I suppose you should, too, but it isn't necessary."

"What about the money you spent on groceries? You can't afford acts of charity, you know. Wait a minute and I'll—"

"Forget it," she snapped. "I can spend my money on whatever I damn well please. I'm my own person, remember? You can just owe me. Buy me dinner sometime." She left before he could say anything else.

Maryanne's own apartment felt bleak and lonely after Nolan's. The first thing she did was walk around turning on all the lights. No sooner had she finished when there was a loud knock at her door. She opened it to find Nolan standing there in his disreputable moth-eaten robe, glaring.

"Yes?" she inquired sweetly.

"You read my manuscript, didn't you?" he boomed in a voice that echoed like thunder off the apartment walls.

"I most certainly did not," she denied vehemently. She straightened her back as if to suggest she found the very question insulting.

Without waiting for an invitation, Nolan stalked into her living room, then whirled around to face her. "Admit it!"

Making each word as clear and distinct as possible, Maryanne said, "I did not read your precious manuscript. How could I possibly have cleaned up, done the laundry, prepared a big kettle of homemade soup, and still had time to read 212 pages of manuscript?"

"How did you know it was 212 pages?" Sparks of reproach shot from his eyes.

"Ah—" she swallowed uncomfortably "—it was a guess, and from the looks of it, a good one."

"It wasn't any guess."

He marched toward her and for every step he took, she retreated two. "All right," she admitted guiltily, "I did look at it, but I swear I didn't read more than a few lines. I was straightening up the living room and . . . it was there, so I turned over the last page and read a couple of paragraphs."

"Aha! Finally, the truth!" Nolan pointed directly at her. "You did read it!"

"Just a few lines," she repeated in a tiny voice, feeling completely wretched.

"And?" His eyes softened.

"And what?"

"What did you think?" He looked at her expectantly, then frowned. "Never mind, I shouldn't have asked."

Rubbing her palms together, Maryanne took one step forward. "Nolan, it was wonderful. Witty and terribly suspenseful and . . . I would have given anything to read more. But I knew I didn't dare because, well, because I was invading your privacy . . . which I didn't want to do, but I did and I really didn't want . . . that."

"It is good, isn't it?" he asked almost smugly, then his expression sobered as quickly as it had before.

She grinned, nodding enthusiastically. "Tell me about it."

He seemed undecided, then launched excitedly into his idea. "It's about a Seattle newspaperman, Leo, who stumbles on a murder case. Actually, I'm developing a series with him as the main character. This one's not quite finished yet—as I'm sure you know."

"Is there a woman in Leo's life?"

"You're kidding, aren't you?"

Maryanne wasn't. The few paragraphs she'd read had mentioned a Maddie who was apparently in danger. Leo had been frantic to save her.

"You had no business going anywhere near that manuscript," Nolan reminded her.

"I know, but the temptation was so strong. I shouldn't have peeked, I realize that, but I couldn't help myself. Nolan, I'm not lying when I say how good the writing was. Do you have a publisher in mind? Because if you don't, I have several New York editor friends I could recommend and I know—"

"I'm not using you or any influence you may have in New York. I don't want anything to do with your father's publishing company. Understand?"

"Of course, but you're overreacting." He seemed to be doing a lot of that lately. "My father wouldn't stay in business long if he ordered the editors to purchase my friends' manuscripts, would he? Believe me, it would all be on the up and up, and if you've got an idea for a series using Leo—"

"I said no."

"But—"

"I mean it, Annie. This is my book and I'll submit it myself without any help from you."

"If that's what you want," she concurred meekly.

"That's the way it's going to be." The stern unyielding look slipped back into place. "Now if you don't mind, I'll quietly go back to my messy little world, sans wife and countless interruptions from a certain neighbor."

"I'll try not to bother you again," Maryanne said sarcastically, since he was the one who'd invaded *her* home this time.

"It would be appreciated," he said, apparently ignoring her tone.

"Your apartment is yours and mine is mine, and I'll uphold your privacy with the utmost respect," she continued, her voice still faintly mocking. She buried her hands in her pockets and her fingers closed around something cold and metallic.

"Good." Nolan was nodding. "Privacy, that's what we need."

"Um, Nolan . . ." She paused. "This is somewhat embarrassing, but it seems I have . . ." She hesitated again, then resolutely squared her shoulders. "I suppose you'd appreciate it if I returned your keys, right?"

"My keys?" Nolan exploded.

"I just found them. They were in my pocket. You see, all you had in your refrigerator was one limp strand of celery and I couldn't very well make soup out of that, so I had to go to the store and I didn't want to leave your door unlocked and—"

"You have my keys?"

"Yes."

He held out his palm, casting his eyes toward the ceiling. Feeling like a pickpocket caught in the act, Maryanne dropped the keys into his hand and stepped quickly back, almost afraid he was going to grab her by the shoulders and shake her. Which, of course, was ludicrous.

Nolan left immediately and Maryanne followed him to the door, staring out into the hallway as he walked back to his own apartment.

The next Thursday, Maryanne was hurrying to get ready for work when the phone rang. She frowned and stared at it, wondering if she dared take the time to answer. It might be Nolan, but every instinct she possessed told her otherwise. They hadn't spoken all week. Every afternoon, like clockwork, he'd arrived at Mom's Diner. More often than not, he ordered chili. Maryanne waited on him most of the time, but she might have been a robot for all the attention he paid her. His complete lack of interest dented her pride; still, his attitude shouldn't have come as any surprise.

"Hello," she said hesitantly, picking up the receiver.

"Maryanne," her mother responded, her voice rising with pleasure. "I can't believe I finally got hold of you. I've been trying for the past three days."

Maryanne immediately felt swamped by guilt. "You didn't leave a message on my machine."

"You know how I hate those things."

Maryanne did know that. She also knew she should have phoned her parents herself, but she wasn't sure how long she could continue with this farce. "Is everything all right?"

"Yes, of course. Your father's working too hard, but that's nothing new. The boys are busy with soccer and growing like weeds." Her mother's voice fell slightly. "How's the job?"

"The job?"

"Your special assignment."

"Oh, that." Maryanne had rarely been able to fool her mother, and she could only wonder how well she was succeeding now. "It's going . . . well. I'm learning so much."

"I think you'll make a terrific investigative reporter, sweetie, and the secrecy behind this assignment makes it all the more intriguing. When are your father and I going to learn exactly what you've been doing? I wish we'd never promised not to check up on your progress at the paper. We're both so curious."

"I'll be finished with it soon." Maryanne glanced at her watch and was about to close the conversation when her mother asked, "How's Nolan?"

"Nolan?" Maryanne's heart zoomed straight into her throat. She hadn't remembered mentioning him, and just hearing his name sent a feverish heat through her body.

"You seemed quite enthralled with him the last time we spoke, remember?"

"I was?"

"Yes, sweetie, you were. You claimed he was very talented, and although you were tight-lipped about it I got the impression you were strongly attracted to this young man."

"Nolan's a friend. But we argue more than anything."

Her mother chuckled. "Good."

"How could that possibly be good?"

"It means you're comfortable enough with each other to be yourselves, and that's a positive sign. Why, your father and I bickered like old fishwives when we first met. I swear there wasn't a single issue we could agree on." She sighed softly. "Then one day we looked at each other, and I knew then and there I was going to love this man for the rest of my life. And I have."

"Mom, it isn't like that with Nolan and me. I . . . I don't even think he likes me."

"Nolan doesn't like you?" her mother repeated. "Why, sweetie, that would be impossible."

Maryanne started to laugh then, because her mother was so obviously biased, yet sounded completely objective and matter-of-fact. It felt good to laugh again, good to find something amusing. She hadn't realized how melancholy she'd become since her last encounter with Nolan. He was still making such an effort to keep her at arm's length for fear . . . She didn't know exactly *what* he feared. Perhaps he was falling in love with her, but she'd noticed precious little evidence pointing to that conclusion. If anything, Nolan considered her an irritant in his life.

Maryanne spoke to her mother for a few more minutes, then rushed out the door, hoping she wouldn't be late for her shift at Mom's Place. Some investigative reporter she was!

At the diner, she slipped the apron around her waist and hurried out to help with the luncheon crowd. Waiting tables, she was learning quite a lot about character types. This could be helpful for a writer, she figured. Some of her customers were pretty eccentric. She observed them carefully, wondering if Nolan did the same thing. But she wasn't going to think about Nolan . . . .

Halfway through her shift, she began to feel light-headed and sick to her stomach.

"Are you feeling all right?" Barbara asked as she slipped past, carrying an order.

"I—I don't know."

"When was the last time you ate?"

"This morning. No," she corrected, "last night. I didn't have much of an appetite this morning."

"That's what I thought." Barbara set the hamburger and fries on the counter in front of her customer and walked back to Maryanne. "Now that I've got a good look at you, you do seem a bit peaked."

"I'm all right."

Hands on her hips, Barbara continued to study Maryanne as if memorizing every feature. "Are you sure?"

"I'm fine." She had the beginnings of a headache, but nothing she could really complain about. It probably hadn't been a good idea to skip breakfast and lunch, but she'd make up for it when she took her dinner break.

"I'm not sure I believe you," Barbara muttered, dragging out a well-used phone book. She flipped through the pages until she apparently found the number she wanted, then reached for the phone.

"Who are you calling?"

She held the receiver against her shoulder. "Nolan Adams, who else? Seems to me it's his turn to play nursemaid."

"Barbara, no!" She might not be feeling a hundred per cent, but she wasn't all that sick, either. And the last person she wanted running to her rescue was Nolan. He'd only use it against her, as proof that she should go back to the cosy comfortable world of her parents. She'd almost proved she could live entirely on her own, without relying on interest from her trust fund.

"Nolan's not at the office," Barbara said a moment later, replacing the receiver. "I'll talk to him when he comes in."

"No, you won't! Barbara, I swear to you I'll personally give your phone number to every trucker who comes into this place if you so much as say a single word to Nolan."

"Honey," the other waitress said, raising her eyebrows, "you'd be doing me a favor!"

Grumbling, Maryanne returned to her customers.

By closing time, however, she was feeling slightly worse. Not exactly sick, but not exactly herself, either. Barbara was watching Maryanne closely, regularly feeling her cheeks and forehead and muttering about her temperature. If there was one thing to be grateful for, it was the fact that Nolan hadn't shown up. Barbara insisted Maryanne leave a few minutes early and shooed her out the door. Had she been feeling better, Maryanne would have argued.

By the time she arrived back at her apartment, she knew

beyond a doubt that she was coming down with some kind of virus. Part of her would've liked to blame Nolan, but she was the one who'd let herself into his apartment. She was the one who'd lingered there, straightening up the place and staying far longer than necessary.

After a long hot shower, she put on her flannel pyjamas and unfolded her bed, climbing quickly beneath the covers. She'd turned the television on for company and prepared herself a mug of soup. As she took her first sip, she heard someone knock at her door.

"Who is it?" she called out.

"Nolan."

"I'm in bed," she shouted.

"You've seen me in my robe. It's only fair I see you in yours," he yelled back.

Maryanne tossed aside her covers and sat up. "Go away."

A sharp pounding noise came from the floor, followed by an equally loud roar that proclaimed it time for "Jeopardy." Apparently Maryanne's shouting match with Nolan was disrupting Mrs. McBride's favorite television show.

"Sorry." Maryanne cupped her hands over her mouth and yelled at the hardwood floor.

"Are you going to let me in, or do I have to get the passkey?" Nolan demanded.

Groaning, Maryanne shuffled across the floor in her giant fuzzy slippers and turned the lock. "Yes?" she asked with exaggerated patience.

For the longest moment, Nolan said nothing. He shoved his hands deep into the pockets of his beige raincoat. "How are you?"

Maryanne glared at him with all the indignation she could muster, which at the moment was considerable. "Do you mean to say you practically pounded down my door to ask me that?"

He didn't bother to answer, but walked into her apartment as though he had every right to do so. "Barbara phoned me."

"Oh, brother! And what exactly did she say?" She continued to hold open the door, hoping he'd get the hint and leave.

"That you caught my bug." His voice was rough with ill-disguised worry.

"Wrong. I felt a bit under the weather earlier, but I'm fine now." The last thing she wanted Nolan motivated by was guilt. He'd succeeded in keeping his distance up to now; if he decided to see her, she wanted to be sure his visit wasn't prompted by an overactive sense of responsibility.

"You look . . ."

"Yes?" she prompted.

His gaze skimmed her, from slightly damp hair to large fuzzy feet. "Fine," he answered softly.

"As you can see I'm really not sick, so you needn't concern yourself."

Her words were followed by a lengthy silence. Nolan turned as though to leave. Maryanne should have felt relieved to see him go; instead, she experienced the strangest sensation of loss. She longed to reach out a hand, ask him to stay, but she didn't have the courage.

She brushed the hair from her face and smiled, even though it was difficult to put on a carefree facade.

"I'll stop by in the morning and see how you're doing," Nolan said, hovering by the threshold.

"That won't be necessary."

He frowned. "When did you get so prickly?"

"When did you get so caring?" The words nearly caught in her throat and escaped on a whisper.

"I *do* care about you," he said.

"Oh, sure, the same way you'd care about an annoying younger sister. Believe me, Nolan, your message came through loud and clear. I'm not your type. Fine, I can accept that, because you're not my type, either." She didn't really think she had a type, but it sounded philosophical and went a long way toward salving her badly bruised ego. Nolan couldn't have made his views toward her any plainer had he rented a billboard. He'd even said he'd taken one look at her and immediately thought, "Here comes trouble."

She'd never been more attracted to a man in her life, and here she was, standing in front of him lying through her teeth rather than admit how she truly felt.

"So I'm not your type, either?" he asked, almost in a whisper.

Maryanne's heartbeat quickened. He studied her as intently as she studied him. He gazed at her mouth, then slipped his hand behind her neck and slowly, so very slowly, lowered his lips to hers.

He paused, their mouths a scant inch apart. He seemed to be waiting for her to pull away, withdraw from him. Everything inside her told her to do exactly that. He was only trying to humiliate her, wasn't he? Trying to prove how powerful her attraction to him was, how easily he could bend her will to his own.

And she was letting him.

Her heart was beating so furiously her body seemed to rock with the sheer force of it. Every throb seemed to drive her directly into his arms, right where she longed to be. She placed her palms against his chest and sighed as his mouth met hers. The touch of his lips felt warm and soft. And right.

His hand cradled her neck while his lips continued to move over hers in the gentlest explorations, as though he feared she was too delicate to kiss the way he wanted.

Gradually his hands slipped to her shoulders. He drew a ragged breath, then put his head back as he stared up at the ceiling. He exhaled slowly, deliberately.

It took all the restraint Maryanne possessed not to ask him why he was stopping. She wanted these incredible sensations to continue. She longed to explore the feelings his kiss produced and the complex responses she experienced deep within her body. Her pulse hammered erratically as she tried to control her breathing.

"Okay, now we've got that settled, I'll leave." He backed away from her.

"Got what settled?" she asked swiftly, then realized she was only making a bigger fool of herself. Naturally he was talking about the reason for this impromptu visit, which had been her health. Hadn't it? "Oh, I see."

"I don't think you do," Nolan said enigmatically. He turned and walked away.

Eight

"Whose turn next?" Maryanne asked. She and her two friends were sitting in the middle of her living room floor, having a "pity party."

"I will," Carol Riverside volunteered eagerly. She ceremonially plucked a tissue from the box that rested in the center of their small circle, next to the lit candle. Their second large bottle of cheap wine was nearly empty, and the three of them were feeling no pain.

"For years I've wanted to write a newspaper column of my own," Carol said, squaring her shoulders and hauling in a huge breath. "But it's not what I thought it'd be like. I ran out of ideas for things to write about after the first week."

"Ah," Maryanne sighed sympathetically.

"Ah," Barbara echoed.

"That's not all," Carol said sadly. "I never knew the world was so full of critics. No one seems to agree with me. I—I didn't know Seattle had so many cantankerous readers. I try, but it's impossible to make everyone happy. What happens is that some of the people like me some of the time and all the rest hate everything I write." She glanced up. "Except the two of you, of course."

Maryanne nodded her head so hard she nearly toppled over. She spread her hands out at either side in an effort to maintain her balance. The wine made her yawn loudly.

Apparently in real distress, Carol dabbed at her eyes. "Being a columnist is hard work and nothing like I'd always dreamed." The edges of her mouth turned downward. "I don't even like writing anymore," she sobbed.

"Isn't that a pity!" Maryanne cried, ritually tossing her tissue into the center of the circle. Barbara followed suit, and then they both patted Carol gently on the back.

Carol brightened once she'd finished. "I don't know what I'd do without the two of you. You and Betty are my very best friends in the whole world," she announced.

"Barbara," Maryanne corrected. "Your very best friend's name is Barbara."

The three of them looked at each other and burst into gales of laughter. Maryanne hushed them by waving her hands. "Stop! We can't allow ourselves to become giddy. A pity party doesn't work if all we do is laugh. We've got to remember this is sad and serious business."

"Sad and serious," Barbara agreed, sobering. She grabbed a fresh tissue and clutched it in her hand, waiting for the others to share their sorrows and give her a reason to cry.

"Whose idea was the wine?" Maryanne wanted to know, taking a quick sip.

Carol blushed. "I thought it would be less fattening than the chocolate ice-cream bars you planned to serve."

"Hey," Barbara said, narrowing her eyes at Maryanne. "You haven't said anything about your problem."

Maryanne suddenly found it necessary to remove lint from her jeans. Sharing what disturbed her most was a little more complicated than being disappointed in her job or complaining about fingernails that cracked all too easily, as Barbara had done. She hadn't sold a single article since she'd quit the paper, or even received a positive response to one of her queries. But worst of all she was falling in love with Nolan. He felt something for her, too—she knew that—but he was fighting her every step of the way. Fighting her and fighting himself.

He was attracted to her, he couldn't deny it, although he'd tried to, more than once. When they were alone together, the tension seemed to throb between them.

He was battling the attraction so hard he'd gone as far as arranging a date for her with another man. Since the evening they'd met, Nolan had insulted her, harangued her and lectured her. He'd made it plain that he didn't want her around. And yet there were times he sought out her company. He argued with her at every opportunity, took it upon himself to be her guardian, and yet . . .

"Maryanne?" Carol said, studying her with concern. "What's wrong?"

"Nolan Adams," she whispered. Lifting her wineglass, she took a small swallow, hoping that would give her the courage to continue.

"I should have guessed," Carol muttered, frowning. "From the moment you moved in here, next door to that madman, I just knew he'd cause you nothing but problems."

Her friend's opinion of Nolan had never been high and Maryanne had to bite back the urge to defend him.

"Tell us everything," Barbara said, drawing up her knees and leaning against the sofa.

"There isn't much to tell."

"He's the one who got you into this craziness in the first place, remember?" Carol pointed out righteously—as if Maryanne needed reminding. Carol then turned to Barbara and began to explain to the older woman how it had all started. "Nolan wrote a derogatory piece about Maryanne in his column a while back, implying she was a spoiled debutante, and she took it to heart and decided to prove him wrong."

"He didn't mean it. In fact, he's regretted every word of that article." This time Maryanne did feel obliged to defend him. As far as she was concerned, all of that was old business, already resolved. It was the unfinished business, the things happening between them now, that bothered her the most.

The denial. The refusal on both their parts to accept the feelings they shared. Only a few days earlier, Maryanne had tried to convince Nolan he wasn't her type, that nothing about them was compatible. He'd been only too eager to agree.

But they'd been drawn together, virtually against their wills, by an attraction so overwhelming, so inevitable, they were powerless against it. Their sensual and emotional awareness of each other seemed more intense every time they met. This feeling couldn't be anything except love.

"You're among friends, so tell us everything," Barbara pressed, handing Maryanne the entire box of tissues. "Remember, I've known Nolan for years, so nothing you say is going to shock me."

"For one thing, he's impossible," Maryanne whispered, finding it difficult to express her thoughts.

"He deserves to be hanged from the closest tree," Carol said scornfully.

"And at the same time he's wonderful," Maryanne concluded, ignoring Carol's comment.

"You're not . . ." Carol paused, her face tightening as if she was having trouble forming the words. "You don't mean to suggest you're falling in—" she swallowed "—*love* with him, are you?"

"I don't know." Maryanne crumpled the soggy tissue. "But I think I might be."

"Oh, no," Carol cried, covering her mouth with both hands, "you've got to do something quick. A man like Nolan Adams eats little girls like you for breakfast. He's cynical and sarcastic and—"

"Talented and generous," Maryanne finished for her.

"You're not thinking clearly. It probably has something to do with that fever you had. You've got to remember the facts. Nolan insulted you in print, seriously insulted you, and then tried to make up for it. You're mistaking that small attack of conscience for something more—which could be dangerous." Awkwardly, Carol rose to her feet and started pacing.

"He's probably one of the most talented writers I've ever read," Maryanne continued, undaunted by her friend's concerns. "Every time I read his work, I can't help being awed."

"All right," Carol said, "I'll concede he does possess a certain amount of creative talent, but that doesn't change who or what he is. Nolan Adams is a bad-tempered egotistical self-centered . . . grouch."

"I hate to say this," Barbara said softly, shaking her head, "but Carol's right. Nolan's been eating at Mom's Place for as long as I've worked there, and that's three years. I feel I know him better than you do, and he's everything Carol says. But," she said thoughtfully, "underneath it all, there's more to him. Oh, he'd like everyone to believe he's this macho guy. He plays that role to the hilt, but after you've been around him awhile, you can tell it's all a game to him."

"I told you he's wonderful!" Maryanne exclaimed.

"The man's a constant," Carol insisted. "Constantly in a bad mood, constantly making trouble, constantly getting involved in matters that are none of his business. Maryanne here is the perfect example. He should never have written that column about her." Carol plopped back down and jerked half a dozen tissues from the box in quick succession. She handed them to

Maryanne. "You've got blinders on where he's concerned. Take it from me, a woman can't allow herself to become emotionally involved with a man she plans to change."

"I don't want to change Nolan."

"You don't?" Carol echoed, her voice low and disbelieving. "You mean to say you like him as he is?"

"You just don't know him the way I do," Maryanne said. "Nolan's truly generous. Did either of you know he's become sort of a father figure to the teenagers in this neighborhood? He's their friend in the very best sense. He keeps tabs on them and makes sure no one gets involved in drugs or is lured into gang activities. The kids around here idolize him."

"Nolan Adams does that?" Carol sounded skeptical. She arched her brows as though she couldn't completely trust Maryanne's observations.

"When Barbara told him I was coming down with a virus, he came over to check on me and—"

"As well he should!" Barbara declared. "He was the one who gave you that germ in the first place."

"I'm not entirely sure I caught it from him."

Carol and Barbara exchanged a look. Slowly each shook her head, and then all three shared a warm smile.

"I think we might be too late," Barbara said theatrically, speaking from the side of her mouth.

"She's showing all the signs," Carol agreed solemnly.

"You're right, I fear," Barbara responded in kind. "She's already in love with him."

"Good grief, no," Carol wailed, pressing her hands to her mouth. "Say it isn't so. She's too young and vulnerable."

"It's a pity, such a pity."

"I can't help but agree. Maryanne is much too sweet for Nolan Adams. I just hope he appreciates her."

"He won't," Carol muttered, reverting to her normal voice, "but then no man ever fully appreciates a woman."

"It's such a pity men act the way they do," Barbara said in a sad voice.

"Some men," Maryanne added.

Carol and Barbara dabbed their eyes and solemnly tossed the used tissues into the growing heap in the middle of their circle.

The plan had been to gather all the used tissues and ceremonially dump them in the toilet, flush their "pity pot," and then celebrate all the good things in their lives.

The idea for this little party had been an impromptu one of Maryanne's on a lonely Friday night. She'd been feeling blue and friendless and decided to look for a little innocent fun. She'd phoned Carol and learned she was a weekend widow; her husband had gone fishing with some cronies. Barbara had thought the idea was a good one herself, since she'd just broken her longest fingernail and was in the mood for a shoulder to cry on.

A pity party seemed just the thing to help three lonely women make it through a bleak Friday night.

Maryanne awoke Saturday morning with a humdinger of a headache. Wine and the ice cream they'd had at the end of the evening definitely didn't mix.

If her head hadn't been throbbing so painfully, she might have recognized sooner that her apartment had no heat. Her cantankerous radiator was acting up again. It did that some mornings, but she'd always managed to coax it back to life with a few well-placed whacks. The past few days had been unusually cold for early November—well below freezing at night.

She reached for her robe and slippers, bundling herself up like a December baby out in her first snowstorm. Cupping her hands over her mouth, she blew until a frosty mist formed.

A quickly produced cup of coffee with two extra-strength aspirin took the edge off her headache. Maryanne shivered while she slipped into jeans, sweatshirt and a thick winter coat. She suspected she resembled someone preparing to join an Arctic expedition.

She fiddled with the radiator, twisting the knobs and slamming her hand against the side, but the only results were a couple of rattles and a hollow clanking.

Not knowing what else to try, she got out her heavy cast-iron skillet and banged it against the top of the rad in hopes of reviving the ageing pipes.

The noise was deafening, vibrating through the room like a jet aircraft crashing through the sound barrier. If that wasn't enough, Maryanne's entire body began to quiver, starting at her arm and spreading outward in a rippling effect that caused her arms and legs to tremble.

"What the hell's going on over there?" Nolan shouted from the other side of the wall. He didn't wait for her to answer and a couple of seconds later came barreling through her front door, wild-eyed and dishevelled.

"What . . . Where?" He was carrying a baseball bat, and stalked to the middle of her apartment, scanning the interior for what Maryanne could only assume were invaders.

"I don't have any heat," she announced, tucking the thin scarf more tightly around her ears.

Nolan blinked. She'd apparently woken him from a sound sleep. He was barefoot and dressed in pyjama bottoms, and although he wore a shirt, it was unbuttoned, revealing a broad muscular chest dusted with curly black hair.

"What's with you? Are you going to a costume party?"

"Believe me, this is no party. I'm simply trying to keep warm."

His gaze lowered to the heavy skillet in her hand. "Do you plan to cook on that radiator?"

"I might if I could get it to work. In case you hadn't noticed, there isn't any heat in this place."

Nolan set the baseball bat aside and moved to the far wall to look at the radiator. "What's wrong with it?"

How like a man to ask stupid questions! If Maryanne had *known* what was wrong with it, she wouldn't be standing there shivering, with a scarf swaddling her face like an old-time remedy for toothache.

"How in heaven's name am I supposed to know?" she answered testily.

"What went on here last night, anyway? A wake?"

She glanced at the mound of tissues and shrugged. He was scanning the area as if it were a crime scene and he should take caution not to stumble over a dead body.

Walking across the living room, he picked up the two empty wine bottles and held them aloft for her inspection, pretending to be shocked.

"Very funny." She put the skillet down and removed the bottles from his hands, to be deposited promptly in the garbage.

"So you had a party and I wasn't invited." He made it sound as though he'd missed the social event of the year.

Maryanne sighed loudly. "If you must know, Carol, Barbara and I had a pity party."

"A what? You're kidding, right?" He didn't bother to hide his mocking grin.

"Never mind." She should've realized he'd only poke fun at her. "Can you figure out how to get this thing working before the next ice age?"

"Here, give me a shot at it." He gently patted the top of the radiator as he knelt in front of it. "Okay, ol' Betsy, we're trusting you to be good." He began fiddling with knobs, still murmuring ridiculous endearments—like a cowboy talking to his horse.

"It doesn't do any good to talk to an inanimate object," she advised primly, standing behind him.

"You want to do this?"

"No," she muttered. Having Nolan in her home, dressed in his nightclothes, did something odd to her, sent her pulse skittering erratically. She deliberately allowed her attention to wander to the scene outside her window. The still-green lawns of Volunteer Park showed in the distance and she pretended to be absorbed in their beauty.

"I thought I told you to keep that door chain in place," he said casually as he worked. "This isn't The Seattle."

"Do you honestly think you need to remind me of that now?" She rubbed her hands together, hoping to generate some warmth before her fingers went numb.

"There," he said, sounding satisfied. "All she needed was a little loving care."

"Thanks," Maryanne said with relief.

"No problem, only the next time something like this happens don't try to fix it yourself."

"Translated, that means I shouldn't try to fix the radiator again while *you're* trying to sleep."

"Right."

She smiled up at him, her eyes alive with appreciation. He really had been good to her from the day she'd moved in— before then, too. Discounting what he'd written about her in his column, of course. And even that had ended up having a positive effect.

It'd been a week since she'd seen him. A long week. A lonely week. Until now, she'd hardly been able to admit, even to herself, how much she'd missed him. Standing there as he was, Maryanne was struck by just how attractive she found him. If only he'd taken the time to button his shirt! She reveled in his lean strength and his aura of unquestionable authority—and that chest of his was driving her to distraction.

She wasn't the only one enthralled. Nolan was staring at her, too. The silence lingered between them, lengthening moment by moment as they gazed into each other's eyes.

"I have to go," he finally said, breaking eye contact by glancing past her, out the window.

"Right. I—I understand," she stammered, stepping back. Her hands swung at her sides as she followed him to the door. "I really do appreciate this." Already she could feel the warmth spilling into her apartment. And none too soon, either.

"Just remember to keep the door locked."

She grinned and mockingly saluted him. "Aye, aye, sir."

He left then. Maryanne hated to see him go, hated to see him walk away from her, and yet it seemed he was always doing exactly that.

Later that same afternoon, after she'd finished her errands, Maryanne was strolling through the park when a soft feminine voice spoke from behind her.

Maryanne turned around and waved when she discovered Gloria, the teenager she'd met here earlier. But this time Gloria wasn't alone.

"This is my little sister, Katie, the pest," Gloria explained. "She's three."

"Hello, Katie," Maryanne said, smiling.

"Why am I a pest?" Katie asked, gazing at Gloria, but apparently not offended that her older sister referred to her that way.

"Because." Looking annoyed, the teenager shrugged in the same vague manner Maryanne had so often seen in her younger brothers. "Katie's three and every other word is 'why.' Why this? Why that? It's enough to drive a person straight to the loony bin."

"I have brothers, so I know what you mean."

"You do?"

"They're several years younger than I am. So trust me, I understand what you're talking about."

"Did your brothers want to go every place you did? And did your mother make you take them even if it was a terrible inconvenience?"

Maryanne tried to disguise a smile. "Sometimes."

"Eddie asked me to come and watch him play basketball this afternoon with Mr. Adams, and I had to drag Katie along because she wanted to come to the park, too. My mom pressured me into bringing her. I didn't even get a chance to say no." Gloria made it sound as if she were being forced to swim across Puget Sound with the three-year-old clinging to her back.

"I'm not a pest," Katie insisted now, flipping her braid over one shoulder in a show of defiance. Looking up at Maryanne, the little girl carefully manipulated her fingers and proudly exclaimed, "I'm three."

"Three?" Maryanne repeated, raising her eyebrows, feigning surprise. "Really? I would've thought you were four or five."

Katie grinned delightedly. "I'm nearly four, you know."

"Mr. Adams is already here," Gloria said, brightening. She frowned as she glanced down at her little sister and jerked the small arm in an effort to hurry her along. "Come on, Katie, we have to go. Eddie wants me to watch him play ball."

"Why?"

Gloria groaned. "See what I mean?"

"You go on," Maryanne said, offering Katie her hand. The youngster obediently slipped her small hand into Maryanne's much larger one, willingly abandoning her cranky older sister. "Katie and I will follow behind."

Gloria looked surprised by the offer. "You mean you don't mind? I mean, Katie's my responsibility and it wouldn't be fair to palm her off on you. You're not going to kidnap her or anything, are you? I mean, I know you're not—you're Mr. Adams's friend. I wouldn't let her go with just anyone, you know. But if anything happened to her, my mother would kill me."

"I promise to take the very best care of her."

Gloria grinned, looking sheepish for having suggested anything else. "You're sure you don't mind?"

"I don't mind in the least. I don't think Katie does, either. Is that right, Katie?"

"Why?"

"Are you *really* sure? Okay, then . . ." Once she'd made a token protest Gloria raced off to join her friends.

Katie was content to skip and hop at Maryanne's side until they reached a huge pile of leaves under a chestnut tree, not far from the basketball court. Almost before Maryanne realized it, Katie raced toward the leaves, bunching as many as she could in her small arms and carrying them back to Maryanne as though presenting her with the rarest of jewels.

"Look," she cried happily. "Leafs."

"Leaves," Maryanne corrected, bending over and grabbing an armful herself. She tossed them in the air and grinned as Katie leapt up to catch as many as she could and in the process dropped the armload she was holding.

Laughing, Maryanne clasped the child by the waist and swung her around, while Katie shrieked with delight. Dizzy, Maryanne leaned against the tree in an effort to regain her equilibrium and her breath.

It was then that she saw Nolan had stopped playing and was standing in the middle of the basketball court, staring at her. The game was going on all around him, boys scattering in one direction and then another, racing to one end of the court and back again. Nolan seemed oblivious to them and to the game—to everything but her.

A tall boy bumped into him from behind and Nolan stumbled. Maryanne gasped, fearing he might fall, but he caught himself in time. Without a pause, he rejoined the game, racing down the court at breakneck speed. He stole the ball and made a slam dunk, coming down hard on the pavement.

Gloria ran back toward Maryanne and Katie. "I thought you said you and Mr. Adams were just friends?" she teased. She was grinning in a way that suggested she wasn't about to be fooled again. "He nearly got creamed because he couldn't take his eyes off you."

With Katie on her lap, Maryanne sat beside the teenage girls watching the game. Together she and the three-year-old became Nolan's personal cheering squad, but whether or not he appreciated their efforts she didn't know. He didn't give a single indication that he heard them.

When the game was finished, Nolan walked breathlessly off the court. His grey sweatshirt was stained with perspiration, and his face was red and damp from the sheer physical exhaustion of keeping up with kids half his age.

For an anxious moment, Maryanne assumed he was planning to ignore her and simply walk away. But after he'd stopped at the water fountain, he came over to the bench where she and Katie were sitting.

He slumped down beside her, dishevelled and still breathing hard. "What are you doing here?" he grumbled.

"I happened to be in the park," she answered, feeling self-conscious now and unsure. "You don't need to worry, Nolan. I didn't follow you."

"I didn't think you had."

"You look nice in blue," he said hoarsely, then cleared his

throat as if he hadn't meant to say that, as if he wanted to withdraw the words.

"Thanks." The blue sweater was one of her favorites. She'd
worn her long wool coat and was surprised he'd even noticed
the periwinkle-blue sweater beneath.

"Hello, Katie."

Katie beamed, stretching out both arms for Nolan to lift
her up, which he did. The little girl hugged him quickly, then
leapt off the bench and ran to her sister, who stood talking to
her boyfriend.

"You're good with children," Nolan said. His voice fell
slightly, as though the fact surprised him.

"I do have a knack with them. I always have." She'd been
much-sought as a babysitter by her parents' friends and for a
time had considered becoming a teacher. If she'd pursued that
field of study she would have preferred to teach kindergarten.
She found five-year-olds, with their eagerness to learn about
the world, delightful. A couple of articles she'd written the
week before were geared toward children's magazines. If only
she'd hear something soon. It seemed to take so long.

"How many years of your life did you lose this time?" Maryanne asked teasingly.

"Another two or three, at least."

He smiled at her and it was that rare special smile he granted
her only in those brief moments when his guard was lowered.
His resistance to the attraction he felt to her was at its weakest
point, and they both knew it.

Maryanne went still, almost afraid to move or speak for fear
of ruining the moment. His eyes, so warm and gentle, continued to hold hers. When she tried to breathe, the air seemed to
catch in her lungs.

"Maryanne." Her name was little more than a whisper.

"Yes?"

He raked his hand through his hair, then looked away. "Nothing. Never mind."

"What is it?" she pressed, unwilling to let the matter drop.

The muscles along the side of his jaw clenched. "I said it was nothing," he answered gruffly.

Maryanne gazed down at her hands, feeling an overwhelming sense of frustration and despair. The tension between them was so thick she could practically touch it, but nothing she could say or do would make any difference. If anything, her efforts would only make it worse.

"Hey, Nolan," Eddie called out, loping toward them. "What's with you, man?" He laughed, tossing his basketball from one hand to the other. "You nearly lost that game 'cause you couldn't take your eyes off your woman."

Nolan scowled at him. "You looking for a rematch?"

"Any time you want."

"Not today." Shaking his head, Nolan slowly pushed the sleeves of his sweatshirt past his elbows.

"Right," Eddie said with a knowing laugh. "I didn't think so, with your woman here and all."

"Maryanne isn't my woman," Nolan informed him curtly, his frown darkening.

"Right," Eddie responded. "Hey, dude, this is me, Eddie. Can't fool me! You practically went comatose when you saw her. I don't blame you, though. She ain't bad. So when are you two getting married?"

Nine

"I've changed my mind," Barbara announced at closing time Monday evening.

Maryanne was busy refilling the salt and pepper shakers and reloading the napkin holders. "About what?" she asked absently, stuffing napkins into the small chrome canisters.

"You and Nolan."

If Barbara hadn't had Maryanne's attention earlier, she did now. Nolan had left the restaurant about forty minutes earlier, after having his customary meal of chili and coffee. He'd barely said two words to Maryanne the whole time he was there. He'd buried his face in the evening edition of the *Sun* and done a brilliant job of pretending he didn't know her.

"What about us?" Maryanne's expression might have remained aloof, but her heart was pounding furiously.

"Since the night of our pity party, I've had a change of heart. You're exactly the right kind of woman for Nolan. The two of you . . . balance each other. At first I agreed with Carol. My opinion of Nolan isn't as negative as hers, but you have to remember that those two work for rival papers. At any rate, I was concerned. You *are* really sweet."

Maryanne winced at the "sweet." It rather sounded as though friendship with her was like falling into a jar of honey.

"And now?"

"I don't know exactly what changed my mind. Partly it was watching Nolan when he was here. I got quite a kick out of him."

"How do you mean?"

Barbara's grin was broad as she continued to wipe the counter. "I swear that man couldn't keep his eyes off you."

Maryanne was puzzled. "What are you talking about? Nolan didn't look my way even once."

"Oh, he'd scowl every time you were close, but behind that cross expression of his was an intensity I've never seen in him before. It was like he had to come in and get his daily fix of you."

Maryanne's heart couldn't decide whether to lift with happiness or sink with doubt. "You're wrong. Other than ordering his meal, he didn't speak to me at all. I might as well have been a robot."

"That's what he'd like you to believe."

"He was reading the paper," Maryanne said. "The same way he reads it every time he comes here."

"Correction," Barbara said, and her face broke into a spontaneous smile. "He *pretended* to be reading the paper, but when you weren't looking his eyes were following you like a hawk."

"Oh, Barbara, really?" It seemed almost more than she dared hope for. He'd hardly spoken to her in the past few days, and he seemed to be avoiding her. The kids in the park had taken to teasing them about being "in love" and asking pointed questions, and Nolan had practically fallen all over himself denying that they were anything other than friends.

"It's more than just the way he was watching you," Barbara said, slipping on to a stool. "Have you read his columns the past couple of weeks?"

Naturally Maryanne had, more impressed by his work every time she did. The range of his talent and the power of his writing were unmistakable. Within a few years, if not sooner, she expected his newspaper column to be picked up for syndication.

"Lately, I've noticed something unusual about his writing," Barbara said, still clutching the dishrag. "That cynical edge of his—it isn't quite as sharp. His writing's less sarcastic now. I heard one of my customers comment earlier today that Nolan's going soft on us. I hadn't thought about it much until then, but Ernie's right. I don't know what's made the difference, but I figure it must be love. Oh, I doubt there's much in this life that's going to change Nolan Adams. He'll always be stubborn as a mule, headstrong and temperamental. That's just part of his nature. But mark my words, he's in love."

"What you said earlier, about us being so different . . ."

"You are, with you so nice and all, and Nolan such a grouch. At least he likes to pretend he's one. You and I know better, but most folks don't."

"And?" Maryanne probed.

"And, well, it seems to me the two of you fit together perfectly. Like two pieces of a puzzle."

It seemed that way to Maryanne, too.

"You heard, didn't you?" Barbara muttered, abruptly changing the subject.

Maryanne nodded. Mom's Place was going to close in a month for remodelling.

"What are you going to do?"

Maryanne didn't know yet. "Find a temporary job, I suppose. What about you?" By then, she should have sold a few of the articles she'd submitted. At least she hadn't been rejected yet. She should be hearing any time.

"I'm not that worried about taking a month or so off work," Barbara returned, her look thoughtful. "I could use a vacation, especially over the holidays. I was thinking of staying home and baking Christmas gifts this year. My fudge is out of this world."

"I suppose I should start looking for another job now." Maryanne was already worried about meeting expenses. Mom's Place couldn't have chosen a worse time to close.

A half hour later, she was waiting for the bus, her mind spinning with what Barbara had said. The diner's closing was a concern, but Barbara's comments about Nolan gladdened Maryanne's heart.

Nolan did feel something for her, something more powerful than he'd let on.

She supposed she should confront him with it, force him to acknowledge his feelings. A brief smile crossed her lips as she envisioned what would happen if she actually did such a thing. She nearly laughed out loud at the thought.

Nolan would deny it, of course, loudly and vehemently, and she'd have to counteract with a loud argument of her own. The smile appeared again. Her decision was made.

Feeling almost light-headed, Maryanne glanced down the street, eager for the bus to arrive so she could get home. The first thing she intended to do was march into Nolan's apartment and demand the truth. If he tried to ignore her, as he usually did, then she had the perfect solution.

She'd kiss him.

A kiss would silence his protests in the most effective way she could imagine. Maryanne almost melted at the memory of being kissed by Nolan, being held in his arms. It was like walking through the gates of an undiscovered paradise. Just remembering those moments made her feel faint with desire, weak with excitement. He seemed to experience the same emotions, Maryanne remembered hopefully.

Cheered by the thought, she nearly applauded when her bus

arrived. The ride passed quickly and she hurried into the building, eager to see Nolan.

Consumed by her sense of purpose, she went directly to his apartment. She stood in front of his door, took several deep breaths, then knocked politely. No answer. She tried again, harder this time.

"Who is it?" Nolan growled from the other side.

"Maryanne. I want to talk to you."

"I'm busy."

She was only a little discouraged by his unfriendliness. "This'll just take a minute."

The door was yanked open with excessive force. Nolan stood before her, dressed in a black tuxedo and white cummerbund, looking so handsome that he caught her completely by surprise. Her mouth sagged open.

"Yes?" he asked crossly.

"Hello, Nolan," she said, aware that her mission had been thwarted. Nothing he could've said or done would have affected her as profoundly as finding him dressed like this. Because it meant he was going out on a date.

"Hello," he said, tugging at the cuffs of his jacket, adjusting the fit. He frowned, apparently waiting for her to say something.

"Uh . . ." She tried to gather her scattered composure, and finally managed to squeak, "You're going out?"

He scowled. "I don't dress like this for a jaunt to the corner store."

"No, I don't suppose you do."

"You wanted something?"

She'd been so confident, so sure she was doing the right thing. But now, seeing Nolan looking more dressed up and formal than he'd ever looked for *her*, she found herself speechless.

She couldn't help wondering where he was going—and with whom. The "with whom" part bothered her the most.

He glanced pointedly at his wristwatch. "How long is this going to take?" he asked coolly. "I'm supposed to pick up Prudence in fifteen minutes."

"Prudence?" His face, tight with impatience, drew her full attention. *Prudence*, her mind repeated. Who was this woman?

Then in a flash, Maryanne knew. It was all she could do not to laugh and inform him that his little plan just wasn't working. No imaginary date was going to make *her* jealous.

He wasn't seeing anyone named Prudence. Good grief, if he had to invent a name, the least he could've done was come up with something a little more plausible than Prudence.

In fact, Maryanne remembered Nolan casually mentioning a week or so earlier that he'd been asked to speak at a Chamber of Commerce banquet. There had also been a notice in the paper. Who did he think he was kidding?

Of course he wanted her to believe he was dating another woman. That was supposed to discourage her, she guessed. Except that it didn't.

"It wasn't important . . ." she said, gesturing vaguely. "The radiators were giving me trouble this morning, but I'll manage. I was planning to go out tonight myself."

His eyes connected with hers. "Another pity party?"

"Not this time." She considered announcing she had a hot date herself, but that would have been carrying this farce a little too far. "Barbara and I will probably go to a movie."

"Sounds like fun."

"I'm sure it will be." She smiled up at him, past the square cut of his jaw to his incredibly dark eyes. "Have a good time with . . . Prudence," she said with a bright knowing smile.

Holding back a laugh, she returned to her own apartment. The rat. The low-down dirty rat! He was pretending to escort some imaginary woman to a fancy affair. Oh, he'd like nothing better than for Maryanne to think he considered her a pest. But she knew that wasn't quite the case.

Where was the man who'd rushed to her rescue when the pipes needed a little coaxing? Where was the man who'd nearly been run over on a basketball court when he saw her standing on the sidelines? Where was the man who'd tried to set her up with someone else he thought more suitable? Nolan Adams had just proved what she'd suspected all along. He was a coward—at least when it came to love.

Suddenly depressed, Maryanne slowly crossed the living room and sank on to her sofa, trying to gather her wits. Ten minutes later, she still sat there, mulling things over and feeling sorry for herself, when she heard Nolan's door open and close. She immediately perked up, wondering if he'd had a change of heart. He seemed to pause for a moment outside her door, but any second thoughts he might be having didn't last long.

Barbara phoned soon after, full of apologies, to cancel their movie plans, so Maryanne spent the evening drowning her sorrows in television reruns and slices of cold pizza.

She must have fallen asleep because a harsh ringing jolted her awake a couple of hours later. She leapt off the sofa and stumbled dazedly around before she realized the sound came from the phone. She rushed across the room.

A greeting had barely left her lips when her father's booming voice assailed her.

"Where the hell are you?"

"Hello, Dad," she muttered, her heart sinking. How like him to get to the subject at hand without anything in the way of preliminaries. "How are you, too?"

"I want to know where you're living and I want to know right now!"

"I beg your pardon?" she asked, stalling for time. Obviously her father had discovered her small deception.

"I talked to the managing editor of the *Seattle Review* this morning and he told me you haven't worked there in weeks. He said you'd quit! Now I want to know what this craziness is you've been feeding your mother and me about a special assignment."

"Uh . . ." By now, Maryanne was awake enough to know her father wasn't in any mood to listen to excuses.

"You lied to us, girl."

"Not exactly . . ." She paused, searching for the right words. "It was more a case of omission, don't you think?"

"You've had us worried sick. We've been trying to get hold of you all afternoon. Where were you? And who the hell is Nolan Adams?"

"Nolan Adams?" she echoed, playing dumb, which wasn't all that difficult at the moment.

"Your mother mentioned his name, and when I called the paper, some woman named . . . Riverside, Carol Riverside, claimed this was his fault."

"Dad, listen, it's all rather complicated, so I think—"

"I don't want excuses, I want facts. You decided to work on the other side of the country. Against my better judgment, I arranged it for you with the promise that I wouldn't intrude— and look where it's gotten me! To have you deceive us by—"

"Dad, please, just settle down."

He seemed to be making an effort to calm himself, but more than likely the effort was thanks to her mother. Maryanne could hear her arguing softly in the background.

"Can I explain?" she asked, waiting a minute for the tension to ease, although she wasn't sure what to say, what excuses she could possibly offer.

"You can try to explain, but I doubt it'll do any good," he answered gruffly.

Now that she had the floor, Maryanne floundered.

"I take it this all revolves around that columnist friend of yours from the *Sun*?" her father asked. "That Adams character?"

"Well, yes," Maryanne admitted reluctantly. But she didn't feel she could place the whole blame on him. "Leaving the paper was my decision—"

"Where are you living?"

That was one of several questions Maryanne was hoping to avoid. "I—I rented an apartment."

"You were in an apartment before. It doesn't make the least bit of sense for you to move. The Seattle has a reputation for excellence."

"Yes, Dad, I know, but moving was necessary." She didn't go on to explain why. She didn't want to mislead her father more than she already had. But at the same time, if she told him she couldn't afford to continue living at The Seattle, he'd certainly demand to know why.

"That doesn't explain a damn thing," Samuel Simpson boomed.

Maryanne held the phone away from her ear and sighed heavily. She was groggy from her nap and discouraged by her relationship with Nolan. To complicate matters, she was truly in love for the first time in her life. Loving someone shouldn't be this difficult!

"I insist you tell me what's going on," her father said, in the tone she remembered from childhood confrontations about missed curfews and other transgressions.

She tried again. "It's not that easy to explain."

"You have three seconds, young lady, to tell me why you've lied to your parents."

"I apologize for that. I've felt horrible about it, I really have, but I didn't want to say anything for fear you'd worry."

"Of course we'd worry! Now tell me exactly what it is we should be worrying about."

"Dad, honestly, I'm over twenty-one. I should be able to live and work where I please. You can't keep me your little girl forever." This conversation was not only reminiscent of several she'd had with Nolan, it was one she should have had with her father years ago.

"I demand to know why you quit the paper!"

Maryanne refused to be intimidated. "I already explained that. I had another job."

"Obviously you're doing something you're too ashamed to tell your parents."

"I'm not ashamed! It's nothing illegal. Besides, I happen to like what I do, and I've managed to live entirely on what I make, which is no small feat. I'm happy, Dad, really happy." She tried to force some cheerful enthusiasm into her voice, but unfortunately she didn't entirely succeed. How she wished she could brag about selling her articles. Surely she'd receive word soon!

"If you're so pleased about this change in jobs, then why do you seem upset?" her mother asked reasonably, joining the conversation from an extension.

"I—I'm fine, really I am."

"Somehow, sweetie, that just doesn't ring true—"

"I don't like the sound of this," her father interrupted impatiently. "I made a mistake in arranging this Seattle assignment for you. It seems to me it'd be best if you quit whatever you're doing and moved back to—"

"Dad, I refuse to quit now."

"I want you to move back home. As far as I can see, you've got one hell of a lot of explaining to do."

"It seems to me," Maryanne said after a moment of strained silence, "that we should both take time to cool down and think this over before one of us says or does something we're all going to regret."

"I'm calm." The voice that roared over the long-distance wires threatened to impair Maryanne's hearing.

"Daddy, I love you and Mom dearly, but I think it would be best if we both slept on this. I'm going to hang up now, not to be rude, but because I don't think this conversation is accomplishing anything. I'll call you first thing in the morning."

"Maryanne . . . Maryanne, don't you dare—"

She didn't allow him to finish, knowing it would do no good to argue with him when he was in this frame of mind. Her heart was heavy with regret as she replaced the receiver. Knowing her father would immediately call again, she unplugged the phone.

Now that her family had discovered she wasn't working at the *Review*, everything would change. And not for the better. Her father would hound her until she was forced to tell him she'd taken a job as a waitress. Once he discovered that, he'd hit the roof.

Still thinking about what had happened, she put on her flannel pyjamas and pulled out her bed. With the demanding physical schedule she kept, sleeping had never been a problem. Tonight, she missed the clatter of Nolan's typing. She'd grown accustomed to its comforting familiarity, in part because it was a sign of his presence. She often lay awake wondering how his mystery novel was developing. Some nights she even fantasized that he'd let her read the manuscript, which to her represented the ultimate gesture of trust.

But Nolan wasn't at his typewriter this evening. He was giving a speech. Closing her eyes, she imagined him standing before the large dinner crowd. How she would have enjoyed being in the audience! She knew beyond a doubt that his eyes would have sought her out . . . .

Instead she was spending the night alone. She lay with her eyes wide open; every time she started to drift off, some small noise would jerk her into wakefulness. She finally had to admit that she was waiting to hear the sounds of Nolan's return.

Some time in the early morning hours, Maryanne did eventually fall asleep. She woke at six to the familiar sound of Nolan pounding on his typewriter.

She threw on her robe, thrust her feet into the fuzzy slippers and began pacing, her mind whirling.

When she could stand it no longer, she banged on the wall separating their two apartments.

"Your typing woke me up!" Which, of course, wasn't fair or even particularly true. But she'd spent a fretful night thinking about him, and that was excuse enough.

Her family had found out she'd quit her job and all hell was about to break loose. Time was running out for her and Nolan. If she was going to do something—and it was clear she'd have to be the one—she'd need to do it soon.

"Just go back to bed," Nolan shouted.

"Not on your life, Nolan Adams!" Without questioning how wise it was to confront him now, Maryanne stormed out of her apartment dressed as she was, and beat hard on his door.

Nolan opened it almost immediately, still wearing the tuxedo from the night before, without the jacket and cummerbund. The sleeves of his shirt were rolled past his elbows and the top three buttons were open. His dishevelment and the shadows under his eyes suggested he hadn't been to bed.

"What now?" he demanded. "Is my breathing too loud?"

"We need to talk," she stated calmly as she marched into his apartment.

Nolan remained standing at the door. "Why don't you come in and make yourself at home?" he muttered sarcastically.

"I already have." She sat on the edge of his sofa and waited until he turned to face her. "So?" she asked with cheerful derision. "How'd your hot date go?"

"Fine." He smiled grimly. "Just fine."

"Where'd you go for dinner? The Four Seasons? Fullers?" She named two of the best restaurants in town. "By the way, do I know Prudence?"

"No," he answered with sharp impatience.

"I didn't think so."

"Maryanne—"

"I don't suppose you have coffee made?"

"It's made." But he didn't offer her any. The fact that he was still standing by the door suggested he wanted her out of his home. But when it came to dealing with Nolan, Maryanne had long since learned to ignore the obvious.

"Thanks, I'll get myself a cup." She walked into the kitchen and found two clean mugs in the dishwasher. "You want one?"

"I have some," he said pointedly, stationing himself in the kitchen doorway. He heaved a long-suffering sigh. "Maryanne, I'm busy, so if you could get on with—"

"My father knows," she said calmly, watching him closely for some sort of reaction. If she'd been looking for evidence of concern or regret, he showed neither. The only emotion she was able to discern was a brief flicker of what she could only assume was relief. That wasn't encouraging. He appeared all too willing to get her out of his life.

"Well?" she probed. "Say something."

"What the hell have you been telling him?"

"Nothing about you, so don't worry. I did mention you to my mother, but you don't need to worry about that, either. She thinks you and I . . . Never mind."

"*What* does your father know?" Nolan asked.

She sipped from the edge of the mug and shrugged. "He found out I wasn't on special assignment for the paper."

"Special assignment? What does that have to do with anything?"

"That's what I told my mother when I moved."

"Why the hell would you tell her something like that?"

"She was expecting me to send her my columns, and call every other day. I couldn't continue to do either of those things. I had to come up with some excuse."

He cocked an eyebrow. "You might have tried the truth."

Maryanne nodded her agreement. If she'd bungled any part of this arrangement, it had been with her parents. However, there wasn't time for regrets now.

"Dad learned I moved out of The Seattle. I didn't tell him where I was living, but that won't deter him. Knowing Dad, he'll have all the facts by noon today. To put it mildly, he isn't pleased. He wants me to return to the East Coast."

"Are you going?" Nolan's question was casual, as though her response was of little concern to him.

"No."

"Why not?" The impatient look was back. "For the love of heaven, Annie, will you kindly listen to reason? You don't be-long here. You've proved your point. If you're waiting for me to admit I was wrong about you, then fine, I'll admit it, and gladly. You've managed far better than I ever dreamed you would, but it's time to get on with your life. It's time to move back into the world where you belong."

"I can't do that now."

"Why the hell not?"

"Because . . . I've fallen—"

"Look, Annie, it's barely seven and I have to go to work," he said brusquely, cutting her off. "Shouldn't you be getting dressed? Walking around the hallway in your pyjamas isn't wise—people might think something."

"Let them."

He rubbed his face wearily, shaking his head.

"Nolan," Maryanne said softly, her heart in her throat. "I know you didn't go out with anyone named Prudence. You made the whole thing up. This game of yours isn't going to work. It's too late. I'm . . . already in love with you."

The whole world seemed to come to an abrupt halt. Maryanne hadn't intended to blurt out her feelings this way, but she didn't know how else to cut through the arguments and the denial.

For one wild-eyed moment Nolan didn't say anything. Then he raised his hand, as though fending off some kind of attack, and retreated from the kitchen.

"You can't be in love with me," he insisted, slowly sinking to the sofa, like a man in the final stages of exhaustion. "I won't allow it."

Ten

"Unfortunately it's too late," Maryanne told him again, no less calmly. "I'm already in love with you."

"Now just a minute," Nolan said, apparently regaining his composure. "You're a nice kid, and to be honest I've been impressed—"

"I am not a kid," she corrected with quiet authority, "and you know it."

"Annie . . . Maryanne," he said, "listen to me. What you feel for me isn't love." His face revealed a bitterness she hadn't seen before. He walked toward her, gripped her shoulders and gazed down at her.

"That won't work, either," she said in the same quiet voice. She wasn't a poor little rich girl who'd only recently discovered who she was. Nor had she mistaken admiration for love. "I know what I feel."

She slipped her arms around his neck and stood on tiptoe, wanting to convince him of her sincerity with a kiss.

But before her mouth could meet his, Nolan jerked his head back, preventing the contact. He dropped his arms and none too gently pushed her away.

"Are you afraid to kiss me?"

"You're damn right I am," he said, burying his hands in his pockets as he hastily moved even farther away.

Maryanne smiled softly. "And with good reason. We both know what would happen if you did. You've done a good job of hiding your feelings, I'll grant you that much. I was nearly fooled."

"Naturally I'm flattered." His expression was darkening by the second. He stalked across the room, his shoulders hunched forward. He didn't say anything else, and Maryanne strongly suspected he was at a loss for words. Nolan was *never* at a loss for words. Words were his stock-in-trade.

But he was confronting emotions now, not words or concepts, and she knew him well enough to realize how uncomfortable that made him.

He'd hidden his feelings behind a mask of gruff annoyance, allowing her to believe she'd become a terrible nuisance in his life. He needed to disguise what he felt for her—to prevent her from learning what everyone else already knew.

Nolan was in love with her.

The mere thought thrilled her and gave her more courage than she'd ever possessed in her life.

"I fully expect you to be flattered," she said gently, "but I'm not telling you this to give your ego a boost. I honestly love you, and nothing my parents say is going to convince me to leave Seattle."

"Maryanne, please . . ."

He was prepared to push her away verbally, as he had so often. This time she wouldn't let him. This time she walked over to him, threw both arms around his waist and hugged him close.

He raised his hands to her shoulders, ready to ease her from him, but the moment they came to rest on her he seemed to lose his purpose.

"This is ridiculous," she heard him mumble. He held himself rigid for a moment or two, then with a muttered curse buried his face in her hair. A ragged sigh tore through his body.

Experiencing a small sense of triumph, Maryanne pressed her ear to his chest and smiled contentedly when she heard his racing uneven heartbeat.

"You shouldn't let me hold you like this." His voice was low and hushed. "Tell me not to," he breathed as his lips moved through her hair and then lower to the pulse point behind her ear and the slope of her neck.

"I don't want you to stop . . ." She turned her head, begging him to touch and kiss her.

"Annie, please."

"I want to be in your arms more than anywhere. More than anything."

"You don't know what you're saying . . . ."

She lifted her head enough for their eyes to meet. Placing her finger on his lips, she shook her head. "I'm a woman, a grown woman, and there's no question of my not knowing what I want."

His hands gently grazed her neck, as though he was still hesitant and unsure. Kissing her was what *he* wanted—she could read it clearly in his dark eyes—but he was holding himself back, his face contorted with indecision.

"Go ahead, kiss me," she urged softly, wanting him so much her whole body seemed to ache. "I dare you to."

His breathing was labored, and Maryanne could sense the forces raging within him. A fresh wave of tenderness filled her.

"You make it so hard to do what's right," he groaned.

"Loving each other is what's right."

"I'd like to believe that, but I can't." He placed his hand on her cheek and their eyes locked hungrily. He searched her face.

"I love you," she whispered, smiling up at him. She didn't want him to question her feelings. She'd say it a thousand times a day if that was what it took to convince him.

Flattening her hands against his hard chest, she leaned into his strength and offered him her mouth. Only moments earlier he'd pushed her away, but not now. His gaze softened and he closed his eyes tightly. He was losing the battle.

It was while his eyes were closed that Maryanne claimed the advantage and kissed him. He moaned and seemed about to argue, but once their mouths met, urgency took hold and Nolan was rendered speechless.

To her delight, he responded with the full-fledged hunger she'd witnessed in his eyes. He slid his hands through her hair, his fingers tangling with the thick auburn mass as he angled her head to one side. Maryanne felt herself savoring the taste of his kiss. It was so long since he'd held her like this, so long since he'd done anything but keep her at arm's length. She wanted to cherish these moments, delight in the rush of sensations.

So many thoughts crowded her mind. So many ideas. Plans for their future.

He tore his mouth from hers and nestled his face in the hollow of her neck as he drew in several deep breaths.

Maryanne clung to him, hugging him as close as humanly possible. "Nolan—"

"It isn't going to work—you and me together . . . it isn't right," he whispered.

"It's more right than anything I've ever known."

"Oh, Annie, the things you do to me."

She smiled gently. "You know what I think?" She didn't give him the opportunity to answer. "I love you and you love me and when two people feel that way about each other, they usually—" she paused and swallowed once "—get married."

"What?" Nolan exploded, leaping away from her as though he'd received an electrical shock.

"You heard me," she said.

"You're a crazy woman. You know that, don't you? Downright certifiable." Nolan backed away from her, eyes narrowed. He began pacing rapidly in one direction, then another.

"Marriage was just a suggestion," she said mildly. "I am serious, though, and if you're at all interested we should move fast. Because once my father gets wind of it there'll be hell to pay."

"I have no intention of even considering the idea! In fact, I think it's time you left."

"Nolan, okay, I'm sorry. I shouldn't have mentioned marriage. I was just thinking, hoping actually, that it was something you wanted, too. There's no need to overreact." He had already ushered her across the living room toward the door. She tried to redirect his efforts, turning in his arms, but he wouldn't allow it.

"We need to talk about this," she insisted.

"Oh, no, you don't," he said, opening the door and steering her into the hallway. "Your idea of talking doesn't seem to coincide with mine. Before I figure out how it happens, you're in my arms and we're—"

"Maryanne!" Her father's voice came like a high-intensity foghorn from behind her.

Maryanne whirled around to discover both her parents standing in the hallway outside her apartment door. "Mom . . . Dad . . ." Frantic, she looked at Nolan, hoping he'd do the explaining part.

"Mr. and Mrs. Simpson," Nolan said formally, straightening. He removed his arms from around Maryanne, stepped forward and held out his hand to her father. "I'm Nolan Adams."

"How do you do?" Muriel Simpson said in a brittle voice as the two men exchanged brief handshakes. Her mother's troubled gaze moved from the men to Maryanne, surveying her attire with a single devastating look.

Until that moment, Maryanne had forgotten she was still in her pyjamas. She closed her eyes and groaned.

"Samuel," Muriel Simpson said in a shocked voice. "Maryanne's coming out of . . . his apartment."

"It's not what it looks like," Maryanne rushed to tell them. "Mom and Dad, please, you've got to listen to me. I didn't spend the night at Nolan's, honest. We just happened to get into a tiff this morning and instead of shouting through the walls and—"

"Samuel." Her mother reached for her father's sleeve, gripping it hard. "I feel faint."

Samuel Simpson clamped his arm about his wife's waist and with Nolan's assistance led her through his open apartment door. Maryanne hurried ahead of them to rearrange pillows on the sofa.

Crouched in front of her mother, Maryanne gently patted her hand. Muriel wasn't given to fainting spells; clearly, she'd been worried sick about her daughter, which increased Maryanne's guilt a hundredfold.

"My little girl is safe, and that's all that matters," Muriel whispered.

"Listen here, young man," Maryanne's father said sternly to Nolan. "It seems you two have some explaining to do."

"Daddy, please." Jumping to her feet, Maryanne stood between her father and Nolan, loving them both so much and not sure which one to confront first. She took a deep breath and blurted out, "I'm in love with Nolan."

"Sir, I know the circumstances look bad, but I can assure you there's nothing between me and your daughter."

"What do you mean there's nothing between us?" Maryanne cried, furious with him. Good grief, she'd just finished spilling out her heart to the man! The least he could do was acknowledge what they shared, what they both felt. Well, if he wasn't so inclined, she was. "That's a bold-faced lie," she announced to her father, hearing Nolan groan behind her as she spoke.

Samuel Simpson, so tall and formidable, so distinguished and articulate, seemed to find himself dumbstruck. He slumped onto the sofa next to his wife and rested his face in both hands.

"Maryanne," Nolan said from between gritted teeth. "Your parents appear to think the worst. Don't you agree it would be more appropriate to assure them that—"

"I don't care what they think. Well, I do, of course," she amended quickly, "but I'm more interested in settling things between you and me."

Nolan frowned impatiently. "This is neither the time nor the place."

"I happen to think it is."

"Maryanne, please," her mother wailed, holding out one hand. "Your father and I have spent a long sleepless night flying across the country. We've been worried half to death about you."

"She didn't answer her phone," Samuel muttered in dire tones, his eyes narrowing suspiciously on the two of them. "If Maryanne had been at her apartment, the way she claims, then she would have picked up the receiver. We must've called fifteen or twenty times. If she was home, why didn't she answer the phone?"

The question seemed to be directed at Nolan, but it was Maryanne who answered. "I unplugged it."

"Why would you do that?" Muriel asked. "Surely you know we'd try to reach you. We're your parents. We love you!"

"That's it, young lady. You're moving back with us."

"You can't force me to leave Seattle. I refuse."

"This place . . ." Muriel was looking around as though the building was likely to be condemned any minute. "Why would you want to live here? Have you rejected everything we've given you?"

"The answer is obvious," her father bellowed. "She's living here to be close to *him*."

"But why didn't her . . . friend move into her apartment building?"

"Isn't it obvious?" Samuel stood abruptly and stalked to the other side of the room. "Adams couldn't afford to live within a mile of The Seattle." He stopped short, then nodded apologetically at Nolan. "I didn't mean that in a derogatory way. You seem like a fine young man, but frankly . . ."

"I wouldn't care where Nolan lived," Maryanne informed them both, squaring her shoulders righteously. Any man she fell in love with didn't need to head a financial empire or be related to someone who did. "I'd live anywhere if it meant we could be together." Her eyes softened at her mother's shocked look.

"Don't you remember what it's like to be young and in love, Mom?" Maryanne asked her. "Remember all those things you told me about you and Dad? How you used to argue and everything? It's the same with Nolan and me. I'm crazy about him. He's so talented and—"

"That's enough," Nolan interrupted harshly. "If you're looking for someone to blame for Maryanne's living in this building and working at Mom's Place—"

"What's Mom's Place?"

"A very nice diner," Maryanne inserted quickly. "We do a brisk lunch trade and carry a limited dinner menu."

Her mother let out a cry of dismay. "You're . . . you're working as a waitress?"

Miserable, Maryanne nodded. "But I'm doing lots of freelance work. None of the feature articles I've written have sold yet, but it's too soon for that. I just found out the community newspaper's buying a couple of my shorter pieces, and I plan on selling them lots more."

"You might have warned me they didn't know about your being a waitress," Nolan muttered under his breath.

Samuel drew a hand across his eyes, as if that would erase the image of his daughter waiting on tables. "Why would you choose to quit the newspaper to work as a waitress?" Asking the question seemed to cause him pain.

"It's honest work, Dad. I don't understand why you're acting like this. You're making it sound like I'm doing something that'll bring disgrace to the family name."

"But your education is being wasted," her mother said, shaking her head. "You could have any job in publishing you wanted."

That much was true when it was her family doing the hiring, but when she was looking on her own her employers were more interested in her job skills than who her father was.

"I'm afraid I'm the one who started this," Nolan interrupted. "I wrote a column about Maryanne," he said bluntly. "It was unfortunate, because I was out of line in some of the things I said, but—"

"Nolan didn't write anything that wasn't true," Maryanne hastened to say. "He made me stop and think about certain aspects of my life, and I decided it was time to prove I could make it on my own."

"By denouncing your family!"

"I never did that, Dad."

Samuel's shoulders sagged with defeat. The long hours her parents had spent travelling were telling on them both. They looked at her blankly, as though they couldn't quite believe, even now, what she'd been doing for the past month and a half.

"I did it for another reason, too." All three of them were staring at her as if they suspected she'd lost her mind. "I'd met Nolan and we had dinner together and I discovered how much

I liked him." She glanced at the man in question and saw him frown, knitting his brow, obviously searching for a way to stop her. "I'm sorry, Mom and Dad. I hated lying to you, but I couldn't see any way around it. I didn't want to worry you," she said, stepping next to Nolan and wrapping her arm around his waist. "I belong here with Nolan." There, she'd said it! "I won't be returning to New York with you."

"Maryanne, sweetie, you can't go on living like this!"

"I have a wonderful life."

Her father was pacing again. "You're in love with this man?"

"Yes, Daddy. I love him so much—enough to defy you for the first time in my life."

Her father's eyes slowly moved from his only daughter to Nolan. "What about you, young man? How do you feel about my daughter?"

Nolan was quiet for so long it was all Maryanne could do not to answer for him. Finally she couldn't stand it any longer and did exactly that. "He loves me. He may not want to admit it, but he does—lock, stock and barrel."

Her father continued to look at Nolan. "Is that true?"

"Unfortunately," he said, gently removing Maryanne's arm, "I don't return her feelings. You've raised a wonderful daughter—but I don't love her, not the way she deserves to be loved."

"Nolan!" His name escaped on a cry of outrage. "Don't lie. Not now, not to my family."

He took her by the shoulders, his face pale and expressionless. She searched his eyes, looking for something, anything to ease the terrible pain his words had inflicted.

"You're sweet and talented, and one day you'll make some man very proud—but it won't be me."

"Nolan, stop this right now. You love me. You're intimidated because of who my father is. But don't you understand that money doesn't mean anything to me?"

"It rarely does to those who have it. Find yourself a nice rich husband and be happy."

She found his words insulting. If she hadn't been so desperate to straighten out this mess, she would have confronted him with it. "I won't be happy without you. I refuse to be happy."

His face was beginning to show signs of strain. "Yes, you will. Now, I suggest you do as your family wants and leave with them."

Every word felt like a kick in the stomach, each more vicious than the one before.

"You don't mean that!"

"Damn it, Maryanne," he said coldly, "don't make this any more difficult than it already is. We don't belong together. We never have. I live in one world and you live in another. I've been telling you that from the first, but you wouldn't listen to me."

Maryanne was too stunned to answer. She stared up at him, hoping, praying, for some sign that he didn't mean what he was saying.

"Sweetie." Her mother tucked an arm around Maryanne's waist. "Please, come home with us. Your friend's right, you don't belong here."

"That's not true. I'm here now and I intend to stay."

"Maryanne, damn it, would you listen to your parents?" Nolan barked. "What do you intend to do once Mom's Place closes for remodeling?"

"Come home, sweetie," her mother pleaded.

Too numb to speak, Maryanne stared at Nolan. She wouldn't leave if he gave the slightest indication he wanted her to stay. Anything. A flicker of his eye, a twitch of his hand, anything that would show her he didn't mean the things he'd said.

There was nothing. Nothing left for her. She couldn't go back to the newspaper, not now. Mom's Place was closing, but the real hardship, the real agony, came from acknowledging that Nolan didn't want her around. Nolan didn't love her.

She turned her back on him and walked to her own apartment. Her mother and father joined her there a few minutes later, trying to hide their dismay at its bleakness.

"I won't need to give my notice," she told them, sorting through the stack of folded clothes for a fresh uniform. "But I'll stay until Mom's closes. I wouldn't want to leave them short-staffed."

"Yes, of course," her mother answered softly, then suggested, "If you like, I can stay with you here in Seattle."

Maryanne declined with a quick shake of her head, trying to conceal how badly Nolan's rejection had hurt. "I'll be fine." She paused, then turned to her family. "He really is a wonderful man. It's just that he's terribly afraid of falling in love—especially with someone like me. I have everything he doesn't—an education, wealth, and perhaps most importantly, parents who love me as much as you do."

Maryanne hadn't known it was possible for two weeks to drag by so slowly. But finally her last day of work arrived.

"The minute I set eyes on Nolan Adams again, I swear I'll give him a piece of my mind," Barbara declared, hands on her hips.

Nolan hadn't eaten at Mom's once in the past two weeks. That didn't surprise Maryanne; in fact, she would've been shocked if he'd decided to show up.

"You keep in touch, you hear? That Nolan Adams—he's got a lot to answer for," Barbara said, her eyes filling. "I'm gonna miss you, girl. Are you sure you have to leave?"

"I'm sure," Maryanne whispered, swallowing back her own tears.

"I suppose you're right. That's why I'm so furious with Nolan."

"It isn't all his fault." Maryanne hadn't told anyone the embarrassing details that had led to her leaving Seattle.

"Of course it is. He should stop you from going. I don't know what's got into that man, but I swear, for two cents I'd give him—"

"A piece of your mind," Maryanne finished for her.

They both laughed, and hugged each other one last time. Although they'd only worked together a short while, they'd become good friends. Maryanne would miss Barbara's down-to-earth philosophy and her reliable sense of humor.

When she arrived home, her apartment was dark and dismal. Cardboard boxes littered the floor. Her packing was finished, except for the bare essentials. She'd made arrangements with a shipping company to come for her things in the morning. Then she'd call a taxi to take her to Sea-Tac Airport in time to catch the noon flight for New York.

The next morning, dressed in jeans and a loose red sweatshirt, Maryanne was hauling boxes out of her living room and stacking them in the hallway when she heard Nolan's door open. She quickly moved back into her own apartment.

"What are you doing?" he demanded, following her in. He was wearing the ever-present beige raincoat, his mood as sour as his look.

"Moving," she responded flippantly. "That was what I thought you wanted."

"Then leave the work to the movers."

"I'm fine, Nolan." Which was a lie. How could she possibly be fine when her heart was broken?

"I guess this is goodbye, then," he said, glancing around the room, looking everywhere but at her.

"Yes. I'll be gone before you get back this afternoon." She forced a trembling smile to her lips as she brushed the dust from her palms. "It's been a pleasure knowing you."

"You, too," he said softly.

"Someday I'll be able to tell my children I knew the famous Nolan Adams when he was a columnist for the *Seattle Sun*." But those children wouldn't be his . . . .

"I wish you only the best." His eyes had dimmed slightly, but she was too angry to see any significance in that.

She didn't reply and the silence stretched, tense and awkward.

"So," she finally said, with a deep sigh, "you're really going to let me go."

"Yes." He spoke without hesitation, but she noticed that his mouth thinned, became taut.

"It may come as a surprise to learn you're not the only one with pride." She spoke as clearly and precisely as she could. "I'm going to do what you asked and leave Seattle. I'll walk away without looking back. Not once will I look back," she repeated, her throat constricting, making speech difficult. She waited a moment to compose herself. "Someday you'll regret this, Nolan. You'll think back to what happened and wish to hell you'd handled the situation differently. Don't you know it's not what you've done that will fill you with regret, but what you haven't done?"

"Annie—"

"No, let me finish. I've had this little talk planned for days and I'm going to deliver it. The least you can do is stand here and listen."

He closed his eyes and nodded.

"I've decided to haunt you."

"What?" His eyes flew open.

"That's right. You won't be able to go into a restaurant without believing you see me there. I'll be hiding behind every corner. I'll follow you down every street. And as for enjoying another bowl of chili, you can forget that, as well." By now her voice was trembling.

"I never meant to hurt you."

She abruptly turned away from him, wiping the tears from her cheeks with both hands.

"Be happy, Annie."

She would try. There was nothing else to do.

Eleven

"Have you had a chance to look over those brochures?" Muriel asked Maryanne two weeks later. They were sitting at the breakfast table, savoring the last of their coffee.

"I was thinking I should find myself another job." It was either that or spend the rest of her life poring over cookbooks. Some people travelled to cure a broken heart, some worked—but not Maryanne. She hadn't written a word since she'd left Seattle. Not one word.

She'd planned to send out new queries, start researching new articles for specialty magazines. Somehow, that hadn't happened. Instead, she'd been baking up a storm. Cookies for the local day-care center, cakes for the senior citizens' home, pies for the clergy. She figured she'd gone through enough flour in the past week to take care of the Midwest wheat crop. Since the holiday season was fast approaching, baking seemed the thing to do.

"But, sweetie, Europe this time of year is fabulous."

"I'm sorry, Mom, I don't mean to be ungrateful, but travelling just doesn't interest me right now."

Her mother's face softened with concern. "Apparently, baking does. Maryanne, you can't bake cookies for the rest of your life."

"I know, I know. If I keep this up I'll look like the Goodyear blimp by Christmas."

Her mother laughed. "That obviously isn't true. If anything, you've been losing weight." She hesitated before adding, "And you've been so quiet."

When she was in pain, Maryanne always withdrew into herself, seeking what comfort she could in routine tasks—such as baking. She was struggling to push every thought of Nolan from her mind. But as her mother said, she had to get out of the kitchen and rejoin the world. Soon she'd write again. Maybe there was a magazine for bakers—she could submit to that, she thought wryly. It would be a place to start, anyway, to regain her enthusiasm. Soon she'd find the strength to face her computer again. Even the sale of three articles hadn't cheered her. She'd stared at the checks and felt a vague sense of disappointment. If only they'd arrived before she left Seattle; then she might have considered staying.

"Is it still so painful?" Muriel asked unexpectedly. Nolan and Maryanne's time in Seattle were subjects they all avoided, and Maryanne appreciated the opportunity to talk about him.

"I wish you and Dad had known him the way I did," she said wistfully. "He's such a contradiction. Rough and surly on the outside, but gentle and compassionate on the inside."

"It sounds as though you're describing your father."

She pondered her mother's words. "Nolan *is* a lot like Daddy. Principled and proud. Independent to a fault. I didn't realize that in the beginning, only later." She laughed softly. "No man could ever make me angrier than Nolan." Nor could any man hope to compete when it came to the feelings he evoked as he kissed her. She came to life in his arms.

"He drove me crazy with how stubborn he could be. At first all I could see was his defensiveness. He'd scowl at me and grumble—he always seemed to be grumbling, as if he couldn't wait to get me out of his hair. He used to look at me and insist I was nothing but trouble. Then he'd do these incredibly considerate things." She was thinking of the day she'd moved into the apartment and how he'd organized the neighborhood teens to haul her boxes up four flights of stairs. How he'd brought her dinner. The morning he'd fixed her radiator. Even the time he'd tried to find her a more "suitable" date.

"There'll be another man for you, sweetie, someone who'll love you as much as you love him."

A bittersweet smile crossed Maryanne's lips. That was the irony of it all.

"Nolan does love me. I know it now, in my heart. I believed him when he said he didn't, but he was lying. It's just that he was in love with someone else a long time ago and he was badly hurt," she said. "He's afraid to leave himself open to that kind of pain again. To complicate matters, I'm Samuel Simpson's daughter. If I weren't, he might've been able to let go of his insecurities and make a commitment."

"He's the one who's losing out."

Maryanne understood that her mother's words were meant to comfort her, but they had the opposite effect. Nolan wasn't the only one who'd lost. "I realize that and I think in some sense he does, too, but it's not much help."

Her mother was silent.

"You know, Mom," Maryanne said, surprising herself with a sudden streak of enthusiasm. "I may not feel like flying off to Paris, but I think a shopping expedition would do us both a world of good. We'll start at the top floor of Sak's and work our way straight down to the basement."

They spent a glorious afternoon Christmas shopping. They arrived home at dinnertime, exhausted yet rejuvenated.

"Where was everyone after school?" Mark, the older of the

Simpson boys, complained. At sixteen, he was already as tall as his father and his dark eyes shone brightly with the ardor of youth. "I had a rotten day."

"What happened?"

Every eye was on him. Mark sighed expressively. "There's this girl—"

"Susie Johnson. Mark's bonkers over her," fourteen-year-old Sean supplied, grinning shrewdly at his older brother.

Mark ignored him. "I've been trying to get Susie's attention for a long time. At first I thought she'd notice me because of my brains."

"What brains? Why would she do anything as dumb as that?"

Samuel tossed his son a threatening glare and Sean quickly returned to his meal.

"Some girls really go for that intelligent stuff. You, of course—" he looked down his nose at Sean "—wouldn't know that, on account of only being in junior high. Which is probably where you'll stay for the rest of your life."

Samuel frowned again.

"Go on," Maryanne urged Mark, not wanting the conversation to get sidetracked by her two brothers trading insults.

"Unfortunately Susie didn't even seem to be aware I was in three of her classes, let alone that I was working my head off to impress her. So I tried out for the soccer team. I figured she'd have to notice me because she's a cheerleader."

"Your skills have been developing nicely," Samuel said, nodding proudly at his eldest son.

"Susie hasn't noticed."

"Don't be so sure," Maryanne said.

"No, it's true." Mark sighed melodramatically, as if the burden of his problem was too heavy to bear. "That was when I came up with the brilliant idea of paying someone—another girl, one I trust—to talk to Susie, ask her a few questions. I figured if I could find out what she really wants in life then I could go out of my way to—" he paused "—you know."

"What you were hoping was that she'd say she wanted to date a guy who drove a red Camaro so you could borrow your mother's to take to school for the next week or so." Samuel didn't succeed in disguising his smile as he helped himself to salad.

"Well, you needn't worry," Mark muttered, rolling his eyes in disgust. "Do you know what Susie Johnson wants most in this world?"

"To travel?" his mother suggested.

Mark shook his head.

"To date the captain of the football team?" Maryanne tried.

Mark shook his head again.

"What then?" Sean demanded.

"She wants thinner thighs."

Maryanne couldn't help it; she started to smile. Her eyes met her younger brother's, and the smile grew into a full-fledged laugh.

Soon they were all laughing.

The doorbell chimed and Maryanne's parents exchanged brief glances. "Bennett will get it," Samuel said before the boys could vault to their feet.

Within a couple of minutes, Bennett appeared. He whispered something to Maryanne's father, who excused himself and hurried out of the dining room.

Maryanne continued joking with her brothers until she heard raised voices coming from the front of the house. She paused as an unexpected chill shot down her spine. One of the voices sounded angry, even defensive. Nevertheless Maryanne had no difficulty recognizing whose it was.

Nolan's.

Her heart did a slow drumroll. Without hesitating, she tossed down her napkin and ran to the front door.

Nolan was standing just inside the entryway, wearing his raincoat. Everything about him, the way he stood, the way he spoke and moved, conveyed his irritation.

Maryanne went weak at the sight of him. She noticed things she never had before. Small things that made her realize how much she loved him, how empty her life had become without him.

"I've already explained," her father was saying. Samuel managed to control his legendary temper, but obviously with some difficulty.

Nolan's expression showed flagrant disbelief. He looked tired, Maryanne saw, as if he'd been working nights instead of sleeping. His face was gaunt, his eyes shadowed. "You don't expect me to believe that, do you?"

"You're damn right I do," Maryanne's father returned.

"What's going on here?" she asked, stepping forward, her voice little more than a whisper. She was having trouble dealing with the reality that he was here, in New York, in her family's home. But from the look of things, this wasn't a social call.

"My newspaper column's been picked up nationally," Nolan said, his gaze narrowing on her. "Doesn't that tell you something? Because it damn well should!"

Maryanne couldn't conceal how thrilled she was. "But, Nolan, that's wonderful! What could possibly be wrong with that? I thought it was a goal you'd set yourself."

"Not for another two years."

"Then you must be so pleased."

"Not when it was arranged by your father."

Before Maryanne could whirl around to confront her father, he vehemently denied it.

"I tell you, I had nothing to do with it." Samuel's eyes briefly met Maryanne's and the honesty she saw there convinced her that her father was telling the truth. She'd just opened her mouth to comment when Nolan went on.

"I don't suppose you had anything to do with the sale of my novel, either," he said sarcastically.

Samuel Simpson shook his head. "For heaven's sake, man, I didn't even know you were writing one."

"Your novel sold?" Maryanne shrieked. "Oh, Nolan, I knew it would. The little bit I read was fabulous. Your idea was wonderful. I could hardly force myself to put it down and not read any more." She had to restrain the impulse to throw her arms around his neck and rejoice with him.

"For more money than I ever thought I'd see in my life," he added, his voice hard with challenge. Although he was speaking to Samuel, his eyes rested on Maryanne—eyes that revealed a need and a joy he couldn't disguise.

"Oh, Nolan, I'm so happy for you."

He nodded absently and turned to her father again. "Do you honestly expect me to believe you had nothing to do with that?" he asked, more mildly this time.

"Yes," Samuel answered impatiently. "What possible reason would I have for furthering your career, young man?"

"Because of Maryanne, of course."

"What?" Maryanne couldn't believe what she was hearing. It was ridiculous. It made no sense.

"Your father's attempting to buy you a husband," Nolan growled. Then he turned to Samuel. "Frankly, that upsets me, because Maryanne doesn't need any help from you."

Her father's eyes were stern, and he seemed about to demand that Nolan leave his home.

Maryanne stepped directly in front of Nolan, her hands on her hips. "Trust me, Nolan, if my father was going to buy me a husband, it wouldn't be you! Dad had nothing to do with your success. Even if he did, what would it matter? You've already made it clear you don't want anything to do with me."

His only response was silence.

"I may have spoken a bit . . . hastily about not loving you," Nolan said a moment later, his voice hoarse.

Samuel cleared his throat, murmuring something about giving the two of them time to talk and promptly left the room.

Maryanne stood gazing up at Nolan, her heart shining through her eyes. Nolan *did* love her; she'd known that for a long time. Only he didn't love her enough to discard the burden of his self-doubts. The boy from the wrong side of the tracks. The self-educated, self-made newsman who feared he'd never fit in with the very people who were awed by his talent.

"You were right," he grumbled, the way he always grumbled, as if he felt annoyed with her.

"About what?"

His smile was almost bitter. "About everything. I love you. Heaven knows I tried not to."

Maryanne closed her eyes, savoring the words she'd never expected to hear. Her heart was pounding so furiously that her head spun. Only . . . only he didn't say he loved her as though it pleased him.

"Is that such a terrible thing?" she asked. "To love me?"

"No . . . yes."

He seemed trapped by indecision, dragged down by their differences, yet buoyed by the need to see her again, hear the sound of her voice, gaze at her freckle-dotted nose and run his fingers through her hair. Nolan didn't have to say the words for Maryanne to realize what he was thinking.

"When everything started happening in my life, I thought—I assumed—your father was somehow involved."

"Did you really?" she asked skeptically. The excuse was all too convenient.

Nolan lowered his gaze. "No, I guess I didn't believe he really had anything to do with the sale of my book. But having my columns picked up nationally came as a surprise. For a while I tried to convince myself your family had to be behind that, but I knew it wasn't true. What *really* happened is exactly what you said would happen. You haunted me, Annie. Every time I turned around I could've sworn you were there. I've never missed anyone in my life the way I've missed you."

She smiled shakily. "That's the most beautiful thing you've ever said to me."

Nolan's look was sheepish. "I tried to tell myself your father was out to buy you a husband. Namely me. Think about it, Annie. He got you that job with the *Review*, and for all I knew he could've made it his primary purpose in life to give you everything you want."

"I thought I'd proved otherwise," she said. "My parents went out of their way to make sure none of us was spoiled. I was hoping I'd convinced you of that."

"You did." He slid his hands into the wide pockets of his raincoat. "I guess what I'm trying to say is that if your father's willing to have me in the family, I'd be more than happy to take you off his hands."

"Take me off his hands. How very kind of you," Maryanne snapped, crossing her arms in annoyance. She was looking for romance, declarations of love and words that came straight from his heart. Instead he was handing out insults.

"Don't get all bent out of shape," he said and the smile that stole across his lips was so devastating Maryanne's breath caught. "The way I figure it," he continued, "you need someone . . ."

Maryanne turned to walk away from him. Not any great distance, of course, just far enough for him to know he wasn't getting anywhere with this argument.

"All right," he amended, catching her by the hand and urging her around to face him again. "*I* need someone."

"Someone?"

"You!" he concluded with a wide grin.

"You're improving. Go on."

"Nothing seemed right after you left. There was this giant hole inside me I couldn't seem to fill. Work didn't satisfy me anymore. Nothing did. Gloria and Eddie asked about you and I didn't know what to say. I was grateful Mom's Place was closed, because I couldn't have eaten there."

A part of her longed for all the romantic words a woman wanted to hear from the man she loved. But it wasn't too likely she'd get them from Nolan. He wasn't telling her he'd heard her name whispered in the wind or seen it written in his heart. Nolan would never say things like that.

"You want me to move back to Seattle so I'll quit haunting you," she finally said.

"No. I want you to come back because I love you."

"And need me?"

He nodded. "I still think you could do a hell of a lot better than marrying an ornery guy like me. I promise to be a good husband—that is, if you're willing to put up with me . . ." He let the rest fade. His eyes grew humble as he slowly, uncertainly, pulled her into his arms. "Would you . . . be willing?"

She smiled, and hot tears gathered in the corners of her eyes. She nodded jerkily. "Yes. Oh, you idiot. I could slap you for putting us through all of this."

"Wouldn't a kiss do just as well?"

"I suppose, only . . ."

But the thought was left unspoken. His kiss was long and thorough and said all the tender words, the fanciful phrases she'd never hear.

It was enough.

More than enough to last her a lifetime.

Epilogue

It was Christmas morning in the Adams household.

The wrapping paper had accumulated in a small mountain on the living-room carpet. The Christmas tree lights twinkled and "Silent Night" played in the background.

Maryanne sat on the sofa next to Nolan with her feet up, her head on her husband's shoulder. The girls were busy sorting through their stash of new toys and playing their favorite game—"being grown-ups." Bailey was pretending to be a young college graduate determined to make a name for herself in the newspaper business. Courtney played a jaded reporter from a rival newspaper, determined to thwart her. It was Maryanne and Nolan's romance all over again. The girls had loved hearing every detail of their courtship.

"They don't seem *too* disappointed about not getting a puppy," he said.

"I'm so proud of them." Maryanne smiled. Both Courtney and Bailey were thrilled about the new baby, and although it had been hard, they'd accepted that there wouldn't be a puppy in the family, after all. Not for a few years, anyway.

"They're adorable," Nolan agreed and kissed the top of her head. "Just like their mother."

"Thank you," she whispered.

"When did you say your parents would—" Nolan didn't get a chance to finish the question before the doorbell rang. "Is that them?" Samuel and Muriel Simpson had come from New York to spend Christmas week with the family.

Maryanne nodded. Sitting up, she called to her oldest daughter, "Courtney, could you please answer the door?"

Both girls raced to the front door, throwing it open. They were silent for just a second, then squealed with delight. "Grandma! Grandpa Simpson!"

"Merry Christmas. Merry Christmas."

Maryanne's parents stepped into the house, carrying a large wicker basket. Inside slept a small black-and-white puppy.

"A puppy?" Courtney said in a hushed voice. She stared at her grandparents, who grinned and nodded.

"We think every family needs a dog," Maryanne's father said.

"Oh, he's *so* cute," Bailey whispered, covering her mouth with both hands.

"He's perfect," Courtney said, lifting the squirming puppy from his bed. "Is he ours? Can we keep him?"

"Oh, yes, this is a special-delivery Christmas gift for my two beautiful granddaughters."

Maryanne came over to take the puppy from Courtney. She cuddled the small, warm body and looked into sleepy brown eyes. "I guess you've come a long way, haven't you?" she murmured. The puppy gazed up at her, unblinking, and Maryanne fell in love. Just like that, all her concerns disappeared. At least this baby would be house-trained well before their son was born. And the girls could help look after him. She looked up to meet Nolan's eyes, and he nodded. So, despite everything, there'd be *two* new additions to the family this next year.

Nolan ushered her parents inside and took their coats. "Sit down and make yourselves comfortable. Maryanne and I have a Christmas surprise, too."

"As good as a new puppy?" her father asked.

"Oh, yes," Courtney told him after a whispered consultation with her sister. She stroked the puppy, still cradled in her mother's arms. "I don't know what we're naming *that* surprise, but we're calling this one Jack."

★ ★ ★ ★ ★

The Forgetful Bride

For Karen Young and Rachel Hauck,
plotting partners and treasured friends.

Prologue

"Not unless we're married."

Ten-year-old Martin Marshall slapped his hands against his thighs in disgust. "I told you she was going to be unreasonable about this."

Caitlin watched as her brother's best friend withdrew a second baseball card from his shirt pocket. If Joseph Rockwell wanted to kiss her, then he was going to have to do it the right way. She might be only eight, but Caitlin knew about these things. Glancing down at the doll held tightly in her arms, she realized instinctively that Barbie wouldn't approve of kissing a boy unless he married you first.

Martin approached her again. "Joe says he'll throw in his Don Drysdale baseball card."

"Not unless we're married," she repeated, smoothing the front of her sundress with a haughty air.

"All right, all right, I'll marry her," Joe muttered as he stalked across the backyard.

"How you gonna do that?" Martin demanded.

"Get your Bible."

For someone who wanted to kiss her so badly, Joseph didn't look very pleased. Caitlin decided to press her luck. "In the fort."

"The fort?" Joe exploded. "No girls are allowed in there!"

"I refuse to marry a boy who won't even let me into his fort."

"Call it off," Martin demanded. "She's asking too much."

"You don't have to give me the second baseball card," she said. The idea of being the first girl ever to view their precious fort had a certain appeal. And it meant she'd probably get invited to Betsy McDonald's birthday party.

The boys exchanged glances and started whispering to each other, but Caitlin heard only snatches of their conversation. Martin clearly wasn't thrilled with Joseph's concessions, and he kept shaking his head as though he couldn't believe his friend might actually go through with this. For her part, Caitlin didn't know whether to trust Joseph. He liked playing practical jokes and everyone in the neighborhood knew it.

"It's time to feed my baby," she announced, preparing to leave.

"All right, all right," Joseph said with obvious reluctance. "I'll marry you in the fort. Martin'll say the words, only you can't tell anyone about going inside, understand?"

"If you do," Martin threatened, glaring at his sister, "you'll be sorry."

"I won't tell," Caitlin promised. It would have to be a secret, but that was fine because she liked keeping secrets.

"You ready?" Joseph demanded. Now that the terms were set, he seemed to be in a rush, which rather annoyed Caitlin. The frown on his face didn't please her, either. A bridegroom should at least *look* happy. She was about to say so, but decided not to.

"You'll have to change clothes, of course. Maybe the suit you wore on Easter Sunday . . ."

"What?" Joseph shrieked. "I'm not wearing any suit. Listen,

Caitlin, you've gone about as far as you can with this. I get married exactly the way I am or we call it off."

She sighed, rolling her eyes expressively. "Oh, all right, but I'll need to get a few things first."

"Just hurry up, would you?"

Martin followed her into the house, letting the screen door slam behind him. He took his Bible off the hallway table and rushed back outside.

Caitlin hurried up to her room, where she grabbed a brush to run through her hair and straightened the two pink ribbons tied around her pigtails. She always wore pink ribbons because pink was a color for girls. Boys were supposed to wear blue and brown and boring colors like that. Boys were okay sometimes, but mostly they did disgusting things.

Her four dolls accompanied her across the backyard and into the wooded acre behind. She hated getting her Mary Janes dusty, but that couldn't be avoided.

With a good deal of ceremony, she opened the rickety door and then slowly, the way she'd seen it done at her older cousin's wedding, Caitlin marched into the boys' packing-crate-and-cardboard fort.

Pausing inside the narrow entry, she glanced around. It wasn't anything to brag about. Martin had made it sound like a palace with marble floors and crystal chandeliers. She couldn't help feeling disillusioned. If she hadn't been so eager to see the fort, she would've insisted they do this properly, in church.

Her brother stood tall and proud on an upturned apple crate, the Bible clutched to his chest. His face was dutifully somber. Caitlin smiled approvingly. He, at least, was taking this seriously.

"You can't bring those dolls in here," Joseph said loudly.

"I most certainly can. Barbie and Ken and Paula and Jane are our children."

"Our children?"

"Naturally they haven't been born yet, so they're really just a glint in your eye." She'd heard her father say that once and it sounded special. "They're angels for now, but I thought they should be here so you could meet them." She was busily arranging her dolls in a tidy row behind Martin on another apple crate.

Joseph covered his face with his hands and it looked for a moment like he might change his mind.

"Are we going to get married or not?" she asked.

"All right, all right." Joseph sighed heavily and pulled her forward, a little more roughly than necessary, in Caitlin's opinion.

The two of them stood in front of Martin, who randomly opened his Bible. He gazed down at the leather-bound book and then at Caitlin and his best friend. "Do you, Joseph James Rockwell, take Caitlin Rose Marshall for your wife?"

"Lawfully wedded," Caitlin corrected. She remembered this part from a television show.

"Lawfully wedded wife," Martin amended grudgingly.

"I do." Caitlin noticed that he didn't say it with any real enthusiasm. "I think there's supposed to be something about richer or poorer and sickness and health," Joseph said, smirking at Caitlin as if to say she wasn't the only one who knew the proper words.

Martin nodded and continued. "Do you, Caitlin Rose Marshall, hereby take Joseph James Rockwell in sickness and health and in riches and in poorness?"

"I'm only going to marry a man who's healthy and rich."

"You can't go putting conditions on this now," Joseph argued. "We already agreed."

"Just say 'I do,'" Martin urged, his voice tight with annoyance. Caitlin suspected that only the seriousness of the occasion prevented him from adding, "You pest."

She wasn't sure if she should go through with this or not. She was old enough to know that she liked pretty things and when she married, her husband would build her a castle at the edge of the forest. He would love her so much, he'd bring home silk ribbons for her hair, and bottles and bottles of expensive perfume. So many that there wouldn't be room for all of them on her makeup table.

"Caitlin," Martin said through clenched teeth.

"I do," she finally answered.

"I hereby pronounce you married," Martin proclaimed, closing the Bible with a resounding thud. "You may kiss the bride."

Joseph turned to face Caitlin. He was several inches taller than she was. His eyes were a pretty shade of blue that reminded her of the way the sky looked the morning after a bad rainstorm. She liked Joseph's eyes.

"You ready?" he asked.

She nodded, closed her eyes and pressed her lips tightly together as she angled her head to the left. If the truth be known, she wasn't all that opposed to having Joseph kiss her, but she'd never let him know that because . . . well, because kissing wasn't something ladies talked about.

A long time passed before she felt his mouth touch hers. Actually his lips sort of bounced against hers. Gee, she thought. What a big fuss over nothing.

"Well?" Martin demanded of his friend.

Caitlin opened her eyes to discover Joseph frowning down at her. "It wasn't anything like Pete said it would be," he grumbled.

"Caitlin might be doing it wrong," Martin offered, frowning accusingly at his sister.

"If anyone did anything wrong, it's Joseph." They were making it sound like she'd purposely cheated them. If anyone was being cheated, it was Caitlin, because she couldn't tell Betsy McDonald about going inside their precious fort.

Joseph didn't say anything for a long moment. Then he slowly withdrew his prized baseball cards from his shirt pocket. He gazed at them lovingly before he reluctantly held them out to her. "Here," he said, "these are yours now."

"You aren't going to *give* 'em to her, are you? Not when she messed up!" Martin cried. "Kissing a girl wasn't like Pete said, and that's got to be Caitlin's fault. I told you she's not really a girl, anyway. She's a pest."

"A deal's a deal," Joseph said sadly.

"You can keep your silly old baseball cards." Head held high, Caitlin gathered up her dolls in a huff, prepared to make a dignified exit.

"You won't tell anyone about us letting you into the fort, will you?" Martin shouted after her.

"No." She'd keep that promise.

But neither of them had said a word about telling everyone in school that she and Joseph Rockwell had gotten married.

One

For the third time that afternoon, Cait indignantly wiped sawdust from the top of her desk. If this remodeling mess got much worse, the particles were going to get into her computer, destroying her vital link with the New York Stock Exchange.

"We'll have to move her out," a gruff male voice said from behind her.

"I beg your pardon," Cait demanded, rising abruptly and whirling toward the doorway. She clapped the dust from her hands, preparing to do battle. So much for this being the season of peace and goodwill. All these men in hard hats strolling through the office, moving things around, was inconvenient enough. But at least she'd been able to close her door to reduce the noise. Now, it seemed, even that would be impossible.

"We're going to have to pull some electrical wires through there," the same brusque voice explained. She couldn't see the man's face, since he stood just outside her doorway, but she had an impression of broad-shouldered height. "We'll have everything back to normal within a week."

"A week!" She wouldn't be able to service her customers, let alone function, without her desk and phone. And exactly where did they intend to put her? Certainly not in a hallway! She wouldn't stand for it.

The mess this simple remodeling project had created was one thing, but transplanting her entire office as if she were nothing more than a . . . a tulip bulb was something else again.

"I'm sorry about this, Cait," Paul Jamison said, slipping past the crew foreman to her side.

The wind went out of her argument at the merest hint of his devastating smile. "Don't worry about it," she said, the picture of meekness and tolerance. "Things like this happen when a company grows as quickly as ours."

She glanced across the hallway to her best friend's office, shrugging as if to ask, *Is Paul ever going to notice me?* Lindy shot her a crooked grin and a quick nod that suggested Cait stop being so negative. Her friend's confidence didn't help. Paul was a wonderful district manager and she was fortunate to have the opportunity to work with him. He was both talented and resourceful. The brokerage firm of Webster, Rodale and Missen was an affiliate of the fastest-growing firm in the country. This branch had been open for less than two years and already they were breaking national sales records. Due mainly, Cait believed, to Paul's administrative skills.

Paul was slender, dark-haired and handsome in an urbane, sophisticated way—every woman's dream man. Certainly Cait's. But as far as she could determine, he didn't see her in a similar romantic light. He thought of her as an important team member. One of the staff. At most, a friend.

Cait knew that friendship was often fertile ground for romance, and she hoped for an opportunity to cultivate it. Willingly surrendering her office to an irritating crew of carpenters and electricians was sure to gain her a few points with her boss.

"Where would you like me to set up my desk in the meantime?" she asked, smiling warmly at Paul. From habit, she lifted her hand to push back a stray lock of hair, forgetting she'd recently had it cut. That had been another futile attempt to attract Paul's affections—or at least his attention. Her shoulder-length chestnut-brown hair had been trimmed and permed into a pixie style with a halo of soft curls.

The difference from the tightly styled chignon she'd always worn to work was striking, or so everyone said. Everyone except Paul. The hairdresser had claimed it changed Cait's cooly polished look into one of warmth and enthusiasm. It was exactly the image Cait wanted Paul to have of her.

Unfortunately he didn't seem to detect the slightest difference in her appearance. At least not until Lindy had pointedly commented on the change within earshot of their absentminded employer. Then, and only then, had Paul made a remark about noticing something different; he just hadn't been sure what it was, he'd said.

"I suppose we could move you . . . ." Paul hesitated.

"Your office seems to be the best choice," the foreman said.

Cait resisted the urge to hug the man. He was tall, easily six three, and as solid as Mount Rainier, the majestic mountain she could see from her office window. She hadn't paid much attention to him until this moment and was surprised to note something vaguely familiar about him. She'd assumed he was the foreman, but she wasn't certain. He seemed to be around the office fairly often, although not on a predictable schedule. Every time he did show up, the level of activity rose dramatically.

"Ah . . . I suppose Cait could move in with me for the time being," Paul agreed. In her daydreams, Cait would play back this moment; her version had Paul looking at her with surprise and wonder, his mouth moving toward hers and—

"Miss?"

Cait broke out of her reverie and glanced at the foreman—the man who'd suggested she share Paul's office. "Yes?"

"Would you show us what you need moved?"

"Of course," she returned crisply. This romantic heart of hers was always getting her into trouble. She'd look at Paul and her head would start to spin with hopes and fantasies and then she'd be lost . . . .

Cait's arms were loaded with files as she followed the carpenters, who hauled her desk into a corner of Paul's much larger office. Her computer and phone came next, and within fifteen minutes she was back in business.

She was on the phone, talking with one of her most important clients, when the same man walked back, unannounced, into the room. At first Caitlin assumed he was looking for Paul, who'd stepped out of the office. The foreman—or whatever he was—hesitated for a few seconds. Then, scooping up her nameplate, he grinned at her as if he found something highly entertaining. Cait did her best to ignore him, flipping needlessly through the pages of the file.

Not taking the hint, he stepped forward and plunked the nameplate on the edge of her desk. As she looked up in annoyance, he boldly winked at her.

Cait was not amused. How dare this . . . this . . . redneck flirt with her!

She glared at him, hoping he'd have the good manners and good sense to leave—which, of course, he didn't. In fact, he seemed downright stubborn about staying and making her as uncomfortable as possible. Her phone conversation ran its natural course and after making several notations, she replaced the receiver.

"You wanted something?" she demanded, her eyes meeting his. Once more she noted his apparent amusement. She didn't understand it.

"No," he answered, grinning again. "Sorry to have bothered you."

For the second time, Cait was struck by a twinge of the familiar. He strolled out of her makeshift office as if he owned the building.

Cait waited a few minutes, then approached Lindy. "Did you happen to catch his name?"

"Whose name?"

"The . . . man who insisted I vacate my office. I don't know who he is. I thought he was the foreman, but . . ." She crossed her arms and furrowed her brow, trying to remember if she'd heard anyone say his name.

"I have no idea." Lindy pushed back her chair and rolled a pencil between her palms. "He is kinda cute, though, don't you think?"

A smile softened Cait's lips. "There's only one man for me and you know it."

"Then why are you asking questions about the construction crew?"

"I . . . don't know. That guy seems familiar for some reason, and he keeps grinning at me as if he knows something I don't. I hate it when men do that."

"Then ask one of the others what his name is. They'll tell you."

"I can't do that."

"Why not?"

"He might think I'm interested in him."

"And we both know how impossible that would be," Lindy said with mild sarcasm.

"Exactly." Lindy and probably everyone else in the office complex knew how Cait felt about Paul. The district manager himself, however, seemed to be completely oblivious. Other than throwing herself at him, which she'd seriously considered more than once, there was little she could do but be patient. One of these days Cupid was going to let fly an arrow and hit her lovable boss directly between the eyes.

When it happened—and it would!—Cait planned to be ready.

"You want to go for lunch now?" Lindy asked.

Cait nodded. It was nearly two and she hadn't eaten since breakfast, which had consisted of a banana and a cup of coffee. A West Coast stockbroker's day started before dawn. Cait was generally in the office by six and didn't stop work until the market closed at one-thirty, Seattle time. Only then did she break for something to eat.

Somewhere in the middle of her turkey on whole wheat, Cait convinced herself she was imagining things when it came to that construction worker. He'd probably been waiting around to ask her where Paul was and then changed his mind. He did say he was sorry for bothering her.

If only he hadn't winked.

He was back the following day, a tool pouch riding on his hip like a six-shooter, hard hat in place. He was issuing orders like a drill sergeant, and Cait found herself gazing after him with reluctant fascination. She'd heard he owned the construction company, and she wasn't surprised.

As she studied him, she realized once again how striking he was. Not because he was extraordinarily handsome, but because he was somehow commanding. He possessed an authority, a presence, that attracted attention wherever he went. Cait was as drawn to it as those around her. She observed how the crew instinctively turned to him for directions and approval.

The more she observed him, the more she recognized that he was a man who had an appetite for life. Which meant excitement, adventure and probably women, and that confused her even more because she couldn't recall ever knowing anyone quite like him. Then why did she find him so . . . familiar?

Cait herself had a quiet nature. She rarely ventured out of the comfortable, compact world she'd built. She had her job, a nice apartment in Seattle's university district, and a few close friends. Excitement to her was growing herbs and participating in nature walks.

The following day while she was studying the construction worker, he'd unexpectedly turned and smiled at something one of his men had said. His smile, she decided, intrigued her most. It was slightly off center and seemed to tease the corners of his mouth. He looked her way more than once and each time she thought she detected a touch of humor, an amused knowledge that lurked just beneath the surface.

"It's driving me crazy," Cait confessed to Lindy over lunch.

"What is?"

"That I can't place him."

Lindy set her elbows on the table, holding her sandwich poised in front of her mouth. She nodded slowly, her eyes distant. "When you figure it out, introduce me, will you? I could go for a guy this sexy."

So Lindy had noticed that earthy sensuality about him, too. Well, of course she had—any woman would.

After lunch, Cait returned to the office to make a few calls. He was there again.

No matter how hard she tried, she couldn't place him. Work became a pretense as she continued to scrutinize him, racking her brain. Then, when she least expected it, he strolled past her and brazenly winked a second time.

As the color clawed up her neck, Cait flashed her attention back to her computer screen.

"His name is Joe," Lindy rushed in to tell her ten minutes later. "I heard one of the men call him that."

"Joe," Cait repeated slowly. She couldn't remember ever knowing anyone named Joe.

"Does that help?"

"No," Cait said, shaking her head regretfully. If she'd ever met this man, she wasn't likely to have overlooked the experience. He wasn't someone a woman easily forgot.

"Ask him," Lindy said. "It's ridiculous not to. It's driving you insane. Then," she added with infuriating logic, "when you find out, you can nonchalantly introduce me."

"I can't just waltz up and start quizzing him," Cait argued. The idea was preposterous. "He'll think I'm trying to pick him up."

"You'll go crazy if you don't."

Cait sighed. "You're right. I'm not going to sleep tonight if I don't settle this."

With Lindy waiting expectantly in her office, Cait approached him. He was talking to another member of the crew and once he'd finished, he turned to her with one of his devastating lazy smiles.

"Hello," she said, and her voice shook slightly. "Do I know you?"

"You mean you've forgotten?" he asked, sounding shocked and insulted.

"Apparently. Though I'll admit you look somewhat familiar."

"I should certainly hope so. We shared something very special a few years back."

"We did?" Cait was more confused than ever.

"Hey, Joe, there's a problem over here," a male voice shouted. "Could you come look at this?"

"I'll be with you in a minute," he answered brusquely over his shoulder. "Sorry, we'll have to talk later."

"But—"

"Say hello to Martin for me, would you?" he asked as he stalked past her and into the room that had once been Cait's office.

Martin, her brother. Cait hadn't a clue what her brother could possibly have to do with this. Mentally she ran through a list of his teenage friends and came up blank.

Then it hit her. Bull's-eye. Her heart started to pound until it roared like a tropical storm in her ears. Mechanically Cait made her way back to Lindy's office. She sank into a chair beside the desk and stared into space.

"Well?" Lindy pressed. "Don't keep me in suspense."

"Um, it's not that easy to explain."

"You remember him, then?"

She nodded. Oh, Lord, did she ever.

"Good grief, what's wrong? You've gone so pale!"

Cait tried to come up with an explanation that wouldn't sound . . . ridiculous.

"Tell me," Lindy said. "Don't just sit there wearing a foolish grin and looking like you're about to faint."

"Um, it goes back a few years."

"All right. Start there."

"Remember how kids sometimes do silly things? Like when you're young and foolish and don't know any better?"

"Me, yes, but not you," Lindy said calmly. "You're perfect. In all the time we've been friends, I haven't seen you do one impulsive thing. Not one. You analyze everything before you act. I can't imagine you ever doing anything silly."

"I did once," Cait told her, "but I was only eight."

"What could you have possibly done at age eight?"

"I . . . I got married."

"Married?" Lindy half rose from her chair. "You've got to be kidding."

"I wish I was."

"I'll bet a week's commissions that your husband's name is Joe." Lindy was smiling now, smiling widely.

Cait nodded and tried to smile in return.

"What's there to worry about? Good grief, kids do that sort of thing all the time! It doesn't mean anything."

"But I was a real brat about it. Joe and my brother, Martin, were best friends. Joe wanted to know what it felt like to kiss a girl, and I insisted he marry me first. If that wasn't bad enough, I pressured them into performing the ceremony inside their boys-only fort."

"So, you were a bit of pain—most eight-year-old girls are when it comes to dealing with their brothers. He got what he wanted, didn't he?"

Cait took a deep breath and nodded again.

"What was kissing him like?" Lindy asked in a curiously throaty voice.

"Good heavens, I don't remember," Cait answered shortly, then reconsidered. "I take that back. As I recall, it wasn't so bad, though obviously neither one of us had any idea what we were doing."

"Lindy, you're still here," Paul said as he strolled into the office. He inclined his head briefly in Cait's direction, but she had the impression he barely saw her. He'd hardly been around in the past couple of days—almost as if he was purposely avoiding her, she mused, but that thought was too painful to contemplate.

"I was just finishing up," Lindy said, glancing guiltily toward Cait. "We both were."

"Fine, fine, I didn't mean to disturb you. I'll see you two in the morning." A second later, he was gone.

Cait gazed after him with thinly disguised emotion. She waited until Paul was well out of range before she spoke. "He's so blind. What do I have to do, hit him over the head?"

"Quit being so negative," Lindy admonished. "You're going to be sharing an office with him for another five days. Do whatever you need to make darn sure he notices you."

"I've tried," Cait murmured, discouraged. And she had. She'd tried every trick known to woman, with little success.

Lindy left the office before her. Cait gathered up some stock reports to read that evening and stacked them neatly inside her leather briefcase. What Lindy had said about her being methodical and careful was true. It was also a source of pride; those traits had served her clients well.

To Cait's dismay, Joe followed her. "So," he said, smiling down at her, apparently oblivious to the other people clustering around the elevator. "Who have you been kissing these days?"

Hot color rose instantly to her face. Did he have to humiliate her in public?

"I could find myself jealous, you know."

"Would you kindly stop," she whispered furiously, scowling at him. Her hand tightened around the handle of her briefcase so hard her fingers ached.

"You figured it out?"

She nodded, her eyes darting to the lighted numbers above the elevator door, praying it would make its descent in record time instead of pausing on each floor.

"The years have been good to you."

"Thank you." *Please hurry*, she urged the elevator.

"I never would've believed Martin's little sister would turn out to be such a beauty."

If he was making fun of her, she didn't appreciate it. She was attractive, she knew that, but she certainly wasn't waiting for anyone to place a tiara on her head. "Thank you," she repeated grudgingly.

He gave an exaggerated sigh. "How are our children doing? What were their names again?" When she didn't answer right away, he added, "Don't tell me you've forgotten."

"Barbie and Ken," she muttered under her breath.

"That's right. I remember now."

If Joe hadn't drawn the attention of her co-workers before, he had now. Cait could have sworn every single person standing by the elevator turned to stare at her. The hope that no one was interested in their conversation was forever lost.

"Just how long do you intend to tease me about this?" she snapped.

"That depends," Joe responded with a chuckle Cait could only describe as sadistic. She gritted her teeth. He might have found the situation amusing, but she derived little enjoyment from being the office laughingstock.

Just then the elevator arrived, and not a moment too soon to suit Cait. The instant the doors slid open, she stepped toward it, determined to get as far away from this irritating man as possible.

He quickly caught up with her and she swung around to face him, her back ramrod stiff. "Is this really necessary?" she hissed, painfully conscious of the other people crowding into the elevator ahead of her.

He grinned. "I suppose not. I just wanted to see if I could get a rise out of you. It never worked when we were kids, you know. You were always so prim and proper."

"Look, you didn't like me then and I see no reason for you to—"

"Not *like* you?" he countered loudly enough for everyone in the building to hear. "I married you, didn't I?"

Two

Cait's heart seemed to stop. She realized that not only the people on the elevator but everyone left in the office was staring at her with unconcealed interest. The elevator was about to close and she quickly stepped forward, stretching out her arms to hold the doors open. She felt like Samson balanced between two marble columns.

"It's not the way it sounds," she felt obliged to explain in a loud voice, her gaze pleading.

No one made eye contact with her and, desperate, she turned to Joe, sending him a silent challenge to retract his words. His eyes were sparkling with mischief. If he did say anything, Cait thought in sudden horror, it was bound to make things even worse.

There didn't seem to be anything to do but tell the truth. "In case anyone has the wrong impression, this man and I are not married," she shouted. "Good grief, I was only eight!"

There was no reaction. It was as if she'd vanished into thin air. Defeated, she dropped her arms and stepped back, freeing the doors, which promptly closed.

Ignoring the other people on the elevator—who were carefully ignoring her—Cait clenched her hands into hard fists and glared up at Joe. Her face tightened with anger. "That was a rotten thing to do," she whispered hoarsely.

"What? It's true, isn't it?" he whispered back.

"You're being ridiculous to talk as though we're married!"

"We were once. It wounds me that you treat our marriage so lightly."

"I . . . it wasn't legal." The fact that they were even discussing this was preposterous. "You can't possibly hold me responsible for something that happened so long ago. To play this game now is . . . is infantile, and I refuse to be part of it."

The elevator finally came to a halt on the ground floor and, eager to make her escape, Cait rushed out. Straightening to keep her dignity intact, she headed through the crowded foyer toward the front doors. Although it was midafternoon, dusk was already setting in, casting dark shadows between the towering office buildings.

Cait reached the first intersection and sighed in relief as she glanced around her. Good. No sign of Joseph Rockwell. The light was red and she paused, although others hurried across the street after checking for traffic; Cait always felt obliged to obey the signal.

"What do you think Paul's going to say when he hears about this?" Joe asked from behind her.

Cait gave a start, then turned to look at her tormenter. She hadn't thought about Paul's reaction. Her throat seemed to constrict, rendering her speechless, otherwise she would have demanded Joe leave her alone. But he'd raised a question she dared not ignore. Paul might hear about her so-called former relationship with Joe and might even think there was something between them.

"You're in love with him, aren't you?"

She nodded. At the very mention of Paul's name, her knees went weak. He was everything she wanted in a man and more. She'd been crazy about him for months and now it was all about to be ruined by this irritating, unreasonable ghost from her past.

"Who told you?" Cait snapped. She couldn't imagine Lindy betraying her confidence, but Cait hadn't told anyone else.

"No one had to tell me," Joe said. "It's written all over you."

Shocked, Cait stared at Joe, her heart sinking. "Do . . . do you think Paul knows how I feel?"

Joe shrugged. "Maybe."

"But Lindy said . . ."

The light changed and, clasping her elbow, Joe urged her into the street. "What was it Lindy said?" he prompted when they'd crossed.

Cait looked up, about to tell him, when she realized exactly what she was doing—conversing with her antagonist. This was the very man who'd gone out of his way to embarrass and humiliate her in front of the entire office staff. Not to mention assorted clients and carpenters.

She stiffened. "Never mind what Lindy said. Now if you'll kindly excuse me . . ." With her head high, she marched down the sidewalk. She hadn't gone more than a few feet when the hearty sound of Joe's laughter caught up with her.

"You haven't changed in twenty years, Caitlin Marshall. Not a single bit."

Gritting her teeth, she marched on.

"Do you think Paul's heard?" Cait asked Lindy the instant she had a free moment the following afternoon. The New York Stock Exchange had closed for the day and Cait hadn't seen Paul since morning. It looked like he really *was* avoiding her.

"I wouldn't know," Lindy said as she typed some figures into her computer. "But the word about your childhood marriage has spread like wildfire everywhere else. It's the joke of the day. What did you and Joe do? Make a public announcement before you left the office yesterday afternoon?"

It was so nearly the truth that Cait guiltily lowered her eyes. "I didn't say a word," she defended herself. "Joe was the one."

"He told everyone you were married?" A suspicious tilt at the corner of her mouth betrayed Lindy's amusement.

"Not exactly. He started asking about our children in front of everyone."

"There were children?"

Cait resisted the urge to close her eyes and count to ten. "No. I brought my dolls to the wedding. Listen, I don't want to rehash a silly incident that happened years ago. I'm more afraid Paul's going to hear about it and put the wrong connotation on the whole thing. There's absolutely nothing between me and Joseph Rockwell. More than likely Paul won't give it a second thought, but I don't want there to be any . . . doubts between us, if you know what I mean."

"If you're so worried about it, talk to him," Lindy advised without lifting her eyes from the screen. "Honesty is the best policy, you know that."

"Yes, but it could prove to be a bit embarrassing, don't you think?"

"Paul will respect you for telling him the truth before he hears the rumors from someone else. Frankly, Cait, I think you're making a fuss over nothing. It isn't like you've committed a felony, you know."

"I realize that."

"Paul will probably be amused, like everyone else. He's not going to say anything." She looked up quickly, as though she expected Cait to try yet another argument.

Cait didn't. Instead she mulled over her friend's advice, gnawing on her lower lip. "You might be right. Paul will respect me for explaining the situation myself, instead of ignoring everything." Telling him the truth could be helpful in other respects, too, now that she thought about it.

If Paul had any feeling for her whatsoever, and oh, how she prayed he did, then he might become just a little jealous of her relationship with Joseph Rockwell. After all, Joe was an attractive man in a rugged outdoor sort of way. He was tall and muscular and, well, good-looking. The kind of good-looking that appealed to women—not Cait, of course, but other women. Hadn't Lindy commented almost immediately on how attractive he was?

"You're right," Cait said, walking resolutely toward the office she was temporarily sharing with Paul. Although she'd felt annoyed at first about being shuffled out of her own space, she'd come to think of this inconvenience as a blessing in disguise. However, she had to admit she'd been disappointed thus far. She had assumed she'd be spending a lot of time alone with him. That hadn't happened yet.

The more Cait considered the idea of a heart-to-heart talk with her boss, the more appealing it became. As was her habit, she mentally rehearsed what she wanted to say to him, then gave herself a small pep talk.

"I don't remember that you talked to yourself." The male voice booming behind her startled Cait. "But then there's a great deal I've missed over the years, isn't there, Caitlin?"

Cait was so rattled she nearly stumbled. "What are you doing here?" she demanded. "Why are you following me around? Can't you see I'm busy?" He was the last person she wanted to confront just now.

"Sorry." He raised both hands in a gesture of apology contradicted by his twinkling blue eyes. "How about lunch later?"

He was teasing. He had to be. Besides, it would be insane for her to have anything to do with Joseph Rockwell. Heaven only knew what would happen if she gave him the least bit of encouragement. He'd probably hire a skywriter and announce to the entire city that they'd married as children.

"It shouldn't be that difficult to agree to a luncheon date," he informed her coolly.

"You're serious about this?"

"Of course I'm serious. We have a lot of years to catch up on." His hand rested on his leather pouch, giving him a rakish air of indifference.

"I've got an appointment this afternoon . . ." She offered the first plausible excuse she could think of; it might be uninspired but it also happened to be true. She'd made plans to have lunch with Lindy.

"Dinner then. I'm anxious to hear what Martin's been up to."

"Martin," she repeated, stalling for time while she invented another excuse. This wasn't a situation she had much experience with. She did date, but infrequently.

"Listen, bright eyes, no need to look so concerned. This isn't an invitation to the senior prom. It's one friend to another. Strictly platonic."

"You won't mention . . . our wedding to the waiter? Or anyone else?"

"I promise." As if to offer proof of his intent, he licked the end of his index finger and crossed his heart. "That was Martin's and my secret pledge sign. If either of us broke our word, the other was entitled to come up with a punishment. We both understood it would be a fate worse than death."

"I don't need any broken pledge in order to torture you, Joseph Rockwell. In two days you've managed to turn my life into—" She paused midsentence as Paul Jamison casually strolled past. He waved in Cait's direction and smiled benignly.

"Hello, Paul," she called out, weakly raising her right hand. He looked exceptionally handsome this morning in a three-piece dark blue suit. The contrast between him and Joe, who was wearing dust-covered jeans, heavy boots and a tool pouch, was so striking that Cait had to force herself not to stare at her boss. If only Paul had been the one to invite her to dinner . . .

"If you'll excuse me," she said politely, edging her way around Joe and toward Paul, who'd gone into his office. Their office. The need to talk to him burned within her. Words of explanation began to form themselves in her mind.

Joe caught her by the shoulders, bringing her up short. Cait gasped and raised shocked eyes to his.

"Dinner," he reminded her.

She blinked, hardly knowing what to say. "All right," she mumbled distractedly and recited her address, eager to have him gone.

"Good. I'll pick you up tonight at six." With that he released her and stalked away.

After taking a couple of moments to compose herself, Cait headed toward the office. "Hello, Paul," she said, standing just inside the doorway. "Do you have a moment to talk?"

He glanced up from a file on his desk. "Of course, Cait. Sit down and make yourself comfortable."

She moved into the room, closing the door behind her. When she looked back at Paul, he'd cocked his eyebrows in surprise. "Problems?" he asked.

"Not exactly." She pulled out the chair opposite his desk and slowly sat down. Now that she had his full attention, she was at a loss. All her prepared explanations and witticisms had flown out of her head. "The rate on municipal bonds has been extremely high lately," she said nervously.

Paul agreed with a quick nod. "They have been for several months now."

"Yes, I know. That's what makes them such excellent value." Cait had been selling bonds heavily in the past few weeks.

"You didn't close the door to talk to me about bonds," Paul said softly. "What's troubling you, Cait?"

She laughed uncomfortably, wondering how a man could be so astute in one area and so blind in another. If only he'd reveal some emotion toward her. Anything. All he did was sit across from her and wait. He was cordial enough, gracious even, but there was no hint of anything more. Nothing to give Cait any hope that he was starting to care for her.

"It's about Joseph Rockwell."

"The contractor who's handling the remodeling?"

Cait nodded. "I knew him years ago when we were just children." She glanced at Paul, whose face remained blank. "We were neighbors. In fact Joe and my brother, Martin, were best friends. Joe moved out to the suburbs when he and Martin were in the sixth grade and I hadn't heard anything from him since."

"It's a small world, isn't it?" Paul remarked affably.

"Joe and Martin were typical young boys," she said, rushing her words a little in her eagerness to have this out in the open. "Full of tomfoolery and pranks."

"Boys will be boys," Paul said without any real enthusiasm.

"Yes, I know. Once—" she forced a light laugh "—they actually involved me in one of their crazy schemes."

"What did they put you up to? Robbing a bank?"

She somehow managed a smile. "Not exactly. Joe—I always called him Joseph back then, because it irritated him. Anyway, Joe and Martin had this friend named Pete who was a year older and he'd spent part of his summer vacation visiting his aunt in Peoria. I think it was Peoria . . . . Anyway he came back bragging about having kissed a girl. Naturally Martin and Joe were jealous and as you said, boys will be boys, so they decided that one of them should test it out and see if kissing a girl was everything Pete claimed it was."

"I take it they decided to make you their guinea pig."

"Exactly." Cait slid to the edge of the chair, pleased that Paul was following this rather convoluted explanation. "I was eight and considered something of a . . . pest." She paused, hoping Paul would make some comment about how impossible that was. When he didn't, she continued, a little let down at his restraint. "Apparently I was more of one than I remembered," she said, with another forced laugh. "At eight, I didn't think kissing was something nice girls did, at least not without a wedding band on their finger."

"So you kissed Joseph Rockwell," Paul said absently.

"Yes, but there was a tiny bit more than that. I made him marry me."

Paul's eyebrows shot to the ceiling.

"Now, almost twenty years later, he's getting his revenge by going around telling everyone that we're actually married. Which of course is ridiculous."

A couple of strained seconds followed her announcement.

"I'm not sure what to say," Paul murmured.

"Oh, I wasn't expecting you to say anything. I thought it was important to clear the air, that's all."

"I see."

"He's only doing it because . . . well, because that's Joe. Even when we were kids he enjoyed playing these little games. No one really minded, though, especially not the girls, because he was so cute." She certainly had Paul's attention now.

"I thought you should know," she added, "in case you happened to hear a rumor or something. I didn't want you thinking Joe and I were involved, or even considering a relationship. I was fairly certain you wouldn't, but one never knows and I'm a firm believer in being forthright and honest."

Paul blinked. Wanting to fill the awkward silence, Cait chattered on. "Apparently Joe recognized my name when he and his men moved my office in here with yours. He was delighted when I didn't recognize him. In fact, he caused a commotion by asking me about our children in front of everyone."

"Children?"

"My dolls," Cait was quick to explain.

"Joe Rockwell's an excellent man. I couldn't fault your taste, Cait."

"The two of us *aren't* involved," she protested. "Good grief, I haven't seen him in nearly twenty years."

"I see," Paul said slowly. He sounded . . . disappointed, Cait thought. But she must have misread his tone because there wasn't a single, solitary reason for him to be disappointed. Cait felt foolish now for even trying to explain this fiasco. Paul was so oblivious about her feelings that there was nothing she could say or do to make him understand.

"I just wanted you to know," she repeated, "in case you heard the rumors and were wondering if there was anything between me and Joseph Rockwell. I wanted to assure you there isn't."

"I see," he said again. "Don't worry about it, Cait. What happened between you and Rockwell isn't going to affect your job."

She stood up to leave, praying she'd detect a suggestion of jealousy. A hint of rivalry. Anything to show he cared. There was nothing, so she tried again. "I agreed to have dinner with him, though."

Paul had returned his attention to the papers he'd been reading when she'd interrupted him.

"For old times' sake," she said in a reassuring voice—to fend off any violent display of resentment, she told herself. "I certainly don't have any intention of dating him on a regular basis."

Paul grinned. "Have a good time."

"Yes, I will, thanks." Her heart felt as heavy as a sinking battleship. Without knowing where she was headed or who she'd talk to, Cait wandered out of Paul's office, forgetting for a second that she had no office of her own. The area where her desk once sat was cluttered with wire reels, ladders and men. Joe must have left, a fact for which Cait was grateful.

She walked into Lindy's small office across the hall. Her friend glanced up. "So?" she murmured. "Did you talk to Paul?"

Cait nodded.

"How'd it go?"

"Fine, I guess." She perched on the corner of Lindy's desk, crossing her arms around her waist as her left leg swung rhythmically, keeping time with her discouraged heart. She should be accustomed to disappointment when it came to Paul, but somehow each rejection inflicted a fresh wound on her already battered ego. "I was hoping Paul might be jealous."

"And he wasn't?"

"Not that I could tell."

"It isn't as though you and Joe have anything to do with each other now," Lindy sensibly pointed out. "Marrying him was a childhood prank. It isn't likely to concern Paul."

"I even mentioned that I was going out to dinner with Joe," Cait said morosely.

"You are? When?" Lindy asked, her eyes lighting up. "Where?"

If only Paul had revealed half as much interest. "Tonight. And I don't know where."

"You are going, aren't you?"

"I guess. I can't see any way of avoiding it. Otherwise he'd pester me until I gave in. If I ever marry and have daughters, Lindy, I'm going to warn them about boys from the time they're old enough to understand."

"Don't you think you should follow your own advice?" Lindy asked, glancing pointedly in the direction of Paul's office.

"Not if I were to have Paul's children," Cait said, eager to defend her boss. "Our daughter would be so intelligent and perceptive she wouldn't need to be warned."

Lindy's smile was distracted. "Listen, I've got a few things to finish up here. Why don't you go over to the deli and grab us a table. I'll meet you there in fifteen minutes."

"Sure," Cait said. "Do you want me to order for you?"

"No. I don't know what I want yet."

"Okay, I'll see you in a few minutes."

They often ate at the deli across the street from their office complex. The food was good, the service fast, and generally by three in the afternoon, Cait was famished.

She was so wrapped up in her thoughts, which were muddled and gloomy after her talk with Paul, that she didn't notice how late Lindy was. Her friend rushed into the restaurant more than half an hour after Cait had arrived.

"I'm sorry," she said, sounding flustered and oddly shaken. "I had no idea those last few chores would take me so long. Oh, you must be starved. I hope you've ordered." Lindy removed her coat and stuffed it into the booth before sliding onto the red upholstered seat herself.

"Actually, no, I didn't." Cait sighed. "Just tea." Her spirits were at an all-time low. It was becoming painfully clear that Paul didn't harbor a single romantic feeling toward her. She was wasting her time and her emotional energy on him. If only she'd had more experience with the opposite sex. It seemed her whole love life had gone into neutral the moment she'd graduated from college. At the rate things were developing, she'd still be single by the time she turned thirty—a possibility too dismal to contemplate. She hadn't given much thought to marriage and children, always assuming they'd naturally become part of her life; now she wasn't so sure. Even as a child, she'd pictured her grown-up self with a career *and* a family. Behind the business exterior was a woman traditional enough to hunger for that most special of relationships.

She had to face the fact that marriage would never happen if she continued to love a man who didn't return her feelings. She gave a low groan, then noticed that Lindy was gazing at her in concern.

"Let's order something," Lindy said quickly, reaching for the menu tucked behind the napkin holder. "I'm starved."

"I was thinking I'd skip lunch today," Cait mumbled. She sipped her lukewarm tea and frowned. "Joe will be taking me out to dinner soon. And frankly, I don't have much of an appetite."

"This is all my fault, isn't it?" Lindy asked, looking guilty.

"Of course not. I'm just being practical." If Cait was anything, it was practical—except about Paul. "Go ahead and order."

"You're sure you don't mind?"

Cait gestured nonchalantly. "Heavens, no."

"If you're sure, then I'll have the turkey on whole wheat," Lindy said after a moment. "You know how much I like turkey, though you'd think I'd have gotten enough over Thanksgiving."

"I'll just have a refill on my tea," Cait said.

"You're still flying to Minnesota for the holidays, aren't you?" Lindy asked, fidgeting with the menu.

"Mmm-hmm." Cait had purchased her ticket several months earlier. Martin and his family lived near Minneapolis. When their father had died several years earlier, Cait's mother moved to Minnesota, settling down in a new subdivision not far from Martin, his wife and their four children. Cait tried to visit at least once a year. However, she'd been there in August, stopping off on her way home from a business trip. Usually she made a point of visiting her brother and his family over the Christmas holidays. It was generally a slow week on the stock market, anyway. And if she was going to travel halfway across the country, she wanted to make it worth her while.

"When will you be leaving?" Lindy asked, although Cait was sure she'd already told her friend more than once.

"The twenty-third." For the past few years, Cait had used one week of her vacation at Christmas time, usually starting the weekend before.

But this year Paul was having a Christmas party and Cait didn't want to miss that, so she'd booked her flight closer to the holiday.

The waitress came to take Lindy's order and replenish the hot water for Cait's tea. The instant she moved away from their booth, Lindy launched into a lengthy tirade about how she hated Christmas shopping and how busy the malls were this time of year. Cait stared at her, bewildered. It wasn't like her friend to chat nonstop.

"Lindy," she interrupted, "is something wrong?"

"Wrong? What could possibly be wrong?"

"I don't know. You haven't stopped talking for the last ten minutes."

"I haven't?" There was an abrupt, uncomfortable silence.

Cait decided it was her turn to say something. "I think I'll wear my red velvet dress," she mused.

"To dinner with Joe?"

"No," she said, shaking her head. "To Paul's Christmas party."

Lindy sighed. "But what are you wearing tonight?"

The question took Cait by surprise. She didn't consider this dinner with Joe a real date. He just wanted to talk over old times, which was fine with Cait as long as he behaved himself. Suddenly she frowned, then closed her eyes. "Martin's a Methodist minister," she said softly.

"Yes, I know," Lindy reminded her. "I've known that since I first met you, which was what? Three years ago now."

"Four last month."

"So what does Martin's occupation have to do with anything?" Lindy asked.

"Joe Rockwell can't find out," Cait whispered.

"I didn't plan on telling him," Lindy whispered back. "I've got to make up some other occupation like . . ."

"Counselor," Lindy suggested. "I'm curious, though. Why can't you tell Joe about Martin?"

"Think about it!"

"I am thinking. I really doubt Joe would care one way or the other."

"He might try to make something of it. You don't know Joe like I do. He'd razz me about it all evening, claiming the marriage was valid. You know, because Martin really *is* a minister, and since Martin performed the ceremony, we must really be married—that kind of nonsense."

"I didn't think about that."

But then, Lindy didn't seem to be thinking much about anything lately. It was as if she was walking around in a perpetual daydream. Cait couldn't remember Lindy's ever being so scatterbrained. If she didn't know better, she'd guess there was a man involved.

Three

At ten to six, Cait was blow-drying her hair in a haphazard fashion, regretting that she'd ever had it cut. She was looking forward to this dinner date about as much as a trip to the dentist. All she wanted was to get it over with, come home and bury her head under a pillow while she sorted out how she was going to get Paul to notice her.

Restyling her hair hadn't done the trick. Putting in extra hours at the office hadn't impressed him, either. Cait was beginning to think she could stand on top of his desk naked and not attract his attention.

She walked into her compact living room and smoothed the bulky-knit sweater over her slim hips. She hadn't dressed for the occasion, although the sweater was new and expensive. Gray wool slacks and a powder-blue turtleneck with a silver heart-shaped necklace dangling from her neck were about as dressy as she cared to get with someone like Joe. He'd probably be wearing cowboy boots and jeans, if not his hard hat and tool pouch.

Oh, yes, Cait had recognized his type when she'd first seen him. Joe Rockwell was a man's man. He walked and talked macho. No doubt he drove a truck with tires so high off the ground she'd need a stepladder to climb inside. He was tough and gruff and liked his women meek and submissive. In that case, of course, she had nothing to worry about; he'd lose interest immediately.

He arrived right on time, which surprised Cait. Being prompt didn't fit the image she had of Joe Rockwell, redneck contractor. She sighed and painted on a smile, then walked slowly to the door.

The smile faded. Joe stood before her, tall and debonair, dressed in a dark gray pin-striped suit. His gray silk tie had *pink* stripes. He was the picture of smooth sophistication. She knew that Joe was the same man she'd seen earlier in dusty work clothes—yet he was different. He was nothing like Paul, of course. But Joseph Rockwell was a devastatingly handsome man. With a devastating charm. Rarely had she seen a man smile the way he did. His eyes twinkled with warmth and life and mischief. It wasn't difficult to imagine Joe with a little boy whose eyes mirrored his. Cait didn't know where that thought came from, but she pushed it aside before it could linger and take root.

"Hello," he said, flashing her that smile.

"Hi." She couldn't stop looking at him.

"May I come in?"

"Oh . . . of course. I'm sorry," she faltered, stumbling in her haste to step aside. He'd caught her completely off guard. "I was about to change clothes," she said quickly.

"You look fine."

"These old things?" She feigned a laugh. "If you'll excuse me, I'll only be a minute." She poured him a cup of coffee, then dashed into her bedroom, ripping the sweater over her head and closing the door with one foot. Her shoes went flying as she ran to her closet. Jerking aside the orderly row of business jackets and skirts, she pulled clothes off their hangers, considered them, then tossed them on the bed. Nearly everything she owned was more suitable for the office than a dinner date.

The only really special dress she owned was the red velvet one she'd purchased for Paul's Christmas party. The temptation to slip into that was strong but she resisted, wanting to save it for her boss, though heaven knew he probably wouldn't notice.

Deciding on a skirt and blazer, she hopped frantically around her bedroom as she pulled on her panty hose. Next she threw on a rose-colored silk blouse and managed to button it while stepping into her skirt. She tucked the blouse into the waistband and her feet into a pair of medium-heeled pumps. Finally, her velvet blazer and she was ready. Taking a deep breath, she returned to the living room in three minutes flat.

"That was fast," Joe commented, standing by the fireplace, hands clasped behind his back. He was examining a framed photograph that sat on the mantel. "Is this Martin's family?"

"Martin . . . why, yes, that's Martin, his wife and their children." She hoped he didn't detect the breathless catch in her voice.

"Four children."

"Yes, he and Rebecca wanted a large family." Her heartbeat was slowly returning to normal though Cait still felt lightheaded. She had a sneaking suspicion that she was suffering from the effects of unleashed male charm.

She realized with surprise that Joe hadn't said or done anything to embarrass or fluster her. She'd expected him to arrive with a whole series of remarks designed to disconcert her.

"Timmy's ten, Kurt's eight, Jenny's six and Clay's four." She introduced the freckle-faced youngsters, pointing each one out.

"They're handsome children."

"They are, aren't they?"

Cait experienced a twinge of pride. The main reason she went to Minneapolis every year was Martin's children. They adored her and she was crazy about them. Christmas wouldn't be Christmas without Jenny and Clay snuggling on her lap while their father read the Nativity story. Christmas was singing carols in front of a crackling wood fire, accompanied by Martin's guitar. It meant stringing popcorn and cranberries for the seven-foot-tall tree that always adorned the living room. It was having the children take turns scraping fudge from the sides of the copper kettle, and supervising the decorating of sugar cookies with all four crowded around the kitchen table. Caitlin Marshall might be a dedicated stockbroker with an impressive clientele, but when it came to Martin's children, she was Auntie Cait.

"It's difficult to think of Martin with kids," Joe said, carefully placing the family photo back on the mantel.

"He met Rebecca his first year of college and the rest, as they say, is history."

"What about you?" Joe asked, turning unexpectedly to face her.

"What about me?"

"Why haven't you married?"

"Uh . . ." Cait wasn't sure how to answer him. She had a glib reply she usually gave when anyone asked, but somehow she knew Joe wouldn't accept that. "I . . . I've never really fallen in love."

"What about Paul?"

"Until Paul," she corrected, stunned that she'd forgotten the strong feelings she held for her employer. She'd been so concerned with being honest that she'd overlooked the obvious. "I am deeply in love with Paul," she said defiantly, wanting there to be no misunderstanding.

"There's no need to convince me, Caitlin."

"I'm not trying to convince you of anything. I've been in love with Paul for nearly a year. Once he realizes he loves me, too, we'll be married."

Joe's mouth slanted in a wry line and he seemed about to argue with her. Cait waylaid any attempt by glancing pointedly at her watch. "Shouldn't we be leaving?"

After a long moment, Joe said, "Yes, I suppose we should," in a mild, neutral voice.

Cait went to the hall closet for her coat, aware with every step she took that Joe was watching her. She turned back to smile at him, but somehow the smile didn't materialize. His blue eyes met hers, and she found his look disturbing—caressing, somehow, and intimate.

Joe helped her on with her coat and led her to the parking lot, where he'd left his car. Another surprise awaited her. It wasn't a four-wheel-drive truck, but a late sixties black convertible in mint condition.

The restaurant was one of the most respected in Seattle, with a noted chef and a reputation for excellent seafood. Cait chose grilled salmon and Joe ordered Cajun shrimp.

"Do you remember the time Martin and I decided to open our own business?" Joe asked, as they sipped a predinner glass of wine.

Cait did indeed recall that summer. "You might have been a bit more ingenious. A lemonade stand wasn't the world's most creative enterprise."

"Perhaps not, but we were doing a brisk business until an annoying eight-year-old girl ruined everything."

Cait wasn't about to let that comment pass. "You were using moldy lemons and covering the taste with too much sugar. Besides, it's unhealthy to share paper cups."

Joe chuckled, the sound deep and rich. "I should've known then that you were nothing but trouble."

"It seems to me the whole mess was your own fault. You boys wouldn't listen to me. I had to do something before someone got sick on those lemons."

"Carrying a picket sign that read 'Talk to me before you buy this lemonade' was a bit drastic even for you, don't you think?"

"If anything, it brought you more business," Cait said dryly, recalling how her plan had backfired. "All the boys in the neighborhood wanted to see what contaminated lemonade tasted like."

"You were a damn nuisance, Cait. Own up to it." He smiled and Cait sincerely doubted that any woman could argue with him when he smiled full-force.

"I most certainly was not! If anything you two were—"

"Disgusting, I believe, was your favorite word for Martin and me."

"And you did your level best to live up to it," she said, struggling to hold back a smile. She reached for a breadstick and bit into it to disguise her amusement. She'd always enjoyed rankling Martin and Joe, though she'd never have admitted it, especially at the age of eight.

"Picketing our lemonade stand wasn't the worst trick you ever pulled, either," Joe said mischievously.

Cait had trouble swallowing. She should have been prepared for this. If he remembered her complaints about the lemonade stand, he was sure to remember what had happened once Betsy McDonald found out about the kissing incident.

"It wasn't a trick," Cait protested.

"But you told everyone at school that I'd kissed you—even though you'd promised not to."

"Not exactly." There was a small discrepancy that needed clarification. "If you think back you'll remember you said I couldn't tell anyone I'd been inside the fort. You didn't say anything about the kiss."

Joe frowned darkly as if attempting to jog his memory. "How can you remember details like that? All of this happened years ago."

"I remember everything," Cait said grandly—a gross exaggeration. She hadn't recognized Joe, after all. But on this one point she was absolutely clear. "You and Martin were far more concerned that I not tell anyone about going inside the fort. You didn't say a word about keeping the kiss a secret."

"But did you have to tell Betsy McDonald? That girl had been making eyes at me for weeks. As soon as she learned I'd kissed you instead of her, she was furious."

"Betsy was the most popular girl in school. I wanted her for my friend, so I told."

"And sold me down the river."

"Would an apology help?" Confident he was teasing her once again, Cait gave him her most charming smile.

"An apology just might do it." Joe grinned back, a grin that brightened his eyes to a deeper, more tantalizing shade of blue. It was with some difficulty that Cait pulled her gaze away from his.

"If Betsy liked you," she asked, smoothing the linen napkin across her lap, "then why didn't you kiss her? She'd probably have let you. You wouldn't have had to bribe her with your precious baseball cards, either."

"You're kidding. If I kissed Betsy McDonald I might as well have signed over my soul," Joe said, continuing the joke.

"Even as mere children, men are afraid of commitment," Cait said solemnly.

Joe ignored her remark.

"Your memory's not as sharp as you think," Cait felt obliged to tell him, enjoying herself more than she'd thought possible.

Once again, Joe overlooked her comment. "I can remember Martin complaining about how you'd line up your dolls in a row and teach them school. Once you even got him to come in as a guest lecturer. Heaven knew what you had to do to get him to play professor to a bunch of dolls."

"I found a pair of dirty jeans stuffed under the sofa with something dead in the pocket. Mom would have tanned his hide if she'd found them, so Martin owed me a favor. Then he got all bent out of shape when I collected it. He didn't seem the least bit appreciative that I'd saved him."

"Good old Martin," Joe said, shaking his head. "I swear he was as big on ceremony as you were. Marrying us was a turning point in his life. From that point on, he started carting a Bible around with him the way some kids do a slingshot. Right in his hip pocket. If he wasn't burying something, he was holding revival meetings. Remember how he got in a pack of trouble at school for writing 'God loves you, ask Martin' on the back wall of the school?"

"I remember."

"I sort of figured he might become a missionary."

"Martin?" She gave an abrupt laugh. "Never. He likes his conveniences. He doesn't even go camping. Martin's idea of roughing it is doing without valet service."

She expected Joe to chuckle. He did smile at her attempted joke, but that was all. He seemed to be studying her the same way she'd been studying him.

"You surprise me," Joe announced suddenly.

"I do? Am I a disappointment to you?"

"Not at all. I always thought you'd grow up and have a house full of children yourself. You used to haul those dolls of yours around with you everywhere. If Martin and I were too noisy, you'd shush us, saying the babies were asleep. If we wanted to play in the backyard, we couldn't because you were having a tea party with your dolls. It was enough to drive a ten-year-old boy crazy. But if we ever dared complain, you'd look at us serenely and with the sweetest smile tell us we had to be patient because it was for the children."

"I did get carried away with all that motherhood business, didn't I?" Joe's words stirred up uncomfortable memories, the same ones she'd entertained earlier that afternoon. She really did love children. Yet, somehow, without her quite knowing how, the years had passed and she'd buried the dream. Nowadays she didn't like to think too much about a husband and family—the life that hadn't happened. It haunted her at odd moments.

"I should have known you'd end up in construction," she said, switching the subject away from herself.

"How's that?" Joe asked.

"Wasn't it you who built the fort?"

"Martin helped."

"Sure, by staying out of the way." She grinned. "I know my brother. He's a marvel with people, but please don't ever give him a hammer."

Their dinner arrived, and it was as delicious as Cait had expected, although by then she was enjoying herself so much that even a plateful of dry toast would have tasted good. They drank two cups of cappuccino after their meal, and talked and laughed as the hours melted away. Cait couldn't remember the last time she'd laughed so much.

When at last she glanced at her watch, she was shocked to realize it was well past ten. "I had no idea it was so late!" she said. "I should get home." She had to be up by five.

Joe took care of the bill and collected her coat. When they walked outside, the December night was clear and chilly, with a multitude of stars twinkling brightly above.

"Are you cold?" he asked as they waited for the valet to deliver the car.

"Not at all." Nevertheless, he placed his arm around her shoulders, drawing her close.

Cait didn't protest. It felt natural for this man to hold her close.

His car arrived and they drove back to her apartment building in silence. When he pulled into the parking lot, she considered inviting him in for coffee, then decided against it. They'd already drunk enough coffee, and besides, they both had to work the following morning. But more important, Joe might read something else into the invitation. He was an old friend. Nothing more. And she wanted to keep it that way.

She turned to him and smiled softly. "I had a lovely time. Thank you so much."

"You're welcome, Cait. We'll do it again."

Cait was astonished to realize how appealing another evening with Joseph Rockwell was. She'd underestimated him.

Or had she?

"There's something else I'd like to try again," he was saying, his eyes filled with devilry.

"Try again?" she repeated. "What?"

He slid his arm behind her and for a breathless moment they looked at each other. "I don't know if I've got a chance without trading a few baseball cards, though."

Cait swallowed. "You want to kiss me?"

He nodded. His eyes seemed to grow darker, more intense. "For old times' sake." His hand caressed the curve of her neck, his thumb moving slowly toward the scented hollow of her throat.

"Well, sure. For old times' sake." She was astonished at the way her heart was reacting to the thought of Joe holding her . . . kissing her.

His mouth began a slow descent toward hers, his warm breath nuzzling her skin.

"Just remember," she whispered when his mouth was about to settle over hers. Her hands gripped his lapels. "Old times' . . ."

"I'll remember," he said as his lips came down on hers.

She sighed and slid her hands up his solid chest to link her fingers at the base of his neck. The kiss was slow and thorough. When it was over, Cait's hands were clutching his collar.

Joe's fingers were in her hair, tangled in the short, soft curls, cradling the back of her head.

A sweet rush of joy coursed through her veins. Cait felt a bubbling excitement, a burst of warmth, unlike anything she'd ever known before.

Then he kissed her a second time . . .

"Just remember . . ." she repeated when he pulled his mouth from hers and buried it in the delicate curve of her neck.

He drew in several ragged breaths before asking, "What is it I'm supposed to remember?"

"Yes, oh, please, remember."

He lifted his head and rested his hands lightly on her shoulders, his face only inches from hers. "What's so important you don't want me to forget?" he whispered.

It wasn't Joe who was supposed to remember; it was Cait. She didn't realize she'd spoken out loud. She blinked, uncertain, then tilted her head to gaze down at her hands, anywhere but at him. "Oh . . . that I'm in love with Paul."

There was a moment of silence. An awkward moment. "Right," he answered shortly. "You're in love with Paul." His arms fell away and he released her.

Cait hesitated, uneasy. "Thanks again for a wonderful dinner." Her hand closed around the door handle. She was eager now to make her escape.

"Any time," he said flippantly. His own hands gripped the steering wheel.

"I'll see you soon."

"Soon," he echoed. She climbed out of the car, not giving Joe a chance to come around and open the door for her. She was aware of him sitting in the car, waiting until she'd unlocked the lobby door and stepped inside. She hurried down the first-floor hall and into her apartment, turning on the lights so he'd know she'd made it safely home.

Then she removed her coat and carefully hung it in the closet. When she peeked out the window, she saw that Joe had already left.

Lindy was at her desk working when Cait arrived the next morning. Cait smiled at her as she hurried past, but didn't stop to indulge in conversation.

Cait could feel Lindy's gaze trailing after her and she knew her friend was disappointed that she hadn't told her about the dinner date with Joe Rockwell.

Cait didn't want to talk about it. She was afraid that if she said anything to Lindy, she wouldn't be able to avoid mentioning the kiss, which was a subject she wanted to avoid at all costs. She wouldn't be able to delay her friend's questions forever, but Cait wanted to put them off until at least the end of the day. Longer, if possible.

What a fool she'd been to let Joe kiss her. It had seemed so right at the time, a natural conclusion to a delightful evening.

The fact that she'd let him do it without even making a token protest still confused her. If Paul happened to hear about it, he might think she really *was* interested in Joe. Which, of course, she wasn't.

Her boss was a man of principle and integrity—and altogether a frustrating person to fall in love with. Judging by his reaction to her dinner with Joe, he seemed immune to jealousy. Now if only she could discover a way of letting him know how she felt . . . and spark his interest in the process!

The morning was hectic. Out of the corner of her eye, Cait saw Joe arrive. Although she was speaking to an important client on the phone, she stared after him as he approached the burly foreman. She watched Joe remove a blueprint from a long, narrow tube and roll it open so two other men could study it. There seemed to be some discussion, then the foreman nodded and Joe left, without so much as glancing in Cait's direction.

That stung.

At least he could have waved hello. But if he wanted to ignore her, well, fine. She'd do the same.

The market closed on the up side, the Dow Jones industrial average at 2600 points after brisk trading. The day's work was over.

As Cait had predicted, Lindy sought her out almost immediately.

"So how'd your dinner date go?"

"It was fun."

"Where'd he take you? Sam's Bar and Grill as you thought?"

"Actually, no," she said, clearing her throat, feeling more than a little foolish for having suggested such a thing. "He took me to Henry's." She announced it louder than necessary, since Paul was strolling into the office just then. But for all the notice he gave her, she might as well have been fresh paint drying on the office wall.

"Henry's," Lindy echoed. "He took you to Henry's? Why, that's one of the best restaurants in town. It must have cost him a small fortune."

"I wouldn't know. My menu didn't list any prices."

"You're joking. No one's ever taken me anyplace so fancy. What did you order?"

"Grilled salmon." She continued to study Paul for some clue that he was listening in on her and Lindy's conversation. He was seated at his desk, reading a report on short-term partnerships as a tax advantage. Cait had read it earlier in the week and had recommended it to him.

"Was it wonderful?" Lindy pressed.

It took Cait a moment to realize her friend was quizzing her about the dinner. "Excellent. The best fish I've had in years."

"What did you do afterward?"

Cait looked back at her friend. "What makes you think we did anything? We had dinner, talked, and then he drove me home. Nothing more happened. Understand? Nothing."

"If you say so," Lindy said, eyeing her suspiciously. "But you're certainly defensive about it."

"I just want you to know that nothing happened. Joseph Rockwell is an old friend. That's all."

Paul glanced up from the report, but his gaze connected with Lindy's before slowly progressing to Cait.

"Hello, Paul," Cait greeted him cheerfully. "Are Lindy and I disturbing you? We'd be happy to go into the hallway if you'd like."

"No, no, you're fine. Don't worry about it." He looked past them to the doorway and got to his feet. "Hello, Rockwell."

"Am I interrupting a meeting?" Joe asked, stepping into the office as if it didn't really matter whether he was or not. His hard hat was back in place, along with the dusty jeans and the tool pouch. And yet Cait had no difficulty remembering last night's sophisticated dinner companion when she looked at him.

"No, no," Paul answered, "we were just chatting. Come on in. Problems?"

"Not really. But there's something I'd like you to take a look at in the other room."

"I'll be right there."

Joe threw Cait a cool smile as he strolled past. "Hello, Cait."

"Joe." Her heart was pounding hard, and that was ridiculous. It must have been due to embarrassment, she told herself. Joe was a friend, a boy from the old neighborhood; just because she'd allowed him to kiss her didn't mean there was—or ever would be—anything romantic between them. The sooner she made him understand this, the better.

"Joe and Cait went out to dinner last night," Lindy said pointedly to Paul. "He took her to Henry's."

"How nice," Paul commented, clearly more interested in troubleshooting with Joe than discussing Cait's dating history.

"We had a good time, didn't we?" Joe asked Cait.

"Yes, very nice," she responded stiffly.

Joe waited until Paul was out of the room before he stepped back and dropped a kiss on her cheek. Then he announced loudly enough for everyone in the vicinity to hear, "You were incredible last night."

Four

"I thought you said nothing happened," Lindy said, looking intently at a red-faced Cait.

"Nothing did happen." Cait was furious enough to kick Joe Rockwell in the shins the way he deserved. How dared he say something so . . . so embarrassing in front of Lindy! And probably within earshot of Paul!

"But then why would he say something like that?"

"How should I know?" Cait snapped. "One little kiss and he makes it sound like—"

"He kissed you?" Lindy asked sharply, her eyes narrowing. "You just got done telling me there's nothing between the two of you."

"Good grief, the kiss didn't mean anything. It was for old times' sake. Just a platonic little kiss." All right, she was exaggerating a bit, but it couldn't be helped.

While she was speaking, Cait gathered her things and shoved them in her briefcase. Then she slammed the lid closed and reached for her coat, thrusting her arms into the sleeves, her movements abrupt and ungraceful.

"Have a nice weekend," she said tightly, not completely understanding why she felt so annoyed with Lindy. "I'll see you Monday." She marched through the office, but paused in front of Joe.

"You wanted something, sweetheart?" he asked in a cajoling voice.

"You're despicable!"

Joe looked downright disappointed. "Not low and disgusting?"

"That, too."

He grinned from ear to ear just the way she knew he would. "I'm glad to hear it."

Cait bit back an angry retort. It wouldn't do any good to engage in a verbal battle with Joe Rockwell. He'd have a comeback for any insult she could hurl. Seething, Cait marched to the elevator and jabbed the button impatiently.

"I'll be by later tonight, darling," Joe called to her just as the doors were closing, effectively cutting off any protest.

He was joking. He had to be joking. No man in his right mind could possibly expect her to invite him into her home after this latest stunt. Not even the impertinent Joe Rockwell.

Once home, Cait took a long, soothing shower, dried her hair and changed into jeans and a sweater. Friday nights were generally quiet ones for her. She was munching on pretzels and surveying the bleak contents of her refrigerator when there was a knock on the door.

It couldn't possibly be Joe, she told herself.

It *was* Joe, balancing a large pizza on the palm of one hand and clutching a bottle of red wine in the other.

Cait stared at him, too dumbfounded at his audacity to speak.

"I come bearing gifts," he said, presenting the pizza to her with more than a little ceremony.

"Listen here, you . . . you fool, it's going to take a whole lot more than pizza to make up for that stunt you pulled this afternoon."

"Come on, Cait, lighten up a little."

"Lighten up! You . . . you . . ."

"I believe the word you're looking for is fool."

"You have your nerve." She dug her fists into her hips, knowing she should slam the door in his face. She would have, too, but the pizza smelled *so* good it was difficult to maintain her indignation.

"Okay, I'll admit it," Joe said, his deep blue eyes revealing genuine contrition. "I got carried away. You're right, I am an idiot. All I can do is ask your forgiveness." He lifted the lid of the pizza box and Cait was confronted by the thickest, most mouthwatering masterpiece she'd ever seen. The top was crowded with no less than ten tempting toppings, all covered with a thick layer of hot melted cheese.

"Do you accept my humble apology?" Joe pressed, waving the pizza under her nose.

"Are there any anchovies on that thing?"

"Only on half."

"You're forgiven." She took him by the elbow and dragged him inside her apartment.

Cait led the way into the kitchen. She got two plates from the cupboard and collected knives, forks and napkins as she mentally reviewed his crimes. "I couldn't believe you actually said that," she mumbled, shaking her head. She set the kitchen table, neatly positioning the napkins after shoving the day's mail to one side. "The least you can do is tell me why you found it necessary to say that in front of Paul. Lindy had already started grilling me. Can you imagine what she and Paul must think now?" She retrieved two wineglasses from the cupboard and set them by the plates. "I've never been more embarrassed in my life."

"Never?" he prompted, opening and closing her kitchen drawers until he located a corkscrew.

"Never," she repeated. "And don't think a pizza's going to ensure lasting peace."

"I wouldn't dream of it."

"It's a start, but you're going to owe me a long time for this prank, Joseph Rockwell."

"I'll be good," he promised, his eyes twinkling. He agilely removed the cork, tested the wine and then filled both glasses.

Cait jerked out a wicker-back chair and threw herself down. "Did Paul say anything after I left?"

"About what?" Joe slid out a chair and joined her.

Cait had already dished up a large slice for each of them, fastidiously using a knife to disconnect the strings of melted cheese that stretched from the box to their plates.

"About me, of course," she growled.

Joe handed her a glass of wine. "Not really."

Cait paused and lifted her eyes to his. "Not really? What does that mean?"

"Only that he didn't say much about you."

Joe was taunting her, dangling bits and pieces of information, waiting for her reaction. She should have known better than to trust him, but she was so anxious to find out what Paul had said that she ignored her pride. "Tell me everything he said," she demanded, "word for word."

Joe had a mouthful of pizza and Cait was left to wait several moments until he swallowed. "I seem to recall he said you explained that the two of us go a long way back."

Cait straightened, too curious to hide her interest. "Did he look concerned? Jealous?"

"Paul? No, if anything, he looked bored."

"Bored," Cait repeated. Her shoulders sagged with defeat. "I swear that man wouldn't notice me if I pranced around his office naked."

"That's a clever idea, and one that just might work. Maybe you should practice around the house first, get the hang of it. I'd be willing to help you out if you're serious about this." He sounded utterly nonchalant, as though she'd suggested subscribing to cable television. "This is what friends are for. Do you need help undressing?"

Cait took a sip of her wine to hide a smile. Joe hadn't changed in twenty years. He was still witty and fun-loving and a terrible tease. "Very funny."

"Hey, I wasn't kidding. I'll pretend I'm Paul and—"

"You promised you were going to be good."

He wiggled his eyebrows suggestively. "I will be. Just you wait."

Cait could feel the tide of color flow into her cheeks. She quickly lowered her eyes to her plate. "Joe, cut it out. You're making me blush and I hate to blush. It makes my face look like a ripe tomato." She lifted her slice of pizza and bit into it, chewing thoughtfully. "I don't understand you. Every time I think I have you figured out you do something to surprise me."

"Like what?"

"Like yesterday. You invited me to dinner, but I never dreamed you'd take me someplace as elegant as Henry's. You were the perfect gentleman all evening and then today, you were so . . ."

"Low and disgusting."

"Exactly." She nodded righteously. "One minute you're the picture of charm and culture and the next you're badgering me with your wisecracks."

"I'm a tease, remember?"

"The problem is I can't deal with you when I don't know what to expect."

"That's my charm." He reached for a second piece of pizza. "Women are said to adore the unexpected in a man."

"Not this woman," she informed him promptly. "I need to know where I stand with you."

"A little to the left."

"Joe, please, I'm not joking. I can't have you pulling stunts like you did today. I've lived a good, clean life for the past twenty-eight years. Two days with you has ruined my reputation with the company. I can't walk into the office and hold my head up any longer. I hear people whispering and I know they're talking about me."

"Us," he corrected. "They're talking about us."

"That's even worse. If they want to talk about me and a man, I'd rather it was Paul. Just how much longer is this remodeling project going to take, anyway?" As far as Cait was concerned, the sooner Joe and his renegade crew were out of her office, the sooner her life would return to normal.

"Not too much longer."

"At the rate you're progressing, Webster, Rodale and Missen will have offices on the moon."

"Before the end of the year, I promise."

"Yes, but just how reliable are your promises?"

"I'm being good, aren't I?"

"I suppose," she conceded ungraciously, jerking a stack of mail away from Joe as he started to sort through it.

"What's this?" Joe asked, rescuing a single piece of paper before it fluttered to the floor.

"A Christmas list. I'm going shopping tomorrow."

"I should've known you'd be organized about that, too." He sounded vaguely insulting.

"I've been organized all my life. It isn't likely to change now."

"That's why I want you to lighten up a little." He continued studying her list. "What time are you going?"

"The stores open at eight and I plan to be there then."

"I suppose you've written down everything you need to buy so you won't forget anything."

"Of course."

"Sounds sensible." His remark surprised her. He scanned her list, then yelped, "Hey, I'm not on here!" He withdrew a pen from his shirt pocket and added his own name. "Do you want me to give you a few suggestions about what I'd like?"

"I already know what I'm getting you."

Joe arched his brows. "You do? And please don't say 'nothing.'"

"No, but it'll be something appropriate—like a muzzle."

"Oh, Caitlin, darling, you injure me." He gave her one of his devilish smiles, and Cait could feel herself weakening. Just what she didn't want! She had every right to be angry with Joe. If he hadn't brought that pizza, she'd have slammed the door in his face. Wouldn't she? Sure, she would! But she'd always been susceptible to Italian food. Her only other fault was Paul. She did love him. No one seemed to believe that, but she'd known almost from the moment they'd met that she was destined to spend the rest of her life loving Paul Jamison. Only she'd rather do it as his wife than his employee . . . .

"Have you finished your shopping?" she asked idly, making small talk with Joe since he seemed determined to hang around.

"I haven't started. I have good intentions every year, you know, like I'll get a head start on finding the perfect gifts for my nieces and nephews, but they never work out. Usually panic sets in Christmas Eve and I tear around the stores like mad and buy everything in sight. Last year I forgot wrapping paper. My mother saved the day."

"I doubt it'd do any good to suggest you get organized."

"I haven't got the time."

"What are you doing right now? Write out your list, stick to it and make the time to go shopping."

"My darling Cait, is this an invitation for me to join you tomorrow?"

"Uh . . ." Cait hadn't intended it to be, but she supposed she couldn't object as long as he behaved himself. "You're welcome on one condition."

"Name it."

"No jokes, no stunts like you pulled today and absolutely no teasing. If you announce to even one person that we're married, I'm walking away from you and that's a promise."

"You've got it." He raised his hand, then ceremoniously crossed his heart.

"Lick your fingertips first," Cait demanded. The instant the words were out of her mouth, she realized how ridiculous she sounded, as if they were eight and ten all over again. "Forget I said that."

His eyes were twinkling as he stood to bring his plate to the sink. "I swear it's a shame you're so in love with Paul," he told her. "If I'm not careful, I could fall for you myself." With that, he kissed her on the cheek and let himself out the door.

Pressing her fingers to her cheek, Cait drew in a deep, shuddering breath and held it until she heard the door close. Then and only then did it seep out in ragged bursts, as if she'd forgotten how to breathe normally.

"Oh, Joe," she whispered. The last thing she wanted was for Joe to fall in love with her. Not that he wasn't handsome and sweet and wonderful. He was. He always had been. He just wasn't for her. Their personalities were poles apart. Joe was unpredictable, always doing the unexpected, whereas Cait's life ran like clockwork.

She liked Joe. She almost wished she didn't, but she couldn't help herself. However, a steady diet of his pranks would soon drive her into the nearest asylum.

Standing, Cait closed the pizza box and tucked the uneaten

portion onto the top shelf of her refrigerator. She was putting the dirty plates in her dishwasher when the phone rang. She quickly washed her hands and reached for it.

"Hello."

"Cait, it's Paul."

Cait was so startled that the receiver slipped out of her hand. Grabbing for it, she nearly stumbled over the open dishwasher door, knocking her shin against the sharp edge. She yelped and swallowed a cry as she jerked the dangling phone cord toward her.

"Sorry, sorry," she cried, once she'd rescued the telephone receiver. "Paul? Are you still there?"

"Yes, I'm here. Is this a bad time? I could call back later if this is inconvenient. You don't have company, do you? I wouldn't want to interrupt a party or anything."

"Oh, no, now is perfect. I didn't realize you had my home number . . . but obviously you do. After all, we've been working together for nearly a year now." Eleven months and four days, not that she was counting or anything. "Naturally my number would be in the Human Resources file."

He hesitated and Cait bent over to rub her shin where it had collided with the dishwasher door. She was sure to have an ugly bruise, but a bruised leg was a small price to pay. Paul had phoned her!

"The reason I'm calling . . ."

"Yes, Paul," she prompted when he didn't immediately continue.

The silence lengthened before he blurted out, "I just wanted to thank you for passing on that article on the tax advantages of limited partnerships. It was thoughtful of you and I appreciate it."

"I've read quite a lot in that area, you know. There are several recent articles on the same subject. If you'd like, I could bring them in next week."

"Sure. That would be fine. Thanks again, Cait. Goodbye."

The line was disconnected before Cait could say anything else and she was left holding the receiver. A smile came, slow and confident, and with a small cry of triumph, she tossed the telephone receiver into the air, caught it behind her back and replaced it with a flourish.

Cait was dressed and waiting for Joe early the next morning. "Joe," she cried, throwing open her apartment door, "I could just kiss you."

He was dressed in faded jeans and a hip-length bronze-colored leather jacket. "Hey, I'm not stopping you," he said, opening his arms.

Cait ignored the invitation. "Paul phoned me last night." She didn't even try to contain her excitement; she felt like leaping and skipping and singing out loud.

"Paul did?" Joe sounded surprised.

"Yes. It was shortly after you left. He thanked me for giving him an interesting article I found in one of the business journals and—this is the good part—he asked if I was alone . . . as if it really mattered to him."

"If you were alone?" Joe repeated, and frowned. "What's that got to do with anything?"

"Don't you understand?" For all his intelligence Joe could be pretty obtuse sometimes. "He wanted to know if *you* were here with me. It makes sense, doesn't it? Paul's jealous, only he doesn't realize it yet. Oh, Joe, I can't remember ever being this happy. Not in years and years and years."

"Because Paul Jamison phoned?"

"Don't sound so skeptical. It's exactly the break I've been waiting for all these months. Paul's finally noticed me, and it's thanks to you."

"At least you're willing to give credit where credit is due." But he still didn't seem particularly thrilled.

"It's just so incredible," she continued. "I don't think I slept a wink last night. There was something in his voice that I've never heard before. Something . . . deep and personal. I don't know how to explain it. For the first time in a whole year, Paul knows I'm alive!"

"Are we going Christmas shopping or not?" Joe demanded brusquely. "Damn it all, Cait, I never expected you to go soft over a stupid phone call."

"But this wasn't just any call," she reminded him. She reached for her purse and her coat in one sweeping motion. "It was from *Paul*."

"You sound like a silly schoolgirl." Joe frowned, but Cait wasn't about to let his short temper destroy her mood. Paul had phoned her at home and she was sure that this was the beginning of a *real* relationship. Next he'd ask her out for lunch, and then . . .

They left her apartment and walked down the hall, Cait grinning all the way. Standing just outside the front doors was a huge truck with gigantic wheels. Just the type of vehicle she'd expected him to drive the night he'd taken her to Henry's.

"This is your truck?" she asked when they were outside. She couldn't keep the laughter out of her voice.

"Something wrong with it?"

"Not a single thing, but Joe, honestly, you are so predictable."

"That's not what you said yesterday."

She grinned again as he opened the truck door, set down a stool for her and helped her climb into the cab. The seat was cluttered, but so wide she was able to shove everything to one side. When she'd made room for herself, she fastened the seat belt, snapping it jauntily in place. She was so happy, the whole world seemed delightful this morning.

"Will you quit smiling before someone suggests you've been overdosing on vitamins?" Joe grumbled.

"My, aren't we testy this morning."

"Where to?" he asked, starting the engine.

"Any of the big malls will do. You decide. Do you have your list all made out?"

Joe patted his heart. "It's in my shirt pocket."

"Good."

"Have you decided what you're going to buy for whom?"

His smile was slightly off-kilter. "Not exactly. I thought I'd follow you around and buy whatever you did. Do you know what you're getting your mother? Mine's damn difficult to buy for. Last year I ended up getting her a dozen bags of cat food. She's got five cats of her own and God only knows how many strays she's feeding."

"At least your idea was practical."

"Well, there's that, and the fact that by the time I started my Christmas shopping the only store open was a supermarket."

Cait laughed. "Honestly, Joe!"

"Hey, I was desperate and before you get all righteous on me, Mom thought the cat food and the two rib roasts were great gifts."

"I'm sure she did," Cait returned, grinning. She found herself doing a lot of that when she was with Joe. Imagine buying his mother rib roasts for Christmas!

"Give me some ideas, would you? Mom's a hard case."

"To be honest, I'm not all that imaginative myself. I buy my mother the same thing every year."

"What is it?"

"Long-distance phone cards. That way she can phone her sister in Dubuque and her high-school friend in Kansas. Of course she calls me every now and then, too."

"Okay, that takes care of Mom. What about Martin? What are you buying him?"

"A bronze eagle." She'd decided on that gift last summer when she'd attended Sunday services at Martin's church. In the opening part of his sermon, Martin had used eagles to illustrate a point of faith.

"An eagle," Joe repeated. "Any special reason?"

"Y-yes," she said, not wanting to explain. "It's a long story, but I happen to be partial to eagles myself."

"Any other hints you'd care to pass on?"

"Buy wrapping paper in the after-Christmas sales. It's about half the price and it stores easily under the bed."

"Great idea. I'll have to remember that for next year."

Joe chose Northgate, the shopping mall closest to Cait's apartment. The parking lot was already beginning to fill up and it was only a few minutes after eight.

Joe managed to park fairly close to the entrance and came around to help Cait out of the truck. This time he didn't bother with the step stool, but clasped her around the waist to lift her down. "What did you mean when you said I was so predictable?" he asked, giving her a reproachful look.

With her hands resting on his shoulders and her feet dangling in midair, she felt vulnerable and small. "Nothing. It was just that I assumed you drove one of these Sherman-tank trucks, and I was right. I just hadn't seen it before."

"The kind of truck I drive bothers you?" His brow furrowed in a scowl.

"Not at all. What's the matter with you today, Joe? You're so touchy."

"I am not touchy," he snapped.

"Fine. Would you mind putting me down then?" His large hands were squeezing her waist almost painfully, though she doubted he was aware of it. She couldn't imagine what had angered him. Unless it was the fact that Paul had called her—which didn't make sense. Maybe, like most men, he just hated shopping.

He lowered her slowly to the asphalt and released her with seeming reluctance. "I need a coffee break," he announced grimly.

"But we just arrived."

Joe forcefully expelled his breath. "It doesn't matter. I need something to calm my nerves."

If he needed a caffeine fix so early in the day, Cait wondered how he'd manage during the next few hours. The stores quickly became crowded this time of year, especially on a Saturday. By ten it would be nearly impossible to get from one aisle to the next.

By twelve, she knew: Joe disliked Christmas shopping every bit as much as she'd expected.

"I've had it," Joe complained after making three separate trips back to the truck to deposit their spoils.

"Me, too," Cait agreed laughingly. "This place is turning into a madhouse."

"How about some lunch?" Joe suggested. "Someplace far away from here. Like Tibet."

Cait laughed again and tucked her arm in his. "That sounds like a great idea."

Outside, they noticed several cars circling the lot looking for a parking space and three of them rushed to fill the one Joe vacated. Two cars nearly collided in their eagerness. One man leapt out of his and shook an angry fist at the other driver.

"So much for peace and goodwill," Joe commented. "I swear Christmas brings out the worst in everyone."

"And the best," Cait reminded him.

"To be honest, I don't know what crammed shopping malls

and fighting the crowds and all this commercialism have to do with Christmas in the first place," he grumbled. A car cut in front of him, and Joe blared his horn.

"Quite a lot when you think about it," Cait said softly. "Imagine the streets of Bethlehem, the crowds and the noise . . ." The Christmas before, fresh from a shopping expedition, Cait had asked herself the same question. Christmas seemed so commercial. The crowds had been unbearable. First at Northgate, where she did most of her shopping and then at the airport. Sea-Tac had been filled with activity and noise, everyone in a hurry to get someplace else. There seemed to be little peace or good cheer and a whole lot of selfish concern and rudeness. Then, in the tranquility of church on Christmas Eve, everything had come into perspective for Cait. There had been crowds and rudeness that first Christmas, too, she reasoned. Yet in the midst of that confusion had come joy and peace and love. For most people, it was still the same. Christmas gifts and decorations and dinners were, after all, expressions of the love you felt for your family and friends. And if the preparations sometimes got a bit chaotic, well, that no longer bothered Cait.

"Where should we go to eat?" Joe asked, breaking into her thoughts. They were barely moving, stuck in heavy traffic.

She looked over at him and smiled serenely. "Any place will do. There're several excellent restaurants close by. You choose, only let it be my treat this time."

"We'll talk about who pays later. Right now, I'm more concerned with getting out of this traffic sometime within my life span."

Still smiling, Cait said, "I don't think it'll take much longer."

He returned her smile. "I don't, either." His eyes held hers for what seemed an eternity—until someone behind them honked irritably. Joe glanced up and saw that traffic ahead of them had started to move. He immediately stepped on the gas.

Cait didn't know what Joe had found so fascinating about her unless it was her unruly hair. She hadn't combed it since leaving the house; it was probably a mass of tight, disorderly curls. She'd been so concerned with finding the right gift for her nephews and niece that she hadn't given it a thought.

"What's wrong?" she asked, feeling self-conscious.

"What makes you think anything's wrong?"

"The way you were looking at me a few minutes ago."

"Oh, that," he said, easing into a restaurant parking lot. "I don't think I've ever fully appreciated how lovely you are," he answered in a calm, matter-of-fact voice.

Cait blushed and glanced away. "I'm sure you're mistaken. I'm really not all that pretty. I sometimes wondered if Paul would have noticed me sooner if I was a little more attractive."

"Trust me, Bright Eyes," he said, turning off the engine. "You're pretty enough."

"For what?"

"For this." And he leaned across the seat and captured her mouth with his.

Five

"I . . . wish you hadn't done that," Cait whispered, slowly opening her eyes in an effort to pull herself back to reality.

As far as kisses went, Joe's were good. Very good. He kissed better than just about anyone she'd ever kissed before—but that didn't alter the fact that she was in love with Paul.

"You're right," he muttered, opening the door and climbing out of the cab. "I shouldn't have done that." He walked around to her side and yanked the door open with more force than necessary.

Cait frowned, wondering at his strange mood. One minute he was holding her in his arms, kissing her tenderly; the next he was short-tempered and irritable.

"I'm hungry," he barked, lifting her abruptly down to the pavement. "I sometimes do irrational things when I haven't eaten."

"I see." The next time she went anywhere with Joseph Rockwell, she'd have to make sure he ate a good meal first.

The restaurant was crowded and Joe gave the hostess their names to add to the growing waiting list. Sitting on the last empty chair in the foyer, Cait set her large black leather purse on her lap and started rooting through it.

"What are you searching for? Uranium?" Joe teased, watching her.

"Crackers," she answered, shifting the bulky bag and handing him several items to hold while she continued digging.

"You're searching for crackers? Whatever for?"

She glanced up long enough to give him a look that questioned his intelligence. "For obvious reasons. If you're irrational when you're hungry, you might do something stupid while we're here. Frankly, I don't want you to embarrass me." She returned to the task with renewed vigor. "I can just see you standing on top of the table dancing."

"That's one way to get the waiter's attention. Thanks for suggesting it."

"Aha!" Triumphantly Cait pulled two miniature bread sticks wrapped in cellophane from the bottom of her purse. "Eat," she instructed. "Before you're overcome by some other craziness."

"You mean before I kiss you again," he said in a low voice, bending his head toward hers.

She leaned back quickly, not giving him any chance of following through on that. "Exactly. Or waltz with the waitress or any of the other loony things you do."

"You have to admit I've been good all morning."

"With one minor slip," she reminded him, pressing the bread sticks into his hand. "Now eat."

Before Joe had a chance to open the package, the hostess approached them with two menus tucked under her arm. "Mr. and Mrs. Rockwell. Your table is ready."

"Mr. and Mrs. Rockwell," Cait muttered under her breath, glaring at Joe. She should've known she couldn't trust him.

"Excuse me," Cait said, standing abruptly and raising her index finger. "His name is Rockwell, mine is Marshall," she explained patiently. She was not about to let Joe continue his silly games. "We're just friends here for lunch." Her narrowed eyes caught Joe's, which looked as innocent as freshly fallen snow. He shrugged as though to say any misunderstanding hadn't been *his* fault.

"I see," the hostess replied. "I'm sorry for the confusion."

"No problem." Cait hadn't wanted to make a big issue of this, but on the other hand she didn't want Joe to think he was going to get away with it, either.

The woman led them to a linen-covered table in the middle of the room. Joe held out Cait's chair for her, then whispered something to the hostess who immediately cast Cait a sympathetic glance. Joe's own gaze rested momentarily on Cait before he pulled out his chair and sat across from her.

"All right, what did you say to her?" she hissed.

The menu seemed to command his complete interest for a couple of minutes. "What makes you think I said anything?"

"I heard you whispering and then she gave me this pathetic look like she wanted to hug me and tell me everything was going to be all right."

"Then you know."

"Joe, don't play games with me," Cait warned.

"All right, if you must know, I explained that you'd suffered a head injury and developed amnesia."

"Amnesia," she repeated loudly enough to attract the attention of the diners at the next table. Gritting her teeth, Cait snatched up her menu, gripping it so tightly the edges curled. It didn't do any good to argue with Joe. The man was impossible. Every time she tried to reason with him, he did something to make her regret it.

"How else was I supposed to explain the fact that you'd forgotten our marriage?" he asked reasonably.

"I did not forget our marriage," she informed him from between clenched teeth, reviewing the menu and quickly making her selection. "Good grief, it wasn't even legal."

She realized that the waitress was standing by their table, pen and pad in hand. The woman's ready smile faded as she looked from Cait to Joe and back again. Her mouth tightened as if she suspected they really were involved in something illegal.

"Uh . . ." Cait hedged, feeling like even more of an idiot. The urge to explain was overwhelming, but every time she tried, she only made matters worse. "I'll have the club sandwich," she said, glaring across the table at Joe.

"That sounds good. I'll have the same," he said, closing his menu.

The woman scribbled down their order, then hurried away, pausing to glance over her shoulder as if she wanted to be able to identify them later in a police lineup.

"Now look what you've done," Cait whispered heatedly once the waitress was far enough away from their table not to overhear.

"Me?"

Maybe she was being unreasonable, but Joe was the one who'd started this nonsense in the first place. No one could rattle her as effectively as Joe did. And worse, she let him.

This shopping trip was a good example, and so was the pizza that led up to it. No woman in her right mind should've allowed Joe into her apartment after what he'd said to her in front of Lindy. Not only had she invited him inside her home, she'd agreed to let him accompany her Christmas shopping. She ought to have her head examined!

"What's wrong?" Joe asked, tearing open the package of bread sticks. Rather pointless in Cait's opinion, since their lunch would be served any minute.

"What's wrong?" she cried, dumbfounded that he had to ask. "You mean other than the hostess believing I've suffered a head injury and the waitress thinking we're drug dealers or something equally disgusting?"

"Here." He handed her one of the miniature bread sticks. "Eat this and you'll feel better."

Cait sincerely doubted that, but she took it, anyway, muttering under her breath.

"Relax," he urged.

"Relax," she mocked. "How can I possibly relax when you're doing and saying things I find excruciatingly embarrassing?"

"I'm sorry, Cait. Really, I am." To his credit, he did look contrite. "But you're so easy to fluster and I can't seem to stop myself."

Their sandwiches arrived, thick with slices of turkey, ham and a variety of cheeses. Cait was reluctant to admit how much better she felt after she'd eaten. Joe's spirits had apparently improved, as well.

"So," he said, his hands resting on his stomach. "What do you have planned for the rest of the afternoon?"

Cait hadn't given it much thought. "I suppose I should wrap the gifts I bought this morning." But that prospect didn't particularly excite her. Good grief, after the adventures she'd had with Joe, it wasn't any wonder.

"You mean you actually wrap gifts before Christmas Eve?" Joe asked. "Doesn't that take all the fun out of it? I mean, for me it's a game just to see if I can get the presents bought."

She grinned, trying to imagine herself in such a disorganized race to the deadline. Definitely not her style.

"How about a movie?" he suggested out of the blue. "I have the feeling you don't get out enough."

"A movie?" Cait ignored the comment about her social life, mainly because he was right. She rarely took the time to go to a show.

"We're both exhausted from fighting the crowds," Joe added. "There's a six-cinema theater next to the restaurant. I'll even let you choose."

"I suppose you'd object to a love story?"

"We can see one if you insist, only . . ."

"Only what?"

"Only promise me you won't ever expect a man to say the kinds of things those guys on the screen do."

"I beg your pardon?"

"You heard me. Women hear actors say this incredible drivel and then they're disappointed when real men don't."

"Real men like you, I suppose?"

"Right." He looked smug, then suddenly he frowned. "Does Paul like romances?"

Cait had no idea, since she'd never gone on a date with Paul and the subject wasn't one they'd ever discussed at the office. "I imagine he does," she said, dabbing her mouth with her napkin. "He isn't the type of man to be intimidated by such things."

Joe's deep blue eyes widened with surprise and a touch of respect. "Ouch. So Martin's little sister reveals her claws."

"I don't have claws. I just happen to have strong opinions on certain subjects." She reached for her purse while she was speaking and removed her wallet.

"What are you doing now?" Joe demanded.

"Paying for lunch." She sorted through the bills and withdrew a twenty. "It's my turn and I insist on paying . . ." She hesitated when she saw Joe's deepening frown. "Or don't real men allow women friends to buy their lunch?"

"Sure, go ahead," he returned flippantly.

It was all Cait could do to hide a smile. She guessed that her gesture in paying for their sandwiches would somehow be seen as compromising his male pride.

Apparently she was right. As they were walking toward the cashier, Joe stepped up his pace, grabbed the check from her hand and slapped some money on the counter. He glared at her as if he expected a drawn-out public argument. After the fuss they'd already caused in the restaurant, Cait was darned if she was going to let that happen.

"Joe," she argued the minute they were out the door. "What was *that* all about?"

"Fine, you win. Tell me my views are outdated, but when a woman goes out with me, I pick up the tab, no matter how liberated she is."

"But this isn't a real date. We're only friends, and even that's—"

"I don't give a damn. Consider it an apology for the embarrassment I caused you earlier."

"Isn't that kind of sexist?"

"No! I just have certain . . . standards."

"So I see." His attitude shouldn't have come as any big surprise. Just as Cait had told him earlier, he was shockingly predictable.

Hand at her elbow, Joe led the way across the car-filled lot toward the sprawling theater complex. The movies were geared toward a wide audience. There was a Disney classic, along with a horror flick and a couple of adventure movies and last but not least, a well-publicized love story.

As they stood in line, Cait caught Joe's gaze lingering on the poster for one of the adventure films—yet another story about a law-and-order cop with renegade ideas.

"I suppose you're more interested in seeing that than the romance."

"I already promised you could choose the show, and I'm a man of my word. If, however, you were to pick another movie—" he buried his hands in his pockets as he grinned at her appealingly "—I wouldn't complain."

"I'm willing to pick another movie, but on one condition."

"Name it." His eyes lit up.

"I pay."

"Those claws of yours are out again."

She raised her hands and flexed her fingers in a catlike motion. "It's your decision."

"What about popcorn?"

"You can buy that if you insist."

"All right," he said, "you've got yourself a deal."

When it was Cait's turn at the ticket window, she purchased two for the Disney classic.

"Disney?" Joe yelped, shocked when Cait handed him his ticket.

"It seemed like a good compromise," she answered.

For a moment it looked as if he was going to argue with her, then a slow grin spread across his face. "Disney," he said again. "You're right, it does sound like fun. Only I hope we're not the only people there over the age of ten."

They sat toward the back of the theater, sharing a large bucket of buttered popcorn. The theater was crowded and several kids seemed to be taking turns running up and down the aisles. Joe needn't have worried; there were plenty of adults in attendance, but of course most of them were accompanying children.

The lights dimmed and Cait reached for a handful of popcorn, relaxing in her seat. "I love this movie."

"How many times have you seen it?"

"Five or six. But it's been a few years."

"Me, too." Joe relaxed beside her, crossing his long legs and leaning back.

The credits started to roll, but the noise level hadn't decreased much. "Will the kids bother you?" Joe wanted to know.

"Heavens, no. I love kids."

"You do?" The fact that he was so surprised seemed vaguely insulting and Cait frowned.

"We've already had this discussion," she responded, licking the salt from her fingertips.

"We did? When?"

"The other day. You commented on how much I used to enjoy playing with my dolls and how you'd expected me to be married with a house full of children." His words had troubled her then, because "a house full of children" was exactly what Cait would have liked, and she seemed a long way from realizing her dream.

"Ah, yes, I remember our conversation about that now." He scooped up a large handful of popcorn. "You'd be a very good mother, you know."

That Joe would say this was enough to bring an unexpected rush of tears to her eyes. She blinked them back, annoyed that she'd get weepy over something so silly.

The previews were over and the audience settled down as the movie started. Cait focused her attention on the screen, munching popcorn every now and then, reaching blindly for the bucket. Their hands collided more than once and almost before she was aware of it, their fingers were entwined. It was a peaceful sort of feeling, being linked to Joe in this way. There was a *rightness* about it that she didn't want to explore just yet. He hadn't really changed; he was still lovable and funny and fun. For that matter, she hadn't changed very much, either . . . .

The movie was as good as Cait remembered, better, even—perhaps because Joe was there to share it with her. She half expected him to make the occasional wisecrack, but he seemed to respect the artistic value of the classic animation and, judging by his wholehearted laughter, he enjoyed the story.

When the show was over, he released Cait's hand. Hurriedly she gathered her purse and coat. As they walked out of the noisy, crowded theater, it seemed only natural to hold hands again.

Joe opened the truck, lifted down the step stool and helped her inside. Dusk came early these days, and bright, cheery lights were ablaze on every street. A vacant lot across the street was now filled with Christmas trees. A row of red lights was strung between two posts, sagging in the middle, and a portable CD player sent forth saccharine versions of better-known Christmas carols.

"Have you bought your tree yet?" Joe asked, nodding in the direction of the lot after he'd climbed into the driver's seat and started the engine.

"No. I don't usually put one up since I spend the holidays with Martin and his family."

"Ah."

"What about you? Or is that something else you save for Christmas Eve?" she joked. It warmed her a little to imagine Joe staying up past midnight to decorate a Christmas tree for his nieces and nephews.

"Finding time to do the shopping is bad enough," he said, not really answering her question.

"Your construction projects keep you that busy?" She hadn't given much thought to Joe's business. She knew from remarks Paul had made that Joe was very successful. It wasn't logical that she should feel pride in his accomplishments, but she did.

"Owning a business isn't like being in a nine-to-five job. I'm on call twenty-four hours a day, but I wouldn't have it any other way. I love what I do."

"I'm happy for you, Joe. I really am."

"Happy enough to decorate my Christmas tree with me?"

"When?"

"Next weekend."

"I'd like to," she told him, touched by the invitation, "but I'll have left for Minnesota by then."

"That's all right," Joe said, grinning at her. "Maybe next time."

She turned, frowning, to hide her blush.

They remained silent as he concentrated on easing the truck into the heavy late-afternoon traffic.

"I enjoyed the movie," she said some time later, resisting the urge to rest her head on his shoulder. The impulse to do that arose from her exhaustion, she told herself. Nothing else!

"So did I," he said softly. "Only next time, I'll be the one to pay. Understand?"

Next time. There it was again. She suspected Joe was beginning to take their relationship, such as it was, far too seriously. Already he was suggesting they'd be seeing each other soon, matter-of-factly discussing dates and plans as if they were longtime companions. Almost as if they were married . . .

She was mulling over this realization when Joe pulled into the parking area in front of her building. He climbed out and began to gather her packages, bundling them in his arms. She managed to scramble down by herself, not giving him a chance to help her, then she led the way into the building and unlocked her door.

Cait stood just inside the doorway and turned slightly to take a couple of the larger packages from Joe's arms.

"I had a great time," she told him briskly.

"Me, too." He nudged her, forcing her to enter the living room. He followed close behind and unloaded her remaining things onto the sofa. His presence seemed to reach out and fill every corner of the room.

Neither of them spoke for several minutes, but Cait sensed Joe wanted her to invite him to stay for coffee. The idea was tempting but dangerous. She mustn't let him think there might ever be anything romantic between them. Not when she was in love with Paul. For the first time in nearly a year, Paul was actually beginning to notice her. She refused to ruin everything now by becoming involved with Joe.

"Thank you for . . . today," she said, returning to the door, intending to open it for him. Instead, Joe caught her by the wrist and pulled her against him. She was in his arms before she could voice a protest.

"I'm going to kiss you," he told her, his voice rough yet strangely tender.

"You are?" She'd never been more aware of a man, of his hard, muscular body against hers, his clean, masculine scent. Her own body reacted in a chaotic scramble of mixed sensations. Above all, though, it felt *good* to be in his arms. She wasn't sure why and dared not examine the feeling.

Slowly, leisurely, he lowered his head. She made a soft weak sound as his mouth touched hers.

Cait sighed, forgetting for a moment that she meant to free herself before his kiss deepened. Before things went any further . . .

Joe must have sensed her resolve because his hands slid down her spine in a gentle caress, drawing her even closer. His mouth began a sensuous journey along her jaw, and down her throat—

"Joe!" She moaned his name, uncertain of what she wanted to say.

"Hmm?"

"Are you hungry again?" She wondered desperately if there were any more bread sticks in the bottom of her purse. Maybe that would convince him to stop.

"Very hungry," he told her, his voice low and solemn. "I've never been hungrier."

"But you had lunch and then you ate nearly all the popcorn."

He slowly raised his head. "Cait, are we talking about the same things here? Oh, hell, what does it matter? The only thing that matters is this." He covered her parted lips with his.

Cait felt her knees go weak and sagged against him, her fingers gripping his jacket as though she expected to collapse any moment. Which was becoming a distinct possibility as he continued to kiss her . . . .

"Joe, no more, please." But she was the one clinging to him. She had to do something, and fast, before her ability to reason was lost entirely.

He drew an unsteady breath and muttered something she couldn't decipher as his lips grazed the delicate line of her jaw.

"We . . . need to talk," she announced, keeping her eyes tightly closed. If she didn't look at Joe, then she could concentrate on what she had to do.

"All right," he agreed.

"I'll make a pot of coffee."

With a heavy sigh, Joe abruptly released her. Cait half fell against the sofa arm, requiring its support while she collected herself enough to walk into the kitchen. She unconsciously reached up and brushed her lips, as if she wasn't completely sure even now that he'd taken her in his arms and kissed her.

He hadn't been joking this time, or teasing. The kisses they'd shared were serious kisses. The type a man gives a woman he's strongly attracted to. A woman he's interested in developing a relationship with. Cait found herself shaking, unable to move.

"You want me to make that coffee?" he suggested.

She nodded and sank down on the couch. She could scarcely stand, let alone prepare a pot of coffee.

Joe returned a few minutes later, carrying two steaming mugs. Carefully he handed her one, then sat across from her on the blue velvet ottoman.

"You wanted to talk?"

Cait nodded. "Yes." Her throat felt thick, clogged with confused emotion, and forming coherent words suddenly seemed beyond her. She tried gesturing with her free hand, but that only served to frustrate Joe.

"Cait," he asked, "what's wrong?"

"Paul." The name came out in an eerie squeak.

"What about him?"

"He phoned me."

"Yes, I know. You already told me that."

"Don't you understand?" she cried, her throat unexpectedly clearing. "Paul is finally showing some interest in me and now you're kissing me and telling anyone who'll listen that the two of us are married and you're doing ridiculous things like . . ." She paused to draw in a deep breath. "Joe, oh, please, Joe, don't fall in love with me."

"Fall in love with you?" he echoed incredulously. "Caitlin, you can't be serious. It won't happen. No chance."

Six

"No chance?" Cait repeated, convinced she'd misunderstood him. She blinked a couple of times as if that would correct her hearing. Either Joe was underestimating her intelligence, or he was more of a . . . a cad than she'd realized.

"You have nothing to worry about." He sipped coffee, his gaze steady and emotionless. "I'm not falling in love with you."

"In other words you make a habit of kissing unsuspecting women."

"It isn't a habit," he answered thoughtfully. "It's more of a pastime."

"You certainly seem to be making a habit of it with me." Her anger was quickly gaining momentum and she was at odds to understand why she found his casual attitude so offensive. He was telling her exactly what she wanted to hear. But she hadn't expected her ego to take such a beating in the process. The fact that he wasn't the least bit tempted to fall in love with her should have pleased her.

It didn't.

It was as if their brief kisses were little more than a pleasant interlude for him. Something to occupy his time and keep him from growing bored with her company.

"This may come as a shock to you," Joe continued indifferently, "but a man doesn't have to be in love with a woman to kiss her."

"I know that," Cait snapped, fighting to hold back her temper, which was threatening to break free at any moment. "But you don't have to be so . . . so casual about it, either. If I wasn't involved with Paul, I might have taken you seriously."

"I didn't know you were involved with Paul," he returned with mild sarcasm. He leaned forward and rested his elbows on his knees, his pose infuriatingly relaxed. "If that was true I'd never have taken you out. The way I see it, the involvement is all on your part. Am I wrong?"

"No," she admitted reluctantly. How like a man to bring up semantics in the middle of an argument!

"So," he said, leaning back again and crossing his legs. "Are you enjoying my kisses? I take it I've improved from the first go-around."

"You honestly want me to rate you?" she sputtered.

"Obviously I'm much better than I was as a kid, otherwise you wouldn't be so worried." He took another drink of his coffee, smiling pleasantly all the while.

"Believe me, I'm not worried."

He arched his brows. "Really?"

"I'm sure you expect me to fall at your feet, overcome by your masculine charm. Well, if that's what you're waiting for, you'll have one hell of a long wait!"

His grin was slightly off center, as if he was picturing her arrayed at his feet—and enjoying the sight. "I think the problem here is that *you* might be falling in love with *me* and just don't know it."

"Falling in love with you and not know it?" she repeated with a loud disbelieving snort. "You've gone completely out of your mind. There's no chance of that."

"Why not? Plenty of women have told me I'm a handsome son of a gun. Plus, I'm said to possess a certain charm. Heaven knows, I'm generous enough and rather—"

"Who told you that? Your mother?" She made it sound like the most ludicrous thing she'd heard in years.

"You might be surprised to learn that I do have admirers."

Why this news should add fuel to the fire of her temper was beyond Cait, but she was so furious with him she could barely sit still. "I don't doubt it, but if I fall in love with a man you can believe it won't be just because he's 'a handsome son of a gun,'" she quoted sarcastically. "Look at Paul— he's the type of man I'm attracted to. What's on the inside matters more than outward appearances."

"Then why are you so worried about falling in love with me?"

"I'm not worried! You've got it the wrong way around. The only reason I mentioned anything was because I thought *you* were beginning to take our times together too seriously."

"I already explained that wasn't a problem."

"So I heard." Cait set her coffee aside. Joe was upsetting her so much that her hand was shaking hard enough to spill it.

"Well," Joe murmured, glancing at her. "You never did answer my question."

"Which one?" she asked irritably.

"About how I rated as a kisser."

"You weren't serious!"

"On the contrary." He set his own coffee down and raised himself off the ottoman far enough to clasp her by the waist and pull her into his lap.

Caught off balance, Cait fell onto his thighs, too astonished to struggle.

"Let's try it again," he whispered in a rough undertone.

"Ah . . ." A frightening excitement took hold of Cait. Her mind commanded her to leap away from this man, but some emotion, far stronger than common sense or prudence, urged the opposite.

Before she could form a protest, Joe bent toward her and covered her mouth with his. She'd hold herself stiff in his arms, that was what she'd do, teach him the lesson he deserved. How dared he assume she'd automatically fall in love with him. How dared he insinuate he was some . . . some Greek god all women adored. But the instant his lips met hers, Cait trembled with a mixture of shock and profound pleasure.

Everything within her longed to cry out at the unfairness of it all. It shouldn't be this good with Joe. They were friends, nothing more. This was the kind of response she expected when Paul kissed her. If he ever did.

She meant to pull away, but instead, Cait moaned softly. It felt so incredibly wonderful. So incredibly right. At that moment, there didn't seem to be anything to worry about—except the likelihood of dissolving in his arms then and there.

Suddenly Joe broke the contact. Her instinctive disappointment, even more than the unexpectedness of the action, sent her eyes flying open. Her own dark eyes met his blue ones, which now seemed almost aquamarine.

"So, how do I rate?" he murmured thickly, as though he was having trouble speaking.

"Good." A one-word reply was all she could manage, although she was furious with him for asking.

"Just good?"

She nodded forcefully.

"I thought we were better than that."

"We?"

"Naturally I'm only as good as my partner."

"Th-then how do you rate me?" She had to ask. Like a fool she handed him the ax and laid her neck on the chopping board. Joe was sure to use the opportunity to trample all over her ego, to turn the whole bewildering experience into a joke. She couldn't take that right now. She dropped her gaze, waiting for him to devastate her.

"Much improved."

She cocked one eyebrow in surprise. She had no idea what to say next.

They were both silent. Then he said softly, "You know, Cait, we're getting better at this. Much, much better." He pressed his forehead to hers. "If we're not careful, you just might fall in love with me, after all."

"Where were you all day Saturday?" Lindy asked early Monday morning, walking into Cait's office. The renovations to it had been completed late Friday and Cait had moved everything back into her office first thing this morning. "I must have tried calling you ten times."

"I told you I was going Christmas shopping. In fact, I bought some decorations for my office."

Lindy nodded. "But all day?" Her eyes narrowed suspiciously as she set down her briefcase and leaned against Cait's desk, crossing her arms. "You didn't happen to be with Joe Rockwell, did you?"

Cait could feel a telltale shade of pink creeping up her neck. She lowered her gaze to the list of current Dow Jones stock prices and took a moment to compose herself. She couldn't admit the truth. "I told you I was shopping," she said somewhat defensively. Then, in an effort to change the topic, she reached for a thick folder with Paul's name inked across the top and muttered, "You wouldn't happen to know Paul's schedule for the day, would you?"

"N-no, I haven't seen him yet. Why do you ask?"

Cait flashed her friend a bright smile. "He phoned me Friday night. Oh, Lindy, I was so excited I nearly fell all over myself." She dropped her voice as she glanced around to make sure none of the others could hear her. "I honestly think he intends to ask me out."

"Did he say so?"

"Not exactly." Cait frowned. Lindy wasn't revealing any of the enthusiasm she expected.

"Then why did he phone?"

Cait rolled her chair away from the desk and glanced around once again. "I think he might be jealous," she whispered.

"Really?" Lindy's eyes widened.

"Don't look so surprised." Cait, however, was much too excited recounting Paul's phone call to be offended by Lindy's attitude.

"What makes you think Paul would be jealous?" Lindy asked next.

"Maybe I'm magnifying everything in my own mind because it's what I so badly want to believe. But he did phone . . ."

"What did he say?" Lindy pressed, sounding more curious now. "It seems to me he must have had a reason."

"Oh, he did. He mentioned something about appreciating an article I'd given him, but we both know that was just an excuse. What clued me in to his jealousy was the way he kept asking if I was alone."

"But that could've been for several different reasons, don't you think?" Lindy suggested.

"Yes, but it made sense that he'd want to know if Joe was at the apartment or not."

"And was he?"

"Of course not," Cait said righteously. She didn't feel guilty about hiding the fact that he'd been there earlier, or that they'd spent nearly all of Saturday together. "I'm sure Joe's ridiculous remark when I left the office on Friday is what convinced Paul to phone me. If I wasn't so furious with Joe, I might even be grateful."

"What's that?" Lindy asked abruptly, pointing to the folder in front of Cait. Her lips had thinned slightly as if she was confused or annoyed—about what, Cait couldn't figure out.

"This, my friend," she began, holding up the folder, "is the key to my future with our dedicated manager."

Lindy didn't immediately respond and looked more puzzled than before. "How do you mean?"

Cait couldn't get over the feeling that things weren't quite right with her best friend; she seemed to be holding something back. But Cait realized Lindy would tell her when she was ready. Lindy always hated being pushed or prodded.

"The folder?" Lindy prompted when Cait didn't answer.

Cait flipped it open. "I spent all day Sunday reading through old business journals looking for articles that might interest Paul. I must've gone back five years. I copied the articles I consider the most valuable and included a brief analysis of my own. I was hoping to give it to him sometime today. That's why I was asking if you knew his schedule."

"Unfortunately I don't," Lindy murmured. She straightened, picked up her briefcase and made a show of checking her watch. Then she looked up to smile reassuringly at Cait. "I'd better get to work. I'll come by later to help you put up your decorations, okay?"

"Thanks," Cait said, then added, "Wish me luck with Paul."

"You know I do," Lindy mumbled on her way out the door.

Mondays were generally slow for the stock market—unless there was a crisis. World events and financial reports had a significant impact on the market. However, as the day progressed, everything ran smoothly.

Cait looked up every now and then, half expecting to see Joe lounging in her doorway. His men had started early that morning, but by noon, Joe still hadn't arrived.

Not until much later did she realize it was Paul she should be anticipating, not Joe. Paul was the romantic interest of her life and it annoyed her that Joe seemed to occupy her thoughts.

As it happened, Paul did stroll past her office shortly after the New York market closed. Grabbing the folder, Cait raced toward his office, not hesitating for an instant. This was her golden opportunity and she was taking hold of it with both hands.

"Good afternoon, Paul," she said cordially as she stood in his doorway, clutching the folder. "Do you have a moment or would you rather I came back later?"

He looked tired, as if the day had already been a grueling one. It was all Cait could do not to offer to massage away the stress and worry that complicated his life. Her heart swelled with a renewed wave of love. For a wild, impetuous moment, it was true, she'd suffered her doubts. Any woman would have when a man like Joe took her in his arms. He might be arrogant in the extreme and one of the worst pranksters she'd ever met; despite all that, he had a certain charm. But now that she was with Paul, Cait remembered sharply who it was she really loved.

"I don't want to be a bother," she told him softly.

He give her a listless smile. "Come in, Cait. Now is fine." He gestured toward a chair.

She hurried into the office, trying to keep the bounce out of her step. Knowing she'd be spending a few extra minutes alone with Paul, Cait had taken special care with her appearance that morning.

He glanced up and smiled at her again, but this time Cait thought she could see a glimmer of appreciation in his eyes.

"What can I do for you? I hope you're pleased with your office." He frowned slightly.

For a second, she forgot what she was doing in Paul's office and stared at him blankly until his own gaze fell to the folder. "The office looks great," she said quickly. "Um, the reason I'm here . . ." She faltered, then gulped in a quick breath and continued, "I went through some of the business journals I have at home and found several articles I felt would interest you." She extended the folder to him, like a ceremonial offering.

He took it from her and opened it gingerly. "Gracious," he said, flipping through the pages and scanning her written comments, "you must've spent hours on this."

"It was . . . nothing." She'd willingly have done a good deal more to gain his appreciation and eventually his love.

"I won't have a chance to look at this for a few days," he said.

"Oh, please, there's no rush. You happened to mention you got some useful insights from the previous article I gave you. So I thought I'd share a few others that seem relevant to what's going on with the market now."

"It's very thoughtful of you."

"I was happy to do it. More than happy," she amended with her most brilliant smile. When he didn't say anything more, Cait rose reluctantly to her feet. "You must be swamped after being in meetings for most of the day, so I'll leave you now."

She was almost at the door when he spoke. "Actually I only dropped in to the office to collect a few things before heading out again. I've got an important date this evening."

Cait felt as if the floor had suddenly disappeared and she was plummeting through empty space. "Date?" she repeated before she could stop herself. It was a struggle to keep smiling.

Paul's grin was downright boyish. "Yes, I'm meeting her for dinner."

"In that case, have a good time."

"Thanks, I will," he returned confidently, his eyes alight with excitement. "Oh, and by the way," he added, indicating the folder she'd worked so hard on, "thanks for all the effort you put into this."

"You're . . . welcome."

By the time Cait got back to her office she felt numb. Paul had an important date. It wasn't as though she'd expected him to live the life of a hermit, but before today, he'd never mentioned going out with anyone. She might have suspected he'd thrown out the information hoping to make her jealous if it hadn't been for one thing. He seemed genuinely thrilled about this date. Besides, Paul wasn't the kind of man to resort to pretense.

"Cait, my goodness," Lindy said, strolling into her office a while later, "what's wrong? You look dreadful."

Cait tried to swallow the lump in her throat and managed a shaky smile. "I talked to Paul and gave him the research I'd done."

"He didn't appreciate it?" Lindy picked up the Christmas wreath that lay on Cait's desk and pinned it to the door.

"I'm sure he did," she replied. "What he doesn't appreciate is me. I might as well be invisible to that man." She pushed the hair away from her forehead and braced both elbows on her desk, feeling totally disheartened. Unless she acted quickly, she was going to lose Paul to some faceless, nameless woman.

"You've been invisible to him before. What's different about this time?" Lindy fastened a silver bell to the window as Cait abstractedly fingered her three ceramic wise men.

"Paul's got a date, and from the way he talked about it, this isn't with just any woman, either. Whoever she is must be important, otherwise he wouldn't have said anything. He looked like a little kid who's been given the keys to a candy store."

The information seemed to surprise Lindy as much as it had

Cait. She was quiet for a few minutes before she asked, "What are you going to do about it?"

"I don't know," Cait cried, hiding her face in her hands. She'd once jokingly suggested to Joe that she parade around naked in an effort to gain Paul's attention. Of course she'd been exaggerating, but some form of drastic action was obviously needed. If only she knew what.

Lindy mumbled an excuse and left. It wasn't until Cait looked up that she realized her friend was gone. She sighed wearily. She'd arrived at work this morning with such bright expectations, and now everything had gone wrong. She felt more depressed than she'd been in a long time. She knew the best remedy would be to force herself into some physical activity. Anything. The worst possible thing she could do was sit home alone and mope. Maybe she should plan to buy herself a Christmas tree and some ornaments. Her spirits couldn't help being at least a little improved by that; it would get her out of the house, if nothing else. And then she'd have something to entertain herself with, instead of brooding about this unexpected turn of events. Getting out of the house had an added advantage. If Joe phoned, she wouldn't be there to answer.

No sooner had that thought passed through her mind when a large form filled her doorway.

Joe.

A bright orange hard hat was pushed back on his head, the way movie cowboys wore their Stetsons. His boots were dusty and his tool pouch rode low on his hip, completing the gunslinger image. Even the way he stood with his thumbs tucked in his belt suggested he was waiting for a showdown.

"Hi, beautiful," he drawled, giving her that lazy, intimate smile of his. The one designed, Cait swore, just to unnerve her. But it wasn't going to work, not in her present state of mind.

"Don't you have anyone else to pester?" she asked coldly.

"My, my," Joe said, shaking his head in mock chagrin. Disregarding her lack of welcome, he strode into the office and threw himself down in the chair beside her desk. "You're in a rare mood."

"You would be too after the day I've had. Listen, Joe. As you can see, I'm poor company. Go flirt with the receptionist if you're trying to make someone miserable."

"Those claws are certainly sharp this afternoon." He ran his hands down the front of his shirt, pretending to inspect the damage she'd inflicted. "What's wrong?" Some of the teasing light faded from his eyes as he studied her.

She sent him a look meant to blister his ego, but as always Joe seemed invincible against her practiced glares.

"How do you know I'm not here to invest fifty thousand dollars?" he demanded, making himself at home by reaching across her desk for a pen. He rolled it casually between his palms.

Cait wasn't about to fall for this little game. "Are you here to invest money?"

"Not exactly. I wanted to ask you to—"

"Then come back when you are." She grabbed a stack of papers and slapped them down on her desk. But being rude, even to Joe, went against her nature. She was battling tears and the growing need to explain her behavior, apologize for it, when he rose to his feet. He tossed the pen carelessly onto her desk.

"Have it your way. If asking you to join me to look for a Christmas tree is such a terrible crime, then—"

"You're going to buy a Christmas tree?"

"That's what I just said." He flung the words over his shoulder as he strode out the door.

In that moment, Cait felt as though the whole world was tumbling down around her shoulders. She felt like such a shrew. He'd come here wanting to include her in his Christmas preparations and she'd driven him away with a spiteful tongue and a haughty attitude.

Cait wasn't a woman easily given to tears, but she struggled with them now. Her lower lip started to quiver. She might have been eight years old all over again—this was like the day she'd found out she wasn't invited to Betsy McDonald's birthday party. Only now it was Paul doing the excluding. He and this important woman of his were going out to have the time of their lives while she stayed home in her lonely apartment, suffering from a serious case of self-pity.

Gathering up her things, Cait thrust the papers into her briefcase with uncharacteristic negligence. She put on her coat, buttoned it quickly and wrapped the scarf around her neck as though it were a hangman's noose.

Joe was talking to his foreman, who'd been unobtrusively working around the office all day. He hesitated when he saw her, halting the conversation. Cait's eyes briefly met his and although she tried to disguise how regretful she felt, she obviously did a poor job of it. He took a step toward her, but she raised her chin a notch, too proud to admit her feelings.

She had to walk directly past Joe on her way to the elevator and forced herself to look anywhere but at him.

The stocky foreman clearly wanted to resume the discussion, but Joe ignored him and stared at Cait instead, with narrowed, assessing eyes. She could feel his questioning concern as profoundly as if he'd touched her. When she could bear it no longer, she turned to face him, her lower lip quivering uncontrollably.

"Cait," he called out.

She raced for the elevator, fearing she'd burst into tears before she could make her grand exit. She didn't bother to respond, knowing that if she said anything she'd make a greater fool of herself than usual. She wasn't even sure what had prompted her to say the atrocious things to Joe that she had. He wasn't the one who'd upset her, yet she'd unfairly taken her frustrations out on him.

She should've known it would be impossible to make a clean getaway. She almost ran through the office, past the reception desk, toward the elevator.

"Aren't you going to answer me?" Joe demanded, following on her heels.

"No." She concentrated on the lighted numbers above the elevator, which moved with painstaking slowness. Three more floors and she could make her escape.

"What's so insulting about inviting you to go Christmas-tree shopping?" he asked.

Close to weeping, she waved her free hand, hoping he'd understand that she was incapable of explaining just then. Her throat was clogged and it hurt to breathe, let alone talk. Her eyes filled with tears, and everything started to blur.

"Tell me," he commanded a second time.

Cait gulped at the tightness in her throat. "Y-you wouldn't understand." Why, oh, why, wouldn't that elevator hurry?

"Try me."

It was either give in and explain, or stand there and argue. The first choice was easier; frankly, Cait didn't have the energy to fight with him. Sighing deeply, she began, "It—it all started when I made up this folder of business articles for Paul . . ."

"I might've known Paul had something to do with this," Joe muttered under his breath.

"I spent hours putting it together, adding little comments, and . . . and . . . I don't know what I expected but it wasn't . . ."

"What happened? What did Paul do?"

Cait rubbed her eyes with the back of her hand. "If you're going to interrupt me, then I can't see any reason to explain."

"Boss?" the foreman called out, sounding impatient.

Just then the elevator arrived and the doors opened, revealing half a dozen men and women. They stared out at Cait and Joe as he blocked the entrance, gripping her by the elbow.

"Joseph," she hissed, "let me go!" Recognizing her advantage, she called out, "This man refuses to release my arm." If she expected a knight in shining armor to leap to her rescue, Cait was to be sorely disappointed. It was as if no one had heard her.

"Don't worry, folks, we're married." Joe charmed them with another of his lazy, lopsided grins.

"Boss?" the foreman pleaded again.

"Take the rest of the day off," Joe shouted. "Tell the crew to go out and buy Christmas gifts for their wives."

"You want me to do *what*?" the foreman shouted back. Joe moved into the elevator with Cait.

"You heard me."

"Let me make sure I understand you. You want the men to go Christmas shopping for their wives? I thought you just said we're on a tight schedule?"

"That's right," Joe said loudly as the elevator doors closed.

Cait had never felt more conspicuous in her life. Every eye was focused on her and Joe, and it was all she could do to keep her head high.

When the tension became intolerable, Cait turned to face her fellow passengers. "We are not married," she announced.

"Yes, we are," Joe insisted. "She's simply forgotten."

"I did not forget our marriage and don't you dare tell them that cock-and-bull story about amnesia."

"But, darling—"

"Stop it right now, Joseph Rockwell! No one believes you. I'm sure these people can figure out that I'm the one who's telling the truth."

The elevator finally stopped on the ground floor, a fact for which Cait was deeply grateful. The doors glided open and two women stepped out first, but not before pausing to get a good appreciative look at Joe.

"Does she do this often?" one of the men asked, directing his question to Joe, his amusement obvious.

"Unfortunately, yes," he answered, chuckling as he tucked his hand under Cait's elbow and led her into the foyer. She tried to jerk her arm away, but he wouldn't allow it. "You see, I married a forgetful bride."

Seven

Pacing the carpet in the living room, Cait nervously smoothed the front of her red satin dress, her heart pumping furiously while she waited for Joe to arrive. She'd spent hours preparing for this Christmas party, which was being held in Paul's home. Her stomach was in knots.

She, the mysterious woman Paul was dating, would surely be there. Cait would have her first opportunity to size up the competition. Cait had studied her reflection countless times, trying to be objective about her chances with Paul based on looks alone. The dress was gorgeous. Her hair flawless. Everything else was as perfect as she could make it.

The doorbell sounded and Cait hurried across the room, throwing open the door. "You know what you are, Joseph Rockwell?"

"Late?" he suggested.

Cait pretended not to hear him. "A bully," she said. "A badgering bully, no less. I'm sorry I ever agreed to let you take me to Paul's party. I don't know what I was thinking."

"You were probably hoping to corner me under the mistletoe," he remarked with a wink that implied he wouldn't be difficult to persuade.

"First you practically kidnap me into going Christmas-tree shopping with you," she raged. "Then—"

"Come on, Cait, admit it, you had fun." He lounged indolently on her sofa while she got her coat and purse.

She hesitated, her mouth twitching with a smile. "Who'd ever believe that a man who bought his mother a rib roast and a case of cat food for Christmas last year would be so particular about a silly tree?" Joe had dragged her to no fewer than four lots yesterday, searching for the perfect tree.

"I took you to dinner afterward, didn't I?" he reminded her.

Cait nodded. She had to admit it: Joe had gone out of his way to help her forget her troubles. Although she'd made the tree-shopping expedition sound like a chore, he'd turned the evening into an enjoyable and, yes, memorable one.

His good mood had been infectious and after a while she'd completely forgotten Paul was out with another woman—someone so special that his enthusiasm about her had overcome his normal restraint.

"I've changed my mind," Cait decided suddenly, clasping her hands over her stomach, which was in turmoil. "I don't want to go to this Christmas party, after all." The evening was already doomed. She couldn't possibly have a good time watching the man she loved entertain the woman *he* loved. Cait couldn't think of a single reason to expose herself to that kind of misery.

"Not go to the party?" Joe repeated. "But I thought you'd arranged your flight schedule just so you could."

"I did, but that was before." Cait stubbornly squared her shoulders and elevated her chin just enough to convince Joe she meant business. He might be able to bully her into going shopping with him for a Christmas tree, but this was entirely different. "*She'll* be there," Cait added as an explanation.

"She?" Joe repeated slowly, burying his hands in his suit pockets. He was exceptionally handsome in his dark blue suit and no doubt knew it. He was as comfortable in tailored slacks as he was in dirty jeans.

A lock of thick hair slanted across his forehead; Cait managed—it was an effort—to resist brushing it back. An effort not because it disrupted his polished appearance, but because she had the strangest desire to run her fingers through his hair. Why she'd think such a thing now was beyond her. She'd long since stopped trying to figure out her feelings for Joe. He was a friend and a confidant even if, at odd moments, he behaved like a lunatic. Just remembering some of the comments he'd made to embarrass her brought color to her cheeks.

"I'd imagine you'd want to meet her," Joe challenged. "That way you can size her up."

"I don't even want to know what she looks like," Cait countered sharply. She didn't need to. Cait already knew everything she cared to about Paul's hot date. "She's beautiful."

"So are you."

Cait gave a short, derisive laugh. She wasn't discounting her own homespun appeal. She was reasonably attractive, and never more so than this evening. Catching a glimpse of herself in the mirror, she was pleased to see how nice her hair looked, with the froth of curls circling her head. But she wasn't going to kid herself, either. Her allure wasn't extraordinary by any stretch of the imagination. Her eyes were a warm shade of brown, though, and her nose was kind of cute. Perky, Lindy had once called it. But none of that mattered. Measuring herself against Paul's sure-to-be-gorgeous, nameless date was like comparing bulky sweat socks with a silk stocking. She'd already spent hours picturing her as a classic beauty . . . tall . . . sophisticated.

"I've never taken you for a coward," Joe said in a flat tone as he headed toward the door.

Apparently he wasn't even going to argue with her. Cait almost wished he would, just so she could show him how strong her will was. Nothing he could say or do would convince her to attend this party. Besides, her feet hurt. She was wearing new heels and hadn't broken them in yet, and if she did go, she'd be limping for days afterward.

"I'm not a coward," she told him, schooling her face to remain as emotionless as possible. "All I'm doing is exercising a little common sense. Why depress myself over the holidays? This is the last time I'll see Paul before Christmas. I leave for Minnesota in the morning."

"Yes, I know." Joe frowned as he said it, hesitating before he opened her door. "You're sure about this?"

"Positive." She was mildly surprised Joe wasn't making more of a fuss. From past experience, she'd expected a full-scale verbal battle.

"The choice is yours of course," he granted, shrugging. "But if it was me, I know I'd spend the whole evening regretting it." He studied her when he'd finished, then gave her a smile Cait could only describe as crafty.

She groaned inwardly. If there was one thing that drove her crazy about Joe it was the way he made the most outrageous statements. Then every once in a while he'd say something so wise it caused her to doubt her own conclusions and beliefs. This was one of those times. He was right: if she didn't go to Paul's, she'd regret it. Since she was leaving for Minnesota the following day, she wouldn't be able to ask anyone about the party, either.

"Are you coming or not?" he demanded.

Grumbling under her breath, Cait let him help her on with her coat. "I'm coming, but I don't like it. Not one darn bit."

"You're going to do just fine."

"They probably said that to Joan of Arc, too."

Cait clutched the punch glass in both hands, as though terrified someone might try to take it back. Standing next to the fireplace, with its garlanded mantel and cheerful blaze, she hadn't moved since they'd arrived a half hour earlier.

"Is *she* here yet?" she whispered to Lindy when her friend walked past carrying a tray of canapés.

"Who?"

"Paul's woman friend," Cait said pointedly. Both Joe and Lindy were beginning to exasperate her. "I've been standing here for the past thirty minutes hoping to catch a glimpse of her."

Lindy looked away. "I . . . I don't know if she's here or not."

"Stay with me, for heaven's sake," Cait requested, feeling shaky inside and out. Joe had deserted her almost as soon as they got there. Oh, he'd stuck around long enough to bring her a cup of punch, but then he'd drifted away, leaving Cait to deal with the situation on her own. This was the very man who'd insisted she attend this Christmas party, claiming he'd be right by her side the entire evening in case she needed him.

"I'm helping Paul with the hors d'oeuvres," Lindy explained, "otherwise I'd be happy to stay and chat."

"See if you can find Joe for me, would you?" She'd do it herself, but her feet were killing her.

"Sure."

Once Lindy was gone, Cait scanned the crowded living room. Many of the guests were business associates and clients Paul had worked with over the years. Naturally everyone from the office was there, as well.

"You wanted to see me?" Joe asked, reaching her side.

"Thank you very much," she muttered, doing her best to sound sarcastic and keep a smile on her face at the same time.

"You're welcome." He leaned one elbow on the fireplace mantel and grinned at her boyishly. "Might I ask what you're thanking me for?"

"Don't play games with me, Joe. Not now, please." She shifted her weight from one foot to the other, drawing his attention to her shoes.

"Your feet hurt?" he asked, frowning.

"Walking across hot coals would be less painful than these stupid high heels."

"Then why did you wear them?"

"Because they go with the dress. Listen, would you mind very much if we got off the subject of my shoes and discussed the matter at hand?"

"Which is?"

Joe was being as obtuse as Lindy had been. She assumed he was doing it deliberately, just to get a rise out of her. Well, it was working.

"Did you see her?" she asked with exaggerated patience.

"Not yet," he whispered back as though they were exchanging top-secret information. "She doesn't seem to have arrived."

"Have you talked to Paul?"

"No. Have you?"

"Not really." Paul had greeted them at the door, but other than that, Cait hadn't had a chance to do anything but watch him mingle with his guests. The day at the office hadn't been any help, either. Paul had breezed in and out without giving Cait more than a friendly wave. Since they hadn't exchanged a single word, it was impossible for her to determine how his date had gone.

It must have been a busy day for Lindy, as well, because Cait hadn't had a chance to talk to her, either. They'd met on their way out the door late that afternoon and Lindy had hurried past, saying she'd see Cait at Paul's party.

"I think I'll go help Lindy with the hors d'oeuvres," Cait said now. "Do you want me to get you anything?"

"Nothing, thanks." He was grinning as he strolled away, leaving Cait to wonder what he found so amusing.

Cait limped into the kitchen, leaving the polished wooden door swinging in her wake. She stopped abruptly when she encountered Paul and Lindy in the middle of a heated discussion.

"Oh, sorry," Cait apologized automatically.

Paul's gaze darted to Cait's. "No problem," he said quickly. "I was just leaving." He stalked past her, shoving the door open with the palm of his hand. Once again the door swung back and forth.

"What was that all about?" Cait wanted to know.

Lindy continued transferring the small cheese-dotted crackers from the cookie sheet onto the serving platter. "Nothing."

"It sounded as if you and Paul were arguing."

Lindy straightened and bit her lip. She avoided looking at Cait, concentrating on her task as if it was of vital importance to properly arrange the crackers on the plate.

"You were arguing, weren't you?" Cait pressed.

"Yes."

As far as she knew, Lindy and Paul had always gotten along. The fact that they were at odds surprised her. "About what?"

"I—I gave Paul my two-week notice this afternoon."

Cait was so shocked, she pulled out a kitchen chair and sank down on it. "You did *what*?" Removing her high heels, she massaged her pinched toes.

"You heard me."

"But why? Good grief, Lindy, you never said a word to anyone. Not even me. The least you could've done was talk to me about it first." No wonder Paul was angry. If Lindy left, it would mean bringing in someone new when the office was already short-staffed. With Cait and a number of other people away for the holidays, the place would be a madhouse.

"Did you receive an offer you couldn't refuse?" Cait hadn't had any idea her friend was unhappy at Webster, Rodale and Missen. Still, that didn't shock her nearly as much as Lindy's remaining tight-lipped about it all.

"It wasn't exactly an offer—but it was something like that," Lindy replied vaguely. She set aside the cookie sheet, smiled at Cait and then carried the platter into the living room.

For the past couple of weeks Cait had noticed that something was troubling her friend. It hadn't been anything she could readily name. Just that Lindy hadn't been her usual high-spirited self. Cait had meant to ask her about it, but she'd been so busy herself, so involved with her own problems, that she'd never brought it up.

She was still sitting there rubbing her feet when Joe sauntered into the kitchen, nibbling on a cheese cracker. "I thought I'd find you in here." He pulled out the chair across from her and sat down.

"Has she arrived yet?"

"Apparently so."

Cait dropped her foot and frantically worked the shoe back and forth until she'd managed to squeeze her toes inside. Then she forced her other foot into its shoe. "Well, for heaven's sake, why didn't you say something sooner?" she chastised. She stood up, ran her hands down the satin skirt and drew a shaky breath. "How do I look?"

"Like your feet hurt."

She sent him a scalding frown. "Thank you very much," she said sarcastically for the second time in under ten minutes. Hobbling to the door, she opened it a crack and peeked out, hoping to catch sight of the mystery woman. From what she could see, there weren't any new arrivals.

"What does she look like?" Cait demanded and whirled around to discover Joe standing directly behind her. She nearly collided with him and gave a small cry of surprise. Joe caught her by the shoulders to keep her from stumbling. Eager to question him about Paul's date, she didn't take the time to analyze why her heartrate soared when his hands made contact with her bare skin.

"What does she look like?" Cait asked again.

"I don't know," Joe returned flippantly.

"What do you mean you don't know? You just said she'd arrived."

"Unfortunately she doesn't have a tattoo across her forehead announcing that she's the woman Paul's dating."

"Then how do you know she's here?" If Joe was playing games with her, she'd make damn sure he'd regret it. Her love for Paul was no joking matter.

"It's more a feeling I have."

"You had me stuff my feet back into these shoes for a stupid feeling?" It was all she could do not to slap him silly. "You are no friend of mine, Joseph Rockwell. No friend whatsoever." Having said that, she limped back into the living room.

Obviously unscathed by her remark, Joe wandered out of the kitchen behind her. He walked over to the tray of canapés and helped himself to three or four while Cait did her best to ignore him.

Since the punch bowl was close by, she poured herself a second glass. The taste was sweet and cold, but Cait noticed that she felt a bit light-headed afterward. Potent drinks didn't sit well on an empty stomach, so she scooped up a handful of mixed nuts.

"I remember a time when you used to line up all the Spanish peanuts and eat those first," Joe said from behind her. "Then it was the hazelnuts, followed by the—"

"Almonds." Leave it to him to bring up her foolish past. "I haven't done that since I was—"

"Twenty," he guessed.

"Twenty-five," she corrected.

Joe laughed, and despite her aching feet and the certainty that she should never have come to this party, Cait laughed, too.

Refilling her punch glass, she downed it all in a single drink. Once more, it tasted cool and refreshing.

"Cait," Joe warned, "how much punch have you had?"

"Not enough." She filled the crystal cup a third time—or was it the fourth?—squared her shoulders and gulped it down. When she'd finished, she wiped the back of her hand across her mouth and smiled bravely.

"Are you purposely trying to get drunk?" he demanded.

"No." She reached for another handful of nuts. "All I'm looking for is a little courage."

"Courage?"

"Yes," she said with a sigh. "The way I figure it . . ." She paused, smiling giddily, then whirled around in a full circle. "There *is* some mistletoe here, isn't there?"

"I think so," Joe said, frowning. "What makes you ask?"

"I'm going to kiss Paul," she said proudly. "All I have to do is wait until he walks past. Then I'll grab him by the hand, wish him a merry Christmas and give him a kiss he won't soon forget." If the fantasy fulfilled itself, Paul would immediately realize he'd met the woman of his dreams, and propose marriage on the spot . . . .

"What is kissing Paul supposed to prove?"

She returned to reality. "Well, this is where you come in. I want you to look around and watch the faces of the other women. If one of them shows signs of jealousy, then we'll know who it is."

"I'm not sure this plan of yours is going to work."

"It's better than trusting those feelings of yours," she countered.

She saw the mistletoe hanging from the archway between the formal dining room and the living room. Slouched against the wall, hands tucked behind her back, Cait waited patiently for Paul to stroll past.

Ten minutes passed or maybe it was fifteen—Cait couldn't tell. Yawning, she covered her mouth. "I think we should leave," Joe suggested as he casually walked by. "You're ready to fall asleep on your feet."

"I haven't kissed Paul yet," she reminded him.

"He seems to be involved in a lengthy discussion. This could take a while."

"I'm in no hurry." Her throat felt unusually dry. She would have preferred something nonalcoholic, but the only drink nearby was the punch.

"Cait," Joe warned when he saw her helping herself to yet another glass.

"Don't worry, I know what I'm doing."

"So did the captain of the *Titanic*."

"Don't get cute with me, Joseph Rockwell. I'm in no mood to deal with someone amusing." Finding herself hilariously funny, she smothered a round of giggles.

"Oh, no," Joe groaned. "I was afraid of this."

"Afraid of what?"

"You're drunk!"

She gave him a sour look. "That's ridiculous. All I had is four little, bitty glasses of punch." To prove she knew exactly what she was doing, she held up three fingers, recognized her mistake and promptly corrected herself. At least she tried to do it promptly, but figuring out how many fingers equaled four seemed to take an inordinate amount of time. She finally held up two from each hand.

Expelling her breath, she leaned back against the wall and closed her eyes. That was her second mistake. The world took a sharp and unexpected nosedive. Snapping open her eyes, Cait looked to Joe as the anchor that would keep her afloat. He must have read the panic in her expression because he moved toward her and slowly shook his head.

"That does it, Ms. Singapore Sling. I'm getting you out of here."

"But I haven't been under the mistletoe yet."

"If you want anyone to kiss you, it'll be me."

The offer sounded tempting, but it was her stubborn boss Cait wanted to kiss, not Joe. "I'd rather dance with you."

"Unfortunately there isn't any music at the moment."

"You need music to dance?" It sounded like the saddest thing she'd ever heard, and her bottom lip began to tremble at the tragedy of it all. "Oh, dear, Joe," she whispered, clasping both hands to the sides of her head. "I think you might be right. The punch seems to be affecting me . . . ."

"It's that bad, is it?"

"Uh, yes . . . The whole room's just started to pitch and heave. We're not having an earthquake, are we?"

"No." His hand was on her forearm, guiding her toward the front door.

"Wait," she said dramatically, raising her index finger. "I have a coat."

"I know. Stay here and I'll get it for you." He seemed worried about leaving her. Cait smiled at him, trying to reassure him she'd be perfectly fine, but she seemed unable to keep her balance. He urged her against the wall, stepped back a couple of paces as though he expected her to slip sideways, then hurriedly located her coat.

"What's wrong?" he asked when he returned.

"What makes you think anything's wrong?"

"Other than the fact that you're crying?"

"My feet hurt."

Joe rolled his eyes. "Why did you wear those stupid shoes in the first place?"

"I already told you," she whimpered. "Don't be mad at me." She held out her arms to him, needing his comfort. "Would you carry me to the car?"

Joe hesitated. "You want me to carry you?" He sounded as though it was a task of Herculean proportions.

"I can't walk." She'd taken the shoes off, and it would take God's own army to get them back on. She couldn't very well traipse outside in her stocking feet.

"If I carry you, we'd better find another way out of the house."

"All right." She agreed just to prove what an amicable person she actually was. When she was a child, she'd been a pest, but she wasn't anymore and she wanted to be sure Joe understood that.

Grasping Cait's hand, he led her into the kitchen.

"Don't you think we should make our farewells?" she asked. It seemed the polite thing to do.

"No," he answered sharply. "With the mood you're in you're likely to throw yourself into Paul's arms and demand that he make mad passionate love to you right then and there."

Cait's face went fire-engine red. "That's ridiculous."

Joe mumbled something she couldn't hear while he lifted her hand and slipped one arm, then the other, into the satin-lined sleeves of her full-length coat.

When he'd finished, Cait climbed on top of the kitchen chair, stretching out her arms to him. Joe stared at her as though she'd suddenly turned into a werewolf.

"What are you doing now?" he asked in an exasperated voice.

"You're going to carry me, aren't you?"

"I was considering it."

"I want a piggyback ride. You gave Betsy McDonald a piggyback ride once and not me."

"Cait," Joe groaned. He jerked his fingers through his hair, and offered her his hand, wanting her to climb down from the chair. "Get down before you fall. Good Lord, I swear you'd try the patience of a saint."

"I want you to carry me piggyback," she insisted. "Oh, please, Joe. My toes hurt so bad."

Once again her hero grumbled under his breath. She couldn't make out everything he said, but what she did hear was enough to curl her hair. With obvious reluctance, he walked to the chair, and giving a sigh of pure bliss, Cait wrapped her arms around his neck and hugged his lean hips with her legs. She laid her head on his shoulder and sighed again.

Still grumbling, Joe moved toward the back door.

Just then the kitchen door opened and Paul and Lindy walked in. Lindy gasped. Paul just stared.

"It's all right," Cait was quick to assure them. "Really it is. I was waiting under the mistletoe and you—"

"She downed four glasses of punch nonstop," Joe inserted before Cait could admit she'd been waiting there for Paul.

"Do you need any help?" Paul asked.

"None, thanks," Joe returned. "There's nothing to worry about."

"But . . ." Lindy looked concerned.

"She ain't heavy," Joe teased. "She's my wife."

The phone rang, waking Cait from a sound sleep. Her head began throbbing in time to the painful noise and she groped for the telephone receiver.

"Hello," she barked, instantly regretting that she'd spoken loudly.

"How are you feeling?" Joe asked.

"About like you'd expect," she whispered, keeping her eyes closed and gently massaging one temple. It felt as though tiny men with hammers had taken up residence in her head and were pounding away, hoping to attract her attention.

"What time does your flight leave?" he asked.

"It's okay. I'm not scheduled to leave until this afternoon."

"It is afternoon."

Her eyes flew open. "What?"

"Do you still need me to take you to the airport?"

"Yes . . . please." She tossed aside the covers and reached for her clock, stunned to realize Joe was right. "I'm already packed. I'll be dressed by the time you get here. Oh, thank goodness you phoned."

Cait didn't have time to listen to the pounding of the tiny men in her head. She showered and dressed as quickly as possible, swallowed a cup of coffee and a couple of aspirin, and was just shrugging into her coat when Joe arrived at the door.

She let him in, despite the suspiciously wide grin he wore.

"What's so amusing?"

"What makes you think I'm amused?" He strolled into the room, hands behind his back, as if he owned the place.

"Joe, we don't have time for your little games. Come on, or I'm going to miss my plane. What's with you, anyway?"

"Nothing." He circled her living room, still wearing that silly grin. "I don't suppose you realize it, but liquor has a peculiar effect on you."

Cait stiffened. "It does?" She remembered most of the party with great clarity. Good thing Joe had taken her home when he had.

"Liquor loosens your tongue."

"So?" She picked up two shopping bags filled with wrapped packages, leaving the lone suitcase for him. "Did I say anything of interest?"

"Oh, my, yes."

"Joe!" She glanced quickly at her watch. They needed to get moving if she was to catch her flight. "Discount whatever I said—I'm sure I didn't mean it. If I insulted you, I apologize. If I told any family secrets, kindly forget I mentioned them."

He strolled to her side and tucked his finger under her chin. "This was a secret, all right," he informed her in a lazy drawl. "It was something you told me on the drive home."

"Are you sure it's true?"

"Relatively sure."

"What did I say? Did I declare my undying love for you? Because if I—"

"No, no, nothing like that."

"Just how long do you intend to torment me with this?" She was rapidly losing interest in his little guessing game.

"Not much longer." He looked exceptionally pleased with himself. "So Martin's a minister now. Funny you never thought to mention that before."

"Ah . . ." Cait set aside the two bags and lowered herself to the sofa. So he'd found out. Worse, she'd been the one to tell him.

"That may well have some interesting ramifications, my dear. Have you ever stopped to think about them?"

Eight

"This is exactly why I didn't tell you about Martin," Cait informed Joe as he tossed her suitcase into the back seat of his car. She checked her watch again and groaned. They had barely an hour and a half before her flight was scheduled to leave. Cait was never late. Never—at least not when it was her own fault.

"It seems to me," Joe continued, his face deadpan, "that there could very well be some legal grounds to our marriage."

Joe was saying that just to annoy her, and unfortunately it was working. "I've never heard anything more ludicrous in my life."

"Think about it, Cait," he said, ignoring her protest. "We could be celebrating our anniversary this spring. How many years is it now? Eighteen? How the years fly."

"Listen, Joe, I don't find this amusing." She glanced at her watch. If only she hadn't slept so late. Never again would she have any Christmas punch. Briefly she wondered what else she'd said to Joe, then decided it was better not to know.

"I heard a news report of a three-car pileup on the freeway, so we'll take the side streets."

"Just hurry," Cait urged in an anxious voice.

"I'll do the best I can," Joe said, "but worrying about it isn't going to get us there any faster."

She glared at him. She couldn't help it. He wasn't the one who'd been planning this trip for months. If she missed the flight, her nephews and niece wouldn't have their Christmas presents from their Auntie Cait. Nor would she share in the family traditions that were so much a part of her Christmas. She *had* to get to the airport on time.

Everyone else had apparently heard about the accident on the freeway, too, and the downtown area was crowded with the overflow. Cait and Joe were delayed at every intersection and twice were forced to sit through two changes of the traffic signal.

Cait was growing more panicky by the minute. She just had to make this flight. But it almost seemed that she'd get to the airport faster if she simply jumped out of the car and ran there.

Joe stopped for another red light, but when the signal turned green, they still couldn't move—a delivery truck in front of them had stalled. Furious, Cait rolled down the window and stuck out her head. "Listen here, buster, let's get this show on the road," she shouted at the top of her lungs.

Her head was pounding and she prayed the aspirin would soon take effect.

"Quite the Christmas spirit," Joe muttered dryly under his breath.

"I can't help it. I have to catch this plane."

"You'll be there in plenty of time."

"At this rate we won't make it to Sea-Tac before Easter!"

"Relax, will you?" Joe suggested gently. He turned on the radio and a medley of Christmas carols filled the air. Normally the music would have calmed her, but she was suffering from a hangover, depression and severe anxiety, all at the same time. Her fingernails found their way into her mouth.

Suddenly she straightened. "Darn! I forgot to give you your Christmas gift. I left it at home."

"Don't worry about it."

"I didn't get you a gag gift the way I said." Actually she was pleased with the book she'd managed to find—an attractive coffee-table volume about the history of baseball.

Cait waited for Joe to mention *her* gift. Surely he'd bought her one. At least she fervently hoped he had, otherwise she'd feel like a fool. Though, admittedly, that was a feeling she'd grown accustomed to in the past few weeks.

"I think we might be able to get back on the freeway here," Joe said, as he made a sharp left-hand turn. They crossed the overpass, and from their vantage point, Cait could see that the freeway was unclogged and running smoothly.

"Thank God," she whispered, relaxing against the back of the seat as Joe drove quickly ahead.

Her chauffeur chuckled. "I seem to remember you lecturing me—"

"I never lecture," she said testily. "I may have a strong opinion on certain subjects, but let me assure you, I never lecture."

"You were right, though. The streets of Bethlehem must have been crowded and bustling with activity at the time of that first Christmas. I can see it all now, can't you? A rug dealer is held up by a shepherd driving his flock through the middle of town."

Cait smiled for the first time that morning, because she could easily picture the scene Joe was describing.

"Then some furious woman, impatient to make it to the local camel merchant before closing, sticks her nose in the middle of everything and shouts at the rug dealer to get his show on the road." He paused to chuckle at his own wit. "I'm convinced she wouldn't have been so testy except that she was suffering from one heck of a hangover."

"Very funny," Cait grumbled, smiling despite herself.

He took the exit for the airport and Cait was gratified to note that her flight wasn't scheduled to leave for another thirty minutes. She was cutting it close, closer than she ever had before, but she'd confirmed her ticket two days earlier and had already been assigned her seat.

Joe pulled up at the drop-off point for her airline and gave Cait's suitcase to a skycap while she rummaged around in her purse for her ticket.

"I suppose this is goodbye for now," he said with an endearingly crooked grin that sent her pulses racing.

"I'll be back in less than two weeks," she reminded him, trying to keep her tone light and casual.

"You'll phone once you arrive?"

She nodded. For all her earlier panic, Cait now felt oddly unwilling to leave Joe. She should be rushing through the airport to her airline's check-in counter to get her boarding pass, but she lingered, her heart overflowing with emotions she couldn't identify.

"Have a safe trip," he said quietly.

"I will. Thanks so much . . . for everything."

"You're welcome." His expression sobered and the ever-ready mirth fled from his eyes. Cait wasn't sure who moved first. All she knew was that she was in Joe's arms, his thumb caressing the softness of her cheek as they gazed hungrily into each other's eyes.

He leaned forward to kiss her. Cait's eyes drifted shut as his mouth met hers.

At first Joe's kiss was tender but it quickly grew in fervor. The noise and activity around them seemed to fade into the distance. Cait could feel herself dissolving. She moaned and arched closer, not wanting to leave the protective haven of his arms. Joe shuddered and hugged her tight, as if he, too, found it difficult to part.

"Merry Christmas, love," he whispered, releasing her with a reluctance that made her feel . . . giddy. Confused. *Happy*.

"Merry Christmas," she echoed, but she didn't move.

Joe gave her the gentlest of nudges. "You'd better hurry, Cait."

"Oh, right," she said, momentarily forgetting why she was at the airport. Reaching for the bags filled with gaily wrapped Christmas packages, she took two steps backward. "I'll phone when I get there."

"Do. I'll be waiting to hear from you." He thrust his hands into his pockets and Cait had the distinct impression he did it to stop himself from reaching for her again. The thought was a romantic one, a certainty straight from her heart.

Her heart . . . Her heart was full of feeling for Joe. More than she'd ever realized. He'd dominated her life these past few weeks—taking her to dinner, bribing his way back into her good graces with pizza, taking her on a Christmas shopping expedition, escorting her to Paul's party. Joe had become her whole world. Joe, not Paul. Joe.

Given no other choice, Cait abruptly turned and hurried into the airport, where she checked in, then went through security and down the concourse to the proper gate.

The flight had already been called and only a handful of passengers had yet to board.

Cait dashed to the counter with her boarding pass. A young soldier stood just ahead of her. "But you don't understand," the tall marine was saying to the airline employee. "I booked this flight over a month ago. I've got to be on that plane!"

"I'm so sorry," the woman apologized, her dark eyes regretful. "This sort of thing happens, especially during holidays, but your ticket's for standby. I wish I could do something for you, but there isn't a single seat available."

"But I haven't seen my family in over a year. My uncle Harvey's driving from Duluth to visit. He was in the marines, too. My mom's been baking for three weeks. Don't you see? I can't disappoint them now!"

Cait watched as the agent rechecked her computer. "If I could magically create a seat for you, I would," she said sympathetically. "But there just isn't one."

"But when I bought the ticket, the woman told me I wouldn't have a problem getting on the flight. She said there're always no-shows."

"I'm so sorry," the agent repeated, looking past the young marine to Cait.

"All right," he said, forcefully expelling his breath. "When's the next flight with available space? Any flight within a hundred miles of Minneapolis. I'll walk the rest of the way if I have to."

Once again, the woman consulted her computer. "We have space available the evening of the twenty-sixth."

"The twenty-sixth!" the young man shouted. "But that's after Christmas and eats up nearly all my leave. I'd be home for less than a week."

"May I help you?" the airline employee said to Cait. She looked almost as unhappy as the marine, but apparently there wasn't anything she could do to help him.

Cait stepped forward and handed the woman her boarding pass. The soldier gazed at it longingly, then moved dejectedly from the counter and lowered himself into one of the molded plastic chairs.

Cait hesitated, remembering how she'd stuck her head out the window of Joe's truck on their drive to the airport and shouted impatiently at the truck driver who was holding up traffic. A conversation she'd had with Joe earlier returned to haunt her. She'd argued that Christmas was a time filled with love and good cheer, the one holiday that brought out the very best in everyone. And sometimes, Joe had insisted, the very worst.

"Since you already have your seat assignment, you may board the flight now."

The urge to hurry nearly overwhelmed Cait, yet she hesitated once again.

"Excuse me," Cait said, drawing a deep breath and making her decision. She approached the soldier. He seemed impossibly young now that she had a good look at him. No more than eighteen, maybe nineteen. He'd probably joined the service right out of high school. His hair was cropped close to his head and his combat boots were so shiny Cait could see her reflection in them.

The marine glanced up at her, his face heavy with defeat. "Yes?"

"Did I hear you say you needed to be on this flight?"

"I have a ticket, ma'am. But it's standby and there aren't any seats."

"Listen," she said. "You can have mine."

The way his face lit up was enough to blot out her own disappointment at missing Christmas with Martin and her sister-in-law. The kids. Her mother . . . "My family's in Minneapolis, too, but I was there this summer."

"Ma'am, I can't let you do this."

"Don't cheat me out of the pleasure."

They approached the counter to effect the exchange. The marine stood, his eyes wide with disbelief. "I insist," Cait said. "Here." She handed him the two bags full of gifts for her nephews and nieces. "There'll be a man waiting at the other end. A tall minister—he'll have a collar on. Give him these. I'll phone so he'll know to look for you."

"Thank you for everything . . . I can't believe you're doing this."

Cait smiled. Impulsively the marine hugged her, then swinging his duffel bag over his shoulder, he picked up the two bags of gifts and jogged over to Security.

Cait waited for a couple of minutes, then wiped the tears from her eyes. She wasn't completely sure why she was crying. She'd never felt better in her life.

It was around six when she awoke. The apartment was dark and silent. Sighing, she picked up the phone, dragged it onto the bed with her and punched out Joe's number.

He answered on the first ring, as if he'd been waiting for her call. "How was the flight?" he asked immediately.

"I wouldn't know. I wasn't on it."

"You missed the plane!" he shouted incredulously. "But you were there in plenty of time."

"I know. It's a long story, but basically, I gave my seat to someone who needed it more than I did." She smiled dreamily, remembering how the young marine's face had lit up. "I'll tell you about it later."

"Where are you now?"

"Home."

He exhaled sharply, then said, "I'll be over in fifteen minutes."

Actually it took him twelve. By then Cait had brewed a pot of coffee and made herself a peanut-butter-and-jelly sandwich. She hadn't eaten all day and was starved. She'd just finished the sandwich when Joe arrived.

"What about your luggage?" Joe asked, looking concerned. He didn't give her a chance to respond. "Exactly what do you mean, you gave your seat away?"

Cait explained as best she could. Even now she found herself surprised by her actions. Cait rarely behaved spontaneously. But something about that young soldier had reached deep within her heart and she'd reacted instinctively.

"The airline is sending my suitcase back to Seattle on the next available flight, so there's no need to worry," Cait said. "I talked to Martin, who was quick to tell me the Lord would reward my generosity."

"Are you going to catch a later flight, then?" Joe asked. He helped himself to a cup of coffee and pulled out the chair across from hers.

"There aren't any seats," Cait said. She leaned back, yawning, and covered her mouth. Why she should be so tired after sleeping away most of the afternoon was beyond her. "Besides, the office is short-staffed. Lindy gave Paul her notice and a trainee is coming in, which makes everything even more difficult. They can use me."

Joe frowned. "Giving up your vacation is one way to impress Paul."

Words of explanation crowded her tongue. She realized Joe wasn't insulting her; he was only stating a fact. What he didn't understand was that Cait hadn't thought of Paul once the entire day. Her staying or leaving had absolutely nothing to do with him.

If she'd been thinking of anyone, it was Joe. She knew now that giving up her seat to the marine hadn't been entirely unselfish. When Joe kissed her goodbye, her heart had started telegraphing messages she had yet to fully decode. The plain and honest truth was that she hadn't wanted to leave him. It was as if she really did belong with him . . . .

That perception had been with her from the moment they'd parted at the airport. It had followed her in the taxi on the ride back to the apartment. Joe was the last person she'd thought of when she'd fallen asleep, and the first person she'd remembered when she awoke.

It was the most unbelievable thing.

"What are you going to do for Christmas?" Joe asked, still frowning into his coffee cup. For someone who'd seemed downright regretful that she was flying halfway across the country, he didn't seem all that pleased to be sharing her company now.

"I . . . haven't decided yet. I suppose I'll spend a quiet day by myself." She'd wake up late, indulge in a lazy scented bath, find something sinful for breakfast. Ice cream, maybe. Then she'd paint her toenails and settle down with a good book. The day would be lonely, true, but certainly not wasted.

"It'll be anything but quiet," Joe challenged.

"Oh?"

"You'll be spending it with me and my family."

"This is the first time Joe has ever brought a girl to join us for Christmas," Virginia Rockwell said as she set a large tray of freshly baked cinnamon rolls in the center of the huge kitchen table. She wiped her hands clean on the apron that was secured around her thick waist.

Cait felt she should explain. She was a little uncomfortable arriving unannounced with Joe like this. "Joe and I are just friends."

Mrs. Rockwell shook her head, which set the white curls bobbing. "I saw my son's eyes when he brought you into the house." She grinned knowingly. "I remember you from the old neighborhood, with your starched dresses and the pigtails with those bright pink ribbons. You were a pretty girl then and you're even prettier now."

"The starched dresses were me, all right," Cait confirmed. She'd been the only girl for blocks around who always wore dresses to school.

Joe's mother chuckled again. "I remember the sensation you caused in the neighborhood when you said Joe had kissed you."

She chuckled, her eyes shining. "His father and I got quite a kick out of that. I still remember how furious Joe was when he learned his secret was out."

"I only told one person," Cait protested. But Betsy had told plenty of others, and the news had spread with alarming speed. However, Cait figured she'd since paid for her sins tenfold. Joe had made sure of that in the past few weeks.

"It's so good to see you again, Caitlin. When we've got a minute I want you to sit down and tell me all about your mother. We lost contact years ago, but I always thought she was a darling."

"I think so, too," Cait agreed, carrying a platter of scrambled eggs to the table. She did miss being with her family, but Joe's mother made it almost as good as being home. "I know that's how Mom feels about you, too. She'll want to thank you for being kind enough to invite me into your home for Christmas."

"I wouldn't have it any other way."

"I know." She glanced into the other room where Joe was sitting with his brother and sister-in-law. Her heart throbbed at the sight of him with his family. But these newfound feelings for Joe left her at a complete loss. What she'd told Mrs. Rockwell was true. Joe was her friend. The very best friend she'd ever had. She was grateful for everything he'd done for her since they'd chanced upon each other, just weeks ago, really. But their friendship was developing into something much stronger. If only she didn't feel so . . . so ardent about Paul. If only she didn't feel so confused!

Joe laughed at something one of his nephews said and Cait couldn't help smiling. She loved the sound of his laughter. It was vigorous and robust and lively—just like his personality.

"Joe says you're working as a stockbroker right here in Seattle."

"Yes. I've been with Webster, Rodale and Missen for over a year now. My degree was in accounting but—"

"Accounting?" Mrs. Rockwell nodded approvingly. "My Joe has his own accountant now. Good thing, too. His books were in a terrible mess. He's a builder, not a pencil pusher, that boy."

"Are you telling tales on me, Mom?" Joe asked as he sauntered into the kitchen. He picked up a piece of bacon and bit off the end. "When are we going to open the gifts? The kids are getting restless."

"The kids, nothing. You're the one who's eager to tear into those packages," his mother admonished. "We'll open them after breakfast, the way we do every Christmas."

Joe winked at Cait and disappeared into the living room once more.

Mrs. Rockwell watched her son affectionately. "Last year he shows up on my doorstep bright and early Christmas morning needing gift wrap. Then, once he's got all his presents wrapped, he walks into my kitchen—" her face crinkled in a wide grin "—and he sticks all those presents in my refrigerator." She smiled at the memory. "For his brother, he bought two canned hams and three gallons of ice cream. For me it was cat food and a couple of rib roasts."

Breakfast was a bustling affair, with Joe's younger brother, his wife and their children gathered around the table. Joe sat next to Cait and held her hand while his mother offered the blessing. Although she wasn't home with her own family, Cait felt she had a good deal for which to be thankful.

Conversation was pleasant and relaxed, but foremost on the children's minds was opening the gifts. The table was cleared and plates and bowls arranged inside the dishwasher in record time.

Cait sat beside Joe, holding a cup of coffee, as the oldest grandchild handed out the presents. While Christmas music played softly in the background, the children tore into their

packages. The youngest, a two-year-old girl, was more interested in the box than in the gift itself.

When Joe came to the square package Cait had given him,
he shook it enthusiastically.

"Be careful, it might break," she warned, knowing there was
no chance of that happening.

Carefully he removed the bows, then unwrapped his gift.
Cait watched expectantly as he lifted the book from the layers
of bright paper. "A book on baseball?"

Cait nodded, smiling. "As I recall, you used to collect baseball cards."

"I ended up trading away my two favorites."

"I'm sure it was for a very good reason."

"Of course."

Their eyes held until it became apparent that everyone in the
room was watching them. Cait glanced self-consciously away.

Joe cleared his throat. "This is a great gift, Cait. Thank you
very much."

"You're welcome very much."

He leaned over and kissed her as if it was the most natural
thing in the world. It felt right, their kiss. If anything, Cait was
sorry to stop at one.

"Surely you have something for Cait," Virginia Rockwell
prompted her son.

"You bet I do."

"He's probably keeping it in the refrigerator," Cait suggested,
to the delight of Joe's family.

"Oh, ye of little faith," he said, removing a box from his shirt
pocket.

"I recognize that paper," Sally, Joe's sister-in-law, murmured
to Cait. "It's from Stanley's."

Cait's eyes widened at the name of an expensive local jew-
elry store. "Joe?"

"Go ahead and open it," he urged.

Cait did, hands fumbling in her eagerness. She slipped off the ribbon and peeled away the gold textured wrap to reveal a white jeweler's box. It contained a second box, a small black velvet one, which she opened very slowly. She gasped at the lovely cameo brooch inside.

"Oh, Joe," she whispered. It was a lovely piece carved in onyx and overlaid with ivory. She'd longed for a cameo, a really nice one, for years and wondered how Joe could possibly have known.

"You gonna kiss Uncle Joe?" his nephew, Charlie, asked, "'Cause if you are, I'm not looking."

"Of course she's going to kiss me," Joe answered for her. "Only she can do it later when there aren't so many curious people around." He glanced swiftly at his mother. "Just the way Mom used to thank Dad for her Christmas gift. Isn't that right, Mom?"

"I'm sure Cait . . . will," Virginia answered, clearly flustered. She patted her hand against the side of her head as though she feared the pins had fallen from her hair, her eyes downcast.

Cait didn't blame the older woman for being embarrassed, but one look at the cameo and she was willing to forgive Joe anything.

The day flew past. After the gifts were opened—with everyone exclaiming in surprised delight over the gifts Joe had bought, with Cait's help—the family gathered around the piano. Mrs. Rockwell played as they sang a variety of Christmas carols, their voices loud and cheerful. Joe's father had died several years earlier, but he was mentioned often throughout the day, with affection and love. Cait hadn't known him well, but the family obviously felt Andrew Rockwell's presence far more than his absence on this festive day.

Joe drove Cait back to her apartment late that night. Mrs.

Rockwell had insisted on sending a plate of cookies home with her, and Cait swore it was enough goodies to last her a month of Sundays. Now she felt sleepy and warm; leaning her head against the seat, she closed her eyes.

"We're here," Joe whispered close to her ear.

Reluctantly Cait opened her eyes and sighed. "I had such a wonderful day. Thank you, Joe." She couldn't quite stifle a yawn as she reached for the door handle, thinking longingly of bed.

"That's it?" He sounded disappointed.

"What do you mean, that's it?"

"I seem to remember a certain promise you made this morning."

Cait frowned, not sure she understood what he meant. "When?"

"When we were opening the gifts," he reminded her.

"Oh," Cait said, straightening. "You mean when I opened your gift to me and saw the brooch."

Joe nodded with exaggerated emphasis. "Right. *Now* do you remember?"

"Of course." The kiss. He planned to claim the kiss she'd promised him. She brushed her mouth quickly over his and grinned. "There."

"If that's the best you can do, you should've kissed me in front of Charlie."

"You're faulting my kissing ability?"

"Charlie's dog gives better kisses than that."

Cait felt more than a little insulted. "Is this a challenge, Joseph Rockwell?"

"Yes," he returned archly. "You're darn right it is."

"All right, then you're on." She set the plate of cookies aside, slid closer and slipped her arms around Joe's neck. Next she wove her fingers into his thick hair.

"This is more like it," Joe murmured contentedly.

Cait paused. She wasn't sure why. Perhaps because she'd suddenly lost all interest in making fun out of something that had always been so wonderful between them.

Joe's eyes met hers, and the laughter and fun in them seemed to disappear. Slowly he expelled his breath and brushed his lips along her jaw. The warmth of his breath was exciting as his mouth skimmed toward her temple. His arms closed around her waist and he pulled her tight against him.

Impatiently he began to kiss her, introducing her to a world of warm, thrilling sensations. His mouth then explored the curve of her neck. It felt so good that Cait closed her eyes and experienced a curious weightlessness she'd never known—a heightened awareness of physical longing.

"Oh, Cait . . ." He broke away from her, his breathing labored and heavy. She knew instinctively that he wanted to say more, but he changed his mind and buried his face in her hair, exhaling sharply.

"How am I doing?" she whispered once she found her voice.

"Just fine."

"Are you ready to retract your statement?"

He hesitated. "I don't know. Convince me again." So she did, her kiss moist and gentle, her heart fluttering against her ribs.

"Is that good enough?" she asked when she'd recovered her breath.

Joe nodded, as though he didn't quite trust his own voice. "Excellent."

"I had a wonderful day," she whispered. "I can't thank you enough for including me."

Joe shook his head lightly. There seemed to be so much more he wanted to say to her and couldn't. Cait slipped out of the car and walked into her building, turning on the lights when she entered her apartment. She slowly put away her things, wanting to wrap this feeling around her like a warm quilt. Minutes later, she glanced out her window to see Joe still sitting in his car, his hands gripping the steering wheel, his head bent. It looked to Cait as though he was battling with himself to keep from following her inside. She would have welcomed him if he had.

Nine

Cait stared at the computer screen for several minutes, blind to the information in front of her. Deep in thought, she released a long, slow breath.

Paul had been grateful to see her when she'd shown up at the office that morning. The week between Christmas and New Year's could be a harried one. Lindy had looked surprised, then quickly retreated into her own office after exchanging a brief good-morning and little else. Her friend's behavior continued to baffle Cait, but she couldn't concentrate on Lindy's problems just now, or even on her work.

No matter what she did, Cait couldn't stop thinking about Joe and the kisses they'd exchanged Christmas evening. Nor could she forget his tortured look as he'd sat in his car after she'd gone into her apartment. Even now she wasn't certain why she hadn't immediately run back outside. And by the time she'd decided to do that, he was gone.

Cait was so absorbed in her musings that she barely heard the knock at her office door. Guiltily she glanced up to find Paul standing just inside her doorway, his hands in his pockets, his eyes weary.

"Paul!" Cait waited for her heart to trip into double time the way it usually did whenever she was anywhere near him. It didn't, which was a relief but no longer much of a surprise.

"Hello, Cait." His smile was uneven, his face tight. He seemed ill at ease and struggling to disguise it. "Have you got a moment?"

"Sure. Come on in." She stood and motioned toward her client chair. "What can I do for you?"

"Nothing much," he said vaguely, sitting down. "Uh, I just wanted you to know how pleased I am that you're here. I'm sorry you canceled your vacation, but I appreciate your coming in today. Especially in light of the fact that Lindy will be leaving." His mouth thinned briefly.

No one, other than Joe and Martin, was aware of the real reason Cait wasn't in Minnesota the way she'd planned. Nor had she suggested to Paul that she'd changed her plans to help him out because they'd be short-staffed; obviously he'd drawn his own conclusions.

"So Lindy's decided to follow through with her resignation?"

Paul nodded, then frowned anew. "Nothing I say will change her mind. That woman's got a stubborn streak as wide as a . . ." He shrugged, apparently unable to come up with an appropriate comparison.

"The construction project's nearly finished," Cait offered, making small talk rather than joining in his criticism of Lindy. Absently she stood up and wandered around her office, stopping to straighten the large Christmas wreath on her door, the one she and Lindy had put up earlier in the month. Lindy was her friend and she wasn't about to agree with Paul, or argue with him, for that matter. Actually she should've been pleased that Paul had sought her out, but she felt curiously indifferent. And she did have work she needed to do.

"Yes, I'm delighted with the way everything's turned out,"

Paul said, "Joe Rockwell's done a fine job. His reputation is excellent and I imagine he'll be one of the big-time contractors in the area within the next few years."

Cait nodded casually, hoping she'd concealed the thrill of excitement that had surged through her at the mention of Joe's name. She didn't need Paul to tell her Joe's future was bright; she could see that for herself. At Christmas, his mother had boasted freely about his success. Joe had recently received a contract for a large government project—his most important to date—and she was extremely proud of him. He might have trouble keeping his books straight, but he left his customers satisfied. If he worked as hard at satisfying them as he did at finding the right Christmas tree, Cait could well believe he was gaining a reputation for excellence.

"Well, listen," Paul said, drawing in a deep breath, "I won't keep you." His eyes were clouded as he stood and headed toward the door. He hesitated, turning back to face her. "I don't suppose you'd be free for dinner tonight, would you?"

"Dinner," Cait repeated as though she'd never heard the word before. Paul was inviting her to dinner? After all these months? Now, when she least expected it? Now, when it no longer mattered? After all the times she'd ached to the bottom of her heart for some attention from him, he was finally asking her out on a date? Now?

"That is, if you're free."

"Uh . . . yes, sure . . . that would be nice."

"Great. How about if I pick you up around five-thirty? Unless that's too early for you?"

"Five-thirty will be fine."

"I'll see you then."

"Thanks, Paul." Cait felt numb. There wasn't any other way to describe it. It was as if her dreams were finally beginning to play themselves out—too late. Paul, whom she'd loved from afar

for so long, wanted to take her to dinner. She should be dancing around the office with glee, or at least feeling something
other than this peculiar dull sensation in the pit of her stomach.
If this was such a significant, exciting, hoped-for event, why
didn't she feel any of the exhilaration she'd expected?

After taking a moment to collect her thoughts, Cait walked
down the hallway to Lindy's office and found her friend on
the phone. Lindy glanced up, smiled feebly in Cait's direction,
then abruptly dropped her gaze as if the call demanded her full
concentration.

Cait waited a couple of minutes, then decided to return later
when Lindy wasn't so busy. She needed to talk to her friend,
needed her counsel. Lindy had always encouraged Cait in her
dreams of a relationship with Paul. When she was discouraged, it
was Lindy who bolstered her sagging spirits. Yes, it was definitely
time for a talk. She'd try to get Lindy to confide in her, too. Cait
valued Lindy's friendship; true, she couldn't help being hurt that
the person she considered one of her best friends would give notice to leave the firm without even discussing it with her. But
Lindy must've had her reasons. And maybe she, too, needed some
support right about now.

Hearing her own phone ring, Cait hurried back to her
office. She was consistantly busy from then on. The New York
Stock Exchange was due to close in a matter of minutes when
Joe happened by.

"Hi," Cait greeted him, her smile wide and welcoming. Her
gaze connected with Joe's and he returned her smile. Her heart
reacted automatically, leaping with sheer happiness.

"Hi, yourself." He sauntered into her office and threw himself down in the same chair Paul had taken earlier, stretching his
long legs in front of him and folding his hands over his stomach.
"So how's the world of finance doing this fine day?"

"About as well as usual."

"Then we're in deep trouble," he joked.

His smile was infectious. It always had been, but Cait had initially resisted him. Her defenses had weakened, though, and she responded readily with a smile of her own.

"You done for the day?"

"Just about." She checked the time. In another five minutes, New York would be closing down. There were several items she needed to clear from her desk, but nothing pressing. "Why?"

"Why?" It was little short of astonishing how far Joe's eyebrows could reach, Cait noted, all but disappearing into his hairline.

"Can't a man ask a simple question?" Joe asked.

"Of course." The banter between them was like a well-rehearsed play. Never had Cait been more at ease with a man—or had more fun with a man. Or with anyone, really. "What I want to know is whether 'simple' refers to the question or to the man asking it."

"Ouch," Joe said, grinning broadly. "Those claws are sharp this afternoon."

"Actually today's been good." Or at least it had since he'd arrived.

"I'm glad to hear it. How about dinner?" He jumped to his feet and pretended to waltz around her office, playing a violin. "You and me. Wine and moonlight and music. Romance and roses." He wiggled his eyebrows at her suggestively. "You work too hard. You always have. I want you to enjoy life a little more. It would be good for both of us."

Joe didn't need to give her an incentive to go out with him. Cait was thrilled at the mere idea. Joe made her laugh, made her feel good about herself and the world. Of course, he possessed a remarkable talent for driving her crazy, too. But she supposed a little craziness was good for the spirit.

"Only promise me you won't wear those high heels of yours," he chided, pressing his hand to the small of his back. "I've suffered excruciating back pains ever since Paul's Christmas party."

Paul's name seemed to leap out and grab Cait by the throat. "Paul," she repeated, sagging against the back of her chair. "Oh, dear."

"I know you consider him a dear," Joe teased. "What has your stalwart employer done this time?"

"He asked me out to dinner," Cait admitted, frowning. "Out of the blue this morning he popped into my office and invited me to dinner as if we'd been dating for months. I was so stunned, I didn't know what to think."

"What did you tell him?" Joe seemed to consider the whole thing a huge joke. "Wait—" he held up his hand "—you don't need to answer that. I already know. You sprang at the offer."

"I didn't exactly spring," she said, somewhat offended by Joe's attitude. The least he could do was show a little concern. She'd spent Christmas with him, and according to his own mother this was the first time he'd ever brought a woman home for the holiday. Furthermore, despite his insisting to all and sundry that they were married, he certainly didn't seem to mind her seeing another man.

"I'll bet you nearly went into shock." A smile trembled at the edges of his mouth as if he was picturing her reaction to Paul's invitation and finding it all terribly entertaining.

"I did not go into shock." She defended herself heatedly. She'd been taken by surprise, that was all.

"Listen," he said, walking toward the door, "have a great time. I'll catch you later." With that he was gone.

Cait couldn't believe it. Her mouth dropped open and she paced frantically, clenching and unclenching her fists. It took her a full minute to recover enough to run after him.

Joe was talking to his foreman, the same stocky man he'd been with the day he followed Cait into the elevator.

"Excuse me," she said, interrupting their conversation, "but when you're finished I'd like a few words with you, Joe." Her back was ramrod stiff and she kept flexing her hands as though preparing for a fight.

Joe glanced at his watch. "It might be a while."

"Then might I have a few minutes of your time now?"

The foreman stepped away, his step cocky. "You want me to dismiss the crew again, boss? I can tell them to go out and buy New Year's presents for their wives, if you like."

The man was rewarded with a look that was hot enough to barbecue spareribs. "That won't be necessary, thanks, anyway, Harry."

"You're welcome, boss. We serve to please."

"Then please me by kindly shutting up."

Harry chuckled and returned to another section of the office.

"You wanted something?" Joe asked.

Boy, did she. "Is that all you're going to say?"

"About what?"

"About my going to dinner with Paul? I expected you to be . . . I don't know, upset."

"Why should I be upset? Is he going to have his way with you? I sincerely doubt it, but if you're worried, invite me along and I'll be more than happy to protect your honor."

"What's the matter with you?" she demanded, not bothering to disguise her fury and disappointment. She stared at Joe, waiting for him to mock her again, but once more he surprised her. His gaze sobered.

"You honestly expect me to be jealous?"

"Not jealous exactly," she said, although he wasn't far from the truth. "Concerned."

"I'm not. Paul's a good man."

"I know, but—"

"You've been in love with him for months—"

"I think it was more of an infatuation."

"True. But he's finally asked you out, and you've accepted."

"Yes, but—"

"We know each other well, Cait. We were married, remember?"

"I'm not likely to forget it." Especially when Joe took pains to point it out at every opportunity. "Shouldn't that mean . . . something?" Cait was embarrassed she'd said that. For weeks she'd suffered acute mortification every time Joe mentioned the childhood stunt. Now she was using it to suit her own purposes.

Joe took hold of her shoulders. "As a matter of fact, our marriage means a lot to me. Because I care about you, Cait."

Hearing Joe admit as much was gratifying.

"I want only the best for you," he continued. "It's what you deserve. All I can say is that I'd be more than pleased if everything worked out between you and Paul. Now if you'll excuse me, I need to talk something over with Harry."

"Oh, right, sure, go ahead." She couldn't seem to get the words out fast enough. When she'd called Martin to explain why she wouldn't be in Minnesota for Christmas, he'd claimed that God would reward her sacrifice. If Paul's invitation to dinner was God's reward, she wanted her airline ticket back.

The numb feeling returned as Cait returned to her office. She didn't know what to think. She'd believed . . . she'd hoped that she and Joe shared a very special feeling. Clearly their times together meant something entirely different to him than they had to her. Otherwise he wouldn't behave so casually about her going out with Paul. And he certainly wouldn't seem so pleased about it!

That was what hurt Cait the most, and yes, she was hurt. It had taken her several minutes to identify her feelings, but now she knew . . .

More by accident than design, Cait walked into Lindy's office. Her friend had already put on her coat and was closing her briefcase, ready to leave the office.

"Paul asked me to dinner," Cait blurted out.

"He did?" Lindy's eyes widened with astonishment. But she didn't turn it into a joke, the way Joe had.

Cait nodded. "He just strolled in as if it was nothing out of the ordinary and asked me to have dinner with him."

"Are you happy about it?"

"I don't know," Cait answered honestly. "I suppose I should be pleased. It's what I'd prayed would happen for months."

"Then what's the problem?" Lindy asked.

"Joe doesn't seem to care. He said he hopes everything works out the way I want it to."

"Which is?" Lindy pressed.

Cait had to think about that a moment, her heart in her throat. "Honest to heaven, Lindy, I don't know anymore."

"I understand the salmon here is superb," Paul was saying, reading over the Boathouse menu. It was a well-known restaurant on Lake Union.

Cait scanned the list of entrées, which featured fresh seafood, then chose the grilled salmon—the same dish she'd ordered that night with Joe. Tonight, though, she wasn't sure why she was even bothering. She wasn't hungry, and Paul was going to be wasting good money while she made a pretense of enjoying her meal.

"I understand you've been seeing a lot of Joe Rockwell," he said conversationally.

That Paul should mention Joe's name right now was ironic. Cait hadn't stopped thinking about him from the moment he'd dropped into her office earlier that afternoon. Their conversation had left a bitter taste in her mouth. She'd sincerely believed their relationship was developing into something . . . special. Yet Joe had gone out of his way to give her the opposite impression.

"Cait?" Paul stared at her.

"I'm sorry, what were you saying?"

"Simply that you and Joe Rockwell have been seeing a lot of each other recently."

"Uh, yes. As you know, we were childhood friends," she murmured. "Actually Joe and my older brother were best friends. Then Joe's family moved to the suburbs and our families lost contact."

"Yes, I remember you mentioned that."

The waitress came for their order, and Paul requested a bottle of white wine. Then he chatted amicably for several minutes, bringing up subjects of shared interest from the office.

Cait listened attentively, nodding from time to time or adding the occasional comment. Now that she had his undivided attention, Cait wondered what it was about Paul that she'd found so extraordinary. He was attractive, but not nearly as dynamic or exciting as she found Joe. True, Paul possessed a certain charm, but compared to Joe, he was subdued and perhaps even a little dull. Cait couldn't imagine her stalwart boss carrying her piggyback out the back door because her high heels were too tight. Nor could she see Paul bantering with her the way Joe did.

The waitress delivered the wine, opened the bottle and poured them each a glass, once Paul had given his approval. Their dinners followed shortly afterward. After taking a bite or two of her delicious salmon, Cait noticed that Paul hadn't touched his meal. If anything, he seemed restless.

He rolled the stem of the wineglass between his fingers, watching the wine swirl inside. Then he suddenly blurted out, "What do you think of Lindy's leaving the firm?"

Cait was taken aback by the fervor in his voice when he mentioned Lindy's name. "Frankly I was shocked," Cait said. "Lindy and I have been good friends for a couple of years now." There'd been a time when the two had done nearly everything together. The summer before, they'd vacationed in Mexico and returned to Seattle with enough handwoven baskets and bulky blankets to set up shop themselves.

"Lindy's resigning came as a surprise to you, then?"

"Yes, this whole thing caught me completely unawares. Lindy didn't even mention the other job offer to me. I always thought we were good friends."

"Lindy *is* your friend," Paul said with enough conviction to persuade the patrons at the nearby tables. "You wouldn't believe what a good friend she is."

"I . . . know that." But friends sometimes had surprises up their sleeves. Lindy was a good example of that, and apparently so was Joe.

"I find Lindy an exceptional woman," Paul commented, watching Cait closely.

"She's probably one of the best stockbrokers in the business," Cait said, taking a sip of her wine.

"My . . . admiration for her goes beyond her keen business mind."

"Oh, mine, too," Cait was quick to agree. Lindy was the kind of friend who would trudge through the blazing sun of Mexico looking for a conch shell because she knew Cait really wanted to take one home. And Lindy had listened to countless hours of Cait's bemoaning her sorry fate of unrequited love for Paul.

"She's a wonderful woman."

Joe was wonderful, too, Cait thought. So wonderful her heart ached at his indifference when she'd announced she would be dining with Paul.

"Lindy's the kind of woman a man could treasure all his life," Paul went on.

"I couldn't agree with you more," Cait said. Now, if only Joe would realize what a treasure *she* was. He'd married her once—well, sort of—and surely the possibility of spending their lives together had crossed his mind in the past few weeks.

Paul hesitated as though at a loss for words. "I don't suppose you've given any thought to the reason Lindy made this unexpected decision to resign?"

Frankly Cait hadn't. Her mind and her heart had been so full of Joe that deciphering her friend's actions had somehow escaped her. "She received a better offer, didn't she?" Which was understandable. Lindy would be an asset to any firm.

It was then that Cait understood. Paul hadn't asked her to dinner out of any desire to develop a romantic relationship with her. He saw her as a means of discovering what had prompted Lindy to resign. This new awareness came as a relief, a burden lifted from her shoulders. Paul wasn't interested in her. He never had been and probably never would be. A few weeks ago, that realization would have been a crushing defeat, but all Cait experienced now was an overwhelming sense of gratitude.

"I'm sure if you talk to Lindy, she might reconsider," Cait suggested.

"I've tried, trust me. But there's a problem."

"Oh?" Now that Cait had sampled the salmon, she discovered it to be truly delicious. She hadn't realized how hungry she was.

"Cait, look at me," Paul said, raising his voice slightly. His face was pinched, his eyes intense. "Damn, but you've made this nearly impossible."

She looked up at him, her face puzzled. "What is it, Paul?"

"You have no idea, do you? I swear you've got to be the most obtuse woman in the world." He pushed aside his plate and briefly closed his eyes, shaking his head. "I'm in love with Lindy. I have been for weeks . . . months. But for the life of me I couldn't get her to notice me. I swear I did everything but turn cartwheels in her office. It finally dawned on me why she wasn't responding."

"Me?" Cait asked in a feeble, mouselike squeak.

"Exactly. She didn't want to betray your friendship. Then one afternoon—I think it was the day you first recognized Joe—we, Lindy and I, were in my office and— Oh, hell, I don't know how it happened, but Lindy was looking something up for me and she stumbled over one of the cords the construction crew was using. Fortunately I was able to catch her before she fell to the floor. I know it wasn't her fault, but I was so angry, afraid she might have been hurt. Lindy was just as angry with me for being angry with her, and it seemed the only way to shut her up was to kiss her. That was the beginning and I swear to you everything exploded in our faces at that moment."

Cait swallowed, fascinated by the story. "Go on."

"I tried for days to get her to agree to go out with me. But she kept refusing until I demanded to know why."

"She told you . . . how I felt about you?" The thought was mortifying.

"Of course not. Lindy's too good a friend to divulge your confidence. Besides, she didn't need to tell me. I've known all along. Good grief, Cait, what did I have to do to discourage you? Hire a skywriter?"

"I don't think anything that drastic was necessary," she muttered, humiliated to her very bones.

"I repeatedly told Lindy I wasn't attracted to you, but she wouldn't listen. Finally she told me if I'd talk to you, explain everything myself, she'd agree to go out with me."

"The phone call," Cait said with sudden comprehension.

"That was the reason you called me, wasn't it? You wanted to talk about Lindy, not that business article."

"Yes." He looked deeply grateful for her insight, late though it was.

"Well, for heaven's sake, why didn't you?"

"Believe me, I've kicked myself a dozen times since. I wish I knew. I suppose it seemed heartless to have such a frank discussion over the phone. Again and again, I promised myself I'd say something. Lord knows I dropped enough hints, but you weren't exactly receptive."

She winced. "But why is Lindy resigning?"

"Isn't it obvious?" Paul asked. "It was becoming increasingly difficult for us to work together. She didn't want to betray her best friend, but at the same time . . ."

"But at the same time you two were falling in love."

"Exactly. I can't lose her, Cait. I don't want to hurt your feelings, and believe me, it's nothing personal—you're a trustworthy employee and a decent person—but I'm simply not attracted to you."

Paul didn't seem to be the only one. Other than treating their relationship like one big joke, Joe hadn't ever claimed any romantic feelings for her, either.

"I had to do something before I lost Lindy."

"I agree completely."

"You're not angry with her, are you?"

"Good heavens, no," Cait said, offering him a brave smile.

"We both thought something was developing between you and Joe Rockwell. Like I said, you seemed to be seeing quite a bit of each other, and then at the Christmas party—"

"Don't remind me," Cait said with a low groan.

Paul's face creased in a spontaneous smile. "Joe certainly has a wit about him, doesn't he?"

Cait gave a resigned nod.

Now that Paul had cleared the air, he seemed to develop an appetite. He reached for his dinner and ate heartily. By contrast, Cait's salmon had lost its appeal. She stared down at her plate, wondering how she could possibly make it through the rest of the evening.

She did, though, quite nicely. Paul didn't even seem to notice that anything was amiss. It wasn't that Cait was distressed by his confession. If anything, she was relieved at this turn of events and delighted that Lindy had fallen in love. Paul was obviously crazy about her; she'd never seen him more animated than when he was discussing Lindy. It still shocked Cait that she'd been so unperceptive about Lindy's real feelings. Not to mention Paul's . . .

Paul dropped her off at her building and saw her to the front door. "I can't thank you enough for understanding," he said, his voice warm. Impulsively he hugged her, then hurried back to his sports car.

Although she was certainly guilty of being obtuse, Cait knew exactly where Paul was headed. No doubt Lindy would be waiting for him, eager to hear the details of their conversation. Cait planned to talk to her friend herself, first thing in the morning.

Cait's apartment was dark and lonely. So lonely the silence seemed to echo off the walls. She hung up her coat before turning on the lights, her thoughts as dark as the room had been.

She made herself a cup of tea. Then she sat on the sofa, tucking her feet beneath her as she stared unseeing at the walls, assessing her options. They seemed terribly limited.

Paul was in love with Lindy. And Joe . . . Cait had no idea where she stood with him. For all she knew—

Her thoughts were interrupted by the phone. She answered on the second ring.

"Cait?" It was Joe and he seemed surprised to find her back so early. "When did you get in?"

"A few minutes ago."

"You don't sound like yourself. Is anything wrong?"

"No," she said, breaking into sobs. "What could possibly be wrong?"

Ten

The flow of emotion took Cait by storm. She'd had no intention of crying; in fact, the thought hadn't even entered her mind. One moment she was sitting there, contemplating the evening's revelations, and the next she was sobbing hysterically into the phone.

"Cait?"

"Oh," she wailed. "This is all your fault in the first place." Cait didn't know what made her say that. The words had slipped out before she'd realized it.

"What happened?"

"Nothing. I . . . I can't talk to you now. I'm going to bed." With that, she gently replaced the receiver. Part of her hoped Joe would call back, but the telephone remained stubbornly silent. She stared at it for several minutes. Apparently Joe didn't care if he talked to her or not.

The tears continued to flow. They remained a mystery to Cait. She wasn't a woman given to bouts of crying, but now that she'd started she couldn't seem to stop.

She changed out of her dress and into a pair of sweats, pausing halfway through to wash her face.

Sniffling and hiccuping, she sat on the end of her bed and dragged a shuddering breath through her lungs. Crying like this made no sense whatsoever.

Paul was in love with Lindy. At one time, the news would have devastated her, but not now. Cait felt a tingling happiness that her best friend had found a man to love. And the infatuation she'd held for Paul couldn't compare with the strength of her love for Joe.

Love.

There, she'd admitted it. She was in love with Joe. The man who told restaurant employees that she was suffering from amnesia. The man who walked into elevators and announced to total strangers that they were married. Yet this was the same man who hadn't revealed a minute's concern about her dating Paul Jamison.

Joe was also the man who'd gently held her hand through a children's movie. The man who made a practice of kissing her senseless. The man who'd held her in his arms Christmas night as though he never intended to let her go.

Joseph Rockwell was a fun-loving jokester who took delight in teasing her. He was also tender and thoughtful and loving—the man who'd captured her heart only to drop it so carelessly.

Her doorbell chimed and she didn't need to look in the peephole to know it was Joe. But she felt panicky all of a sudden, too confused and vulnerable to see him now.

She walked slowly to the door and opened it a crack.

"What the hell is going on?" Joe demanded, not waiting for an invitation to march inside.

Cait wiped her eyes on her sleeve and shut the door. "Nothing."

"Did Paul try anything?"

She rolled her eyes. "Of course not."

"Then why are you crying?" He stood in the middle of her living room, fists planted on his hips as if he'd welcome the opportunity to punch out her boss.

If Cait knew why she was crying nonstop like this, she would have answered him. She opened her mouth, hoping some intelligent reason would emerge, but the only thing that came out was a low-pitched moan. Joe was gazing at her in complete confusion. "I . . . Paul's in love."

"With *you*?" His voice rose half an octave with disbelief.

"Don't make it sound like such an impossibility," she said crossly. "I'm reasonably attractive, you know." If she was expecting Joe to list her myriad charms, Cait was disappointed.

Instead, his frown darkened. "So what's Paul being in love got to do with anything?"

"Absolutely nothing. I wished him and Lindy the very best."

"So it is Lindy?" Joe murmured as though he'd known it all along.

"You didn't honestly think it was me, did you?"

"Hell, how was I supposed to know? I *thought* it was Lindy, but it was you he was taking to dinner. Frankly it didn't make a whole lot of sense to me."

"Which is something else," Cait grumbled, standing so close to him, their faces were only inches apart. Her hands were on her hips, her pose mirroring his. It occurred to Cait that they resembled a pair of gunslingers ready for a shootout. "I want to know one thing. Every time I turn around, you're telling anyone and everyone who'll listen that we're married. But when it really matters you—"

"When did it really matter?"

Cait ignored the question, thinking the answer was obvious. "You casually turn me over to Paul as if you can't wait to be rid of me. Obviously you couldn't have cared less."

"I cared," he shouted.

"Oh, right," she shouted back, "but if that was the case, you certainly didn't bother to show it!"

"What was I supposed to do, challenge him to a duel?"

He was being ridiculous, Cait decided, and she refused to take the bait. The more they talked, the more unreasonable they were both becoming.

"I thought dating Paul was what you wanted," he complained. "You talked about it long enough. Paul this and Paul that. He'd walk past and you'd all but swoon."

"That's not the least bit true." Maybe it had been at one time, but not now and not for weeks. "If you'd taken the trouble to ask me, you might have learned the truth."

"You mean you don't love Paul?"

Cait rolled her eyes again. "Bingo."

"It isn't like you to be so sarcastic."

"It isn't like you to be so . . . awful."

He seemed to mull that over for a moment. "If we're going to be throwing out accusations," he said tightly, "then maybe you should take a look at yourself."

"What exactly do you mean by that?" As usual, no one could get a reaction out of Cait more effectively than Joe. "Never mind," she answered, walking to the door. "This discussion isn't getting us anywhere. All we seem capable of doing is hurling insults at each other."

"I disagree," Joe answered calmly. "I think it's time we cleared the air."

She took a deep breath, feeling physically and emotionally deflated.

"Joe, it'll have to wait. I'm in no condition to be rational right now and I don't want either of us saying things we'll regret." She held open her door for him. "Please?"

He seemed about to argue with her, then he sighed and dropped a quick kiss on her mouth. Wide-eyed, she watched him leave.

* * *

Lindy was waiting in Cait's office early the next morning, holding two cups of freshly brewed coffee. Her eyes were vulnerable as Cait entered the office. They stared at each other for a long moment.

"Are you angry with me?" Lindy whispered. She handed Cait one of the cups as an apparent peace offering.

"Of course not," Cait murmured. She put down her briefcase and accepted the cup, which she placed carefully on her desk. Then she gave Lindy a reassuring hug, and the two of them sat down for their much-postponed talk.

"Why didn't you tell me?" Cait burst out.

"I wanted to," Lindy said earnestly. "I had to stop myself a hundred times. The worst part of it was the guilt—knowing you were in love with Paul, and loving him myself."

Cait wasn't sure how she would have reacted to the truth, but she preferred to think she would've understood, and wished Lindy well. It wasn't as though Lindy had stolen Paul away from her.

"I don't think I realized how I felt," Lindy continued, "until one afternoon when I tripped over a stupid cord and fell into Paul's arms. From there, everything sort of snowballed."

"Paul told me."

"He . . . told you about that afternoon?"

Cait grinned and nodded. "I found the story wildly romantic."

"You don't mind?" Lindy watched her closely as if half-afraid of Cait's reaction even now.

"I think it's wonderful."

Lindy's smile was filled with warmth and excitement. "I never knew being in love could be so exciting, but at the same time cause so much pain."

"Amen to that," Cait stated emphatically.

Her words shot like live bullets into the room. If Cait could have reached out and pulled them back, she would have.

"Is it Joe Rockwell?" Lindy asked softly.

Cait nodded, then shook her head. "See how much he's confused me?" She made a sound that was half sob, half giggle. "Sometimes that man infuriates me so much I want to scream. Or cry." Cait had always thought of herself as a sane and sensible person. She lived a quiet life, worked hard at her job, enjoyed traveling and crossword puzzles. Then she'd bumped into Joe. Suddenly she found herself demanding piggyback rides, talking to strangers in elevators and seeking out phantom women at Christmas parties while downing spiked punch like it was soda pop.

"But then at other times?" Lindy prompted.

"At other times I love him so much I hurt all the way through. I love everything about him. Even those loony stunts of his. In fact, I usually laugh as hard as everyone else. Even if I don't always want him to know it."

"So what's going to happen with you two?" Lindy asked. She took a sip of coffee and as she did, Cait caught a flash of diamond.

"Lindy?" Cait demanded, jumping out of her seat. "What's that on your finger?"

Lindy's face broke into a smile so bright Cait was nearly blinded. "You noticed."

"Of course I did."

"It's from Paul. After he had dinner with you, he came over to my apartment. We talked for hours and then . . . he asked me to marry him. At first I didn't know what to say. It seems so soon. We . . . we hardly know each other."

"Good grief, you've worked together for ages."

"I know," Lindy said with a shy smile. "That's what Paul told me. It didn't take him long to convince me. He had the ring all picked out. Isn't it beautiful?"

"Oh, Lindy." The diamond was a lovely solitaire set in a wide band of gold. The style and shape were perfect for Lindy's long, elegant finger.

"I didn't know if I should wear it until you and I had talked, but I couldn't make myself take it off this morning."

"Of course you should wear it!" The fact that Paul had been carrying it around when he'd had dinner with her didn't exactly flatter Cait's ego, but she was so thrilled for Lindy that seemed a minor concern.

Lindy splayed her fingers out in front of her to better show off the ring. "When he slipped it on my finger, I swear it was the most romantic moment of my life. Before I knew it, tears were streaming down my face. I still don't understand why I started crying. I think Paul was as surprised as I was."

There must have been something in the air that reduced susceptible females to tears, Cait decided. Whatever it was had certainly affected her.

"Now you've sidetracked me," Lindy said, looking up from her diamond, her gaze dreamy. "You were telling me about you and Joe."

"I was?"

"Yes, you were," Lindy insisted.

"There's nothing to tell. If there was, you'd be the first person to hear. I know," she admitted before her friend could bring up the point, "we have seen a lot of each other recently, but I don't think it meant anything to Joe. When he found out Paul had invited me to dinner, he seemed downright delighted."

"I'm sure it was all an act."

Cait shrugged. She wished she could believe that. Oh, how she wished it.

"You're sure you're in love with him?" Lindy asked hesitantly.

Cait nodded and lowered her eyes. It hurt to think about Joe. Everything was a game to him—a big joke. Lindy had been right about one thing, though. Love was the most wonderful experience of her life. And the most painful.

The New York Stock Exchange had closed and Cait was punching some figures into her computer when Joe strode into her office and closed the door.

"Feel free to come in," she muttered, continuing her work. Her heart was pounding but she dared not let him know the effect he had on her.

"I will make myself at home, thank you," he answered cheerfully, ignoring her sarcasm. He pulled out a chair and sat down expansively, resting one ankle on the opposite knee and relaxing as if he was in a movie theater, waiting for the main feature to begin.

"If you're here to discuss business, might I suggest investing in blue-chip stocks? They're always a safe bet." Cait went on typing, doing her best to ignore Joe—which was nearly impossible, although she gave an Oscar-winning performance, if she did say so herself.

"I'm here to talk business, all right," Joe said, "but it has nothing to do with the stock market."

"What business could the two of us possibly have?" she asked, her voice deliberately ironic.

"I want to resume the discussion we were having last night."

"Perhaps you do, but unfortunately that was last night and this is now." How confident she sounded, Cait thought, mildly pleased with herself. "I can do without hearing you list my no doubt numerous flaws."

"Your being my wife is what I want to talk about."

"Your wife?" She wished he'd quit throwing the subject at her as if it meant something to him. Something other than a joke.

"Yes, my wife." He gave a short laugh. "Believe me, it isn't your flaws I'm here to discuss."

Despite everything, Cait's heart raced. She reached for a stack of papers and switched them from one basket to another. Her entire filing system was probably in jeopardy, but she needed some activity to occupy her hands before she stood up and reached out to Joe. She did stand then, but it was to remove a large silver bell strung from a red velvet ribbon hanging in her office window.

"Paul and Lindy are getting married," he said next.

"Yes, I know. Lindy and I had a long talk this morning." She took the wreath off her door next.

"I take it the two of you are friends again?"

"We were never not friends," Cait answered stiffly, stuffing the wreath, the bell and the three ceramic wise men into the bottom drawer of her filing cabinet. Hard as she tried to prevent it, she could feel her defenses crumbling. "Lindy's asked me to be her maid of honor and I've agreed."

"Will you return the favor?"

It took a moment for the implication to sink in, and even then Cait wasn't sure she should follow the trail Joe seemed to be forging through this conversation. She leaned forward and rested her hands on the edge of the desk.

"I'm destined to be an old maid," she said flippantly, although she couldn't help feeling a sliver of real hope.

"You'll never be that."

Cait was hoping he'd say her beauty would make her irresistible, or that her warmth and wit and intelligence were sure to attract a dozen suitors. Instead he said the very thing she could have predicted. "We're already married, so you don't need to worry about being a spinster."

Cait released a sigh of impatience. "I wish you'd give up on that, Joe. It's growing increasingly old."

"As I recall, we celebrated our eighteenth anniversary not long ago."

"Don't be ridiculous. All right," she said, straightening abruptly. If he wanted to play games, then she'd respond in kind. "Since we're married, I want a family."

"Hey, sweetheart," he cried, throwing his arms in the air, "that's music to my ears. I'm willing."

Cait prepared to leave the office, if not the building. "Somehow I knew you would be."

"Two or three," he interjected, then chuckled and added, "I suppose we should name the first two Ken and Barbie."

Cait's scowl made him chuckle even louder.

"If you prefer, we'll leave the names open to negotiation," he said.

"Of all the colossal nerve . . ." Cait muttered, moving to the window and gazing out.

"If you want daughters, I've got no objection, but from what I understand that's not really up to us."

Cait turned around, crossing her arms. "Correct me if I'm wrong," she said coldly, certain he'd delight in doing so. "But you did just ask me to marry you. Could you confirm that?"

"All I want is to make legal what's already been done."

Cait sighed in exasperation. Was he serious, or wasn't he? He was talking about marriage, about joining their lives, as if he were planning a bid on a construction project.

"When Paul asked Lindy to marry him, he had a diamond ring."

"I was going to buy you a ring," Joe said emphatically. "I still am. But I thought you'd want to pick it out yourself. If you wanted a diamond, why didn't you say so? I'll buy you the whole store if that'll make you happy."

"One ring will suffice, thank you."

"Pick out two or three. I understand diamonds are an excellent investment."

"Not so fast," she said, holding out her arm. It was vital she maintain some distance between them. If Joe kissed her or started talking about having children again, they might never get the facts clear.

"Not so fast?" he repeated incredulously. "Honey, I've been waiting eighteen years to discuss this. You're not going to ruin everything now, are you?" He advanced a couple of steps toward her.

"I'm not agreeing to anything until you explain yourself." For every step he took toward her, Cait retreated two.

"About what?" Joe was frowning, which wasn't a good sign.

"Paul."

His eyelids slammed shut, then slowly rose. "I don't understand why that man's name has to come into every conversation you and I have."

Cait decided it was better to ignore that comment. "You haven't even told me you love me."

"I love you." He actually sounded annoyed, as if she'd insisted on having the obvious reiterated.

"You might say it with a little more feeling," Cait suggested.

"If you want feeling, come here and let me kiss you."

"No."

"Why not?" By now they'd completely circled her desk. "We're talking serious things here. Trust me, sweetheart, a man doesn't bring up marriage and babies with just any woman. I love you. I've loved you for years, only I didn't know it."

"Then why did you let Paul take me out to dinner?"

"You mean I could've stopped you?"

"Of course. I didn't want to go out with him! I was sick about having to turn you down for dinner. Not only that, you didn't even seem to care that I was going out with another man. And as far as you were concerned, he was your main competition."

"I wasn't worried."

"That wasn't the impression I got later."

"All right, all right," Joe said, drawing his fingers through his hair. "I didn't think Paul was interested in you. I saw him and Lindy together one night at the office and the electricity between them was so thick it could've lit up Seattle."

"You knew about Lindy and Paul?"

Joe shrugged. "Let me put it this way. I had a sneaking suspicion. But when you started talking about Paul as though you were in love with him, I got worried."

"You should have been." Which was a bold-faced lie.

Somehow, without her being quite sure how it happened, Joe maneuvered himself so only a few inches separated them.

"Are you ever going to kiss me?" he demanded.

Meekly Cait nodded and stepped into his arms like a child opening the gate and skipping up the walkway to home. This was the place she belonged. With Joe. This was home and she need never doubt his love again.

With a sigh that seemed to come from the deepest part of him, Joe swept her close. For a breathless moment they looked into each other's eyes. He was about to kiss her when there was a knock at the door.

Harry, Joe's foreman, walked in without waiting for a response. "I don't suppose you've seen Joe—" He stopped abruptly. "Oh, sorry," he said, flustered and eager to make his escape.

"No problem," Cait assured him. "We're married. We have been for years and years."

Joe was chuckling as his mouth settled over hers, and in a single kiss he wiped out all the doubts and misgivings, replacing them with promises and thrills.

Epilogue

The robust sound of organ music surged through the Seattle church as Cait walked slowly down the center aisle, her feet moving in time to the traditional music. As the maid of honor, Lindy stood to one side of the altar while Joe and his brother, who was serving as best man, waited on the other. The church was decorated with poinsettias and Christmas greenery, accented by white roses.

Cait's brother, Martin, stood directly ahead of her. He smiled at Cait as the assembly rose and she came down the aisle, her heart overflowing with happiness.

Cait and Joe had planned this day, their Christmas wedding, for months. If there'd been any lingering doubts that Joe really loved her, they were long gone. He wasn't the type of man who expressed his love with flowery words and gifts. But Cait had known that from the first. He'd insisted on building their home before the wedding and they'd spent countless hours going over the architect's plans. Cait was helping Joe with his accounting and would be taking over the task full-time when they started their family. Which would be soon. The way Cait figured it, she'd be pregnant by next Christmas.

But before they began their real life together, they'd enjoy a perfect honeymoon in New Zealand. He'd wanted to surprise her with the trip, but Cait had needed a passport. They'd only be gone two weeks, which was all the time Joe could afford to take, since he had several large projects coming up.

As the organ concluded the "Wedding March," Cait handed her bouquet to Lindy and placed her hands in Joe's. He smiled down on her as if he'd never seen a more beautiful woman in his life. Judging by the look on his face, Cait knew he could hardly keep from kissing her right then and there.

"Dearly beloved," Martin said, stepping forward, "we are gathered here today in the sight of God and man to celebrate the love of Joseph James Rockwell and Caitlin Rose Marshall."

Cait's eyes locked with Joe's. She did love him, so much that her heart felt close to bursting. After all these months of waiting for this moment, Cait was sure she'd be so nervous her voice would falter. That didn't happen. She'd never felt more confident of anything than her feelings for Joe and his for her. Cait's voice rang out strong and clear, as did Joe's.

As they exchanged the rings, Cait could hear her mother and Joe's weeping softly in the background. But these were tears of shared happiness. The two women had renewed their friendship and were excited about the prospect of grand-children.

Cait waited for the moment when Martin would tell Joe he could kiss his bride. Instead he closed his Bible, reverently set it aside, and said, "Joseph James Rockwell, do you have the baseball cards with you?"

"I do."

Cait looked at the two men as if they'd both lost their minds. Joe reached inside his tuxedo jacket and produced two flashy baseball cards.

"You may give them to your bride."

With a dramatic flourish, Joe did as Martin instructed. Cait stared down at the two cards and grinned broadly.

"You may now kiss the bride," Martin declared.

Joe was more than happy to comply.

★ ★ ★ ★ ★